Jackson

USA TODAY & WSJ BESTSELLING AUTHOR
SIOBHAN DAVIS

BOOK DESCRIPTION

The devil came to me in disguise. Too bad I didn't notice until it was far too late.

Vanessa

The devil doesn't always wear an evil mask.
Sometimes, he appears in the most beautiful form.
Like the super-hot bad boy with the dirty-blond hair and a wicked glint in his blue eyes who swept in out of nowhere, stealing all the air from my lungs.
I thought he was my savior.
But he's my ruination.
And he's just taken a machete to my heart.

Jackson

For years, my rage seethed under the surface. Hidden behind a cloudy haze of my poison of choice.
But now, the fog has cleared.
And I'm out for blood.
I will annihilate those responsible for taking my sister from me.
Except *he's* not here, so I go for the next best target.
The woman he abandoned.
Until it suited him to drag her into this messed-up elite world.
Sucks to be her.
Because when I'm done with Vanessa, she'll wish she was dead.

A Note from the Author

This is a dark romance only suitable for readers aged eighteen and older. Some scenes may be triggering. For a list of triggers, refer to my website.

While you don't need to read the previous books in this series, as this is a **stand-alone romance** featuring a new couple, it is highly recommended as there are spoilers in this book pertaining to the previous books.

If you are following the series, this book overlaps, in parts, with *Sweet Retribution* and *Charlie* (timeline and some scenes.)

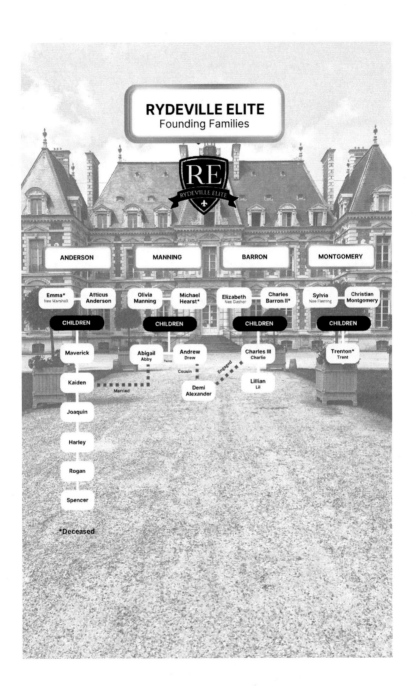

RYDEVILLE ELITE
Founding Families

ANDERSON | **MANNING** | **BARRON** | **MONTGOMERY**

| Emma* Nee Marshall | Atticus Anderson | Olivia Manning | Michael Hearst* | Elizabeth Nee Gasher | Charles Barron II* | Sylvia Nee Fleming | Christian Montgomery |

CHILDREN | **CHILDREN** | **CHILDREN** | **CHILDREN**

Maverick

Abigail Abby — Twins — Andrew Drew

Cousin

Charles III Charlie

Trenton* Trent

Kaiden — Married — Demi Alexander — Engaged

Lillian Lil

Joaquin

Harley

Rogan

Spencer

*Deceased

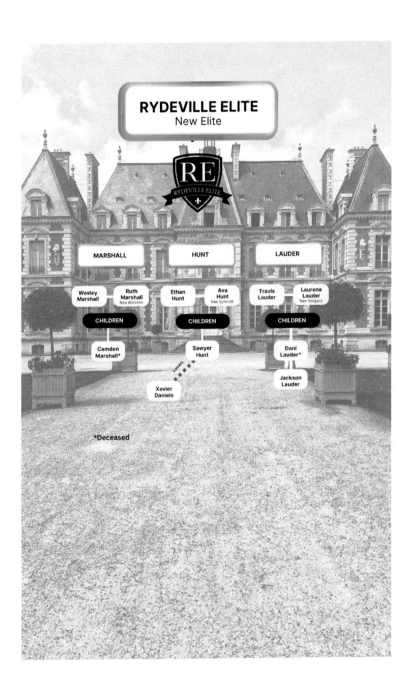

RYDEVILLE ELITE
New Elite

RE
RYDEVILLE ELITE

MARSHALL   **HUNT**   **LAUDER**

Wesley Marshall — Ruth Marshall (Nee Winston)

Ethan Hunt — Ava Hunt (Nee Synnott)

Travis Lauder — Laurena Lauder (Nee Vergara)

CHILDREN (Marshall)

Camden Marshall*

CHILDREN (Hunt)

Sawyer Hunt

Lovers

Xavier Daniels

CHILDREN (Lauder)

Dani Lauder*

Jackson Lauder

*Deceased

Jackson

Prologue
Vanessa

A cold breeze swirls against my bare legs, and the subtle whooshing of air tickles my eardrums, rousing me from sleep. Fingernails dig into my upper arm as I'm dragged out of bed. My eyes blink open as fear, thick and cloying, presses down on my chest. "Get off!" I rasp while swatting at his chest and wriggling in his hold.

He tosses my ass on the carpeted floor like trash. "You have ten minutes to pack your things and get the fuck out of my house," Aaron Breen demands, hovering over me like a dark, shadowy, menacing creature from hell. It wouldn't surprise me to discover my stepfather shares DNA with the devil himself, because there is little that is human about the man.

Faint light trickles through the uncovered window, confirming it's still early out. I'd retreated to my bedroom the instant I returned from The Hamptons last night, crawling into bed in my cutoffs and tank, allowing myself to succumb to the pain of Cam's and Sawyer's rejections for a short while, before hiding behind the inner cage I've perfected over the years. As soon as those bars go up, I am numb to all feeling, and I don't

1

hurt anymore. No one or nothing can get to me when I'm protected behind those steel walls, and it's my number one go-to survival tool.

I scramble to my feet, folding my arms across my chest as I glare at my mother's monster of a husband. "You want me out? Fine. I'll go."

I'd throw a party to celebrate if it wasn't for Kayleigh. My sister is only nine, and I'm scared for her. My jaw tightens as I narrow my eyes on him. "But if you lay a finger on my sister or my brother," I add, including Kayleigh's twin Hunter, because I don't trust Aaron with either of his kids, "I'll fucking bury you."

I have considered it. A lot. But it would be my word against his, and my track record won't help. His expensive lawyers would destroy me in court, but I doubt my stepmonster would walk away with his reputation intact. And *that* is the only thing I can hold over him.

Darting forward, he grabs my chin, pinching my skin with his nails. "Don't fucking threaten me, you stupid cunt. I can end you. Just like that." He shoves me away, snapping his fingers. "I don't want to see you ever again. You're not welcome here. And stay away from my children." He stalks toward me, backing me up against my bedroom wall. "I won't warn you again."

"Why now?" I ask although I'm guessing it's because I've just turned eighteen. I thought he would let me stay until I graduated high school. If I hadn't fucked up spectacularly when I was a freshman, and been forced to repeat the year, I'd be completely free right now.

"I don't have to explain myself to you. My house. My rules." His hands curl around my throat, and he tilts my head back. "If I'd known." His eyes darken with unconcealed rage as his grasp tightens on my throat.

I slowly lift my knee, ready to strike.

"If I'd known, this would've happened years earlier," he supplies. I've got no clue what he's talking about, but that's the least of my worries as I struggle to breathe. In a surprising move, he lets me go before I've had time to embed my knee in his balls. "He'd be so disappointed if he knew." His gaze roams me from head to toe, his face etched in disgust, but he can't disguise the glimmer of desire that radiates from his eyes.

Bile swims up my throat, and I cross my arms over my chest again as a shiver creeps up my spine.

I hate him with the intensity of a thousand suns.

Anger twists and turns in my gut, and I renew my silent vow: I will make him suffer.

Someday, somehow, that bastard will pay for all the ways he has broken me.

"Ticktock." He glances at my walk-in closet. "Start packing." He exits my bedroom, and I exhale heavily. I don't know what has prompted this decision at this moment, but I'm not hanging around to find out.

I hadn't unpacked from my Hamptons vacation, so I grab some more suitcases and throw a bunch of my clothes and personal belongings in. I retrieve the cash pile I've been collecting the past couple years from the shoebox hidden underneath one of the floorboards in my closet, along with my passport and the small handgun a guy at school acquired for me last year.

I hold the cold metal in my palm, feeling more assured knowing I have it and I know how to use it. It was worth the hefty price I'd paid for it, because I knew this day would come, and I've tried to be as prepared as possible.

Placing the gun in my purse, I check I have my cell and my wallet before I get dressed. Pulling an off-the-shoulder sweater down over my head, I slip my feet into my white and gold Vans

3

and take one final look around my childhood bedroom, not feeling any sorrow at saying goodbye.

This bedroom holds nothing but bad memories, and I'm not sorry to be leaving it behind.

The asshole watches as I haul my suitcases downstairs. It takes two trips, but he does nothing to help. He just stands in the large, circular lobby of his massive home, wearing a bored expression, while he repeatedly checks the flashy gold Rolex on his wrist.

Briefly, I wonder where Mom is, but I'm not surprised she isn't here to wave me off.

She checked out on me, on life, a long time ago.

I walk toward the front door with my head held high, holding onto my last suitcase, damping down the fear that prickles my skin for my little sister. As soon as I get out of here, and find some place to call home, I'll work out a plan for protecting Kayleigh.

"Nessa." Her tiny voice infiltrates the layers wrapped around my heart, and I gulp over the messy ball of emotion clogging my throat. I school my features into a pleasant mask before turning to face my sister. She's on the stairs, standing on the bottom step, dressed in her *Frozen* pajamas, rubbing sleep from her eyes. Her shoulder-length honey-blonde hair is in a mass of tangles, covering half of her face, obscuring her cute button nose and those big blue eyes a few shades paler than mine. "You're going away again?" She pushes hair out of her face, staring at me with hurt shining in her eyes.

I walk in her direction, crouching down in front of her. "I'm eighteen now, little princess. It's time to spread my wings."

"You're not coming back?" Her voice elevates a few decibels, and tears cling to her long lashes.

"Not for a while." I hate lying to her, and I'm being as vague as possible without making promises I can't commit to.

4

Fuck that bastard.

I fucking hate him so much.

I pull her into my arms, and warmth filters through my limbs when she curls her small body against mine.

"I don't want you to go. I'll miss you too much." She sobs into my neck, and cracks start splintering my heart.

"I don't have a choice, but I'll find a way to see you," I whisper in her ear. "I'll miss you too," I say more loudly to disguise our hushed conversation. I lower my voice again. "But it's our secret. You can't tell anyone. Not even Hunter."

"Enough," the asshole barks, and she jumps in my arms before subtly nodding.

I kiss her soft little cheeks. "I love you." I love my little brother too, but asking to say goodbye to him is a futile exercise, because I know the asshole won't permit it.

He wants to shove me out the door and pretend like I don't exist.

Like I never lived here or was ever a part of this family.

In his eyes, I never have been, because his blood doesn't flow through my veins, and I was an unwelcome part of the package when he met and married my mom.

"Vanessa needs to leave, sweetie," he adds, deliberately softening his tone as he lifts Kayleigh out of my arms. He presses a kiss to her temple. "And you'll be fine. You've got me and Mom and Hunter. That's all that matters."

My hands twitch with the urge to punch him, and I draw deep breaths to steady myself. Blowing my sister a kiss, I swiftly turn around before I do something I'll regret.

Like remove my gun and put a bullet between that asshole's eyebrows.

I take a shuddering breath as I step outside, closing the door behind me. Relief is sharp but bittersweet because I'm not here to run interference anymore.

Daylight is creeping across the skyline, casting a glorious golden hue on the land below. In a bit of a daze, I stare at the impressive manicured lawn in front of me. This moment is longed for but still surreal. We live in an affluent area of New York, in an exclusive gated community that houses celebrities, attorneys, businesspeople, and several politicians.

It's beautiful here, but, for me, it's an illusion.

I'd rather be broke and happy than rich and living a lie.

Leaving my suitcases by the water fountain, I walk around the side of the massive two-story property and into the ten-car garage. I guess I should count my blessings he has let me keep my Range Rover Evoque. It was my parents' gift on my sweet sixteenth.

I know I only got it so they could keep up appearances.

Aaron Breen values his reputation above anything and everything in his life.

He turned the legacy his parents left him into a hugely successful business. His parents established and managed a chain of grocery stores across the state of New York, but their only offspring turned it into a global brand that rakes in millions and millions every year.

He likes to play the part in every aspect of his life. From his stunning trophy wife to his picture-perfect blond-haired blue-eyed kids.

I've always been the odd one out. Trouble with a capital T. His reckless, selfish, stepdaughter who tarnishes his image with her out-of-control behavior.

Behavior *he* caused.

Not that he sees it that way.

On the surface, it looks like I want for nothing.

Behind the veil, I've been deprived of everything most girls my age take for granted.

Pain slices across my chest, so I reinforce my steel walls and

6

dull my emotions until there is only a calm emptiness in its place.

Climbing in my car, I start the engine as a shadowy form in the corner of the garage catches my eye. Mom ghosts toward me, the layers of her pink silk nightgown floating behind her as she approaches. She's walking with an obvious limp, and acid crawls up my throat. I lower the window when she reaches me, my eyes skimming the myriad of fresh bruises across her chest and arms. They're strategically placed to be hidden under clothes, but that's nothing new.

"Here." She hands me a thick, padded envelope. "That's all I've been able to get. Any more and he'd notice." I peek inside at the bundles of hundred-dollar bills. I don't even consider turning it down. I'll need every cent I can get my hands on. And this woman owes me so much more.

I decide on one last-ditch attempt. "It's not too late to take the twins and come with me. We can plan it. We can—"

"Stop, Van. You know he won't let me go." Her words are clear and un-slurred, and it's a rarity. Lucid moments between us have been few and far between lately. "There's no place we can run to where we can hide." She grabs my arm, looking at me with tear-filled eyes. "I know why you don't want to go, and I'll keep her safe."

A harsh laugh bursts from my lips. She's so fucking delusional.

"I'm sorry I failed you," she adds in a whisper, tears coursing down her cheeks. "You deserve so much more."

"I do, Mom. But this isn't about me anymore."

It's too late for me but not for my sister.

I clutch her arm, pinning her with a somber expression. "Don't fail Kayleigh, Mom, or I swear to God, I won't just be coming back for that monster."

Part One
Summer after High School

Chapter One
Jackson – eleven months later

"Thanks, man," Hunt says, as I step out of the elevator directly into the hallway of the New York penthouse apartment I share with him. He's shaking hands with a tall, skinny dude with glasses, both looking all serious and shit.

"Sup, dude." I jerk my head in acknowledgment at the geek when I reach them.

His nose wrinkles in distaste as he quickly scans my sweaty form.

It's hot as hell out today, so I ran my usual route in Central Park in minuscule training shorts and sneakers. Sweat has plastered hair to my brow, and it glistens on my upper torso, gliding a path down my spine. I wipe my slick brow with the back of my arm, sending a wave of stinky air in mystery dude's direction. His face pales, and I grin, chuckling when he takes a step away from me.

"Jamison was just leaving," Hunt confirms, ushering the guy toward the elevator I've just stepped out of.

I walk into our large open-plan living space, grab a bottle of water from the refrigerator, and stalk to the wide ceiling-to-floor window, looking out at the vast expanse of Central Park down below. I guzzle water as I survey the hustle and bustle of summertime life in New York.

Never thought I'd say it, but I miss Rydeville, and it's only been three weeks since we graduated high school and headed back to New York for summer break. I miss the more laid-back lifestyle, my other best bud Anderson, his wife Abby, and our group of friends. But I sure as shit don't miss all the elite crap we got caught up in.

"Do you have to be so obnoxious?" Hunt asks, appearing at my side.

I flash him my pearly whites. "Did I offend your fuck buddy?"

He rolls his eyes. "I'm not fucking Jamison. He's the guy I told you about. The one I've been paying handsomely to dig into Gerald Allen Junior's background. To see if he could find some link to Dani."

Pain prods at my heart, like it always does any time my sister is mentioned. I still struggle to believe she's gone. Even though it's been almost five years, the agony of losing her isn't fading. I spent years using weed, booze, and sex to numb the pain of her loss, but it also numbed me to most everything else.

Including the ability to properly mourn, and it denied me revenge.

It was Abigail Hearst-Manning—now Abigail Anderson, after she wed my buddy Kaiden last Christmas—who altered my way of thinking. Abby's strength and resolve pulled me out of my head. She fought to regain control of her life and to make her father and those elite bastards pay for what they did to her and others, and it ignited a spark that grew to a flame inside me.

Now, that flame is an inferno, raging wildly, barely

controlled, and the only thing that will tame it is finding the bastard who destroyed my sister and making him pay.

Dani may have taken her own life, but it was the things they did, *he* did, to her that broke her spirit and ended her will to live. Dani may have jumped off the roof of my parents' penthouse in downtown Manhattan, but it was Christian Montgomery who pushed her.

And I won't stop until that bastard is dead.

"Lauder." Hunt waves his hand in front of my face. "Did you hear anything I just said?"

"Sorry, man." I sigh, rubbing the tense spot in my chest. "I zoned out. Did the nerd find anything?"

"He found ... something," he cryptically replies, crossing to the large leather sectional and dropping down onto it. He grabs a paper file from the coffee table. "Not the something we were looking for, and I'm not sure how it helps or if it helps at all." He claws his hands through his dark hair, his brow furrowing.

It's not often I see Sawyer Hunt perplexed or so ill at ease.

"What is it?" I sink onto the couch beside him.

Wordlessly, he hands me the file, and I start reading. I'm vaguely aware of Hunt getting up, but I'm too engrossed in the shit the nerd uncovered to pay any attention. The room pulses with tense silence as I take it all in. "Holy fucking shit." I slam the file down beside me when I've finished reading it. "You didn't know?" I ask, glancing at my buddy's back. He's standing in front of the window, nursing an old-fashioned in his hand.

He turns around, shaking his head. "I had no idea."

"Where is she now?"

"In New York." He sips his drink, eyeing me warily.

"You got an address?" I ask, my foot tapping off the ground.

"Why? What're you planning?"

I scrub a hand over my prickly jaw. "I'm not sure yet. I need to think it through."

Hunt sighs, walking back to me. He sits down on the edge of the large coffee table. "I know you don't like her."

I snort out a laugh. "That's an understatement. In all the years we've vacationed in The Hamptons, I've never once wet my dick in her pussy. What does that tell you?"

"That she's clingy and even you don't go there."

"Exactly." I prop my feet up on the coffee table, ignoring Hunt's scowl. "Look how scary she was after Anderson fucked her that one time." A shudder works its way through me. "Desperate is not a good look on Vanessa, and it's a shame because she's hot as fuck. Pity she's so batshit crazy."

"I've always felt sorry for her," Hunt admits.

"Save me the speech," I snap, guessing where he's going with this.

"I wonder if she knows," he muses, draining the last of his whiskey.

"There's only one way to find out."

Hunt narrows his eyes. "What are you going to do?"

"I think it's time I paid Vanessa Breen a little visit, don't you?"

"You got her address yet?" I ask a couple days later when Hunt returns from a hard day at the office. His dad insists he puts the hours in at Techxet, the multibillion-dollar global technology company he will one day inherit.

Hunt has mad tech skills, and access to a whole team full of expert brains, and he's our go-to guy when we need something. When you add Xavier Daniels to the mix—he's another IT genius and Hunt's sometime bed partner—it feels like we're unstoppable.

Which is why the lack of intel on this one simple matter

14

has me all kinds of suspicious. Hunt could get Vanessa's address in minutes without resorting to his IT skills. One phone call to his parents would do the job.

"Do you have to be such a slob?" Hunt grumbles, pursing his lips as he bends down to pick up some crumpled soda cans from the floor. I briefly scan the room, wondering what he's bitching and whining about. Sure, it's a little messy, but it's not that bad.

My wet towel still lies in a heap where I deposited it after my post-run shower, and my sweaty shorts and sneakers rest by the window. The coffee table is littered with used cups and plates and empty cookie and chip packets. Tons of files and papers surround me as I sit on the floor. I had started my investigative work on the couch, but I needed more space to go through all the evidence nerdy Jamison has dug up these past couple months.

"Florentina will be here tomorrow to clean up," I remind him. "No need to get your panties in a bunch."

Hunt and I lived together for the past year, but it was easier in Rydeville because my house there is over ten-thousand-square feet of prime real estate, and it was easy to forget I was cohabiting. Hunt's penthouse is more confined, and it shows. His anal ways are grating on my nerves as much as my messiness and lack of care are grating on his.

"All I ask is that you fucking tidy up after yourself." He holds his nose while picking up my towel, grimacing like he's holding soiled boxers. "I cannot live like this all summer."

"Don't take your blue balls out on me," I shout after him as he walks toward the laundry room. "Tomorrow's Friday. Call Xavier and get his ass up here. You need to get laid."

Hunt glares at me when he returns with a large black garbage bag. "Do not fucking push me, Lauder. And for the last time, Xavier and I are casual and nonexclusive. We have barely fucked around and it's not something I'll be making a habit of."

"If you say so." I smirk, crawling to the table and tossing some crap into the garbage bag. "Call up one of your secretaries or that bartender chick you had the hots for last summer. Just find someone to fuck, because you're already getting on my very last nerve."

"You want her address or not?" Hunt snaps, clearing away the dirty dishes.

"So, you're admitting you have it?"

"We both know I have it," he calls over his shoulder. "Whether I'll give it to you is another thing."

I climb to my feet, tying a knot in the bag once all the garbage is cleared.

"What's your problem?" I ask, dumping the bag in the laundry room. Florentina can dispose of it tomorrow.

"I need to know your intentions," he admits, grabbing a couple of mugs from the overhead cupboard in the kitchen. He switches the Keurig on, loosening his tie as he waits for the coffee to brew.

"Why? You want in her panties again?"

"You can't hurt her," he says, ignoring my question.

I quirk a brow, snatching creamer from the refrigerator. "Who said anything about hurting her?"

Hunt crosses his arms and narrows his eyes at me. "Don't act dumb. We've been friends long enough for me to know the way that fucked-up brain of yours works."

"I'll take that as a compliment."

"It wasn't meant as one."

I chuckle as I take the mug of steaming coffee from his hand. "I'm making no promises, dude. And don't pretend you care. Anderson was a complete prick to Vanessa, and I didn't notice you stepping in."

"It's different now," he says, leaning back against the counter.

"How?" I take a sip of the bitter liquid, enjoying the burn as it glides down my throat.

"Her stepdad kicked her out last summer. She's on her own."

"Can't say I blame him. She's been out of control for years."

Hunt stares me out of it. "You are such a fucking hypocrite."

"It's not the fucking same," I hiss. Anger claws at my insides. "I thought you wanted to help? It's why I came to you. Why I haven't said a fucking word to Anderson about what we're doing."

The other reason is Kai is all loved up, and I don't want to drag him or Abby into this. They've dealt with enough shit to last a lifetime. They deserve to be happy, and I know if they knew what I had planned, they'd want in. I don't want that for them. Which is why only Hunt and I are in the know. It's why we're using fucking Jamison to help and not Xavier.

If Hunt is having second thoughts, I'll need to revisit my strategy. I'm not holding back this time.

Atticus fucking Anderson—Kai's dad—dropped the truth on me just before we moved to Rydeville at the start of senior year. He made me promise to keep that intel to myself and not to take matters into my own hands.

The bigger picture was more urgent.

Taking Michael Hearst down had to happen first.

I understood, but I hated it. However, Atticus promised Christian would be our next priority, and I stupidly believed him. The selfish asshole was lying to all of us. Now, he's fled overseas, and Christian is MIA too, and I'm kicking myself over all my lost chances.

I could have taken Christian out on any number of occasions, but I didn't, and now, I'm full of regret and brimming with hatred.

"Don't pull that shit on me." Hunt slams his mug down, coffee spilling over the edges. "I loved Dani as if she was my big sister too. I want vengeance as much as you do."

I know that's the truth. Sawyer is an only child, and he spent a huge amount of time hanging out at our house when we were kids. Our parents have been friends for years, and we did most things together. Sawyer looked up to Dani the same way I did. What happened to her killed him too.

But she was *my* flesh and blood.

My sister.

I should have protected her and kept her safe.

And after she died, I should have taken my revenge. Instead, I spent years wallowing in grief and self-pity, wasting the opportunity to take care of that bastard Montgomery. Now, he's hiding overseas, a wanted fugitive, and I'm only one of a number of people searching for his ass.

"He needs to pay," Hunt adds.

"So, what's the fucking issue?" I shout, throwing my hands in the air.

"I don't want you taking any of this out on her. *That's* my issue."

"I never fucking said that!" I'm fudging on purpose. Truth is, I have realized the last couple nights that the best way of getting to Christian Montgomery is through her.

I'm prepared to do whatever it takes.

I couldn't care less about Vanessa Breen.

She's a means to an end.

And if she gets trampled on the way to my end goal, I sure as fuck won't lose any sleep over it.

Chapter Two
Vanessa

"I hate being cooped up inside on days like this," Chloe says in between puffing on her cigarette.

"I used to spend most of my summers at The Hamptons," I admit, leaning my head back against the wall and bathing my face under the beating hot sun.

The small diner I work at, in the heart of the city, is situated on a corner, and there is only a single-story building at the back of us, so there's no looming monstrosity towering over us, blocking out the light. This tiny alley serves as our meeting point when we're on a break. Paul, the owner, is a really good guy, and he even put a few tables and chairs out here so we can eat our lunch outside if we want. "So, I basically lived on the beach. I miss it," I add with a sad smile. "I didn't properly appreciate it until it was gone."

Truth is, I was usually hungover on my lounge chair most days, hiding behind huge sunglasses to mask my bloodshot eyes.

"Lucky bitch." Chloe throws her cigarette butt to the ground, stomping on it. "I've never been to The Hamptons. I've heard it's wild."

"It can be." Taking a swig from my bottle of water, I reminisce about summers past.

"What was it like?" she asks, tucking her short red hair behind her ears as she glances at me.

"The Hunts, and the Lauders, and a whole host of other wealthy families mixed in the same circles as my parents, and it became an unwritten rule that we would spend our summers together," I start explaining. "Everyone congregated at The Hamptons during summer break. The men would leave during the week to attend to work while the women and kids stayed in their vacation homes. When our teen years hit, the partying started hard. Money was in endless supply. As was booze, weed, prescription pills, and hardcore drugs. I spent most summers high, drunk, or hungover."

"Sounds fun." She waggles her brows.

"It was, and it wasn't." I take another sip of water, not wanting to elaborate. I've blocked a lot of it out for a variety of reasons.

"And you can't repair things with your folks?" Curiosity lingers in her tone.

Chloe is the first real best friend I've had in a long time, and while I've opened up to her a little, she doesn't know anything about my past, and that's the way I want to keep it.

I vigorously shake my head. "It's complicated, and trust me, it's for the best."

This past year has been tough but liberating. I stayed at a hostel the first few nights until I found this job and Paul agreed to rent the small studio apartment above the diner to me. After I sold my car, I had enough money to cover my rent for the year, and my salary and tips cover everything else.

I expected the funding for my private school to be cut, but I wasn't hugely surprised when it wasn't. My despicable step-monster is on the board at West Lorian High, and it wouldn't

20

look good if I didn't finish my schooling there. I graduated with a three-point-five GPA which I'm proud of, because my academic record is patchy, to say the least.

"Ladies." Paul pokes his head out the back door. "We're swamped in here."

"We're coming," Chloe says as I recap my water and follow her back inside.

The next couple hours go by in a blur. The diner is popular with locals, and it's pretty much always tourist season in New York, so we have a constant line out the door.

"Couple hotties at the end booth are asking for you," Mara says while I fix drinks for the family at table ten.

I raise a brow. "You sure they were talking about me?"

"They asked for you by name, sweetie," the older waitress says, placing a hand over her heart. "If I was only younger, I'd make a play for them myself."

Chloe nudges Mara with her hip. "Get over yourself, old woman. We both know you've already hit on them."

I smile when Mara shrugs. "Can't blame a gal for trying." She winks at me. "When you get to my age, you've got to take your thrills where you can get them!" She walks off, cackling.

"She's crazy." Chloe shakes her head, her lips twitching.

"Certifiable," I agree, but we mean it affectionately.

Mara is like your mom and friend rolled into one. Always good for a laugh, and she doesn't take herself too seriously, but she's also the first one to offer sage advice.

Mara and Paul are siblings, and they've owned and run this place the past twenty years. Neither is married, so we are the only family they have. They both have big hearts and a penchant for rescuing strays and orphans, like me.

There's no doubt I lucked out when I found this place last summer.

"Whatcha waiting for?" Chloe asks, swiping my tray. "I'll deliver this. You go check out the man candy."

Tucking some stray strands of my dark-blonde hair behind my ears, I tighten my ponytail and wipe my sweaty hands down the front of my apron. Then, I grab my pen and pad and walk toward the end booth.

I spot Sawyer Hunt first. Difficult not to when he's facing my way. His tall frame is upright against the backrest, his features fixed on me, and his stare is intense like a heat-seeking missile.

Even though I can only see his back, it's not challenging to figure out who Sawyer's lunch buddy is. The dirty-blond hair, broad shoulders, and deep chuckle give Jackson Lauder away.

Nerves punch me in the gut, but I force them aside, plastering a smile on my face. "Hey, guys. Long time, no see."

"Hey, Van." Sawyer smiles. "It's good to see you."

"You too. I didn't realize you were back in New York."

My skin tingles when I feel Jackson Lauder's hot gaze on the side of my face.

"Just for the summer," Sawyer adds, sipping a soda Mara obviously brought him.

"We're planning to hit The Hamptons next month," Jackson says, speaking for the first time. "You in?"

I turn my head toward him, smothering my shocked gasp. Jackson has always been good-looking, but he has matured into one hot as fuck sexy bastard. His hair is longer at the front, falling stylishly into blue eyes as deep as the ocean. He's sporting a thin layer of scruff on his chin and jawline, and my fingers itch to explore the angled planes of his face. With a strong nose, high cheekbones, and lips I've always longed to taste, Jackson Lauder is sex on a stick.

My long-forgotten libido awakens, and lust pools low in my belly.

22

In a lightning-fast move, Jackson extends his arm, tipping my chin up with his finger. "Careful you don't catch flies." He winks, gracing me with the full extent of his killer smile, and I consciously snap myself out of whatever trance I'm in.

Heat creeps up my neck and on to my cheeks. "Still a cocky asshole," I mutter.

"Still cocky," he agrees, grabbing his crotch suggestively. "You never got up close and personal. We should rectify that."

It wasn't for lack of trying. I cringe as I recall the number of times I threw myself at him. Or the number of times he rebuked me. Which was humiliating because Jackson Lauder is a walking STD. He only has to trip and his cock impales a pussy.

The queen bees of The Hamptons loved rubbing my nose in it.

Even though I was besties with Sawyer—a situation our parents forced—and I hung out with him, Jackson, and Camden a lot, they treated me like I had the plague.

Except for the time I took Sawyer's virginity. And that one night, the summer before junior year, when I pounced on a very drunk Camden Marshall and he fucked me. Every other time, they kept me at arm's length while they happily took other girls for a ride on their cocks.

"Are you ... hitting on me?" Disbelief underscores my tone.

"What if I am?" Jackson leans his elbows on the table, and his biceps flex and roll with the motion. It's obvious he has sorted his shit out since I last saw him. I guess that is something we've got in common. Although I'm still a work in progress.

"Then I'd tell you you're wasting your time," I lie. "Because I'm not the same person you knew."

"Is that right?" He dazzles me with a panty-melting smile.

Paul calls my name, and I glance over my shoulder, grateful

for the interruption. My boss gestures with his hands, urging me to hurry up.

"You want to order something?" I grip my pen, keeping it poised over my notepad, purposely ending the flirtatiousness.

"The older waitress took our order," Sawyer confirms.

"She's something else," Jackson adds, and my lips twitch.

"I've got to get back to work. I'm not part of The Hamptons' crew anymore, so I won't be there, but have fun," I say, moving to walk away.

"Van, wait." Sawyer slides out of the booth, gently taking my elbow. He slips a card into my hand. "That's my number. Text me so I have yours, and if you need anything, call me."

"Why?" I blurt, looking up at him as I drop the card into the front pocket of my apron.

"I don't know what's happened, but I know you're on your own." His earnest hazel eyes drill into mine. "We were good friends one time."

"When we were like ten." Honestly, every other summer, he avoided me as much as he could.

He lets my elbow go, holding his hands up. "I have no agenda, Van. If you find yourself in need of a friend, call me."

I search his eyes and his gorgeous face, and I detect no hint of a lie. His offer is sincere, and only an idiot would turn him down. "Okay, thanks." I cast one last glance at Jackson, and his eyes are fixated on my bare legs. I'm the tallest of all the waitresses here, and the pink-and-white-plaid dress uniform is shorter on me than most of the women, so I'm flashing a fair amount of skin.

Without overthinking it, I grab a napkin off the table and dab the corner of Jackson's mouth. "You had a little drool."

Sawyer's deep laughter follows me from the booth, and I'm fighting a grin as I head back to work.

I didn't see the guys leave because it was a crazy busy shift, and I was late finishing up, which means I'm late arriving at Kayleigh's class.

Every Thursday at five, I sneak into the auditorium on Fifty-ninth Street where she takes weekly ballet classes. Mom lets me have an hour after ballet ends to take her out. I don't know what lies she's told her bastard husband, but I don't care because this time is precious, and I'll take it for as long as I can get it. I only wish I had time to spend with Hunter too, but it's far too risky because he's close with his dad and he's not as street smart as his twin sister. Without me or Mom having to explain it, Kayleigh understands her father can never know she still sees me or these visits will stop.

I slink into a seat in the back row of the auditorium, watching my little sister command the stage like a pro.

She skips out of the changing area after the session has finished, throwing herself into my arms, and I hold her tight, closing my eyes as I drink in her comforting warmth.

"Can we get ice cream?" she asks, her blue eyes sparkling with expectation.

"Sure can." I grab her hand, swinging our arms together as we walk out of the auditorium. "But practice first."

She nods, humming to herself as we walk toward the south midtown entrance to Central Park. Kayleigh chatters away as we head to our usual place, and I hold her hand tighter, smiling as she regales me with tales of her week. She's like a little ray of sunshine in an otherwise dark world, and I cherish our time together. So far, I detect nothing to indicate he's preying on her. She's her usual bright, bubbly self, and I offer up a silent prayer it continues to stay that way.

We drop our bags behind the large elm tree and begin our lesson. I've been taking Krav Maga classes since I was fifteen, and that was the last time that bastard put his hands on me. I hate that I need to instruct my ten-year-old sister in basic self-defense techniques, but I was only slightly older than her when Aaron started crawling into my bed at night.

I don't know if the fact she is his flesh and blood will make a difference. To me, once a predator, always a predator, and I won't take any chances. Mom stood by and let her husband sexually assault and rape me for years, so I can't rely on her to keep Kayleigh safe. The only person who can do that is Kayleigh, so I'm trying to find a way to help her without going into all the reasons why.

When we're done, I take her to the ice cream stand, and then, we sit on the bench close to the exit, eating our ice cream and sipping from bottles of water, chatting as we wait for Mom to collect her.

"Romy says Mitchell thinks I'm pretty," she admits, peeking at me through her lashes. A faint blush stains her cheeks. Romy is her best friend at school, but this is the first time I'm hearing about Mitchell.

"That's sweet, and he's right. You're such a pretty little princess." I smile at her, sweeping a stray strand of hair out of her face before it lands in her ice cream. "And what about him? Is he cute?"

She shrugs, but by the way her cheeks flare up, I'm guessing she thinks so. "Romy said he wants to be my boyfriend."

I almost choke on my water. "I think you're a little young to be thinking about boyfriends." I kiss the top of her head. "There will be plenty of time for that when you're older." I just want to bundle my sister up and keep her away from guys until she's old enough.

"Boys are kinda gross anyway," she adds, dipping her tongue into her ice cream, licking the very last remnants of her cone.

"Truth, girl." I kiss the top of her head again. "And when they don't feel gross is when you know you're ready to date." I'm not sure I'm the best person to be advising her, but I'm all she's got. My phone pings with a text, and I sigh, rubbing the sudden sharp pain that pierces my chest cavity. I stand, holding out my hand. "Time to go, little princess."

"I hate this part." Sadness clouds her eyes.

"Me too." I kiss the tip of her nose. "But it won't be forever." I dump our trash and turn to her with a sad smile.

"I love you, Nessa." She flings her arms around me.

My heart blossoms to life behind my chest. "I love you too, Kayleigh." I hug her close. "So, so much."

My cell pings a second time, and I grind my teeth to my molars as I reluctantly extricate myself from my sister and walk her out of the park.

Mom's car is idling by the curb. I kiss and hug Kayleigh once more before opening the door to the back seat, watching her climb in. "Enjoy the beach," I say, because they are heading to The Hamptons this weekend, and I won't see her for a few weeks. The thought makes my heart ache, but I keep a smile plastered on my face, purely for Kayleigh's benefit.

Mom lowers the passenger side window, and I poke my head in. "How are you?" she asks, hiding her eyes behind large sunglasses.

"I'm okay." She's wearing a long-sleeved patterned blouse in the height of summer. "How are you?"

"Fine." She removes an envelope from the glove box, stretching across the console to hand it to me. "It's not much, but I have to be careful."

"I know, Mom." I take the envelope and stuff it in my bag.

I fucking hate this.

I hate how weak she is.

How she let herself get trapped like this.

27

How she let that monster control every aspect of her life.

How she abandoned her kids and checked out on life instead of fighting.

But another part of me understands because I spent years trying to numb myself to everything too.

The difference is she was an adult with responsibilities.

Still, she's trying now, in the only way she knows how.

"Thanks, Mom." I glance at the back seat. "Keep him away from her," I whisper so Kayleigh doesn't hear.

She nods. "Stay safe, honey."

I step back from the curb, watching with a heavy heart as Mom eases back out into traffic.

"Cute kid," a deep, masculine voice says at my ear, and I jump in fright.

"Are you trying to give me a coronary!" I shriek, eyeing Jackson in disbelief. "Are you following me?" Grabbing the strap of my bag, I take a step away from him.

"No need to freak the hell out, Nessa. It's not like I'm some fucking serial killer." He grabs his white wifebeater from the back pocket of his running shorts, using it to wipe a light sheen of sweat from his brow. "Someone got me all hot and bothered earlier, and I needed a run." His eyes twinkle with mischief.

My eyes roam over his sculpted chest and down over his carved abs. I lick my lips at the sight of the defined V-indents at his hips and the trail of dark-blond hair sneaking under the waistband of his shorts. "I don't remember you looking like that," I blurt, instantly cursing myself for having zero game. Jackson was always toned with lean muscle, but this is a new look for him.

One I like.

A lot.

He presses warm lips to my ear, making my knees tremble and my legs turn to Jell-O. "Liking what you see, babe?"

"You know you look good," I admit, refusing to look into his eyes. "You were never shy about that."

"I know who I am, and I own it." He brushes some strands of hair off his brow. "Although, I wasn't in control back then."

I startle at his admission, meeting his gaze dead on.

"You're not the only one who has changed," he adds, his voice gentling.

I'm momentarily speechless.

"You got plans?" he asks, and I shake my head. "Have dinner with me?"

"What?"

Have I wandered into some alternate realm? What the hell is going on here?

His answering smile almost knocks me off my feet. "Let me take you to dinner."

"Why?" The word has left my lips before I can stop it. I'm acting like a total idiot, and it's embarrassing.

"Because I want to enjoy the company of a beautiful woman, and I owe you an apology for all those times I was a dick to you."

"You don't have to buy me dinner to apologize. Apology accepted."

He chuckles. "Are you always like this when someone asks you out on a date?"

"I wouldn't know," I whisper, averting my eyes. "No one has ever asked me out before." My cheeks flare at that admission.

It's pathetic.

I'm nineteen.

I've been sexually active for years.

I've done things most girls my age haven't done or are unlikely to ever do.

Yet, I have never been on a proper date.

"Then, it's decided." He takes my hand, bringing it to his lips. His mouth brushes against my knuckles, and I feel his featherlight kiss all over my body. "I'm taking you out, and I won't take no for an answer."

Chapter Three
Jackson

Vanessa is standing outside the front of the diner where she works when I pull up in my SUV a few minutes before eight. I park at the curb and hop out as she walks toward me.

Fuck, she looks beautiful. She's wearing a long summery pink dress with a white flower pattern, and it clings to her gorgeous curves in all the right places. The material flows from the hips down, and it swishes around her thighs and legs as she approaches. On top, it has thin straps, and it dips a little at the cleavage. Not enough to show me the goods, but enough to show a hint of flesh that already has my cock stirring behind the zipper of my shorts. Her hair is hanging in soft waves down her back, and she's not wearing much make up.

If she wasn't such a nutjob, and I didn't have ulterior motives, she would be my dream girl.

"Hey." Her cheeks flush, and her smile is tentative. She looks nervous, and that surprises me a little. Although, she did tell me this was her first-ever date. That shocked me. I know most guys at The Hamptons just wanted to fuck her, but she had plenty of admirers at West Lorian High.

We purposely kept our distance from her at school. I only shared one class with her, and I spent a few years ambling my way through life, perpetually stoned, so I missed a lot of shit. But I'm still shocked no one asked her out.

I lean in, brushing my lips against her cheek. "You are stunning."

The stain on her cheeks darkens. "Thank you. You look nice too." Her cheeks are flaming red now. "I mean, you look hot," she stutters.

Man, this is going to be a cakewalk.

I chuckle, taking her hand. "C'mon. We don't want to be late." I help her into the passenger seat of my car before sliding behind the wheel. I ease the car back out into the traffic. "I hope you like cocktails and pizza," I say, honking my horn at some asshat who cuts out in front of me.

"Sounds perfect." She shoots me another shy smile, and I have to admit I'm intrigued. Anytime I've been around Vanessa in the past, she's been either hungover and mute or drunk and cray-cray.

I'm not sure what to make of this version of her.

Not that it matters.

I have one goal here, and one goal only: To make her fall for me.

I told Hunt it was so I could get close enough to find out where that bastard Montgomery is hiding, but there is a possibility she doesn't know. If that's the case, then I have a Plan B—ruin her like he ruined my sister so he can't use her to further his elite aims.

Just to be clear, Hunt *isn't* aware of Plan B. He's already unhappy with Plan A, and if he knew how far I was prepared to take this, there's no way in hell he'd help me.

Jackson

I don't care that she's innocent in all this. So was Dani, and that didn't stop Christian Montgomery. It's time he got a taste of his own medicine.

"Wow. I love this place." Vanessa's big blue eyes are out on stalks as she casts her gaze around New York's hottest new it place.

I only managed to get last-minute reservations because Dad is one of the investors in Glitter. It's primarily a cocktail bar, but it offers casual dining options too. After midnight, the basement club opens its doors to partygoers. In the ten months since it opened, it has become a popular spot with rich brats and celebs. "I can't believe you haven't been here before," I say, breaking off a piece of bread and popping it in my mouth.

"I don't get out much." She shrugs, sipping on her sparkling water.

"How come? You're eighteen, free of high school and parental bonds, living in central New York, and I know you like to party."

"I'm nineteen, actually, and I'm trying to turn over a new leaf." She sips her water, eyeing me carefully.

"I never realized you were older than us," I truthfully admit.

She bites down on her lower lip, and I try to ignore how sexy she looks chewing on her mouth. "I ended up having to repeat freshman year," she adds.

My eyes pop wide. "Wow. That's almost unheard of. What'd you do? Murder someone or something?" I joke.

Her eyes lower to the table, and she fidgets with her napkin. I reach across the table, unknotting her fingers. "Hey. I was only teasing. We don't have to talk about it."

"I want to," she says, raising her eyes and staring at me. "It's just hard to look back at certain things from my past and not feel depressed."

I'm beginning to realize I don't know a fucking thing about this girl, and she's definitely piqued my curiosity. "I'm a judgment-free zone," I say, slurping some of my Coke. "And you certainly didn't write the book on reckless behavior. I've done plenty of crazy shit I'm not proud of."

She props her elbows on the table and rests her chin in her hands, staring off into space, like she's contemplating how much to tell me.

I wait her out, grabbing another piece of bread from the basket and breaking it up with my fingers.

"I kinda had a mini breakdown during freshman year. Went off the rails. Barely showed up at school. Normally, they would have expelled me, but my stepfather got involved." Her jaw tightens, and her eyes flash with undecipherable emotion.

Interesting.

There's some beef between them although she wouldn't be the first stepkid to have issues with her stepparent.

"He's on the school board, right?" I vaguely remember that.

"Yeah, and he fixed it so I could repeat the year. That's how I ended up at school with all of you."

"Cool." I don't pry because it's obvious she doesn't want to elaborate. I'm supposed to be romancing her, and forcing her to remember fucked-up shit will not help my cause. "So, where do you usually party?"

She shrugs. "I'm not much of a party girl anymore."

"Wow. You really have turned over a new leaf."

"I needed to make changes for my sanity," she quietly says, sipping from her water again. "And, besides, I don't have the money for going out."

I open my mouth but clamp it shut when I see the waiter

returning with our appetizers. We are silent as he places plates in front of us.

"Thank you." Nessa smiles, and he grins, his eyes lowering to her tits for a fleeting second.

I clear my throat, narrowing my eyes at him. "That will be all."

"Of course, sir," he grits out, backing away, shooting one last flirtatious smile at Vanessa.

"Hunt told me you weren't living at home anymore. I just assumed that was by choice," I say, placing a napkin on my lap.

"My stepfather threw me out and cut me off. It happened just after Sawyer sent me home from The Hamptons last summer. I had some money saved, but that's mostly gone, so I'm living on what I earn and tips. I don't have the luxury of nights out anymore," she supplies, picking up her silverware. "Except for movie nights with some of the girls from the diner, and I've gone to a few house parties."

"If you need money—"

"I'm not taking money off you!" The red stain on her cheeks isn't embarrassment this time. "I'm doing fine by myself." Her eyes blaze with determination as she holds her head up. "I have a job, a roof over my head, food in my refrigerator, and a lock on my door to keep the monsters out."

What the fuck? Has Christian made his presence known already? Could he be in New York?

"What kind of monsters?" I inquire before digging into a chicken wing.

Her tongue darts out, wetting her plump lips, and my eyes greedily follow the motion. "I was speaking metaphorically," she says, and I know it's a lie because she won't look me in the eye.

"I admire you," I say, and her eyes pop wide. "What?" I ask.

"You can't stand me," she replies, cutting into her salad. "I still don't get why you asked me out."

Perhaps, she's more astute than I've given her credit for. I stare into her beautiful, big blue eyes. "We've both changed, and we're not dumb teenagers anymore. It's summer in New York. You're beautiful. I'm hot." I shoot her a cocky smile. "And I want to get to know this new Vanessa. She has me intrigued, and that doesn't happen a lot." That's only half a lie. I disarm her with another dazzling smile, and she stares at me in a bit of a daze.

"This new you scares me."

"What's not to love?" I gesture at myself. "And I haven't completely changed." I waggle my brows.

She rolls her eyes. "The hot comment hadn't gone unnoticed, thank you." She grins, popping another forkful of salad into her tempting mouth.

"So, why are you scared?"

"I'm scared of feeling, and you, Jackson Lauder, have the potential to make me feel all kinds of feels."

"You want to get out of here?" I ask after we have finished eating. I wouldn't mind heading to the basement club, but it will be loud as fuck down there and full of assholes ogling my date.

Vanessa has garnered her fair share of admirers tonight, but she seems oblivious. She's not at all what I was expecting, and I'm surprised at how easy our conversation flows. She's not the out-of-control airhead exuding clinger-slash-stalker vibes anymore. That will make this easier to endure. *Hell, who am I kidding?* My cock's been hard as a brick all night.

There appears to be little about fake seducing Vanessa I won't like.

"I don't mind." She's way more easygoing than I remember.

"How about a drive to Coney Island? We could go on some rides or take a walk?"

"A walk sounds good." She beams at me, and her entire face lights up. Her eyes are glowing, and her face is full of life, and I am momentarily spellbound, staring at her like I've never seen a pretty girl before.

"I haven't been to Coney Island in years," she adds. "I hear they cleaned it all up."

"I haven't been back there since Dani died," I admit, breaking out from under her spell and snapping my fingers at the sleazy waiter, gesturing for the check.

"I still can't believe she's gone," Vanessa says in a soft tone. "She was always super sweet to me. Especially when some of her friends were being mean. She always stood up for me."

"I didn't know that," I admit, my mouth turning dry. We all hung out as kids, but Dani wasn't close to Vanessa, or at least, not that I noticed.

The waiter hands me the check on a circular silver plate, and I hand him my platinum card without even looking at it. He scurries off to swipe it.

"I was shocked when I found out she'd taken her own life," Vanessa continues, pinning me with compassionate eyes. "Dani always seemed happy and so together. I guess you never know what's going on inside someone's head."

"Or what's been done to someone to push them to that point," I blurt.

Her brow puckers in confusion.

The waiter returns, handing me the printout and a pen. I'm tempted to leave no tip because the guy's been drooling over my date all night, but even I'm not that miserable. I smirk as I fill it in and add my signature. I hand it back to him and stand, extending my hand for Vanessa. Her tiny, warm hand lands in mine, and her touch sends shards of electricity shooting up my arm, surprising me.

"Is this a joke?" the waiter hisses, glaring at me.

I tuck Vanessa into my side and lean into the guy, staring pointedly at him. "I'd have left more than a dollar tip if you hadn't been eye-fucking my date all night," I retort.

"Fuck you, asshole." He looks like he wants to punch me.

I cluck my tongue. "I suggest you look at the name on that receipt and shut your fucking mouth before I have you fired." His face pales when he checks out my surname, and I almost feel sorry for him.

Almost.

"I'm so sorry, Mr. Lauder. Sir. I apologize for my disrespect. It won't happen again."

What a tool. "I suggest you avoid ogling the clientele if you want to hold on to your job." I offer some parting advice before escorting Vanessa to the underground parking garage.

"I adore the beach," Vanessa says, leaning over the railing on the boardwalk, examining the sandy stretch of shoreline with a wistful look on her face. She tips her face up a little, inhaling deeply. "I could never live anywhere too far from the ocean."

"I agree." I come up behind her, caging her in with my arms, maintaining a small gap between our bodies. We stare at the ocean in amicable silence. All around us, people are enjoying everything Coney Island has to offer. Although it's almost eleven, the place is still thrumming with activity.

"How are you feeling being back here?" she asks, angling her body a little and turning her head up to face me.

My eyes automatically drop to her lips, and an urge to kiss her arises out of nowhere.

"I'm doing okay," I truthfully admit. "It's a beautiful, balmy night. The scent of the ocean is calling to me. And I've a gorgeous girl on my arm. What's not to like?"

She squeezes my arm. "Thank you for taking me."

"My pleasure." Wispy strands of her hair blow across her face, and I tuck them behind her ears, pretending I don't feel the crackle of electricity zipping in the space between us or the tingle in my fingertips where my touch grazes her silky-smooth skin. "Want to walk in the ocean?" I blurt, stepping back and breaking the spell before I do something crazy like kiss her for real.

"Sure." A brief flash of disappointment races across her face, and the smug inner predator lingering under my skin silently fist pumps the air.

I lace my fingers in hers, and we hold hands until we step off the boardwalk and down onto the shore. Vanessa removes her bejeweled, white flat-heeled sandals while I toe off my Nikes. We walk to the water, and Vanessa fists her dress in one hand, lifting it until it reaches her knees.

The water is cool, with a hint of warmth, as it swirls around my toes.

"It's warmer than I expected," she says, smiling at me as we walk along the water's edge.

"If there weren't so many people around, I'd suggest skinny-dipping." I wink suggestively.

"Of course, you would." She giggles. "Remember that time we went skinny-dipping and Melania got stung by a jellyfish on her boob?"

I crack up laughing. "Fuck, yeah. She was screaming and shrieking so bad I thought she'd been attacked by a shark. Man, that was nasty. She had blisters all over her tits for days after." I remember because I'd hooked up with her a few nights later, and the sight of the raised, red skin on her chest had almost cost me my hard-on.

I already admitted I was a dick, right?

Vanessa's smile fades. "Couldn't have happened to a more deserving person. She was a bitch, and I happen to think karma was at work that night."

"They were all bitches," I admit, slinging my arm around her shoulder. "And we were dicks for not defending you."

Vanessa's reckless behavior didn't win her any fans. The girls chose not to associate with her because she was such a hot mess. They enjoyed ridiculing her any chance they got. Guys ran a mile because she exuded scary clinger vibes. Didn't stop most of them from wetting their dicks in her pussy, but she was tossed to the curb after they got what they wanted.

We could've done more.

Should've done more.

But we were pissed Hunt's dad kept foisting her on us, insisting we hang out with her and look after her, and we tended to do the opposite. She was annoying to be around. Always drunk or high or pawing at us. Hunt was the most patient, but even he struggled to deal with her when she was out of control.

Like I said, we were dicks.

She shrugs, but I know if it wasn't so dark out I'd see hurt written all over her face. I need to lighten the sudden tense atmosphere. "But seriously, what's a guy to do to get you naked?"

She shoves me off, but she's grinning. "You're an asshole."

"Never said I wasn't."

"But you're also a good guy, Jackson."

Yeah, I'm so not. Something twists and turns in my gut, and it feels a lot like guilt.

Her amusement transforms as she looks at me with serious eyes. "I see the good in you, and whatever baggage you're carrying because of what happened to Dani, you should let it go. That's not on you. You were a great brother, and she adored you."

"We should head back. It's getting late, and you have work tomorrow." Her words are cutting too close to the bone, and I need to shut this shit down now.

We wade out of the water, retrieve our shoes, and head back to my car.

"I'll walk you to your door," I offer after I've parked at the curb alongside the diner and killed the engine. I still can't believe she lives in a tiny hovel over her place of work, but I've kept those thoughts to myself.

I'm trying to woo her, not piss her off.

Although, I wasn't lying when I said I admired her. She's taken the shitty hand she's been dealt, and she's trying to make the best of it. I admire her strength and her determination, and I never would've believed she had it in her, but she has changed.

Vanessa giggles, and the sound does funny things to my insides. "I think I can manage."

"I'm trying to be a gentleman here," I quip.

"Perhaps, you should avoid talking about how to get me naked in that case," she teases.

"Duly noted." I brush my thumb along one side of her face, and she visibly shivers. "Wait there. I'll get the door."

I climb out, rounding the hood of my SUV and opening the door for her. I take her hand and help her out.

We hold hands as I walk her to her door, and I find myself wishing the night wasn't coming to an end.

But that's exactly why it should.

She stops at her door, turning to face me. "Thank you for a wonderful first date, Jackson. I had a really great time."

"It's my pleasure, Nessa." I move in closer until our chests brush.

She tilts her head up, pinning me with those hypnotizing baby blues.

"Would you be up for a second date, and possibly a third, and maybe more?" I rub my nose along the side of hers, smiling as she gasps.

"I'd like that," she whispers, her warm breath fanning across my cheek. The subtle scent of her light floral perfume wafts around me, and I've a sudden, unexpected urge to bundle her into my arms and hold her tight. If I didn't know her rep, I'd mistake her for a sweet, virginal princess. But I *do* know her rep, and she's as far removed from an innocent virgin as you can get.

"I'll text you," I promise, easing back a little to look at her. Her face is still angled toward me, her eyes swimming in expectation. Slowly, I lower my face, lining our mouths up, staring into her eyes, giving her a way out, before I close that last tiny gap between us and brush my lips against hers.

Her eyes shutter, and she presses into me as my arms circle her slim waist. I tilt my head to the side and plant my lips more firmly on hers, deepening the kiss as I hold her close. She kisses me back with the same skill and enthusiasm, and my cock strains painfully against my zipper. I moan into her mouth as my hands leave her waist, traveling up her body and winding into her beautiful hair.

She tastes divine, like liquid temptation and a tangible slice of heaven. Lust thunders through my veins, and the need to consume her rides me hard. Damn, her kisses are addictive, and her mouth fits against mine with ease, like we were made for one another.

That thought has me breaking the kiss before it can turn into anything else.

"You want to come up?" she asks in a breathy tone.

Fuck yes.

Hell no.

"Not tonight, babe." I cup her cheeks firmly. Hurt and disappointment wage war on her face. I kiss her softly, just once, because I don't trust myself right now. "I want to, Nessa. So bad, but I want to do this right." I peer into her eyes. "You're not the only one with little experience in dating." As the words leave my mouth, I realize how much we have in common. It makes me uncomfortable, but I press on. "You deserve to be romanced and cherished and worshiped."

Her disappointment flees, replaced with bright excitement.

And I feel like the biggest dick.

Chapter Four
Vanessa

"When can I meet the hottie?" Chloe asks me the next day at work. We're sitting outside in the back alley, enjoying lunch al fresco.

"If he's still around in a few weeks, I'll introduce you."

"Don't do that." She shakes her head. "Don't assume he won't stick around."

"You don't know him, and you don't really know me."

"What's that supposed to mean?" She arches a brow, stabbing a piece of chicken like it has offended her.

"Jackson was a total manwhore back in the day, and I ..." I worry my lip between my teeth. I don't want Chloe thinking less of me, but I don't want to hide the truth either, because friends should be honest with one another, right? "I was a total slut," I admit.

"For the record, I despise those labels." She jabs the air with her fork. "So what if you were both sexually promiscuous? Provided it was consensual, there's no harm in it."

I carefully school my features so I give nothing away. "It doesn't exactly bode well for a relationship. Both of us are novices." I remember girls bragging about dates with Jackson, but I can't recall anyone going out with him more than once or twice. His dating record is almost as bad as mine.

"You can learn together." She takes a drink of her soda. "And stop putting yourself down. I've noticed you do that a lot. You're a great catch, Van. Jackson is lucky to be dating you."

"Wanna turn gay?" I joke, shoveling a piece of pasta in my mouth.

"I love The D too much. And from the sounds of it, you do too!"

I howl with laughter, and it feels so good.

"What's so funny? Talk to Mamma Mara." The older waitress pulls up a chair and sits down.

"Van's dating one of the hotties that came into the diner yesterday."

"Well, blow me down with a feather, Missy." Mara tweaks my cheeks. "I didn't pin you for such a fast worker, but I'm damn proud."

My cheeks flare up. "Oh my God, stop it. We only went on one date, and he probably won't even call for a second."

"Which of them was it?" she asks, leaning in, her eyes glinting with excitement. "Mr. Tall, Dark, and Handsome or the sinful blond with the gorgeous smile and Heartbreak City stamped on his brow?"

"Which one do you think?" I say, quirking a brow. Mara's assessment is dead on. There's no denying Sawyer Hunt is a much surer bet, but we have zero chemistry, and he's as much of a commitment-phobe as Jackson is. Plus, he's bi, and I can't ever see Sawyer ending up in a traditional relationship. Not that there is anything wrong with that. You should be free to love who you love and live your life however the hell you want, but he's not the man for me is all I'm saying.

Not that Jackson is either, but ... Ugh. I'm getting carried away, and these two idiots are feeding my insanity.

"I'd be all over that blond hottie like a rash," Mara says. "And I want deets. How big is his cock? I bet he knows how to use it too."

"Calm the jets. We went on one date, and it wasn't like that. He was a perfect gentleman." I was upset for a split second when he turned me down, but after he explained, I floated through my door on a cloud. And don't get me started on that kiss that almost knocked me flat on my ass.

I've *never* been kissed like that. I didn't realize kisses were an even better high than hardcore drugs. I already feel a new addiction forming, and that terrifies me.

"The man clearly knows a good thing when he sees it," Mara loyally replies. "You're a knockout, honey, and you've got the biggest heart. You deserve to be treated like a princess, and any man is lucky to date you."

Chloe juts out her chin, folding her arms across her chest and sending me an "I told ya" look.

"Is it normal to be scared?" I ask, because this new Jackson Lauder scares the crap out of me.

"Totally," Chloe agrees. "When I first dated Jon, I was terrified. Like bona fide scared shitless. He made me feel things I'd never felt before, and that's the scariest fucking feeling. But it's also the absolute best feeling once you get over yourself and learn to take a risk."

"What if he breaks my heart?" I voice my real fear.

"Every girl experiences heartbreak, at least once, before she finds true love," Mara says.

"That sounds like something you'd read in a fortune cookie," Chloe jokes.

"Doesn't make it any less true," Mara says, looking a little wistful, and I wonder what her story is. "Or the fact all a woman may know is heartbreak, but that doesn't mean it's something one should shy away from. If that's all a woman gets to experience, then, I say grab that with both hands, and tell your fear to take a running leap off a tall cliff, because having loved and lost is heaps better than having never loved at all."

"Enjoy your day off, bitch," Chloe says as we pull down the blinds and lock the diner up after another busy day.

"Don't work too hard," I singsong. I'm in a great mood because I get to sleep late in the morning and I have a full day off to myself.

A throat clearing interrupts our banter. "Is this a good or bad time?" Jackson asks, and the rich undertones in his voice send shivers dancing up my spine.

"Oh, this is a good time," Chloe answers for me, and I spot a devilish glint in her eye. "A very good time." She thrusts her hand out. "I'm Chloe. Van's best friend. You must be Jackson."

I glare at her. Okay, I've got zero game, but that doesn't mean Chloe has to rub it in.

"You told your bestie about me." He smirks, and I can't decide which one of them I want to punch more.

"Didn't you tell Sawyer?" I ask.

"Guilty. Guess that makes us even." He flashes me that panty-melting smile, and my lace thong evaporates from my body. Like poof, and it's gone.

"Oh fuck," Chloe murmurs, totally getting it now.

"Yep," I reply, not removing my eyes from Jackson.

"You're fucked, girl," she adds, her eyes shamelessly raking over every inch of Jackson's semi-naked torso. He's in shorts and sneakers again, and damn, if that isn't such a good look on him.

"Not yet she isn't," Jackson purrs, "but if she keeps looking at me like that, I'll have my cock buried balls deep inside her before we've even gotten upstairs."

I fan my face while Chloe looks like she might faint. "I'm trying to work out if that's a threat or a promise," Chloe admits.

"It's a promise," Jackson says, winking at me. "I don't do threats."

"He's a keeper," Chloe decides, tugging on my arm. "And I'm detouring to Jon's place because I need his dick *now*."

I fight a smile.

"Tell him he's welcome," Jackson calls out, chuckling, as she rushes off.

"Let me guess," I say. "You were in the neighborhood?"

He steps closer, and I work hard to remain upright. "Something like that."

"How often do you run?"

"Usually once a day. Sometimes more." He lifts his hand, tracing the tip of his finger along my jawline. "I can't stop thinking about you."

"You can't?" I'm sure he hears the disbelief in my tone.

He shakes his head. "Is this normal? I have no idea, and Hunt is fuck all help."

I laugh. "Don't ask me. I'm zero help too."

We smile at one another, and it's as if the ground is swaying under my feet.

Is this what it feels like when you're falling? And can it happen this fast?

"Please tell me you have no plans."

"For when?" I ask, licking my lips as his eyes suck me deeper into his orbit.

"The rest of your life," he whispers, sliding his hand to my neck. His thumb skates back and forth across my throbbing pulse, and I'm putty in his hands.

"Jackson." His name comes out in a whisper.

"I'm scaring you." He removes his hand and steps back. "I'm sorry."

"Don't apologize. I have no experience with all this, and it's just you've come out of nowhere."

"I'm a lot to handle," he agrees, nodding. "How about takeout at our place later? I can come back for you."

"Will Sawyer be there?"

He shrugs. "I don't know his plans."

"How about takeout at my place?" I suggest. "I mean, it's not much, but it's private, and I have a little balcony out back. We can eat there."

"Perfect." He tweaks my nose. "I'll bring the food. You just bring your delectable self."

"Okay."

He leans down, pressing the softest, sweetest kiss to my lips, and I swoon on my feet. "See you in a couple hours, babe."

The one good thing about living in a postage-sized studio apartment is the fact it is easy to keep it clean and tidy. I've always kept my shit neat anyway, but I don't have to spend ages making my place presentable for Jackson, which means I have time to put new sheets on my bed, take a long hot shower, shave everywhere, put on a facemask, paint my nails, and set the small table out on the balcony before he arrives.

He is punctual, arriving one minute before eight, and I buzz him up, opening the small door at the top of the stairs, smiling as he locks the entrance door down below and climbs the steps two at a time.

"You look fucking gorgeous," he says, his eyes skimming over the casual black knee-length summer dress I'm wearing with obvious admiration. I let my hair dry naturally, and it's still a little damp, cascading in soft waves over my shoulders. I put tinted moisturizer on my face and added a touch of gloss, blush, and mascara.

"Thank you." I stretch up, ignoring the butterflies in my chest and the slight knot in my stomach, pressing a light kiss to his lips. It feels so natural to do it, and I hope he's feeling that too.

He kisses me back, just once, but it's everything. His eyes bore into mine. "What are you doing to me, Nessa? Hmm." With his free hand, he threads his fingers through my hair.

"I like when you call me that," I admit. "The only other person who calls me Nessa is Kayleigh." Jackson knows who my sister is although I doubt he's ever spoken to Kayleigh or Hunter because they are so much younger than us.

"She's going to be a stunner when she grows up," he says. "Just like her big sister." His fingers clasp the back of my head, sending a wave of heat rolling through me.

"Flattery will get you everywhere," I tease, kissing the corner of his mouth.

He groans. "*Never* tell me that."

He drops his forehead to mine, and I drink in the scent and feel of him. Jackson is all man, and I can't believe he's the same guy who used to avoid me, the same guy who used to irritate the fuck out of me with his stupid, immature behavior.

I'm seeing him in a whole new light, and I hope he's seeing me in a new light too.

I ease back a little, smiling at him in what I hope is a flirtatious manner. "Come in." We've been standing at my door like lovesick fools, and I'm sure the food is getting cold. I step aside and let him enter.

"It's a lot nicer than I was expecting," he admits, inspecting the space with surprise in his eyes.

While my apartment is only four hundred and fifty square feet, it is well proportioned and tastefully decorated.

"Paul, who owns the diner, only bought this place eighteen months ago. Initially, he gutted and refitted the space, intending on using it himself on occasion instead of traveling to and from New Jersey every day, but then, I came along, and he offered it to me," I explain.

On the left is my bed with surrounding fitted wardrobes and matching bedside tables. Beside that, just inside the front door, is the small bathroom with shower. It is the only enclosed area in the room. On the right-hand side is the living area with two brown leather couches positioned around a small coffee table and wall-mounted TV. In the middle of the open-plan space is a square gray ash table with four matching chairs. Behind us is the kitchen, consisting of one row of cupboards, a stove, washer-slash-dryer, and refrigerator, and there's even a slim dishwasher. The island unit facing the kitchen, and cutting off that space from the main living area, is where I prepare my meals and where Jackson drops the takeout bag.

"I'm glad I came here now," he says. "I worried you were living in some grungy, neglected shithole. This puts my mind at ease." My heart swells at his words, and it feels good to be cared about. "I didn't bring beer or wine because you said you don't drink, and I've been trying to abstain. Hope these are okay." He hands me a large bottle of sparkling water and a large bottle of Coke.

"Great, thanks." He's observant and thoughtful, and I add it to the growing list of his attractive qualities.

He pulls out one of the stools, watching as I unpack the paper cartons, emptying mouthwatering food into bowls and plates. "I set the table outside," I explain, urging him to grab what he wants and take it outside.

We carry our meal out and sit across from one another. "There isn't much of a view, but at least, it's private."

"There is a lot to be said for privacy in a place like New York City," he agrees, tucking into shrimp stir fry. "You must come over to our place next time. Hunt has the penthouse suite, and we have an awesome rooftop garden. We can grill steaks."

"Sounds good, provided Sawyer won't mind."

"He won't mind. Sawyer feels very ... protective of you. It might be good for him to see I'm not eating you alive." He chuckles as my mouth hangs open.

"What exactly have you been telling him?"

"Nothing." He laughs again. "I swear. He just wants to know I'm treating you right."

"Is he dating anyone?" I ask, taking a bite of spicy chicken. Jackson shakes his head. "Not really."

"I sense a story." I urge him to continue with my eyes.

"He's been hooking up with this guy we hung around with in Rydeville. I think there's more to it than he's saying, but I could be wrong."

"I heard you moved. The gossip mill was in full swing at West Lorian when none of you showed up for senior year."

"I'll bet." He grins.

"Did you really have an orgy with Ms. Rowling?" She was one of the youngest teachers in our private school, and all the guys were in heat around her. When she didn't return, and neither did the guys, all kinds of rumors were circulating.

"If you call me, Anderson, and Hunt taking turns with her and her friend an orgy, then yeah."

"You're all dogs," I murmur, but there's no malice in my tone.

"I seem to recall someone engaging in a few threesomes and foursomes during summer break unless those assholes were lying about fucking you."

I know exactly which assholes he's referring to even if half my summers in The Hamptons are a blur.

"They weren't lying, and I wasn't criticizing." I hold up a hand. "No judgment in this corner."

"Nor in this one." He reaches across the small table, lacing his fingers in mine. "I'm glad we never hooked up back then."

"Yeah. I think that much is obvious." I force a laugh out, so it sounds lighthearted.

He squeezes my hand. "Not in the way you're thinking."

"What do you mean then?"

"It's like I said last night. I want to do things right. If we'd screwed back then, it would've been meaningless like every other nameless, faceless encounter that I barely even remember. But this, now?" He peers deep into my eyes, and I lean forward, my heart beating ninety miles to the hour. "This means something, right?"

I nod, swallowing over the messy ball of emotion in my throat.

"When I make love to you, it will be for the right reasons, at the right time, in the right place, and it will mean everything, Nessa." He brings my hand to his lips, kissing my knuckles. "Everything. You feel me?"

Chapter Five
Jackson

"You're meeting Van again?" Hunt asks the following morning as we're eating breakfast in the kitchen.

"Yep." I shovel the last spoonful of cereal in my mouth. "She can't get enough of me." I flash him one of my signature grins.

"I still don't like this."

"Bite me."

"If she's changed, like you've said, I don't get why you can't just ask her." He scrubs a hand along his jaw.

"It's too risky. She's vulnerable, and if he's reached out to her, she might already have loyalty to him. I want to catch him unawares, not tip him off."

"Can't you drop some hints?"

Dude is starting to get on my nerves again. "I don't see what the big issue is. I'm treating her like a princess. She'll get some great sex out of it and learn a valuable lesson about how to protect her heart in the future." I walk to the sink and dump my bowl and spoon in. "She should probably be thanking me."

"You really are an asshole."

I shrug. "Think what you like, Hunt. This is about Dani. She is all that matters."

"Dani wouldn't want you trampling all over innocent girls in a quest for revenge. She'd hate that."

I see red, yanking him up off his stool and shoving him back against the counter. "Don't fucking tell me what my sister would or wouldn't think. And Vanessa is far from innocent."

He shoves me back, glaring at me. "I'm not talking about her virginity or lack thereof. I *was* there the night we gave it up to one another," he says, smirking.

I don't hide my scowl fast enough, and he scrutinizes my face like I'm a puzzle he desperately wants to figure out. I flip him off, annoyed at him for bringing that up. It's never bothered me before that Hunt took Vanessa's virginity. It never even factored on my radar, but I don't like how it's making me feel now. I rub at the tightness in my chest. Fuck this shit. I need to get with the program.

"I'm talking about how she's innocent in all of this," he adds in a less angry tone.

I fold my arms across my chest, drilling a hole in his forehead. "You can't say that definitively. We don't know what involvement she's had with him."

"If any," he adds. "You're making assumptions, and everyone knows what's said about that."

"Fuck you, Hunt. You want out, just say the word, and I'll do this myself."

He sighs. "I don't want you handling this yourself. I'm as invested as you. I just don't like that you're duping Vanessa."

"If you have other options, I'm all ears!" I shout, grabbing fistfuls of my hair. I'm sick of having the same conversation on repeat. "We've had guys searching the web for months. Paid a small fucking fortune to that PI, and we've still got zilch. Unless you want to defer freshman year at RU, and join me on a fruitless global search for the prick, I don't see that I have any other choice. This is the only tangible lead we have."

He sighs again, looking up at the ceiling. I wait him out, rubbing a sudden tense spot between my brows.

"Fine," he admits. "You're right, but just ... try not to hurt her too bad. Something doesn't feel right about the whole scenario with her parents, and I have a gut feeling there's a lot we don't know about Vanessa. She's cleaning up her act, and I don't want your actions to send her spiraling."

"You know I can't make any promises, but I hear ya. Okay?"

"I am *so* unfit," Nessa admits, her voice all breathless as she flops down on the grass under the tree in Central Park. She looks utterly fuckable in her tight yoga pants and cropped sports top. Girl has legs for miles and perfect curves, and keeping my hands off her is becoming a real challenge.

"You should come running with me every day," I suggest, handing the bellboy from our building a hundred-dollar bill. It's his day off, but he agreed to take the picnic blanket and basket here and wait until we showed up. Dude nods, smiling and whistling under his breath as he saunters off.

"You'd be amazed how quickly you can improve your stamina and speed," I add, laying the blanket down on the grass. "I used to run a fair bit, but my party lifestyle definitely impacted my fitness levels. Then, I cut back on booze, cut out weed, and started running consistently every day, and it really didn't take long to improve."

"I'd have to get up early to run because I'm usually too wrecked after work to do much of anything," she admits.

I extend my arm to her, and she takes my hand. I pull her

up and into my arms, uncaring we're both a little sweaty. "I can force my lazy ass out of bed early to go with you." I rub my nose against hers.

"You don't have to do that. I can run by myself."

I swat her ass. "No fucking way, babe. Jogging around CP by yourself is not happening. I know there are lots of people around, even early, but it's still not safe." I kiss her cheek. "I'd only worry."

She practically swoons in my arms, and my stomach churns unsteadily. "You say all the right things," she murmurs, zeroing in on my lips.

She wouldn't say that if she knew the truth.

Even if my words just now *were* sincere.

I kiss her, because I don't want to be thinking the things I'm thinking right now. "Hungry?" I ask when we break for air, nuzzling into her neck.

"Yeah. But not just for food." She clutches my shoulders, staring at me, making her intent clear. I think my shy Nessa is getting a little braver.

"Food first, and then, we'll see," I tease, pulling her down onto the blanket. We unpack all the food my favorite deli prepared, and then, we lean back against the trunk of the tree, eating and drinking as we people watch.

"Leave some room for dessert," I say when we make fast work on the gorgeous salads and wraps. "We have chocolate strawberries."

"You trying to fatten me up?" she asks, nudging my shoulder.

"Hey, I could've brought brownies. And we burned some calories from our run." I lift a strawberry from the container, deliberately licking my lips as I home in on her beautiful face. "We can always burn more off later if we need to." I waggle my brows suggestively. When I bring the strawberry to her mouth, her lips part, and her warm breath trickles over my fingers.

"I like the sound of that." She opens her mouth wider, biting down on the strawberry as her eyes lock on mine. Fuck, that shouldn't be so hot.

"Me too." I grab another strawberry, ready to pop it in my mouth but she takes it from me.

Her smile is wide as she brings it to my lips, urging me to open for her. I dart my tongue out, licking along the side of her finger, and she sucks in a gasp. Her eyes darken with molten heat, and my cock wakes up. I open my mouth, biting into the strawberry, without breaking eye contact.

We silently feed one another, and the air crackles with sexual tension. Our faces are close, our bodies side by side, and I'd challenge anyone to pry me away from her in this moment. I let her have the last strawberry, but she bites it in half, offering the last bit to me. Little bits of fleshy strawberry sit on her bottom lip, and I can't ignore the temptation any longer. I lap at the strawberry remnants with my tongue as I pull her into my arms. She repositions herself on my lap so she's straddling me, leaning down, and kissing me. Her tongue swirls into my mouth, and the kiss quickly grows heated.

My cock is like a block of wood behind my flimsy jogging shorts as she grinds against me in a way that should be outlawed in public. The tiny moans she emits are like a shot of liquid lust straight to my dick, and I'm seconds away from pulling her behind the tree and burying myself deep inside her.

She pulls back first. "Damn. You make me so horny I forgot we were in broad daylight." She laughs, and it does weird things to me. "The fact I haven't had sex in a year might have something to do with it too."

"Seriously?" I ask, not masking my surprise. I readjust myself in my shorts when she climbs off me.

"Told you I've turned over a new leaf." Pride glimmers in her tone. She sits beside me, resting her head on my shoulder, and I press a kiss to the top of her hair. "I worked my butt off this year. My grades have always been a bit up and down, but I was determined to graduate on a high, so I really knuckled down. Between school, work, and study, I had no downtime, which suited me. I don't miss much about my old life," she adds in a lower tone. "Except my sister and brother. And sex." She laughs again, and the tinkling sound sends a rake of shivers coasting over my body.

And what the fuck is up with that?

I shake myself out of that pansy-ass thought. "So, what's next? You planning on college?"

Silence greets my questions, and I lift her head, cupping her face and forcing her gaze to mine. "Did I say something wrong?"

"No. Of course not." Her smile is sad. "I want to go to college, but I wasn't approved for any of the scholarships I applied for."

"Won't your parents pay for it?"

She shakes her head. "They've washed their hands of me, and I wouldn't be surprised if Aaron suppressed all my applications."

"Shit's that bad?"

She nods. "He hates me." She averts her gaze, and prickles of apprehension raise goose bumps on my arms.

"You want to talk about it?"

She plucks at the grass with her long, slim fingers. "It's the classic scenario. I'm not his flesh and blood. He was stuck with me when he married my mom. And I've done nothing but cause him trouble and damage his precious reputation." She barks out a bitter laugh. "What a fucking joke. If—" She pushes to her feet. "Actually, I don't want to talk about him anymore. I'll only get in a bad mood. I need to shower."

Hmm. I'm sensing there's more she's not saying, but I'm not going to push her on it. "Hang on." I jump up. "Let me clear this up, and I'll walk you home."

"You live in the opposite direction. It's fine, Jackson."

"How about an early movie then?" I suggest. "We can both head home, get changed, and I'll come get you."

"You don't have to spend your entire day with me. I'm sure you've got other stuff to do," she says, shuffling awkwardly on her feet. She chews on the corner of her mouth as her shoulders slump and her lips pull down.

Why does she look so insecure all of a sudden?

It feels like whatever progress we were making has suffered a setback, but I can't work out why.

I place my hands lightly on her hips, pulling her into me. "You're the only one I want to do," I tease before remembering my role. That is not something Prince Charming would say. More like his douchebag evil arch nemesis. "I'll rephrase," I add even though her lips are already curving up. "I can't think of anything I'd rather do than spend my free time with you. I'm not ready to let you go, babe." She laughs, and I wrap my arms around her, pulling her into a hug. My eyes close momentarily. "I like being with you. Please say yes." I press my mouth to her ear. "Say yes; say yes."

"You're incorrigible." She looks up at me through long, thick lashes. "And yes. I'll go to the movies with you."

Chapter Six
Vanessa

"Oh my God. That was so cheesy," I say, leaning my head against his shoulder as we walk home from the movie theater. We ended up catching a later show because Jackson had to go somewhere with Sawyer, but I didn't mind. I spent my afternoon on the balcony reading and dozing before taking a long shower and spending time getting ready for my date.

"I thought girls loved all that mushy shit." Jackson places a soft kiss on my temple.

"I must be missing that gene," I joke. "That part where he was confessing his love in that hideous flowery language, in front of all those people, at the top of the Eiffel Tower had me cringing. I actually had to look away from the screen and block my ears."

"Man, it was corny as fuck," Jackson agrees, "but for my first chick flick, it wasn't as bad as I imagined it would be."

"I like some chick flicks, but they can be a bit hit or miss. *The Notebook* and *Sweet Home Alabama* are two of my favorite movies, but the most romantic movie I've watched is *The*

English Patient." I place a hand over my heart. "Forbidden love at its finest. It's tragically beautiful." I look up at him, blushing at the intent look on his face. "Have you ever watched it?"

"Can't say I've even heard of it."

"That's a tragedy in itself." I cling to his arm, smiling up at him. "I'm sure I can stream it from somewhere. You want to come over one night this week and watch it with me? I'll make dinner too."

"It's a date," he says, and my lady parts swoon.

"You want to come up?" I ask when we reach my door, hoping he doesn't turn me down again.

He nips at my earlobe. "Try stopping me," he whispers in my ear, and I shiver in anticipation.

We head up to my apartment, and I deposit my purse on the kitchen counter as Jackson closes the door. "Do you want something to eat or drink?" I ask.

"Nope." He stalks toward me with that infamous cocky swagger of his. "There's only one thing I want." He reels me against his toned body. Leaning his face down, he lines our mouths up so there's only a sliver of a gap between us. "You," he whispers in a husky voice.

He slams his lips down on mine, and we devour one another without hesitation. I'm clawing at him, desperately needing to get closer, as his wicked lips and tongue whip me into a frenzy. I tighten my arms around his neck, rocking my pelvis against his erection, letting him know I'm down with this.

Without breaking our lip-lock, he grabs my hips and lifts me onto the counter. My thighs automatically spread to accommodate him, and I moan into his mouth at the feel of his hard cock pressing against my pussy. I wrap my legs around his waist, tugging him in closer, grinding my crotch against him in a pathetic attempt to ease the friction building in my core.

I want him so bad, and my panties are already damp with need.

I've heard the gossip about him over the years. Jackson is an awesome fuck, according to his previous hookups, and I want to experience that for myself.

His hands roam my body, fondling my breasts through my dress, and it isn't long before my nipples are as hard as bullets. He tugs the spaghetti strap down on one side, revealing my bare flesh. "Fuck, Nessa," he says, playing with my breast. "You're perfect."

"Jackson." I tilt my head back and arch my body, pushing my boob into his hand. "I need you."

"You're so hot like this," he rasps, rolling my taut nipple between his fingers.

I grab his shoulders just as he lowers his head, sucking my nipple into his warm mouth. I cry out as a dart of desire shoots through my core. I dig my heels into his back, desperate for more. No man's touch has ever felt this good or made me feel so alive. I want to drown in the sensations Jackson is wrenching from my body and never come up for air.

His mouth leaves my breast as he trails a line of wet kisses up over my collarbone and on to my neck. He sucks on that sensitive spot just below my ear, and I squirm on the counter, hot and needy and dying to come.

If he keeps touching and kissing me like he's doing, I'm likely to come without his fingers even brushing my clit, and that would be a first. "You feel so damn good, baby," he whispers into my ear while his fingers slowly push the hem of my knee-length dress up.

I silently fist pump the air until that horrible inner voice sneers in my ear, attempting to shake my confidence.

What if he can tell you are damaged goods? What if you're not good enough? Not tight enough? A disappointment?

A whole host of familiar taunts races through my brain, pulling me out of the euphoric bubble I was encased in. I flinch. It's barely discernible, but he notices, his hand stalling on my bare thigh, his head lifting from my neck.

"Hey." Worried eyes penetrate mine. "What happened? You want me to stop?"

"I ... No." I pull myself together, remembering Mara and Chloe's advice. Every part of opening myself up to this man is scary, but I will never truly move forward unless I'm brave. Unless I take a risk and trust him. I pull his head to mine, planting a hard kiss on his lips. "Don't stop, Jackson. Please."

He threads his hand through my hair, firmly clasping the back of my neck. "We're still gonna go slow, but I want to make you feel good. Let me make you come."

I nod.

"Words, babe. I need to hear the words."

"I want you to do that. I need to come real bad."

"I'll look after you, babe." His kiss is sweet and tender, and tears prick the back of my eyes. "Lie back and close your eyes," he commands, and I do as he says.

Cool air brushes over my thighs and my panties as he pushes my dress up, bunching it at the waist. Lifting my left leg, he begins trailing kisses up my calf, along the bend in my knee, and over my thigh. My pussy is pulsing with need, and I grip the edges of the counter when Jackson presses his mouth against my mound.

"So fucking sweet," he murmurs, nuzzling into my panty-covered pussy. His hands roam up and down my legs, and I am completely at his command. He could tell me to jump off a cliff right now, and I'd do it. I have lost control of my body and my mind, and he's the puppet master pulling the strings.

His fingers brush my hipbones, sending darts of pleasure

ricocheting through me as he gently pulls my lace panties down my legs.

"So fucking sweet," he repeats, parting my pussy folds with his thumbs. I open my eyes and look down at him. He's staring at my most intimate parts, licking his lips with fire dancing in his eyes.

Before my inner demons have time to plague me with doubts, he leans in and licks me. My eyes shutter again as I cry out. His tongue goes to work on my pussy, trailing a line up and down my slit, before plunging inside me.

My hips buck off the counter, and he places his palm on my lower belly holding me in place. "Keep still, babe. I want to make this so fucking good for you."

"It already is," I pant, a little embarrassed at how breathless I sound. I cry out again when he pushes two fingers inside me, easing them in and out of my wet channel while his tongue flicks against my clit. "Jackson," I warn, as the pressure intensifies inside me, building and building.

"Let go, baby," he demands, curling his fingers inside me, hitting all the right places. "Come for me, Nessa," he adds, sucking fiercely on my clit, and I go off like a rocket leaving NASA for outer space.

The orgasm rips through me, and Jackson's strong palm holds me in place as I buck and writhe, screaming as wave after wave of liquid bliss streaks through me like a comet in the night sky. He continues pumping his fingers in and out of me, and sucking on my clit, until I'm sated, lying motionless on my kitchen counter, limbless and missing a small piece of my heart and soul.

"What was that?" I murmur as he scoops me up, cradling me in his arms.

He chuckles as I fight a yawn. My body is gently jostled as he walks. "That, baby, was the Jackson Lauder experience." He places me in bed, carefully removing my dress before pulling the comforter up over me. "Also known as ruining you for all other men."

And that's the last thing I hear before I conk out.

The next couple of weeks fly by in a blur where I'm consumed with work and all things Jackson. It's safe to say I'm obsessed and falling head over heels for the one guy I never seriously considered. He stays true to his word, showing up at my door at six thirty a.m. every morning so we can run together. Every evening, he is waiting outside the diner when my shift finishes. We spend every night together, either eating out or staying in, cuddled up on the couch watching movies.

It feels so comfortable, as if we've been doing this forever, and I never want it to end.

Although we are kissing and making out like crazy, we still haven't fucked, and he refuses to spend the night. But I can't fault him for being a gentleman, and, honestly, it makes me feel special in a way I've never felt before.

I'm used to men taking what they want from my body and discarding me when they've had their fill. Jackson makes me feel like I'm worth more, and I'm starting to believe it.

"You have that look on your face again," Chloe says, yanking me out of my head.

"Do I dare ask?" I pull another couple of designer dresses out of my wardrobe and place them on the bed.

"The look of love, babe." She loops her arm through mine.

"Or maybe, it's the look of lust," I quip, needing to deflect this conversation because I'm so not ready for it.

"You've finally done the deed?" she questions, holding up the red Prada dress I wore to a function hosted by the stepmonster's company the Christmas before last.

"No." The longing is obvious on my face. "But I'm staying at his place this weekend, so I'm hopeful."

I was delighted when Jackson asked me, because Sawyer's boyfriend, or hookup, or whatever Xavier is, is also staying the weekend.

That Jackson wants me to meet his other friends, and to become immersed in his life, seems like an important next step.

One I'm eager to take.

"You need new lingerie," she says, like I can magically pull it out of thin air.

"You know I don't have the money for that." I wave at the dresses, shoes, and jewelry on my bed. "Hence why I'm selling some of my best stuff online."

"I'm sorry, babe." She gives me a quick hug. "Sometimes my mouth opens before my brain has engaged."

"It's okay. You're right. I wish I could afford to buy something sexy, but I'll just have to make do."

"You could wear a garbage bag and still be sexy as hell."

I snort. "I doubt anyone could pull off sexy in a garbage bag."

"You could." She has no idea how much her support and loyalty mean to me. Even the fact she is here, helping me to choose the best items to sell, instead of going to see her boyfriend Jon play a gig with his band, means everything. "I'm not joking, Van. You could be a model. You have the face, the height, and the body. You turn heads every place we go."

"Don't be ridiculous." I shake my head, unwrapping a gorgeous pair of black Jimmy Choos I hate to part with, but I know they'll fetch a good price even if they aren't the latest season.

Out of nowhere, an image of me with Jackson surges to the forefront of my mind. I'm wearing the strappy black sandals and nothing else, sitting on the edge of a bed, with my legs spread wide. He's crouched in front of me, running one hand up my leg as he trails hot kisses up my other leg. It's hot as fuck, and the visual is so vivid my core pulses with raw need, wishing it was reality and not a figment of my imagination.

I put the shoes back in the box and replace them in the closet, unwilling to part with them now.

"You're oblivious to it, but it's true." Chloe takes hold of my elbow, forcing me to focus on her. "Someone did a real number on you, and I'd love to know who so I could kick their ass."

I swallow over the lump lodged in my throat. I wish I could tell her, but I'm terrified if I open those floodgates, if I let it all pour out, that I'll never be able to close them again. I've survived the only way I know how, and I haven't come this far only to undo all my good work. Leaving that shit in the past is for the best. Chloe does not need to hear that horror story, and I sure as fuck don't want Jackson to find out. I doubt he'd be so keen if he knew his girlfriend let her stepmonster abuse her for years.

"Shit happens, girl. And I'm crawling my way out of the hole. But modeling is not the answer." I don't elaborate, and she knows me well enough to drop it.

Chapter Seven
Jackson

"**B**efore we go up," I say, taking her hand in mine over the console of my SUV. "I need to explain about Xavier."

"Okay." She waits for me to continue.

"He's a little *out there*."

"In what way?"

"Well, his hair is green for starters."

"Wow. That's a deal breaker right there," she jokes.

I tweak her nose. "Saucy. Me likey." Leaning forward, I lick her cheek, like a dog in heat.

"Eww." She pushes me off, half-laughing. "You're weird."

I chuckle. "That's a first." I flash her one of my trademark grins, and she swoons, as usual.

"What else?" she asks.

"He has a wacky sense of style, zero filter, and he spews the most random shit at times. He's also loud as fuck when he fucks."

"Do I even want to know?"

"Nope. Not going there." My grin expands.

"If you're trying to scare me, it's not working."

"Not scare. Prepare." I tweak her nose again, and she swats my hand away. "He's good people. For all his eccentric ways, he's also loyal as fuck, highly fucking intelligent, and very entertaining company. He's just … loud and in your face. Don't take offense to it."

"I'm intrigued. Can't wait to meet him."

"Hunt has walked over to Grand Central Station to pick him up. They won't be long." I take her hand, kissing her knuckles. "You look edible, by the way."

"Edible?" She chokes on a laugh. "Please tell me you mean that literally."

"If you want me to eat you out again, baby, you only have to ask." I flash her another wicked smile, knowing it'll get her all worked up.

"As much as I enjoy your talented tongue and your talented fingers, it's your talented cock I'm more interested in."

I love this more confident side to my girl. "My cock *is* talented." My smug grin is off the Richter Scale. "Patience you must have, my young padawan."

"Weird," she murmurs, giggling, and I cup her face.

"That's another Xavier trait. He has a host of movie quotes at the tip of his tongue, and he's a total Star Wars and Marvel nerd. Don't even get me started on the Batman leathers he has for his Harley." I shake my head, grinning as I visualize the time I saw him in that ridiculous outfit. Man, Xavier Daniels is a unique experience everyone needs to see at least once in their lifetime.

"I can't fucking wait to meet him. Might even ditch you for him," she quips.

"Sorry to disappoint, babe, but you've got the wrong equipment. Women don't do it for Xavier." Hell, I'm surprised Hunt does. They are polar opposites, and they annoy the shit out of one another, but there's chemistry there too. I don't know what's going on with them, because we don't talk about shit like that, but I suspect Hunt is battling his feelings for Xavier.

I climb out of the car, removing Nessa's small weekend bag from the back, before opening the door for her. It sucks she has to work for a few hours tomorrow. I tried bribing her boss, but he was having none of it. The best he could do was cut her hours, so at least, she doesn't have to be up early in the morning.

"Another thing. They bicker like an old married couple. I've learned to tune them out, but they'll probably irritate you to no end. You might need to self-medicate."

"I'm a strictly drug-free zone these days, so I'll take my chances."

Dumping her bag, I haul her into my arms. "I'm proud of you, you know."

Her brows climb to her hairline. "You are?" The disbelief in her tone is something I've heard before. Vanessa has quite low self-esteem. I never realized until I started hanging out with her. If I allow myself to be honest for a second, I hate that she does, because she is a sweet girl with a good heart.

Which is why this is becoming complicated for me.

I thought I could do this because she'd annoy the fuck out of me and I wouldn't catch feelings. But she's nothing like I expected. She's genuinely sweet, and I like hanging out with her, and I'm fighting my burgeoning feelings.

I should walk away now, but I can't. I'm in this too deep, and my thirst for revenge outweighs my concerns.

I searched every inch of Vanessa's apartment the night she fell asleep in my arms, and I found jack shit. No cards or letters or messages or hidden phones. If Christian has reached out to her, he's being extra careful.

And that's why I've got to last the distance.

"Jackson?" Her worried gaze meets mine.

I kiss her softly. "Sorry, I zoned out for a minute. I'm proud of you for battling your demons and coming out the other side. I know from personal experience how hard it is, and you've done it all alone." I cup her gorgeous face, trying not to drown in those mesmerizing baby blues.

"Thank you, Jackson." Her eyes turn glassy, and panic bubbles up my throat. *Not tears.* I abso-fucking-lutely cannot handle female tears. "And I'm proud of you too." She wipes moisture from her eye. "I'm proud of us."

I both love and hate the sound of that.

"It's exquisite," Vanessa says ten minutes later after I've given her the grand tour of the penthouse. I haven't taken her up to the roof yet because Grumpy and Happy are on their way up in the elevator, so I'm waiting to make introductions first. She strides to the window. "This view is to die for."

I walk toward her, caging her in from behind. "I couldn't agree more," I say, tipping her face back and staring at her so she gets my meaning.

"I think I'll start calling you Casanova," she quips, arching her back into me.

My cock jerks in my jeans when I press my body against her. I don't know when I've ever exercised this much restraint. I have the worst case of blue balls known to man. I am dying, and I mean *literally dying*, to sink inside her, but I've held back for the perfect moment, and it's fast approaching because I've used up most of my patience reserves by now.

Vanessa gets me so hot.

When she sucked me off the first time, fireworks exploded

behind my eyes. I thought I was having an out-of-body experience.

It was *that* good.

Girl's got mad skills, and after we fuck, I already know I'll have problems keeping my hands off her and my dick out of her pussy.

I need to bring this show to a speedy climax before I end up hurting myself in the process.

"Ahem." A throat clearing behind us brings me back into the moment.

"Don't all rush me at once," Xavier says, and I hear the grin in his tone.

"Ready, babe?" I whisper into her ear.

She nods, smiling, and I push off the window, taking her hand and turning us around. "You disappoint me, dude. I was looking forward to the Batman leathers."

"No point bringing the Harley to the city, and I'm wearing Superman boxer briefs. I'd show you, but it'd be rude in front of the pretty lady." He winks at Vanessa.

"Since when has that ever stopped you?" Hunt retorts, already poking and prodding.

"Oh well then. If you insist." Before any of us can stop him, Xavier has dropped his shorts, confirming that he is, indeed, wearing teeny-tiny blue briefs with Superman's head superimposed on them.

Vanessa bursts out laughing, and, in typical Daniels' fashion, the ice is broken.

"You are one crazy motherfucker." I walk toward him, shaking my head as he pulls up his shorts.

"I'm not sure my eyes will ever recover," Hunt drawls, and the look of disgust in his eyes cannot be faked.

These two are fucking priceless.

"You've seen a lot worse," Xavier replies, drilling him with a smug look. It's obviously some private joke.

"Smutty bedroom jokes are off the table this weekend," I say, pulling Vanessa in front of me. "We have a lady in our presence, and I'd rather you didn't scare her away."

I have already warned Hunt not to breathe a word to Xavier about me fake-dating Nessa. Xavier can't keep anything secret from Abby, and the last thing I need is this getting back to Anderson.

I make introductions. "Xavier, meet Vanessa."

"It's lovely to meet you," Nessa says. "Jackson has told me all about you."

"Well, that's not scary." Xavier winks, darting in to kiss her cheek. "Don't believe a word of it. It's all lies."

"Even the part where he said you were loyal as fuck, highly fucking intelligent, and very entertaining company?" she asks, clasping my arms.

Xavier grins, looking pleased. "Those parts are all true. It's everything else that's a lie."

We head up to the rooftop garden where we spend a pleasant night chatting over takeout and beer. Vanessa sticks to water, and I contain myself to two beers. While I haven't completely cut booze out like she has, I know my limits, and I try to stick to them.

I need a clear head to take that bastard Montgomery down.

"How did you two meet?" Xavier asks, casually throwing his arm over Hunt's shoulder. They are sitting on the couch across from us. Vanessa giggles when Hunt shoves Xavier's arm off, and she snuggles in closer to me. I curl my arm more protectively around her shoulder, deflecting yet another invisible dagger Hunt throws my way.

"We go way back," I explain. "We all spent family vacations at The Hamptons."

"I lost my virginity to Van," Hunt blurts, and I want to smack him upside the head.

Nessa squirms, a blush dotting her cheeks, and I glare at my best friend.

"Well, that was awkward." Xavier slams his hand down on Hunt's thigh. "And extremely rude. If it was for my benefit, it was also unnecessary."

"Not everything is about you," Hunt says. "In fact, most things aren't."

"Ouch." Xavier withdraws his hand. "I'm beginning to wonder why you bothered inviting me for the weekend."

"I didn't," Hunt hisses, and Xavier turns to him with a frown.

"I stole his cell and sent you the text," I admit. "Because his cranky ass needs to get laid."

Xavier's legendary smile drops away. "Asshole move, Lauder."

"Was it?" I glance at Hunt. "He's had all week to call it off, but he didn't. Maybe, ask him about that." I stand, pulling Nessa with me. "We're heading to bed. Enjoy the rest of your night."

"What the hell was all that about?" Nessa asks as soon as we're out of earshot of the others.

"I've got no idea," I lie. "Hunt's been a bit of an ass lately. I thought having Xavier here might help. Maybe, I was wrong."

We step into the kitchen, and I grab two bottles of water from the refrigerator.

"Does he regret it?" Nessa asks when we enter my bedroom.

I close and lock the door. "Regret what?" I kick my Vans off and they fly across the room.

Vanessa sits on the edge of the freshly made bed. Our

cleaning lady, Florentina, was here today, so the place is immaculate and perfect for entertaining my girlfriend.

"Losing his virginity to me." She looks like someone just kicked her puppy.

I kneel in front of her. "I'm sure he doesn't. This wasn't about you. It was about me."

"He doesn't want us to be together?"

I run my hands up her smooth, bare legs. "He's just nervous because we're both new to this whole relationship shit." I'm fudging the truth on purpose, concentrating on the feel of her under my hands. Her skin is like silk to the touch. My hand slips under the hem of her dress, but her fingers curl around my wrist, stopping me. "What? You don't want me to touch you?"

She leans down, kissing me. "You know I love how you touch me, but I want to take care of you." She pulls me to my feet, staring up at me through hooded eyes as she unzips my shorts. She pushes my shorts and boxers down my legs, freeing my cock. I'm already sporting a semi, and as soon as she wraps those delicate fingers around the base of my shaft, I harden like magic. "Wow. Zero to sixty in less than a second. Impressive." She grins.

I chuckle, delving my hands in her hair. "Your touch is impressive, and my cock loves you."

She slowly pumps my dick, looking up at me with a devilish glint in her eye.

How can a girl look so innocent and so wicked at the same time?

"What would you like me to do?" she asks in a breathy voice that has my cock jerking in her hand.

"I want to fuck your mouth," I admit without pause. "And I need to feel your tits."

She slides her dress down to her waist, exposing her bare chest. My hands glide down her body, cupping both tits.

"These are so fucking perfect." It's the truth. They are a perfect handful, round and soft, with small, neat rosy tips.

Every inch of her is perfect.

She is flawless with delicate curves in all the right places, and her body is so responsive to me, which is another huge turn-on. I squeeze her tits, and her nipples harden instantly. I pluck at them with more force than usual, anger still lingering in my veins thanks to Sawyer fucking Hunt.

When she takes me in her lush mouth, I lose all control, rocking my hips back and forth while I grope her tits. She widens her mouth, taking me all in, skillfully moving her lips up and down my shaft. The look in her eyes assures me she is enjoying this as much as I am.

I want to rip my cock from her mouth and bury it deep in her pussy, so deep we both forget who we are and that this is all a means to an end.

Guilt slaps me in the face, and in this moment, I pretty much hate myself.

Shuttering my eyes, I swallow back bile as that thought competes with the tingle zipping up my spine, and I concentrate on the way Nessa is sucking me off, blanking my mind of everything else, until I blow in her mouth, shooting salty cum directly down her throat.

Chapter Eight
Vanessa

I smile as I listen to Jackson singing to himself in the shower. Putting the hairdryer down, I stretch my arms up over my head, thinking back to last night, my smile expanding as I remember curling up in bed against Jackson after we pleasured one another, falling into the sort of deep, contented sleep that usually eludes me.

If I'm honest, there's a tinge of disappointment we didn't sleep together, but he was in a bit of a funny mood after that altercation on the rooftop, so I didn't push the agenda.

Besides, there's always tonight.

I'm still grinning as I stand, grab my brush, and walk to his dresser to fix my hair for work. I'll have to wrench myself away today even if it's only for a few hours. I'm lucky Jackson managed to sweet talk Paul into letting me start late. It means my shift will go extra fast, and I'll be back here before I know it.

I'm smoothing my hair into a ponytail when my eyes flit to the pretty card on his dresser. I glance quickly at the en suite bathroom, chewing on the corner of my lip. The sound of water hitting tiles mingles with Jackson's deep singing voice, confirming he is still showering. My gaze returns to the card, curiosity lighting a fire in my veins. I shouldn't snoop, but it's not like it's hidden away. If he didn't want me to see it, he wouldn't have left it out in plain sight.

I open the card and read. It's an invitation to Kaiden and Abby's wedding in Alabama. I read online they got married in New York last Christmas, so I don't know why they are having a second ceremony.

It's so weird to think of him as Kaiden, because I've only ever known him as Camden or Cam. But that's a story for another day.

The water stops the same time the singing does, and I hurriedly place the card back in the same spot.

I have never visited Alabama, and I'm sure it's beautiful in August. The invitation includes a plus one, so he must be going to ask me, right?

Excitement bubbles up my throat, and I wonder if I should mention it. I contemplate it quickly. I don't want to jump to conclusions or force him to ask me before he's ready, so I hurriedly step away from the dresser before he catches me, deciding to wait for him to bring it up.

Work flies by in a blur of orders and customers, and before I know it, Jackson is waiting outside to escort me to his place.

"Missed you," he says the second I exit the diner, reeling me into his arms and kissing me deeply.

"Goodnight, love birds," Chloe calls out as she leaves.

We break our kiss, and I wave at her as she walks off.

"We're going out tonight," Jackson says, frowning a little as he watches Chloe disappear in the opposite direction. He rests his arm around my shoulder. "You need to grab anything from your apartment?"

"Where are we going, and how dressy will it be?"

"Dinner at a Michelin-starred Mexican restaurant that also serves the best fucking steaks on the planet. Then, drinks at Glitter," he confirms.

"Okay, let me grab an outfit real quick."

Jackson walks across the road to his SUV to wait for me.

I glance briefly at the familiar silver Honda Accord, parked in front of him. I have noticed it a couple times before. The windows are tinted, so I can't make out the person sitting behind the wheel.

"Get a move on, babe," Jackson hollers through cupped hands.

I blow him a kiss before racing upstairs to my apartment. I rummage quickly through my closet, grabbing a sexy pink mini dress and those black Jimmy Choos. Who knows, maybe my fantasy will become reality tonight.

"Van." Xavier yanks me into a bone-squeezing hug the second I arrive at the penthouse. "Thank fuck, you're back. We need some estrogen to balance out the overpowering testosterone."

"And which category are you putting yourself in?" Jackson asks.

Xavier rolls his eyes. "I'm pumped full of testosterone, dude." He grabs his junk, waggling his brows. "Because I'm *gay*, not female," he adds, tut-tutting at Jackson as he tucks me in under his arm. He smiles at me. "Ready to par-tay?"

"Lemme grab a shower, and I'm there."

"Sweet." He kisses my cheek. "Make sure you wear your dancing shoes."

"Release my girl." Jackson tugs on my hand. "And keep your paws to yourself."

Xavier beams. "Jealousy is a good look on you, Lauder."

Jackson flips him the bird, threading his fingers through mine and leading me out to the bedrooms. "Close your eyes," he says, placing his hands over my eyes when we reach his bedroom door.

"Why?"

"I have a surprise for you."

My heart jumps in my chest as he walks me into his room. Jackson keeps one hand over my eyes as he removes the strap from my shoulder, dumping the bag with my dress and shoes on the ground. "You can open your eyes now."

A gorgeous black mini dress hangs on a mobile rail in front of me. The dress is strapless black satin with layers of ruffles that uncurl at the front. It's cinched at the waist with a thick gold and black sash, and it's one of the most gorgeous dresses I've ever seen.

"It's Alexander McQueen. Do you like it?" he asks, and I'm surprised at the hint of anxiety underscoring his tone.

"I love it," I whisper, walking toward it as if in a trance. On the odd occasion, I have missed having a limitless budget to spend as I desire. But mostly, I haven't missed money. Freedom from that bastard is the only currency I need. Provided I have a roof over my head, and food in my belly, I'm good.

I had far too many clothes and possessions anyway. It was obscene. However, I can't deny the buzzing in my veins at the prospect of wearing such an exquisite gown tonight. Getting glammed up for a night out with my boyfriend and his friends is the most fun I've had in ages.

"You sure?" Jackson asks, watching me trail my fingers along the satiny material.

"You bought this for me?" I choke out, keeping my fingers on the dress while I turn to look at him.

"Yep."

"Why?"

He walks right up to me, gently cupping the back of my head. "Because a beautiful woman deserves a beautiful dress, and I want to spoil you. You're my girl. I want you to want for nothing."

My heart swells to the point I'm afraid it might explode. Words loiter at the tip of my tongue, and I want to tell him how I feel, but I am scared I'll chase him off. Instead, I fling my arms around his neck, clinging to him. "You're so good to me, Jackson. I love it so much. Thank you."

"You're welcome." He swats my ass as he pecks my lips. "We're leaving in an hour, so get your tempting ass in the shower. We'll be up on the roof. Come join us when you're ready."

I'm floating on cloud nine as I get ready. I blow-dry my hair straight, adding some serum so it hangs in perfect, sleek sheets down my back. I go smoky with my eyes, adding lashings of mascara while keeping my lips nude and dusting peach blush over my cheeks.

I strap on my Jimmy Choos first and then pull the dress on in front of the long mirror in Jackson's bathroom. The dress is short, hitting me mid-thigh, but it's so beautiful, and my legs look endless in the high stiletto sandals. I wonder if he had help picking this out or if he chose it himself. It's sexy, in an understated, sophisticated way, and it's not something I imagined he would pick. Given his rep, one would think he'd choose something more obviously sexy, but I haven't given him enough credit.

I smile over the lump in my throat as I stare at my reflection.

Jackson is the best thing to happen to me, and I really hope I don't fuck it up.

My fingers dance along my bare collarbone, and I wish I'd thought to bring jewelry with me. At least, I had the sense to bring a small glittery black purse, and it works perfectly with this outfit.

A few spritzes of Hypnotic Poison by Christian Dior and I'm done.

It's time to make my grand entrance.

Nerves prick at me as I step out of the bedroom, smoothing a hand down over my hair as I make my way up to the roof. I keep my shoulders back and my head high, ignoring the butterflies in my tummy as I step out onto Sawyer's rooftop haven.

The guys are seated on the couches, drinking and chatting, and my heels make a subtle clicking sound as I walk toward them. As one, their heads turn in my direction.

Xavier whistles, and Sawyer blinks a couple times, but it's Jackson's reaction that has my heart doing the samba behind my chest cavity. My boyfriend can't keep his eyes off me, and the lust-drenched look on his face is obvious in the extreme as he rakes his gaze over me from head to toe.

He stands, stepping toward me as if on autopilot. His intense attention causes tiny goose bumps to sprout on my arms, and the butterflies descend to my stomach, running amok. His Adam's apple bobs in his throat as he takes my hand, bringing it to his lips, his hot gaze locked on mine. It's as if it's just the two of us up here. Our friends, and the outside world, have ceased to exist.

"You have stolen all the breath from my lungs, Nessa," he rasps, brushing his lips along the back of my knuckles. "You look incredible. I don't have the words to express how fucking beautiful you are."

My cheeks heat with pleasure, and that sentiment from earlier is back in full force. "Thank you again," I whisper.

"Having you on my arm tonight is all the thanks I need." He takes my hand, steering me toward the others.

"Wow," Xavier says. "You are straight fire, Van. It's almost enough to turn me hetero." He winks, and I giggle.

Sawyer stands. "You are stunning, Van." He kisses my cheeks, staring at Jackson. "Far too good for that asshole." There's a little bite to his words that would ordinarily surprise me if I wasn't already aware there is some tension between him and my boyfriend.

"Thank you, Sawyer. And Jackson's not an asshole. He's one of the best guys I've ever known. I know you know that deep down," I say, feeling the need to defend him.

"I agree that, deep down, Jackson knows the right thing to do," he cryptically replies.

Xavier's brow creases, and his gaze bounces between Jackson and Sawyer.

Before I can dwell on Sawyer's strange comment, Jackson has pulled me down on the couch beside him. "I have something else for you."

I shake my head. "You have already given me too much." Without knowing the exact price, I know this dress was expensive.

Jackson opens a large black velvet box, and my eyes almost bug out of my head.

"Let me put it on," he says, removing the gold and black choker-style Dior necklace from the box. I hold my hair up as he puts it on me. "Gorgeous." He plants a light kiss on my lips. "You look like a goddess." He slides the matching cuff band on my wrist, and I *feel* like a goddess. Like a million dollars. Emotion clogs my throat, and my heart races as a myriad of different feelings lay siege to my body.

"We should move," Sawyer says. "I practically had to offer up my firstborn child to get this reservation."

"Shall we?" Jackson takes my hand and helps me to my feet.

"Let the party begin," Xavier says, rubbing his hands in glee.

Chapter Nine
Vanessa

"Having a good time?" Jackson inquires, gliding his lips across my ear as his hands land on my waist.

"The best." The restaurant was sublime, and then, we moved on to Glitter, where I'm currently draining my third virgin cocktail.

"Let's go dancing!" Xavier finishes his vodka cranberry, eyeballing Sawyer with a look that dares him to say no.

Sawyer looks to Jackson, quirking a brow. They've been coolly civil all night, which I guess is progress. "Is there time?"

Jackson glances at his Tag Heuer watch. "We have an hour or so."

"Before what?" I inquire, sipping my drink through my straw.

He tweaks my nose. "Another surprise."

Setting my drink down, I twist around in his arms. My hands slide up his delectable chest. He looks so fucking hot tonight in his snug white button-down shirt, dark jeans, and black Yeezys. His shirt is rolled up to his elbows, showcasing drool-worthy arm porn. "I think you're spoiling me." I plant a kiss on the underside of his prickly jawline. He smells fucking divine, like orange blossom and mint and cinnamon, and good enough to eat.

"It's my job," he jokes, moving his palms to cup my ass.

"Well, you're very good at it," I murmur, pressing featherlight kisses along his jawline.

"And you're very good at making me so fucking hard for you." He subtly rocks his hips into mine, drilling the point home.

I coyly bite down on my lip, palming one side of his face. "I can't hold out much longer, Jackson." I pull his body into mine. "I need you."

He grabs fistfuls of my ass. "Ditto, babe, and I'll look after you when we get home. I promise."

Our eyes meet, and it's like looking in a mirror. My desire is reflected at me in the stunning azure depths of his eyes.

A surge of emotion crests over me, knocking everything else aside. Three little words beg to be let out, and I want to say them, so badly, but I'm scared.

We move at the same time, angling our heads perfectly in sync, our mouths colliding in a melting pot of pent-up desire and potent lust. Calling this a kiss is a bit of an understatement. We ravish one another, tongues invading, lips bruising, and bodies connecting in all the right places. I claw at him, needing him even closer, and I'm drowning in sensations I never want to emerge from.

When we finally come up for air, Sawyer and Xavier are nowhere to be seen. Jackson rests his forehead against mine, and we stare at one another as our chests rise and fall. "What are you doing to me, Nessa?" he whispers. "It's like you've cast a spell on me." A tormented streak flits across his face, but it's gone so fast I'm not sure I didn't imagine it.

"I feel the same way." I circle my arms around his neck,

holding him close, never wanting to let him go. "I've never felt this way about anyone ever before," I whisper into his ear. "It scares me as much as it thrills me." And that's as close to the truth as I'm brave enough to admit.

"I'm right there with you, babe." His arms slide around my waist, holding me in his warm, tight embrace. "It's ... confusing." He keeps his arms locked around me, and I rest my head on his chest, feeling more cherished than I ever have.

We stay like that as the party rages on around us, but we might as well exist on a different plane.

After an indeterminable amount of time, he eases out of my embrace. "Let's find the others. Xavier won't let me live it down if I don't let you dance with him."

Jackson keeps me close as we move through the bar out to a door at the back of the room. He flashes a card at the bouncers, and they step aside to let us pass through. We climb down mirrored stairs that lead to the basement club.

Heavy beats pulse through the crowded space as we enter the club. Jackson strides confidently through the masses, flashing his card again to gain entry to the VIP area where Xavier and Sawyer are waiting for us.

The instant he spots us, Xavier jumps up, grabbing hold of my arm and pulling me out onto the private dance floor. The dance floor faces a row of floor-to-ceiling windows that look out into the main club. "We can see out, but they can't see in," he explains.

We dance for a few songs, and I'm having the time of my life. Xavier is fantastic company and the easiest person to grow comfortable with. It feels like I have known him forever.

When familiar hands land on my hips and a warm body presses into me from behind, I almost melt on the spot. I lean back against Jackson, moving my body in tune with his as we work up a sweat on the dance floor.

Xavier persuades Sawyer to join him, but every attempt he makes to dirty dance with his lover ends with him being shoved away.

Jackson chuckles in my ear, and I honestly don't know what to make of those two. It's no secret Sawyer is bisexual. I've seen him kiss girls and guys during parties in The Hamptons, so I don't know why he's deflecting Xavier's advances in public.

It's not because Xavier is protective of his sexuality. He's clearly comfortable in his own skin, and he wears his homosexuality with pride. I know they shared a room last night, because I bumped into Xavier coming out of Sawyer's master bedroom this morning, and it was obvious from his state of undress and his messed-up hair they weren't just sleeping. Sawyer isn't the type to get embarrassed or to let other's opinions affect him, so I wonder why he's keeping Xavier at arm's length.

We leave just after one a.m., climbing into Jackson's SUV. He insisted on driving, and he has been drinking water all night.

When we pull up to the gas station on the outskirts of Queens, I understand why. "You're racing?" I turn to face him as he maneuvers the SUV into an empty space in the alleyway to the left of the gas station.

"Yep." His eyes light up as he kills the engine.

I bounce in my seat, clapping my hands. "Oh yay! I've always wanted to see you race," I truthfully admit.

In the back seat, Xavier snorts out a laugh. "You look like a bona fide groupie, Van."

I glance over my shoulder, grinning at him. "I don't care. Jackson's a fucking legend in the underground racing scene." I refocus on my boyfriend. "I didn't think you raced anymore, not since—"

"I got arrested?" he asks, smirking. I nod. I'm only privy to that information because I hung around the guys most summers, eavesdropping on conversations. "I haven't raced in a couple years, because I was too much of a mess, but the itch hasn't gone away," he confesses.

Hands slam down on the hood of the SUV, and I shriek, jumping in my seat. Jackson chuckles before opening the door and hopping out.

He greets the guy standing in front of his hood like a long-lost buddy, engaging in some elaborate hug-slash-hand maneuver with the big dude with dreads and a wide grin. The guy's jeans are hanging so low on his hips they look like they might fall off any second. His sheer size is intimidating, but the jovial, friendly expression on his face implies he's about as dangerous as a giant teddy.

"Who is *that*?" Xavier asks, peering between the console to get a better look.

"You're better off not knowing," Sawyer replies in a clipped tone. "You need to curb your inquisitive nature here. They don't like strangers asking questions even if they have rocked up with Hustle."

"Hustle?" I inquire, casting a glance over my shoulder.

"That's Lauder's street name." Sawyer curls his hand around the door handle. "Stick close to me tonight. Place is gonna get crazy when word gets out Hustle is racing again." He pins Xavier with a warning look. "These are not the kind of people you want to get on the wrong side of."

Xavier flips him the bird. "I don't need a fucking lesson or a babysitter. I know how to handle myself."

Sawyer climbs out as Jackson opens the passenger door for me. He lifts me out by my waist, carefully placing my feet on the ground.

The big, scary dude peruses me from head to toe, whistling under his breath, but it's not leery or disrespectful. "Damn, Hustle. You're boxing above your weight."

"Damn fuckin' straight." Jackson takes my hand. "Nessa, meet Comet. The second-best streetcar racer in New York."

Comet thumps Jackson in the upper arm, and I wince in sympathy. The guy's hand is almost as big as my head, so that's got to hurt. "We'll see about that real soon, Hustle." Comet dips his head a little. "Pleasure to meet you. If you ever get tired of this jackass, call me up."

I smile.

"Is everything set up?" Sawyer asks, coming to stand on my other side.

"Sup, man." Comet jerks his head at Sawyer in greeting, raising an inquisitive brow in Xavier's direction.

"He's a friend," Sawyer says, answering some unspoken question.

Xavier's face drops a little, but he quickly recovers. "Hey, man. Good to meet you." He shoots Comet a flirty smile before inspecting him from head to toe in a deliberate move I'm certain is for Sawyer's benefit.

Comet looks a little flustered and unsure what to make of the newcomer. Jackson subtly takes a step back, making a throat-slitting motion, warning Xavier to back down with his eyes. Jackson slaps his hand on Comet's shoulder. "Where's my baby?" he asks, bouncing on his feet, barely containing his excitement.

"This way." Comet lifts one shoulder, eyeing Xavier a little warily as he takes off.

Jackson locks the SUV, keeping hold of my hand as we follow Comet out of the alleyway and around into the gas station where a dozen souped-up cars are lined up in two rows. Mobs of guys and girls crowd the cars, some smoking, some drinking, and others just talking. The scent of MJ wafts through the air, mingling with raucous laughter, and there's a laid-back vibe I wasn't expecting to find at an illegal street race.

Jackson brings me with him as he says hi to the other drivers. Most are guys, but it looks like there are a couple of female racers too.

I'm a little self-conscious in my expensive dress and strappy stilettos, because most of the girls are wearing jeans or cutoffs or short dresses with sneakers.

Jackson keeps me close, introducing me to some of the other racers as his girl, and warmth blooms in my chest. I love how good it feels to be part of a couple, and I love that he brought me here tonight. I don't miss the hostile looks directed my way from several females, but it's of little surprise and something I'll have to get used to.

Jackson is hot, charming, rich, and desirable. To most girls, he's the ultimate prize. To me, he is so much more than a fuckable, wealthy guy. He is also sweet, loving, funny, and attentive, and those qualities far outweigh his other traits.

Winning his affection is one thing. Holding on to it will be the challenge.

I hate that thought the instant it lands in my brain, working hard to shake off the sudden melancholy.

"Wow," Xavier murmurs in my ear. "If looks could kill, you'd be mincemeat, girl."

I shrug. "Being on the receiving end of those kinds of looks is nothing new for me." I'm not the kind of girl who has tons of female friends. It's the opposite. Most girls dislike me, and I can count on one hand the number of girls I have called a friend over the years.

"My sweet ride! Hells yeah." Jackson drops my hand, fist pumping the air when he reaches a car at the end of the first row. It's a sleek, black Ford Mustang, I think, but it's obviously had work done. Two red stripes intersect the center of the hood, and there are matching red stripes on both doors. The windows are tinted, and the wheels are the biggest alloy wheels I have ever seen on a car.

Jackson leans down, kissing the hood like it's the most precious thing in the world. I suppose, to him, it probably is. He does an elaborate arm shake with a tall, skinny dude wearing a garish illuminous green T-shirt and ripped jeans, grinning excitedly as they talk.

"He's in his element," I murmur to Sawyer.

"Racing is in his blood," Sawyer agrees. "Although his dad would prefer he sign to one of his teams and race legitimately."

"Why doesn't he?" I inquire, watching as Jackson accepts keys from the skinny dude.

"Travis is insisting Jackson gets his business degree first. He wants him to have something to fall back on."

Mention of a degree reminds me that my time with Jackson has an expiration date. In a month, he will be starting at Rydeville University while I'll be stuck here. We haven't talked about what happens then, and I don't know if he'll want to try a long-distance relationship or just end things.

A deep ache slices across my chest at that thought, and for the second time in minutes, melancholy has a vise grip on my heart.

Chapter Ten
Vanessa

"Hey, girl. Whatever hideous thought just put that sad look on your face should be wiped immediately from your memory." Xavier circles his arm around my shoulder. "This is gonna be *epic*."

"Babe." Jackson approaches, taking my hand and hauling me toward his car. "Meet my other girl." He pecks my lips, grinning. "Isn't she a beauty?"

"Gorgeous," I agree, admiring the car up close.

"I'll take you out in her sometime," he says, jumping up onto the hood and pulling me into his lap. He cups one side of my face, his expression sobering a little. "You okay with all this?"

"I'm more than okay with it," I reply, forcing my melancholy aside. "I've never been to a street race. It's exciting."

Holding the nape of my neck, he crashes his mouth against mine, kissing me like we're not in the middle of a packed gas station in Queens, surrounded by a boisterous crowd and the revving of several engines. "Wish me luck," he says, breaking the kiss and planting my feet on the ground.

"Good luck!" I kiss the corner of his mouth. "Although I'm sure the legendary Hustle won't need it." I grace him with a full-blown smile.

He pulls me to him, nipping at my earlobe. "I love that you're here." His eyes latch on mine, sincerity radiating from his gaze.

"I'm happy I'm here too."

He brushes his lips against my brow. "Stay with Hunt and Xavier. Most of the crowd are cool, but there's always a few assholes, and I've picked up a few enemies over the years. They'd love nothing more than to get to me through you." His eyes flick over my body. "I made a mistake bringing you here looking like that. Every man will want to put his hands on you. Don't leave Hunt's side, not even to pee. You hear me?"

"Stop worrying. I know how to handle myself, and I won't go anywhere. I promise. Don't worry about me. Just focus on whipping Comet's ass."

"You can count on it!" Jackson lifts me up, swinging me around, and I giggle. I love seeing him like this. All passionate and excited. And I'm so proud to be here with him tonight.

He puts me back on the ground, tweaking my nose before hopping up on the wall beside his car, placing two fingers in his mouth, and shrilly whistling. "Listen up, assholes," he shouts. "Touch my girl, and I'll cut your dick off and feed it to your mama."

A chorus of taunts and catcalls ring out as every set of eyes land on me. I'm grateful it's relatively dark under the dim lighting so no one can see how red my cheeks are.

Jackson throws his hands in the air, moving them up and down. "The Hustle is back, bitches! And I'm ready to reclaim my throne!" he roars.

The crowd goes insane, chanting his name, and Jackson laps it up like a media whore.

"He's obnoxious." Sawyer shakes his head, but there's a hint of amusement shining in his eyes.

"He's fucking awesome." Xavier grins like a lunatic. "I think I picked the wrong friend." Sawyer flips him the bird, and Xavier blows him a kiss. "Only joking, my love. I've seen Lauder's cock. Yours is much bigger."

I should probably defend my man, but I'm too busy laughing and clutching my stomach to form words.

Jackson jumps off the wall, dipping me down low as he plants a passionate kiss on my lips one final time before sliding into his car and revving the engine so loud he almost bursts my eardrums.

Sawyer clasps my hand, and Xavier moves to my other side. "Over here." Sawyer guides me out of the gas station and across the road. "We'll have a much better vantage point on the street."

We walk for a bit, passing small groups congregated on the sidewalk, stopping halfway down the road and claiming a spot. Sawyer leans back against the wall, pulling me around in front of him. His hands lightly hold my hips as Xavier walks to the other side of him.

The race cars roll out of the gas station, two at a time, lining up behind one another on the road in front of us, and adrenaline courses through my veins. I wish I was riding with him although I'd probably pee my pants.

"Bitch," a girl hisses under her breath as she walks past. Her two female companions glare at me, eyes roaming me with unconcealed envy.

"Jealous much, skank?" Xavier retorts as Sawyer bores a hole in the side of his skull, urging him to shut up.

"Forget them." I touch Xavier's arm. "I don't care what they think."

I wasn't always this unaffected. The taunts and insults

hurled at me almost daily used to tear strips off my fragile heart, but I'm stronger now, because I've come through the hell that was my high school years and I'm out the other side.

Not untarnished but strong enough that snarky comments from jealous strangers don't hurt.

A few more guys and girls walk past us, all of them sizing me up, but I ignore them, focusing on my man. We are almost level with Jackson's car, and I can't help the massive grin that spreads over my mouth when Jackson rolls the passenger side window down and blows me a kiss.

Music blares from a large mobile speaker, and the crowds lining both sides of the road start singing and dancing. Xavier and I grin at one another, and I step out of Sawyer's protective hold, swaying my body and shimmying my hips up and down to the rhythmic beats.

A guy climbs onto an upturned crate, holding a loud-speaker to his mouth. He rallies the crowd, getting them more amped up when he announces that Jackson and Comet are up first. Chants of Hustle and Comet ring out around us, and Xavier and I join in, shouting our support for Jackson.

When the announcer begins a countdown, the crowd joins in. I'm shouting out numbers as my eyes lock on Jackson's car. Adrenaline weaves a path through my body, and I'm bouncing on my feet, almost overexcited as Jackson and Comet rev their engines repeatedly, their cars chomping at the bit to run free.

The announcer reaches one, and another guy waves a flag, and then, it's on.

Brakes screech and engines thrum as they take off to the sounds of an adoring crowd, leaving wisps of cloudy smoke behind them. The crowd shouts words of encouragement, and I peer forward, cupping my hands as I watch Jackson and Comet speeding up the empty road, side by side. "Go win back your throne, baby!" I yell. Xavier grabs me, spinning me around, and we're laughing, high on the infectious atmosphere, while Sawyer eyes us like we're a strange alien species.

That dude is so fucking uptight sometimes, and it's not how I remember him.

Jackson and Comet disappear around the bend at the top of the road, and I switch my attention to the other drivers. They are still lined up, waiting for their cue, revving their engines impatiently.

Finally, the rest of the cars take off after them, in timed intervals. I am very impressed at how organized it is.

Across the way, money is exchanging hands as bets are laid. If I had spare cash, I'd put it all on my man, because my guy is a fucking winner.

The party continues raging while the race hurtles through the streets of Queens. Xavier and I dance and mess around, ignoring curious gazes, and we mainly keep to ourselves. A few guys and girls stop to talk to Sawyer from time to time, and it's obvious he's as well-known on the circuit as Jackson is. I hear mention of Cam or Kai a couple times too, which isn't surprising. Those three were always tight.

"They're coming around!" someone screeches from farther back on the road. Sawyer glances down, gripping my hand and gesturing for Xavier to move. We dash across the road just as a car careens around the corner, racing toward the gas station.

I poke my head out, staring ahead, but it's too dark to see who it is. I'm on edge, with my stomach in knots and my breath faltering in my throat, as we wait to discover who has come out on top. My heart pumps furiously as a second car appears, and there isn't much of a gap between them at all.

The crowd turns insane.

Like fucking nuts.

People are jumping around, screaming and hollering.

Xavier grips my hand, his excited gaze mirroring my own.

The crowd chants a mix of encouragement for Hustle and Comet. I hold my breath as the cars speed up the road, almost neck and neck. I spot Jackson, just as he edges slightly ahead, and I'm screaming from the pit of my lungs as he crosses the finish line literally two seconds ahead of his rival.

"He won!" I scream, jumping up and down. Xavier spins me around again. Even Sawyer is grinning, having ditched his grumpy demeanor. I fling my arms around Sawyer's neck. "He won!"

"He's fucking unbeatable. Imagine what he'll do when he goes pro." Pride shines in his voice, and I'm glad to hear it, because I hate seeing them arguing so much.

Jackson is swamped the instant he emerges from his car. Someone lifts him up, and he fist pumps the air as he's carried around on several shoulders. His eyes seek me out, his body relaxing a little when he spots me safely cocooned between Sawyer and Xavier. I blow him a kiss and mouth my congratulations. His eyes remain locked on mine as he's jostled around, as if he can't tear his gaze away, and my heart thumps to a new beat.

There is no use denying it to myself anymore.

Jackson isn't just the reigning champion of the street racing scene.

He has also claimed title to my heart.

Chapter Eleven
Jackson

"Dude, you're a legend," Xavier says, handing me a beer as soon as we reconvene on the rooftop garden of the penthouse an hour later. "I bow at your feet." He bends from the waist, sweeping his arm out in a typical dramatic fashion.

"Man, that felt good," I admit, enjoying the feel of the cold beer gliding down my parched throat. It's almost three thirty, but I'm too wired to sleep. Nessa isn't working tomorrow, so we can sleep in late.

"You were amazing," she says, circling her arm around my waist. "It was such a rush watching it. I can only imagine how you must feel."

"It's the greatest feeling in the world," I admit as Hunt appears with a couple bowls of chips and dips.

"You belong out there," Hunt says, clinking his bottle against mine.

His praise is a welcome reprieve from the tension marring our friendship in recent weeks. "Thanks, man."

I sink another beer, and then, we call it a night. Nessa is

fighting a yawn as I walk us to my bedroom. "Tired, babe?" I murmur, pressing a kiss to that ticklish spot just under her ear.

"Nope," she lies, her eyes lighting up as she stares at me with expectation. "I could party for hours."

I chuckle. "Good," I whisper into her ear as I open my bedroom door. "Because you're going to need lots and lots of stamina."

She visibly shivers, and my heart jumps around a little. I close the door and pull her into my arms, needing to feel her close. I press kisses into her hair. "I've never brought a girl to a race before, and I fucking loved having you there." Being a couple has come a lot more naturally to me than I expected. I thought it'd be a chore to act the part of a loving, affectionate boyfriend, but the truth is, I haven't had to force anything.

And it's all because of her.

She's getting under my skin, and I'd be lying if I said I wasn't concerned.

"I loved it. Thank you for taking me." She snuggles into me, and her tiny hands wind around my waist. My cock thickens at the feel of her pressed up against me. "I'm so proud of you," she adds, and a lump wedges in my throat.

"Thanks, babe," I choke out.

She looks up at me through hooded eyes, and I'm a goner.

Every part of me wants every part of her.

I couldn't halt this train wreck even if I wanted to.

"Do you want to race? Is that what you plan to do with your life?" she asks.

I nod. "More than anything, but Dad wants me to get my degree first." The usual aggression bubbles up my throat at the thought of Dad. We've been estranged since I moved to Rydeville. Because of the things I discovered. I feel bad for Mom, because she's caught in the middle and she doesn't understand why. I can't tell her why I'm so pissed at him, because I know how much it will hurt her to hear he's known who was responsible for Dani's murder all along.

And he did *nothing*.

Disgust trickles through my veins.

"And you don't?" Nessa asks, trailing her fingers up my chest and pulling me out of my head.

"I'd rather race," I admit, smoothing a hand up and down her back. "But I get why he wants me to get a degree. He wants me to take over the business once I retire from racing."

"Is that what you want?" She wriggles against me, making my cock throb with need.

"I suppose so." I shrug. "I mean, I'm interested in managing the racing teams, but he has tons of other businesses and investments I know nothing about, and he works all the fucking time. I don't want that for my life."

"You could always hire people to help you manage it all," she suggests.

"I can," I say, lifting her, "but that's not something I need to decide now." I flash her a panty-melting grin. "Especially when I have a sexy woman in my bedroom dying for a ride on my cock."

She giggles. "I love your dirty mouth."

Her legs automatically wrap around my waist as I walk us toward the bed. I lay her down, hovering over her. Brushing hair off her face, I ask, "You still want to do this?"

"Fuck, yeah."

Is it wrong that hearing her cuss cranks my arousal up a few levels?

She reaches a hand down between us, cupping my boner. "I want your cock inside me, Jackson." She rolls her hips. "I need it like I need air to breathe."

"Then, it's so on, babe." I rock my hips against her, and the guttural moan that escapes her lips has precum leaking from my crown. "Get naked, sexy. I need to devour you."

We pull our clothes off like it's a new Olympic sport, grinning at one another as expectation pulses in the air. "Leave the heels," I demand when she moves to take them off. "I want to fuck you with them on." She's sitting on the edge of the bed, bending down, her fingers lingering at her ankle. She looks up at me with flushed cheeks and a certain something in her eyes. "What?" I ask, kicking my jeans and boxers off, standing before her totally nude.

"I had a fantasy about this moment."

Well, damn. I like the sound of that. Wrapping my hand around my cock, I slowly pump my shaft. "Oh yeah?" She nods as I reach around and unclasp her bra. It falls away, and I cup her tit with my free hand. "Tell me."

"I was sitting on the edge of the bed, just like this, naked except for these shoes. My legs were spread, and you were crouched in front of me, feeling my legs and..." Her cheeks flare up.

I play with her tits as I continue to stroke my cock. "And what, babe. You can tell me."

She lifts her chin, staring me in the face. "You were eating my pussy."

I drop my hands to her panties, and she lifts her hips letting me pull her underwear down her legs. I kneel before her, spreading her gorgeous legs wide. "You want me to make your fantasy come true?"

She nods eagerly. "So damn much."

I stretch up and kiss her mouth. "You never have to beg. Anything you want, you got it." I thread my fingers through her silky hair. "You feel me?"

"I do." She grabs hold of my hair, pulling me to her. Our

kiss is savage and needy and blistering with weeks of curtailed longing.

I pull back, sitting on my heels, grinning as I start running my hands up her shapely legs. "Were you sitting or lying back in this fantasy of yours?" I ask.

"Sitting."

"Okay. Hold still." I move my hands up higher and higher, rubbing my thumbs back and forth across her inner thighs, licking my lips at the prospect of tasting her pussy. She tastes like heaven on my tongue, and I've lost count of the number of times I've eaten her out, each time even more delicious than the last.

We've done everything except fuck, but that changes tonight.

I put her out of her misery, ravishing her with my fingers and my tongue until she's a writhing mess on my bed. She comes with a scream, and I'm hoping Hunt hears this. God knows I owe him payback.

Nessa is lying sated, with a dreamy smile on her face, as I lift her farther up the bed. She reaches for my cock, but I push her away. "I need inside you." I snatch a condom from my bedside table and roll it on. Precum is oozing from my tip, and I doubt I'm going to last very long.

I position myself over her, parting her legs and lining my cock up at her entrance. She looks up at me with glaring trust and adoration in her eyes, and I hold myself still, battling a sudden attack of conscience.

This is wrong.

I squeeze my eyes shut.

"What's wrong?" she softly asks.

Everything.

I'm not supposed to want this. Or care about her feelings or feel guilty for abusing her trust. This should be like countless other meaningless fucks.

But it's not.

It's going to mean something to both of us, and for the first time, this feels so fucking wrong.

"Jackson, please don't stop. Please don't have second thoughts." She reaches up, caressing my face, and my eyes blink open. I don't like what I see in her gaze. Disappointment, hurt, and a multitude of other things I can't decipher. "Don't you want me?" Her voice cracks, and her eyes well up.

Ah, fuck. No.

"Of course, I want you." I peer deep into her eyes. "I just don't want to hurt you." That's the only truth I can give her, and it *is* the truth. I don't want to hurt her even though I know I already have.

"You'll do that if you reject me," she quietly admits, and she might as well have stabbed me straight through the heart. Her body hums with need as her eyes plead with me, and I can't ignore that.

No matter what decision I make, I'm going to hurt her. I can at least give her some pleasure before the inevitable pain.

Fuck it. I lean down and kiss her softly. "Tell me if you want me to stop," I whisper, pressing the tip of my cock inside her.

She grabs hold of my ass cheeks, pulling me in deeper. "I don't want you to stop," she moans, rocking her hips against me. "I don't ever want you to stop." Her eyes penetrate mine. "Fuck me, Jackson. Please."

I can't take it anymore.

This is happening.

Consequences be damned.

I slide the rest of the way in, holding myself still as I kiss her. "You're sure?" I ask again.

"Yes," she says, through gritted teeth, jerking her hips up. "Now, fuck me." Her hot walls grip my cock, and I lose the last vestiges of guilt, giving in to the pleasure waiting in the wings.

I slam in and out of her as I devour every inch of her with my lips, my tongue, and my cock. I fuck her mercilessly, and she takes it all, revels in it, and I can't get enough of her.

Nessa is consuming me, bewitching me, and I'm feeling things I've never felt before.

Everything is breath-stealing and new.

The way she feels hugging my cock.

The way my skin tingles in every place her fingers touch me.

The deep ache that lodges in my core at every whimper, every moan, and every wriggle.

This girl *has* cast a spell on me, and I'm fucked. I am *so* fucked, and that is a major problem.

I pull her legs up to my shoulder, and my cock jerks at the sight of those fuck-me shoes. I pound into her with a new fierceness, pouring all my frustration and helplessness into every thrust of my hips. My balls tighten just as a lick of fire shoots up my spine. I rub her clit vigorously as my body strains, sinewy muscle locking up, preparing to explode. Sweat glides down my spine, and she's bucking and writhing, crying and whimpering, as I slam into her, consumed by need and anger and frustration.

"Come for me, babe. Right fucking now," I gruffly demand, pinching her clit hard as my orgasm rips through me like a tidal wave. I shout out, flexing my hips, driving into her deep as cum shoots into the condom. She screams, clenching around me, and my cock jerks another couple times.

I collapse on her, holding her through the last few waves of her release, and then, I roll to my side, taking her with me, hugging her sweat-slickened body against mine.

"Jackson," she rasps in a breathy tone. My eyes lower to her glassy-filled gaze. "That was—"

"Everything," I blurt.

She nods as tears roll down her face, but she's smiling and gazing at me like I hung the fucking moon in the night sky.

I press her face into my chest, unable to look her in the eye any longer, feeling like the biggest piece of shit to ever walk the earth.

Chapter Twelve
Jackson

I rise first the following morning after a fitful sleep. Nessa slept soundly all night, cradled to my front, unaware of the torment twisting and turning my stomach into knots.

Somehow, I've caught feelings for her, and that wasn't supposed to happen. All it will do is make this so much worse when it comes to an end.

And it will come to an end.

It has to.

Because she's the daughter of my enemy. The man who destroyed my sister, forcing her to take her own life.

There is no scenario where this ends well.

"Ugh." I rest my head on the counter in the kitchen, wishing things could be different, but they can't.

"I thought we agreed you weren't going to fuck her," Hunt says, entering the kitchen and growling at me.

"I never agreed to that," I say, lifting my head.

"What the fuck are you doing?" he snaps, crossing his arms and glaring at me.

"I wish I fucking knew."

"Something smells good," Xavier says, coming up behind Hunt at the grill and placing his hands on his hips.

"Can you grab the salad from the kitchen and the bread from the oven," Hunt says, his voice tense.

"Sure, babe." Xavier pecks his lips, walking off before Hunt can bitch at him.

"I'll help," Nessa says, putting her e-reader down.

"Stay. I'll help." I clamp a hand on her leg, keeping her on the couch. It's the first time I've touched her all day, because I can scarcely look at her without almost choking. I shouldn't have slept with her, because now, I'm royally fucked. I can't stop thinking about the way it feels to be inside her, and I'm struggling to stick to my agenda.

"Thank you." She smiles at me, seemingly oblivious.

Before I get away, she pulls me close, kissing me. "Hurry back," she whispers.

I feel Hunt's disapproving gaze as I silently follow Xavier to the kitchen, pulling out plates while he grabs the bread from the oven.

"I really like her," he says. "She is so sweet."

"I know." I remove the salad from the refrigerator, ignoring the acid climbing up my throat.

"Sawyer thinks you're going to hurt her."

My muscles tighten. "Why would he say that?" I ask, needing to know what he's said. If he has told him, I have an even bigger problem.

"He doubts your ability to commit long-term. He thinks you'll grow bored with her."

My muscles relax. "He needs to butt out of my relationship and concentrate on his own," I hiss.

"We don't have a relationship," Xavier says, his tone a little off. "We're fuck buddies. He's made it very clear that is all we'll be."

I set the salad down beside the plates. "What do you want?"

He doesn't answer straightaway. "Honestly, I'm not sure." He rubs the back of his neck. "I like him. A lot. I mean, he drives me fucking crazy too, but I think we could have something real, you know?"

Yeah, I do. I nod.

"But he's holding out on me. I don't know why, and if he doesn't get his act together, I'm out." He eyeballs me. "I won't be anyone's dirty little secret."

"This steak is almost as good as the one from last night," Nessa says, smiling at Hunt.

"Only almost?" Hunt feigns hurt.

"You want me to lie?" she teases.

"Never." Hunt's jaw tenses as his mood sours again. "Lying never ends well."

That's it. I'm fucking moving out.

"No, it doesn't." She looks away, picking up on the change in his temperament, and the atmosphere around the table is awkward as fuck.

"So, Van, have you got your dress for the wedding yet?" Xavier asks, attempting to change the subject and lift the tension.

He has no clue he's just added to it.

Could this day get any worse? I rub at my throbbing temples, wishing the ground would open and swallow me.

"Wedding?" Her gaze bounces between me and Xavier. "What wedding?"

Xavier turns to me with a frown. "You haven't asked her?"

"I hadn't mentioned it. No." My smile is tight. "For a

reason." I soften my tone, twisting in my chair so I'm facing her. My knee brushes Nessa's. "Abby and Kai are getting married next month."

"Aren't they already married?" She places her silverware down, dabbing the side of her mouth with a napkin.

"They are, but they pretty much eloped, and now, they want to have a proper ceremony with their family and friends there."

"Ah, I see." She smiles. "That makes sense." Anticipation is heavy in the air, and I have no choice but to say this now.

Thanks a fucking bunch, Xavier.

"Babe." I take her hands in mine. "I can't ask you to come with me."

"What?" Her smile fades. "Why?"

"Think about it." I plead with my eyes, urging her to catch my drift, but I'm met with a mask of confusion. "I can't bring you to a wedding where you've fucked the groom. It's a small, intimate wedding, for family and close friends only, and I don't think Abby would appreciate it if I brought a girl who fucked her husband."

Xavier's eyes pop wide. Hunt obviously didn't blurt that truth.

"Of course." Nessa fakes a smile, but we can all tell it's not real. "It's totally fine."

Hunt sends imaginary daggers at me, and I don't blame him this time. I've hurt her, and she's embarrassed. I wasn't planning on telling her anything about the wedding. I was just going to disappear on family business and then come back with her none the wiser. I thought it would be easier that way. But Xavier forced my hand, and now, she's upset.

We eat in silence, and I feel like the biggest dick. But there is nothing I can say or do that will make it better.

What the hell was I thinking asking her to stay here this

weekend? I should be keeping more of a distance. I need to back off a little.

"Thanks for dinner, Sawyer," Nessa says, standing abruptly a few minutes later. My eyes drop to her half-eaten steak. "It's delicious, but I'm not feeling so hot. I think I picked up a little heatstroke. I'm going to head home."

"Nessa."

"It's fine, Jackson." She can barely even look me in the eye. "Enjoy your dinner. I'll get an Uber."

"You're not getting an Uber," I persist. "I'll drive you home. Just let me know when you're ready."

She nods, and I watch her walk away with a pain in my chest.

"You're an asshole," Hunt spits out when she's out of earshot.

"Me? I wasn't going to mention a fucking thing about the wedding." I glare at Xavier even though it's not really his fault.

"I didn't know she slept with Kai," he replies. "Although, if you explained it to Abby, I don't think she'd have a huge issue with it. Unless they like dated or something."

"It was one time. They were both trashed. I doubt either of them remember it," Hunt says. "That's only an excuse."

Xavier narrows his eyes at me. "Not cool, dude."

"I know, but it's for the best."

Hunt's chair squeals as he shoves it back. "I'm going to see if she's okay."

That should be me, but I doubt she wants me anywhere near her.

Xavier and I clear away the ruined dinner in silence. His displeasure swirls around me, adding to my bad mood. After the table is cleaned and the dishwasher is stacked, Xavier leaves to pack his bag. His train is in a couple hours.

I tiptoe toward my bedroom, debating whether to make

myself known when I spot the door ajar. Hunt and Nessa are sitting on the bed, talking. He has his arm wrapped around her, and I want to rip it away. My natural instinct is to rush in there, shove Hunt off my girl, and comfort her.

But what would I say? What could I say?

The obvious solution is to speak to Abby and clear it for Nessa to come as my plus one. But that will only invite a whole host of questions I can't answer. I've kept Kai and Abby out of this for a reason. Bringing Nessa with me will let the cat out of the bag. I can't do it. I can't go there. Which means there is nothing I can say to her now to make her feel better.

Perhaps, Hunt can bring her some peace. So, I flatten my back to the wall and listen.

"Don't get attached, Van," Hunt says, and my hands clench into fists.

"I already am," she admits in a whisper.

"Then, detach yourself."

"Is that what he wants? Is he planning on dumping me, and that's why he didn't ask me to the wedding?"

Her words rip through my heart, shattering it into pieces. I hang my head, disgusted with myself.

"I don't know what's going through his head. He's dealing with stuff, and..." Hunt sighs, trailing off before he goes too far. "He likes you, Van. He does, but you know him. He's not the commitment type. He doesn't do relationships. I don't want you to get hurt. He'll be leaving for college, there's pussy on tap at RU, and you know he won't be able to keep it in his pants."

The veins in my arms tense and my pulse throbs in my neck as liquid rage whittles through me. I want to wrestle my best friend to the ground and punch his fucking lights out, but I hold myself back.

I guess this is what I get for eavesdropping.

"Just treat this for what it is," Hunt continues. "Casual fun with no strings attached and an expiration date. That way, you'll protect your heart."

I want to be mad at Hunt, but the truth is, I can't be mad at him for trying to protect her. He's looking out for her although the reality is there isn't much he can do.

She's already invested.

And I'm invested too—in my plan.

I don't want to hurt her, and I wish things could be different, but they can't because I need that bastard to pay and Vanessa is the only way I can get to him.

I have fucked up spectacularly. I have let my walls down. I have let her in. And I've got to pull back and remember my goal. I have one month until I leave New York for Rydeville. One month to find out if Vanessa knows where he is. I can't lose sight of that, because otherwise, this has all been for nothing.

It doesn't matter that I have feelings for her, because feelings have no place in the bigger picture.

She is understandably quiet in the car as I drive her home. I pull up to the curb outside the diner and kill the engine. I stare through the windshield, too cowardly to look at her face and see the hurt I know is residing there. "I know I've upset you, and I'm sorry."

"It's fine." She curls her hand around the door handle. "I get it. I do." Her voice wobbles. "It seems no matter how hard I try to leave the past in the past it always comes back to haunt me." She gets out, and I hop out my side, grabbing her bag from the back. "Thanks."

She refuses to look at me as I give it to her. "Nessa." I take her hand, lacing my fingers in hers. "Let me make it up to you."

She tips her head up, pinning red-rimmed eyes on me.

I swallow over the messy ball in my throat. "Come to The Hamptons next weekend with me."

She shakes her head. "I don't think so, Jackson." She tries to remove her hand, but I hold on to it.

Surely, she's not going to break up with me because I won't take her as my plus one? "Why not?"

She holds the bag to her chest. "I have my reasons."

"Like what, babe?" I pull her in closer, pleased when she doesn't push me away. She lets the bag drop to the ground. "C'mon. It'll be fun. And I can make up for ruining this weekend."

"I don't know." She looks over my shoulder, and I glance behind me, wondering why she's staring at the silver Honda Accord parked across the road.

"If you're worried about running into Melania or any of those other bitches, you don't need to concern yourself with them. You'll be staying with me, and I won't let any of them even look funny at you."

"It's not just that." She wets her lips, noticeably gulping.

"Your family will be there," I supply as realization dawns. At least, *I* don't have to worry about that. My parents haven't returned to The Hamptons since Dani died.

She nods.

"I know things are shitty with your parents, but isn't this a good opportunity to see your brother and sister? I know how much you miss them."

Her eyes brighten with hope, and I know I have her. "We'll figure out a way for you to spend time with them." I rub my thumb along her lower lip. "Please, come. I will worship at your feet all weekend."

"I'll have to ask for time off."

"You have vacation days to take," I remind her.

"I know, but it's super busy right now. I'm not sure Paul can release me."

"It can't do any harm to ask though, right?"

"No. It can't." She shoots me a timid smile, and I breathe a sigh of relief. "Okay. I'll ask."

"Thanks, babe." I bring her hand to my lips, kissing her knuckles. "You won't regret it."

Chapter Thirteen
Vanessa

We drive out of the city, heading toward The Hamptons at eleven on Friday morning. I'm not sure how Chloe managed it, but she convinced Paul to approve three vacation days around my scheduled day off, which means I have four days in a row to myself.

Sheer bliss.

Our plan is to stay in East Hampton until Monday morning before coming back to the city.

I'm excited for some alone time with my boyfriend because I haven't seen him much this week, and things are still a little strained between us.

Now that I've had time to think about it, I'm not as upset as I was last Sunday. Jackson is right. I can't show up to Kaiden's wedding and upset his wife. It'd be different if it was a big society wedding, where I could blend into the crowd, but I'd be front and center at an intimate gathering, and I don't want to make things awkward for Jackson or upset Kaiden and Abby.

I am disappointed, but I've made my peace with it.

"Hey. You doing okay over there?" Jackson asks, patting my knee.

"I'm good." I smile, tipping my face up, letting the warm breeze skate over my skin. Jackson showed up in a sleek, dark-gray open-top BMW, and I'm reaping the benefits of the glorious day. My hair is scraped back off my face into a messy bun, and I'm wearing my black and gold Chanel sunglasses. "I can't remember the last time I had this much time off."

I'm looking forward to the weekend, but I'm also a little anxious. I desperately want to see Hunter and Kayleigh, but that means risking contact with the stepmonster. I haven't seen him since the day he kicked me out, and I'd be lying if I said I wasn't worried. I don't want to see him and be reminded of a past I've worked so hard to forget.

But Jackson will be with me, and that bastard can't hurt me anymore. He also can't stop me from hanging out on the beach with my brother and sister—no matter how much he might like to. Mom usually brings the twins to Main Beach on Saturday mornings, and I'm praying she hasn't broken with tradition. It will be my only opportunity to "bump" into my siblings at a time when that bastard shouldn't be there.

"You work too hard." Jackson flashes me his signature grin, showcasing his perfectly straight, glistening white teeth.

His hair is a mess of golden waves falling over his brow and onto his shades. He's wearing a black designer T-shirt, stretched across his impressive chest, over knee-length denim shorts.

He's so fucking hot, and I'm already wet for him.

Memories of last Saturday night resurrect in my mind, and I squirm in my seat as liquid lust pools low in my belly. I'm dying for a repeat performance, and I'm planning on jumping him any chance I get this weekend.

"Earth to Nessa." He snaps his fingers at me, taking his eyes off the road for a second. "You zoned out on me."

"I'm here."

"Happy, babe?" He threads his free hand in mine.

"Very." I lean over and kiss his cheek, inhaling his divine spicy, minty, fruity scent. "I'm getting to spend all weekend with you. What's not to love?"

We make good time, driving along the main street a little before one. "Should we stop for something to eat?" I suggest as we roll past familiar high-end boutiques and designer stores. East Hampton is a historic community with some of the best shops, finest restaurants, and world-class beaches. I have always loved it here even if my summer experiences weren't always the happiest. There is something about this place that speaks to me on a whole other level.

"I thought we'd eat at the house. I had the housekeeper stock the refrigerator, and the place has been cleaned."

I place my hand over his on the gearshift. "That was thoughtful."

"We can eat out too, but I thought it'd be nice to have the option."

"What time is Hunt arriving?"

"He should be here by dinnertime. He's leaving the office early."

"Will Xavier be with him?" I inquire, waving at an acquaintance of my mom's as we pass her on the street.

"I don't think an invitation was extended."

"Pity. He's fun."

"He's good people," Jackson agrees, turning off the main street and picking up speed.

We drive for a few miles before Jackson stops at an enclosed property that is at the back of the beach. I've been to his house a few times over the years, but I've never seen it from the front.

We drive up a long, sweeping stone driveway, past manicured lawns, leafy shrubs, and colorful flowerbeds. Rays of sunshine beat down on the car, illuminating the gorgeous surroundings, and heating every part of my exposed skin.

Jackson swings the car around in front of the stunning modern two-story building. He jumps out, stretching his arms and moving his neck from side to side. I gather my purse and climb out as he opens the trunk, extracting our weekend bags. "I didn't hire any of the staff for the weekend," he says. "I thought you'd prefer privacy."

"I do, and if the place is clean and we have food and drink, we don't need anything else."

He slings his arm over my shoulder, holding our bags with his other hand. "Come on. Let's get inside and get something to eat. I'm starving."

"Your house is beautiful," I admit, glancing up at the cream, stone, and glass house as we head toward the front door.

"Mom has good taste," he says, unlocking the door and stepping aside to let me enter first.

The inside temp is perfectly regulated, and the cool air is welcome against my hot skin.

The kitchen is gorgeous with its glossy white cupboards, stainless-steel appliances, and gray-speckled-marble countertop. Jackson dumps our bags on the island unit, heading straight for the refrigerator. I continue walking through the large barn-like open-plan living and dining room, with its high ceilings and overhead beams, toward the tall windows stretching across the length of the back of the room. The sheer white gossamer curtains are already open, highlighting the breathtaking scenery outside.

I unlock and open the sliding glass door, stepping out on the flagstone patio, admiring the view.

My eyes ghost over Jackson's large infinity pool, elegant manicured grounds with the vine-covered pergola protecting a long dining area, and out beyond the steps leading to the shore. I stare in awe at the clear, cloudless sky, miles of clean, sandy beach, and the calm blue ocean with barely a ripple in sight. I inhale deeply, sucking the familiar salty air into my lungs, and my limbs relax as a layer of stress flitters away.

Jackson's house opens out onto a private beach, shared by the adjoining properties.

The house at the very top of this private strip is my parents' vacation house. We are separated from them by a host of gorgeous homes. All the mansions on this secluded end of the beach are nestled on sizable plots of land, so there is enough of a distance between us for me to hide out here all weekend should I desire it.

Hunt's vacation home is the gorgeous three-story property two houses up from here, and it was where most of the parties took place during summer break.

One would think, with his rep, that Jackson's house would be party central. Especially when his parents stopped coming here, and he was mostly alone. But he was picky about who he let into his house, and this place was strictly a party-free zone. I remember attending a couple of dinner parties here with my parents when I was younger, and the only other times I've been inside was when I was with Sawyer and Cam...Kaiden.

"The housekeeper prepared some chicken salads, and there are fresh bread rolls. Will that do?" Jackson asks, popping his head outside.

"Sounds delicious," I say over my shoulder, smiling.

"You want to eat outside or inside?"

I plant my hands on my hips and lift a brow. "You have to ask?"

He grins. "Outside it is."

I help him carry food, dinnerware, and silverware outside. We don't eat at the formal dining area under the pergola, choosing the smaller dining area to the left side of the patio. Jackson erects the umbrella to keep us shaded while we eat.

"This is fantastic," I admit, stabbing a forkful of chargrilled chicken and popping it in my mouth.

"That was delicious," Jackson agrees, pushing his empty plate away and patting his flat stomach. He pours more sparkling water into our glasses, lifting his glass and drinking as he stares at me.

"What?" I ask as soon as I've finished chewing, thinking I must have some lettuce in my teeth or something.

"You look really pretty today."

"I do?" I wanted to be comfortable for the journey, so I threw on a cute white knee-length summer dress with silver flip-flops. My face is devoid of makeup, apart from some tinted sunscreen and lip gloss, and my hair is still in a messy bun. I'm not what I'd consider pretty. At all.

"You don't need all that crap on your face," he adds as if he's read my mind. "You are naturally beautiful. You could model." He crosses one leg over the other. "Mom still has contacts in the business. I could ask her for you?"

I blush at his praise. "Chloe says the same, but it's not something I'm interested in. Thanks for the compliment, though." I don't like the idea of random men ogling my body or the thoughts of perverts jerking off to pics of me, so modeling is not something I would ever consider.

"Anytime, babe. And I meant every word." He flashes me his trademark cheeky grin.

"How is your mom? I haven't seen her or your dad in years."

A soft smile graces his mouth. "Mom's good. Still painting and dancing, and she's heavily involved in her charity work."

"And your dad?"

The smile drops off his mouth. "We don't speak that much." He looks off into space.

"How come?"

He shrugs, and awkward silence bleeds into the air. "He let Dani down," he finally says, "and I can't let it go."

I nod, understanding even though I don't have all the facts. I've seen what Dani's death did to Jackson. How badly he self-destructed. "I'm sorry."

His chest heaves, and he shoots me a tentative smile. "Yeah, me too."

When I have finished eating, we clear the table and head back inside to unpack and change into swimwear.

"It looks exactly how I remember it," I say as we walk through the living area, past white couches centered around a large open fireplace with a massive TV mounted overhead. The maple floors perfectly contrast with the white, gray, and blue color scheme. We stride beyond the long maple table that seats twelve in comfy white leather tub chairs and past the ornate plant pots, eclectic rugs, ornaments, and frames on the wall.

I stop at the end of the angled stairway, admiring the striking blue, green, and purple canvas. "Your mom did this?" I squint at the messy scrawled signature on the bottom right side of the painting.

"She did. She's into all that abstract shit." Jackson tilts his head, his gaze roaming the creation. "Still can't figure it the fuck out, but I like the vibrancy of the colors." He takes my hand, tugging me up the wooden stairs. I hold on to the glass balustrade as we walk upstairs.

I've never been to this part of his house before. The landing is wide and airy with more high ceilings. On our left is a little recreational area with a window seat and a wall of shelving crammed with books. Sunlight pours into the space, and I make a silent promise to find a sneaky hour or two to read my book up here.

My flip-flops snap off the maple floors as I follow Jackson past several closed doors. Family photos adorn the walls, and I smile at pictures of a younger Jackson, remembering his cheeky face and sparkling blue eyes so well. I come to a halt at the framed photo of a ballerina. "Is this your mom?" I ask, pointing at it.

Jackson opens a door and dumps our bags inside before walking back to me. He pulls me into his body, resting his hands on my hips and his chin on top of my hair. "Yeah. It's when she performed *Swan Lake* for the Bolshoi Ballet at The Met. That was the night she met my dad. He swept her off her feet, and they were married three weeks later. She continued to perform with the Bolshoi for a year after their wedding, but then, she gave it up for love. She missed my father too much when she was traveling."

"Is that when she took up modeling?" I ask. Jackson's mom Laurena was a top super model in her day, and she is still a stunningly beautiful woman, regularly photographed on the New York social scene.

"Yeah."

"That's such a romantic story." I'm conscious my voice has this dream-like quality to it.

He steers me into the master suite. "Pity Dad didn't remember that." His tone drips with bitterness.

"What happened?" I inquire.

"They have an open marriage, and I'm pretty sure my father is the driving force behind it."

"I bet that's more common than you think." I peruse the well-proportioned room we'll be staying in. It's decorated in calming whites and greens with pale wooden furniture. The space contains a large king-sized bed dressed in white linens, two matching tables, a matching dresser, a walk-in closet, and another door I'm guessing leads to the en suite bathroom.

Yet it's the outside space that is most impressive. Beyond the long floor-to-ceiling window lies a two-tier decked area with a hot tub, a couple of lounge chairs, a small table and chairs, and exquisite views of the beach and the ocean.

This place is a world away from my parents' more traditional vacation house. I found it hard to relax there, yet this house already feels like home.

"I'm sure it is, but it's not how I'd like things for my mom." He rests his head against the window, sighing as he stares outside.

I walk to him, draping myself around him from behind. "Thank you for taking me here."

He twists around, pulling me into his arms and kissing the top of my head. "I'm glad you came." His thumb brushes the side of my neck as we hug. The steady thumping of his heart is comforting as I rest my head on his broad chest. All I'm thinking is how much I love him and that I need to summon the courage to tell him.

Chapter Fourteen
Vanessa

I grab a quick shower in the opulent bathroom before changing into a strapless black and red Chanel bikini that Melania would throw shade at me for, because it's *so* last season.

I have zero fucks to give.

I like the way the padded top makes my boobs look, I'm comfortable in it, and I don't have cash for a new one, so screw her.

I slather sunscreen on my exposed skin and join Jackson out on the deck. He's wearing black board shorts that hang dangerously low on his hips, highlighting those V-indents I love and the tempting trail of dark-blond hair sneaking under his waistband.

"There is juice and water in the mini fridge," he says, pointing at the corner as he removes his shades. His eyes roam my body while he shamelessly ogles me from head to toe. "Fuck me," he mutters under his breath.

What a great idea!

I drop down in front of him on the lounge chair, handing him the slim gold bottle. "Could you put sunscreen on my back?" I lick my lips, sending him my most seductive smile.

He sits up, planting his feet on either side of the wide, sturdy lounge chair as he takes the bottle from me.

Our fingers brush, and an electrical charge zips up and down my arm. He inches closer, and heat from his body rolls off him in waves, digging under my skin, sending delicious tremors coasting all over my body. Desire shoots straight to my core the instant his hand lands on my shoulder, and I unclasp my bikini top, letting it fall to my waist, before I've had time to second-guess myself.

He sucks in a breath, his hand stalling on my shoulder, and a victorious smile creeps over my mouth. His hands move after a couple of beats, gliding firmly over my back and along my sides.

He's very diligent as he goes about his task, and my nipples pebble, straining with the need to be touched. Moisture dampens my bikini bottoms as his touch ignites a slow-burning fire inside me. A needy whimper escapes my lips when his fingers accidentally brush the side of my boob. He stops, and I hold my breath, waiting to see what he does when I move my butt back, pressing against his dick.

Butterflies scatter in my chest, and that slow-burning fire ruptures into a boisterous inferno when I feel his hardness press against my ass.

Jackson is the only one who can fan the flames, and I want him, need him.

Right now.

I arch my back, putting the rest of my body flush against him, moaning as I grab his hand, placing it over my breast. My nipples are already hard enough to cut glass, and I ache for him everywhere.

"What are you doing?" he asks, his voice thick with lust, his cock jerking against my ass.

"What do you think?" I rasp, pressing my breast into his hand as his fingers start kneading my sensitive flesh.

"Jesus. Fuck." He rests his forehead against my shoulder blade as his free hand creeps around my front, cupping my other breast. "I'm trying to be good, and you're making it very difficult for me."

"I don't want you to be good," I groan, pressing against his solid hard-on as his fingers tweak my nipples. "I want you to be really, really bad."

He grabs my hips and turns me around so I'm straddling him.

"You will be the death of me," he says before lowering his mouth to my breast and sucking hard.

I rock against him, grinding against his hard length, needing the friction to ease the raw throbbing in my core. Grabbing fistfuls of his hair, I yank his face into my breasts, letting him play with them. His fingers, lips, and tongue work my sensitive flesh until I'm sure they're red and bruised. I pick up the pace, rubbing my pussy against his cock, clutching his shoulders. "Jackson. Fuck me. Fuck me right here and now."

He lifts his head from my breasts, trailing his fingers up and down my spine. "You're a very naughty girl, Nessa." He slaps my ass, and liquid gushes from my pussy, staining my bikini bottoms. "Lucky for you, I like it." He waggles his brows, and his eyes scream wicked intent.

Hell yeah.

I silently fist pump the air, yanking his head back and crashing my mouth down on his. His tongue slips into my mouth, and we mutually groan as I flex my hips, grinding down on him.

"I haven't stopped thinking about your pussy," he murmurs

when his mouth leaves my lips, trailing along the side of my neck.

"I haven't stopped thinking about your cock." I cry out as his dick prods my entrance through our swim clothes. "I need you inside me now, Jackson. Please."

He grips my chin. "You never have to beg. I told you that." He lifts me off him to shove his shorts down and kick them away. He takes hold of his cock, stroking it in quick pumps as I shimmy my bikini bottoms down my legs. Thank fuck, we're up high enough the people down on the beach can't see us.

I climb over him, positioning my entrance in the right place, ready to impale myself on his cock, when his hand lands on my hip, stalling me just at the moment of impact. "Shit. Condom."

"I have the implant, and I'm clean." He stares at me for a few seconds, and I can almost see the wheels churning in his head. "Jackson," I plead, hovering over him like a needy shrew. "I want to feel you inside me. Skin to skin."

His free hand moves to my other hip while his eyes never leave mine. Indecision flashes in his eyes, quickly replaced with steely determination. Clasping my hips, he slams me down on top of him in one superfast move, and I scream at the intrusion.

He half-laughs, half-groans. "Babe, there are probably kids down there. We don't want to scar them for life."

I doubt they can hear us from here, but I would hate to be proven wrong. "I'll try to be quiet," I say, thrusting against him.

"Goddamn." His eyes shutter as he holds me in place with his strong hands. "That feels so fucking good."

"It'd feel better if you let me ride you."

His eyes pop open. "Come here, my little temptress." He pulls me down, claiming my lips in a searing-hot kiss I feel all the way to the tips of my toes. We continue kissing, with him stationary inside me, and it's one of the most erotic moments of my life.

I can feel him pulsing inside me, and my walls clench around him of their own accord. Feeling his hot skin deep inside me, filling me up, heating me from within, is like nothing I've experienced before.

His lips are swollen when we finally break our lip-lock. "Ride me, goddess. Make me bend to your will."

I take control, moving up and down on his cock in a slow torturous fashion. His hands roam my body as I ride him, and he moves closer, his tongue darting out, laving my nipples. I pick up speed, bobbing up and down on him, groaning at the feel of his big cock gliding in and out of me. His lips suction on my breast, and he sucks hard in a way I know will bruise me, but I'm enjoying this too much to care.

Sex has never felt this good for me, and no one has cared as much to make sure my needs are fulfilled. Jackson is a generous lover, and he always ensures I get off. I grab his hair while he worships my breasts, reveling in all the sensations he's coaxing from my body.

His touch sets my body on fire.

His kiss alters me.

And his cock, his cock is *life*.

I angle my hips, desperate to feel him deeper, needing him to fill me all the way up. I toss my hair down my back, grinding and writhing on top of him, moaning and whimpering, as his lips trail a blazing path down my body. "You are so fucking hot like this, babe." His hands palm my ass, and he fondles my cheeks before his fingers trek up and down my crack.

"Oh, fuck." I cry out as his finger prods my puckered hole, and I move faster, trying to push him deeper and deeper inside me.

Instinctively, he knows what I need. Letting go of my ass, he grabs hold of my hips again, directing my movements, slamming me up and down on him until I see stars. He keeps up this punishing pace as my climax builds and builds, reaching for that heavenly peak.

Sliding one hand across my belly, he rubs my clit, and I shatter as his thumb presses down on that sensitive bundle of nerves, tumbling over wave after wave as liquid bliss rips through my body.

"Fuck, babe. You are so sexy when you come." He presses a kiss to the underside of my jaw, and a shudder works its way through me at the feel of his warm lips on my overheated skin.

My body feels like liquified jelly when I come down from my erotic high, and I stop moving on top of him, unable to force my limbs into action. He flips us around, until I'm lying underneath him on the lounge chair, and then, he pounds into me like a madman. My legs encircle his waist, and I dig my heels into his ass as I press a slew of open-mouthed kisses all over his chest.

He comes apart in my arms, growling and cussing as he thrusts his hips into me, continuing to pump until he has expelled every last drop of cum. "Fucking hell." He collapses on top of me. "I think you rode me to death."

We maneuver until we are on our sides, facing one another. "Sex with you is incredible," I admit.

"Ditto." He presses the softest of kisses to my lips. "I've never gone bareback before. That was ... out of this world." He caresses my face. "You're so beautiful. So sexy. So sweet. How did I not notice this before?"

His words and the adoring look on his face unchain the padlock on my heart, and the floodgates open. "I love you," I blurt, reaching up to touch his handsome face. "I love you so fucking much, Jackson. You're my everything."

Silence greets my outburst, and a heavy weight presses down on my chest as I watch various emotions flicker in his eyes. "Nessa." His tone is soft. "I care about you. I—"

"It's fine." I cut across him, my cheeks heating up and not from the sun. "I didn't say it so you'd say it back," I lie. Because, come on? No girl says it unless she thinks she's going to hear it in return. Not unless she's a brainless idiot who spews the truth without thinking it through.

Why do I keep putting my foot in my mouth?

I jump up, scooping up my bikini.

"Nessa." He pulls me down into his arms. "Don't be upset."

"I'm not upset," I lie again. "I'm fine. I just think we should get dressed. Don't want to scar those kids for life, right?" I joke, working hard to sound lighthearted despite the pain ripping through my chest.

I get up before Jackson the following morning to cook breakfast. We ended up eating takeout burgers with Sawyer at his place last night instead of going out, which suited me fine since I was feeling a little fragile after my stupid, unrequited confession. It's super awkward when you tell someone you love them for the first time and their response is they *care* about you. It hurts that he doesn't love me back, but what did I expect? I'm not exactly easy to love. I know that.

Sawyer's words seem prophetic.

I'm going to get hurt unless I protect myself.

I have clearly reverted to form, throwing myself at Jackson, reading more into our relationship, and desperately needing that connection to feel whole.

But I'm better than that.

Stronger than that.

So, I'll do as Sawyer advised. I'll keep my feelings securely under lock and key. Keep things casual. And pretend like

Jackson hasn't left me broken, with my heart in pieces on the floor, when he eventually walks away from me.

Chapter Fifteen

Jackson

"Something smells good," I say, ambling into the kitchen in a pair of black running shorts and bare feet. I walk to the stove, pressing up against her, sliding my arm around her slim waist.

"I hope you like your bacon crispy." I can tell it takes effort to keep her tone light, and I hate that I've hurt her again. Her confession has erected another wall between us, yet I'm not sorry for my response. I thought about returning the sentiment, but that is sinking to a level even I won't go to.

I brush her hair aside, kissing that delicate spot under her ear. "That's my favorite kind."

I leave her alone to plate up our food, setting the table on the patio. I watch the first signs of life on the beach below as I wait for Nessa to join me. It's another glorious day in The Hamptons. There isn't a cloud in the sky, the sun is already bathing the ground below in a warm, balmy heat, and the gentle swaying of the ocean calls out invitingly. Perhaps, I can persuade Nessa to take a swim with me later.

She's quiet as we eat, not that I blame her.

"So, what's the plan?" I ask after we have finished eating.

"Mom usually brings the twins to Main Beach early so the stepmonster can sleep off his hangover without the screams and giggles of his offspring waking him. She probably won't stay past noon," she adds, glancing at the time on her cellphone.

"Stepmonster?" I arch a brow, my lips fighting a smile. It's not exactly original, and the guy is an ass, but it still sounds funny tumbling from her lips.

She shrugs, dismissing the question. "I say we take an hour to chill, let our food settle, and then head out?"

"Perfect." I start clearing away the plates, and she stands to help. I shake my head. "You cooked. I'll clean. Why don't you read in the nook upstairs? I saw your greedy eyes when we arrived and you spotted it," I add, answering her unspoken question.

"Sounds good." She finishes her orange juice, staring over my shoulder at the ocean.

She avoided eye contact while we ate too, and her vulnerability is showing again. I know that's my fault, and guilt stirs in my gut. "Thanks for breakfast." I lean across the table, kissing her softly. It's getting harder and harder to pull away from her, from this connection drawing me in, but I do, because she's still upset, and I need to give her some space.

"You're welcome." She shoots me a tight smile before snatching her cell and e-reader and heading inside.

I finish cleaning with a frown on my face, trying to understand it. *What is it with women and those three words? Like, does it really matter what label is applied?* Nessa was happy until she tried to force us into a box. All her declaration has done is upset her, made me feel like an even bigger piece of shit, and further complicated things.

Jackson

We head off jogging in the direction of Main Beach an hour later as planned. Nessa pulls her cap down lower on her head when we pass her parents' vacation house. Dark emotion flares in her eyes as she runs, and I wonder again what happened between them. I know she was out of control for a few years, and she admitted she had a mini breakdown freshman year, but what kind of asshole kicks their daughter out, leaving her completely to her own defenses, and tells her she can't see her brother and sister because she's too much trouble? And if this is Aaron Breen's doing, why hasn't Ruth—Nessa's mom—intervened?

I haven't exactly been a model son these past few years, and while things are strained with Dad, I know I'm welcome at the house, the track, and his office building downtown, anytime. No matter how many cruel words I hurl at him, he always tells me he loves me. If shit rained down on me in the morning, I know I could turn to my dad, and he'd bend over backwards to help me.

Which is why his lack of action regarding Dani makes no sense and frustrates the hell out of me.

It hurts we're no longer close, and I miss him even though it's partly my fault.

I push my legs harder, my mind uneasy at my train of thought. One might say I'm a heartless, selfish prick for the way I've treated Dad, but I can't get over the fact he knew Christian Montgomery was the one who kidnapped and tortured Dani and he's done nothing to retaliate. He told me it's complicated but refused to elaborate, igniting my rage and sending me running in the opposite direction from him.

If there is one thing I can't go to Dad about, it's my plan of revenge. He warned me not to interfere. Told me to drop it.

But he clearly doesn't know me that well if he expected me to listen.

"There they are," Nessa says, panting and slowing to a walk.

I stop running, wiping my slick brow with the back of my hand. I hadn't even realized we had moved onto Main Beach or noticed the crowds of sunbathers lying on the hot sand or the kids playing at the water's edge.

I glance in the direction of her gaze, spotting Ruth Breen and the twins at the side of the raised area where the café, bathrooms, and rental place are.

Nessa's mom's thin frame looks nearly skeletal in her black and gold one-piece as she lies stretched out on a lounge chair under the large umbrella. Hunter and Kayleigh are building sandcastles in front of her, so intent on their task they don't notice us approaching.

"Come on." Nessa's eyes are alive, and it's good to see a smile on her face again. She strides through the hot sand, making a beeline for her siblings.

Kayleigh spots her first, her eyes popping wide, blinking repeatedly, as if she doesn't trust what she's seeing. "Nessa!" she screams, jumping up, sandcastle forgotten. Ruth jerks upright on her lounge chair, quicker than I would have thought she could move.

Nessa races toward Kayleigh as she runs to her. Hunter is climbing to his feet, smiling. Ruth is also on the move, a large scowl planted on her face. I had planned to hold back, to grab a soda while Nessa spent time with her brother and sister, but I'm not liking the vibes Ruth is emitting, so I trail behind my girlfriend, ready to intervene if necessary.

Kayleigh flings herself into Nessa's arms, and Nessa lifts her up, hugging her as her small legs wrap around her waist. "I can't believe you're here!" Kayleigh cries tears of joy as she clings to her sister.

"What the hell do you think you're doing!" Ruth hisses, glaring at Nessa.

"There is no need to make a scene," Nessa coolly replies, hugging her sister close, while her mom glances nervously around. Ruth does a double take when she spots me, shoving her sunglasses to the top of her head, narrowing her eyes suspiciously.

Guess it's showtime. I fix her with a firm gaze as I walk toward them, stopping behind Nessa as she lets Kayleigh down. My hands land gently on Nessa's hips, and I force a smile on my face. "Hello, Mrs. Breen. It's good to see you looking so well," I lie.

"Hello, Jackson," she says, deliberately lowering her voice, looking confused. Her eyes drift to my hands, still resting on her daughter's hips. Her head whips to Nessa. "What is going on?"

Nessa leans back into me. "I'm here with Jackson for a few days. We were running on the beach when I spotted you. I didn't think I needed an invitation to say hi to my brother and sister."

"Of course, you don't." Her smile is as fake as her personality. "I was just taken aback to see you. And with Jackson Lauder, of all people."

"What's that supposed to mean?" Nessa asks, her tone prickly.

"Nothing." Ruth tries to laugh it off. "I didn't know you were dating."

"We are." I slide my arms around her waist, holding her tight to my body, feeling an overwhelming need to protect her.

"I see." Her lips pinch tight, and I can't help pushing her buttons.

"You don't approve?"

She pulls her shades back down over her eyes. "It's not

that." She turns to Kayleigh. She's been quietly listening to all this while holding Nessa's hand. "Go back and play with your brother. I need to speak to your sister alone."

"But, Mom, I—"

"Now, Kayleigh." Her tone is firm as she points to where Hunter is holding back, taking everything in with a frown on his face.

"I'm not leaving," Nessa reassures her sister. "Let me talk to Mom, and I'll come build sandcastles with you. 'Kay?"

"You promise?" Kayleigh asks, and the pain in her eyes slays me. *How the fuck can this woman keep her older sister from her?* Something about this does not add up.

"I promise." Nessa leans down, kissing her cheek. "Run to Hunter. I'll be right there."

Kayleigh trots off, casting little looks over her shoulder, as she walks back to her brother, as if she's afraid her big sister will disappear.

"What?" Nessa snaps, stepping forward, out of my embrace, and squaring up to her mom.

"You know what," Ruth murmurs. She opens her mouth but shuts it again, glancing in my direction.

"You can speak freely in front of my boyfriend."

"I'm not sure dating Jackson is a wise choice, honey," she says.

Nessa snorts out a laugh. "Oh, this I've got to hear." She folds her arms over her chest. "Why not, Mother?"

"Two addicts dating is never a good idea."

"How fucking dare you." I step up beside Nessa. "Not that it's any of your business, considering you kicked your daughter out of your life, but we are both clean and sober, and who we date is of no concern to you." I pull my girlfriend into my side, and she wraps her arms around me.

"Any other objections, because I'd like to spend some time

with my siblings now." Nessa is shaking in my arms, and I know it's not from nerves.

"This isn't a good idea." Ruth rubs a hand across her chest. "He'll find out. Hunter will tell him."

"It's a public beach. We ran into you. You can feed him that line."

"He won't care. You know that."

"That's not my problem." Nessa squeezes my waist, and I hold her tighter.

"Not anymore."

Nessa stiffens, and tension bleeds into the air. No one speaks, and it's awkward as fuck. Behind Ruth, Hunter and Kayleigh watch the interaction with observant eyes.

"We done here?" Nessa says after a few more silent beats.

"I'm leaving at noon," Ruth replies, fixing her shoulders back. "You have until then."

Nessa relaxes against me. She nods, and I'm glad she doesn't thank that bitch.

Ruth stalks back to her lounge chair without another word. "What the fuck was that?" I murmur.

"That is basically my entire life," she cryptically replies, turning in my arms.

I open my mouth to pry before that snarly inner voice reminds me it's none of my business. Delving deeper into Nessa's life will only add further complications. I need to keep my distance. "I'm going to grab a soda and sit on the bench." I gesture at the wooden structure behind us. "Unless you need me to stay?"

"Nope. I'm good." She pecks my lips. "I'll see you later."

"Call me if anything changes," I say before walking off. I cast a final glance over my shoulder as I plow through the sand, smiling as Hunter wraps his arms around Nessa with the biggest smile on his face.

I spend an hour sitting on the bench, sipping a few sodas, people watching, and fighting my thoughts. My eyes keep drifting to the gorgeous girl with the blinding smile building sandcastles with her siblings. I'm having trouble keeping my eyes off her, and that's an issue. My thoughts are jumbled, my head a giant mess of shit I'm not equipped to decode. Thankfully, Nessa calls to say she's ready to leave before my head implodes.

"Hey. What's wrong?" I ask when I reach her, noting her trembling lower lip and her paler complexion.

Tears pool in her eyes as she stares through me.

"Nessa." I stroke her cheek with my thumb. "What is it?"

She swipes at an errant tear that sneaks out of the corner of her eye. "I just hate saying goodbye," she eventually says, averting her gaze and staring out at the ocean.

Chapter Sixteen

Jackson

We arrive at East Avenue, the main bar-slash-nightclub in East Hampton, a little after midnight. You can get into this place once you are over eighteen, but the bands on our wrists dictate it'll be a strictly alcohol-free night. In the past, we used to sneak in with fake IDs and booze, flying under the radar as we got trashed. We had some crazy nights here.

Nessa immediately goes to the restroom while a waitress brings us to the booth Hunt reserved in the front bar section. "What did you do now?" Hunt inquires as soon as we are situated at our table.

"Nothing," I say, through gritted teeth. "She's been quiet since hanging with the twins at the beach."

"What's up with that?" Hunt asks, and I shrug.

"No clue."

He snorts. "And you obviously don't care."

"Do not fucking start with me, Hunt." I glare at him. "You're the one who told me to keep my distance. To keep this casual. So, I'm not prying." I dig my nails into my thigh, just needing this shit to be over soon.

"You need to end this. It's clear she doesn't know anything. It's a waste of time, and the longer you prolong it, the harder it will be for her."

I lean my head back against the booth. "I know." I've come to the same conclusion. I haven't seen anything that leads me to believe she's in contact with Christian.

He examines my face. "Do you have feelings for her?"

"Not the kind you're implying," I lie, offering the waitress a tight smile as she leaves sodas on her table. "But I care about her. She's not at all what I expected."

Hunt stares at me in that creepy all-knowing way. I know he's burrowing deep, attempting to push past the lie and get to the truth. He's buying my feeble protests about as much as I am. "She's changed," Hunt eventually agrees, dropping his intensive lens. Air whooshes out of my mouth in grateful relief. "This Van is a far cry from the drugged-up drunk party girl we knew," he adds.

"We've all grown up." I rub at a tense spot between my brows. "I know I have." Or woken up, more like.

"Well, well, well. Look what the cat dragged in."

I glance up, stifling a groan as my eyes lock on the gorgeous blonde hovering over our table. Her hands are on her hips as she eye fucks me with no hesitation. Melania is a stunner. Curves in all the right places and a face that could grace magazine covers. But she's a class-A bitch and more trouble than she's worth. I fucked her a few times, but that's firmly in my past.

"Melania." Hunt says her name like it bores him to even utter the word. "Fuck off."

"As charming as ever, Sawyer," she deadpans, sliding into

the booth beside me, uninvited. "Is that any way to treat an old friend?"

"We were never friends." Hunt drills her with a look.

She waves her hands about. "Fuck buddies. Whatever." Hunt must have banged her too at some point. It's no surprise I don't remember. I spent a lot of summers high or drunk, so my memory is hazy. She drapes herself around me. "I'm thinking a reunion is in the cards." She runs her finger down my cheek as her hand lands heavily on my upper thigh, making her intent known. I grab her wrist, stopping her upward trajectory, as a cold voice rings out loud and clear.

"I'm thinking you're in my seat," Nessa says, shooting daggers at her arch nemesis.

"You heard my girlfriend," I say, prying Melania off me. "It's time for you to go."

"Girlfriend!?" Her incredulous gaze bounces between me and Nessa. "This is fucking priceless!" She cracks up laughing, slapping her hand on my thigh again.

"Get your hands off him, bitch." Nessa grabs her arm.

"Get your filthy disease-ridden paws off me!" Melania screeches, removing Nessa's grip from her arm.

Hunt looks at me, and I nod, both of us ready to jump in if it turns physical.

"I don't want any trouble," Nessa says, calming down. "Jackson and I are dating, so I'd appreciate it if you'd just fuck off and leave us alone."

"Dating." She snickers. "Wait till the girls hear this." She turns her face to me. "Surely, things aren't so bad you have to slum it?"

"Melania." Hunt's tone carries considerable warning as he slides out his side of the booth, ushering Nessa in.

"Don't be a bitch." I place my arm around Nessa's shoulder,

keeping her close. "And everyone knows I'm boxing above my weight with Vanessa."

"I think all the weed you've smoked has impaired your cognitive ability. She's a slut, and you're far too good for her."

"Let me guess," Nessa snarls, straining across the table at her. "You'd be a more suitable match."

"Honey, Jackson already knows the truth. Why do you think I was the only girl he kept coming back to?" Her eyes glint maliciously. "The only one he fucked countless times?"

Nessa turns rigid in my arms, and I'm done with this shit. "Don't flatter yourself. I was stoned or drunk every time I fucked you, and trust me, it meant nothing. Less than nothing." I eye her with disdain. "Nessa is worth a thousand of you."

Her eyes narrow, and her lips pinch. "You wouldn't say that if you knew the truth."

"Fuck off, Melania. This is your final warning. I don't care what it is you think you know. Get lost." I tighten my hold on Nessa.

She fixes her deadly glare on Nessa. "If you think your secret is safe, think again. I'll ruin you. I'll tell everyone how you—"

Nessa throws her soda at her, cutting her off.

Melania screams, jumping up and staring, horror-struck, at the large Coke stain on the front of her white dress.

"You stupid bitch." She lunges at Nessa over the table, but Hunt grabs her before she can lay a finger on my girlfriend. "This is Michael Kors, and it hasn't even hit stores yet. You will pay for this. I'll tell everyone! I'll put it online. I'll take out a full-page ad in the New York Times. I will destroy you." She continues to hurl abuse at Vanessa as Hunt tries to drag her away from the table.

I spot a bouncer approaching with the manager. Fuck.

"You need to get out of here, babe. Go wait for me outside. Hunt and I will make this go away."

Nessa's face is as white as a ghost, and she's immobile, staring absently into space, so I drag her out of the booth and escort her outside. I place her at the corner of the building under the full illumination of the canopy. Holding her upper arms, I stare into her eyes. "Stay there. I'll be right back." I kiss her brow before walking away.

When I return, Melania is still spewing vitriol and making threats about lawsuits. The bouncer is holding her back as Hunt talks in hushed tones to the manager. The only reason she hasn't been automatically kicked out is because her uncle is one of the club's main suppliers. But we still outrank her, and she fucking knows it.

"I'd like a word with her," I tell the burly bouncer. He looks at me as if he'd like to squash me with his boot. I flash him my ID. The Lauder name carries a lot of weight around here. His entire demeanor changes in a nanosecond. "I won't hurt her. I just want to talk. You can stand over there."

He walks a few feet away, out of earshot but close by if needed.

Melania opens her mouth to speak, but I shut her up with a cutting glare. "Listen up, bitch, and listen up good. If you make one move to hurt Vanessa, Hunt and I will come after you, guns blazing. We trade in secrets, and I bet it wouldn't take long to find the skeletons in your closet."

A brief flash of fear flickers across her retinas before she composes herself, opening her mouth to speak.

"I'm not done." I narrow my eyes at her, and her mouth pulls tight. "I mean it. You hurt my girl, and I will hurt you one hundred times over. Consider this your only warning."

I walk off as Hunt appears at my shoulder. "Is that handled?" I ask him.

"It is." He casts a look over his shoulder. "I don't trust that bitch."

"Neither do I. Will you look into it, or should I ask Xavier?"

"I'll talk to Xavier. We'll investigate it together."

"Send me the file when you have it. I'll send Melania a little teaser should she be tempted to open that big fat mouth of hers."

"Agreed," Hunt says as we step outside.

I look to the corner, cursing at the empty space.

"Where is she?" Hunt looks around, his brow puckered in worry.

"I told her to wait right there," I say, pointing.

"Get your hands off me!" Nessa shouts, and fear floods my system.

Hunt and I share a brief look before we take off running, heading in the direction of her voice.

Chapter Seventeen
Vanessa

The stepmonster grips my chin hard, his nails tearing through flesh while his knee digs painfully into my groin. He pins me to the wall with his body, his full weight locking me in place, meaning I can't use any maneuver to break free.

If I hadn't been so lost in thought—terrified Melania has discovered the truth and fearful she'll carry through on her threat—he never would've been able to creep up on me, drag me around the corner into the alleyway undetected, and incapacitate me so fast.

"You go near my kids again, and I will fucking end you," he hisses, spittle landing on my face.

"I saw the bruises," I snap. "If you touch my sister again, I will go to the police. I will tell them everything you did to me. I'll show them the photos I kept documenting my injuries. I'll tell them you're the reason I had a mini breakdown when I was fourteen."

His hands move to my throat, and he squeezes. "Go near the police, and you're dead. Besides, they won't believe you. I'm a respectable member of the business community, and you're a deadbeat junkie whore. They would've thrown your ass in juvie if I hadn't intervened. I bailed you out, smoothed things over with West Lorian High, and provided a roof over your head even after all the shit you put us through. I'm the hero in this story, sweetheart. You're the villain." He smirks, loosening his hold on my throat to brush his thumb along my neck.

"Fuck you, asshole." I try to move to no avail.

"You've already been there, sweetheart." His hand replaces his knee, and a violent shudder passes through me as he cups my pussy through my dress. "I don't miss your ugly mouth, but your sweet pussy still gets me hard." He flexes his hips, pushing his erection into me.

Bile swims up my throat, and fear trundles through my veins. "Get your hands off me!" I yell, hoping someone will hear and show up to rescue me.

He inches my dress up my thigh, his eyes dark with familiar intent, and I scream. Lust has distracted him, and I manage to work one of my hands free, dragging my long nails down his cheek and drawing blood.

He roars, his hands automatically going to his face, as he staggers back. I seize the opportunity, sliding out from under him and running as the sound of approaching footfalls tickles my eardrums.

"Nessa!" Jackson shouts, rounding the corner to the alley.

Relief mixes with fear as I slam to a halt.

I don't want Jackson to know. It will change how he feels about me. It will ruin everything.

"Oh my God." Jackson clasps my upper arms, inspecting the hand marks around my neck, scratches on my chin, and my wild eyes. His gaze roams over the rest of my body before he gently pulls me into his arms as Sawyer barrels past us. "Are you okay?"

I nod against his chest, unable to speak.

"You fucking asshole!" Sawyer slams his fist into the step-monster's jaw, and that unmutes my tongue.

"Stop!" I wriggle out of Jackson's embrace, running to Sawyer's side. I tug on his arm, pulling him back. "Don't. It was a misunderstanding, but we've worked it out now."

Aaron's threat still lingers in my ear, and I can't do anything that might put Kayleigh in even greater harm. I've been locked in my head all afternoon, going over my options. Ever since I found the yellowed bruising on her upper inner arm, I've been in a state of near hysterics. I asked her how she got them, and I can still vividly recall the dazed look in her eyes as she lied and said she fell off the monkey bars at the playground.

I can't let the same thing happen to her.

I won't.

I just need to figure out a plan and put it in place before he takes her innocence and shatters her forever.

"Nessa." Jackson comes up behind me, pulling me into his side. "What the ever-loving fuck is going on?"

"I'd like to know that too," Sawyer says, flexing his knuckles and glowering at the stepmonster.

"This is family business that doesn't concern either of you," Aaron says, recovering his composure.

"You hurt my girlfriend," Jackson spits, nostrils flaring. Shock splays across Aaron's face. Mom obviously didn't tell him, and it's a relief to know she has *some* good judgment. "That *is* my business."

"She hurt me," he retorts, dabbing at his cheek.

"I doubt she lashed out first," Jackson snaps.

"You never lay your hand on a woman. Ever," Sawyer adds in a clipped tone. "I don't fucking care what Van did, or is alleged to have done, there is nothing that justifies you putting your hands on her."

I gulp over the messy ball of emotion clogging my throat. I wish I could tell them. I bet they could help. But they might insist I go to the police, and I'm scared he would take that out on Kayleigh.

I don't know what to do. And my head is too cluttered to think clearly. I just need to get out of here. I grip Jackson's shirt. "Can we go? Please."

He presses a kiss to my head, holding me tight, and I feel so safe in his arms. But it's only an illusion. A temporary safety net.

I can't rely on Jackson or Sawyer because they won't be in my life much longer.

The only person I can rely on is myself.

The only person who can rescue Kayleigh is me.

"Stay away from her," Jackson growls.

"Fuck off, Lauder. You don't scare me."

"He should," Sawyer replies. "We both should." He cocks his head to the side. "Or have you forgotten what it is I know how to do?"

The bravado slips off Aaron's face for a fleeting second. He pins a warning look at me. "Remember what I said. Don't push this, or you'll be sorry." I shiver in Jackson's arms as Aaron storms off, leaving a wake of devastation behind him.

I walk on autopilot as Jackson guides me out of the alleyway and across the road to his car. I lean my head against the passenger side window, absently glancing at the side mirror as Jackson moves out onto the road, vaguely aware of the silver car that pulls out from the curb behind us.

The mood is somber when we arrive back at Jackson's house. Jackson takes the stairs two at a time, heading to the bathroom to retrieve the first aid kit. "Whatever is going on," Sawyer says, taking my hand and leading me to the couch, "you can trust us."

"I know," I quietly say, wishing it was true. "But there's nothing to tell," I lie. "We have never seen eye to eye. He thinks I'm a bad influence, and he wants me to stay away from the twins."

I can tell from the look in his eyes that he doesn't believe me. I was too rattled for that to be the only truth. But it's all I'm giving him, so it'll have to be enough. "He can't stop you from seeing your brother and sister." Sawyer rubs his thumb back and forth across my hand. "We have access to lawyers and money to burn. If you want to challenge him legally, you only have to say the word."

Tears prick my eyes as feet pound down the stairs. "Thank you, but I can't take your money."

"Why the fuck not?" Jackson says, sitting on my other side.

"It wouldn't be right and it's not necessary. I'll work this out my own way."

Jackson and Sawyer share a look, but they say nothing. Jackson opens the first aid kit, withdrawing a bottle of rubbing alcohol and some cotton balls. "This may sting a little," he says, cleaning the scratches on my chin.

It does, but I barely feel it. The shock of today's events has done a number on me.

"Nessa?" Jackson lifts his eyes to mine as he applies some arnica cream to my chin. "Has he put his hands on you before?"

Everything locks up tight inside me, and I stop breathing. Tension oozes in the air, thick and cloying. "No," I lie. "We fight a lot but never like that." I want to throw up, because I can tell he's not buying it. "I'm tired," I add, averting my gaze. "I'd like to go to bed."

I can feel the weight of Jackson's stare bearing down on me as I stand, and that's all the more reason to curl up in bed and avoid his inquisition.

I tiptoe downstairs in the middle of the night, leaving Jackson softly snoring in the bed behind me. I pretended to be asleep when he eventually came upstairs, but I haven't slept a wink all night.

I'm petrified for my sister, shaken by the altercation with the stepmonster, and feeling lost and helpless because I don't know what to do. All I know is I want to stop thinking about it, so I grab a bottle of vodka from the liquor cabinet in the living room and curl up on the couch with my demon of choice.

The colorless, odorless liquid soothes my anxiety as it slips down my throat, and I huddle under a blanket as I drain the bottle dry, grateful when the hazy numbness blanks my mind of all logical thought and a welcoming darkness swoops in and lays claim to me.

"Nessa." A soft voice croons in my ear as Jackson shakes my shoulders. "Baby. Wake up. Please." Concern drips from his tone in spades.

I blink my eyes open, wincing at the bright light spearing through the window. My throbbing temples, queasy tummy, and parched mouth remind me I fell off the wagon last night, along with all the reasons why. I close my eyes, wanting to retreat to that blank space again.

"Nessa." Jackson cups my face. "Babe. It's after two. I'm worried about you."

"*We're* worried about you," Sawyer adds, and I force my eyes open, meeting his troubled gaze.

I sit up, clutching my sensitive stomach. "Stop worrying. Everything's fine."

"Everything is *not* fine," Jackson says, working hard to keep his tone soft. "You crept out of bed in the middle of the night, ended a year's sobriety, and passed out until the middle of the day. Trust me, that doesn't suggest things are fine." He drags a hand through his hair.

"Why the fuck does it matter?" I glare at him. "You can stop pretending like this is anything more than a casual fling. You'll both be gone in a few weeks, and I'll be the one left to pick up the pieces." I stand, clutching the arm of the couch when my legs threaten to go out from under me.

"Don't fucking do that." Sawyer moves toward me. "No matter what happens, we're your friends. That will never change."

I harrumph. "Friends. That's a joke! I was an annoyance and nothing more." I quietly seethe until the truth explodes from my mouth. "You never intervened when I was being bullied, and none of you ever asked if I was okay because you didn't care! That is not how friends treat friends."

I spent every summer with those guys, and walked past them in the halls at West Lorian daily, and not once did any of them ask me how I was. Not once did any of them notice the dark shadows under my eyes, the bruises and bitemarks on my body, or the pain I literally and figuratively carried in every bone, every muscle, every sinew, and every part of my psyche.

"You're right," Sawyer says, looking pained. "I'm sorry we didn't do more."

"We failed you," Jackson adds, torment etched across his face. "But we're here for you now."

How dare Jackson Lauder swoop into my life now, giving me false hope, making me believe he loved me, only to saunter back out of my life when it suits him.

I'm an idiot for falling for him.

For buying into the bullshit.

For believing someone like me would ever be worthy of someone like him.

I lost sight of the things that matter. Like protecting my sister from that monster.

"I'd like to go home," I blurt. "If you can't take me, I'll take the bus."

Jackson and Sawyer share another one of their secret looks. Jackson stands. "If that's what you really want, then I'll take you home."

"Thank you." I swat his arm away. "I'll go get my things."

Chapter Eighteen
Vanessa

I pace the floor of my living room, waiting for Jackson to arrive to pick me up for our date. It's been two weeks since the awful weekend in The Hamptons, and I'm living on a razor's edge. I have hardly seen my boyfriend—if that's what he still is. At first, that was my fault. I kept him at arm's length as I sunk into depression. I'm drinking again, because it's the only way I can sleep at night now the nightmares have returned with a vengeance. The control I have worked so hard for is slowly slipping away, and I need to cling to something to give me strength.

I was wrong to push Jackson away.

I'm not sorry I haven't told him the truth about my past and what's going on with Kayleigh, but I need him as much as I need air to breathe. I fucking miss him so much. I love him so much. My heart pines for him. I lie awake at night crying without his protective arms around me. More than that, I just miss his company. His cheeky smile. His ability to make me laugh. I don't want to lose him, so I'm going to fight for him even if it could be too late.

He's been in Alabama the past four days, but he got back to the city last night. I had planned on contacting him today, asking to meet up, but he beat me to it. When he called late last night and asked me to dinner, a layer of stress lifted from my shoulders, knowing he hasn't given up on us.

That's not the reason why I'm presently on edge though. I am happy we're going out, and I'm excited to see Jackson, but I'm so fucking terrified, and it consumes everything else.

A week ago, I made an anonymous phone call to social services, and I've been on tenterhooks ever since. Judging from the slew of panicked messages Mom has been leaving on my cell today, I know they must have paid the house a visit. I haven't returned her calls or texts, because I'm afraid she'll know it was me. Yet, I want to know what's happened too, so I'm trapped in this limbo state, and the uncertainty is killing me.

The bell chimes, alerting me to Jackson's presence down-stairs. Forcing my fear aside, I grab my purse and pull the door closed behind me. Hopefully, after a night with my man, I'll feel more relaxed and I'll know what to do.

I open the entrance door to my boyfriend and instantly stop breathing. The early evening light casts a golden hue over his tall form, highlighting his sexy blond hair, those twinkling blue eyes I love to get lost in, the cute dimples in his cheeks, and the flirty smile on his lips. He's wearing a tight shirt and jeans, and man, is he a sight for sore eyes.

"Hey." I smile shyly at him, suddenly overcome with nerves.

"Nessa." His gaze rakes up and down my body, and I shuffle on my feet, feeling self-conscious. "I've missed you."

"You have?" I squeak.

He reaches out, maneuvering his hand through my hair,

clasping the nape of my neck, and reeling me into his chest. "Why would you question that?"

I shrug, biting on my lip. "We haven't exactly been on good terms."

"It doesn't change the fact I missed you."

"I missed you too," I softly admit. "I'm sorry for my odd behavior. The argument with the stepmonster shook me, and I haven't been doing so well. I should never have pushed you away."

"I know, babe. It's okay." He leans down, pressing his lips to mine, and I get lost in his kisses, emptying my mind of all troubling thoughts, focusing on how good it feels to touch him and hold him. His eyes are tender but troubled when he breaks our lip-lock. "We should move before we lose our dinner reservation."

The Thai place he takes me to is a recent addition to the city's dining options. I have heard they are booked out for three months solid, but I'm not surprised Jackson got a reservation. The Lauder name carries clout, and there aren't many doors it doesn't open.

We are escorted to a private booth in the back, and after placing our orders, we settle back to catch up. "How was the wedding?" I ask, sipping my water.

"Good."

"Just good?"

He shrugs. "It was a wedding on the beach. Abby wore a white dress. Anderson put on a monkey suit. We ate cake, got drunk, and danced." He arches a brow. "That better?"

"I was only asking. You don't need to be a dick." There's a subtle bite to my tone.

He sighs, closing his eyes for a second. "I'm sorry. It's just there's not much to tell."

"Okay." I decide to drop the subject.

"Tell me what's been going on with you?" he asks, stretching his hand across the table and threading his fingers in mine.

His touch is comforting, but I still can't relax. He was quiet in the car on the way here, and now, he's prickly when I was only asking a question. It's obvious he doesn't want to discuss it, and his snippy attitude frustrates me. Yet he expects me to talk? Perhaps, going out tonight wasn't such a good idea. Not when he's clearly tired and moody and I'm worried and distracted over what's going down with the stepmonster.

"Not much to tell," I say. "I've been working a lot although I did go to a party with Chloe and her boyfriend last weekend." I don't divulge that I got smashed and passed out on some stranger's couch, waking up with the hangover from hell. Although, I was grateful I still had my clothes on. It beats the times I woke up naked in a stranger's bed with zero recollection of the night before.

Our appetizers arrive, and Jackson frowns as he looks down at our conjoined hands, almost like he can't remember reaching out for me. We eat in silence, and I don't like the sudden awkwardness or the lingering tension simmering in the air.

"Have you had any contact with Aaron or your mom or seen Kayleigh and Hunter?" he asks after the waitress has cleared our plates away.

I shake my head, gulping down a mouthful of sparkling water.

"What are you going to do?"

"I don't know," I lie. "I'm still thinking it over." I place my glass down and knot my hands in my lap, needing to distract myself from this train of thought before I throw up. "What about you? When do you leave for RU?"

"Ten days."

"What happens then?" I blurt, digging my nails into my thigh through my dress.

His brow creases. "What do you mean?"

"With us."

A multitude of emotions flashes across his face before he puts his mask on. He smiles, but it doesn't meet his eyes. "We don't have to talk about this now. Let's just enjoy our dinner."

My stomach twists into anxious knots, and I can't enjoy dinner because I have an unerring sense of impending doom and the dark cloud hovering over my head is souring my mood.

He gets out of the car when we arrive back at my place, opening the car door for me. He takes my hand, and I swallow over the nervous lump in my throat. "Can I come up?" he asks when we reach the front door.

"Sure," I croak. My hands shake as I fumble with the key.

He takes the key from me, inserting it into the lock.

We walk up to my apartment in silence.

A blanket of dread crawls over me. He's going to dump me. I feel it in my bones. And I need to get in there to say my piece first, in the hope it might sway him.

I place my purse on the counter, turning to face him. "Would you like something to drink?"

"No. Come here." He crooks his fingers at me.

"What?" I splutter.

"Come. Here." He reaches out, hauling me into his chest. His muscular arms wrap around me as he peers into my eyes. I gulp back my panic, confused as he just stares at me. I stifle a gasp as he lowers his head and his lips descend.

I startle at the intensity of his kiss. It feels like a plea and a goodbye at the same time. I cling to him, kissing him back with the same passion, the same need, pouring my heart and soul into every sweep of my lips. His erection presses against my stomach, and I palm his ass, grabbing hold of him, needing him to soothe the raw ache coursing through my body.

He pulls away, abruptly ripping his lips from mine. "I'm sorry. I shouldn't have done that." Pained eyes meet mine for a brief second before he turns around, cursing under his breath as he grabs fistfuls of his hair.

"Jackson," I whisper, and his spine stiffens. I walk to him, gently placing my hand on his waist.

He grabs hold of it, bringing my hand to his lips and kissing my knuckles. It's his signature show of affection, and my chest heaves as naked emotion lays siege to my body. "We need to talk," I blurt before he says anything. "There are things I need to say. I know you're leaving, but I don't want to lose you. We share a real connection. I know you feel it the way I do, and we haven't even properly explored it yet."

Silence resonates for a couple beats. He releases my hand, turning around to face me. He takes a step back, creating distance between us. "What are you saying?"

"I don't want to break up. I want to try the long-distance thing. We're not that far away. It's workable."

Conflict rages in his eyes, and I can sense his inner turmoil. "Nessa." He closes the gap between us, winding his fingers through my hair as he pins me with a soft expression. "We'll both be busy. It won't leave much time to see one another."

"I've already spoken to Paul. I can work Monday to Friday so I have my weekends free. I can travel to you, or you can travel to me." It's not exactly a done deal yet, but he doesn't need to know that.

He sighs, and his expression turns troubled again. "I'm an all-or-nothing kinda person, babe." He toys with strands of my hair. "It'd kill me being away from you so much. I don't think I can do it."

Jackson

The first splinter appears in my heart. "Can't you at least try?"

Dropping his hand, he steps back, rubbing a spot over his chest. "I'm sorry, Nessa. I think that would end up hurting both of us more."

I reclaim the space, clutching his arm. "Please, Jackson. I love you." Desperation threads through my tone, but I'm too panicked to care about how needy I sound. "Let's just see how the first month goes." I cup his face. Indecision flickers across his eyes, igniting a spark of hope. "For me?"

His eyes skim my face as he battles some inner war. He squeezes his eyes shut for a moment. When he reopens them, he steps back, and my hands fall away. "This isn't about you, Nessa. You're amazing, and you're going to make some guy really happy one day, but that guy isn't me." He averts his eyes while another splinter tears through my heart. "I'm not ready to settle down. I'm too selfish." He shoves his hands deep in his pockets, staring at the floor. "I'm going to college, and I don't want to be held back."

"You think I'd hold you back?" I hate how my voice wobbles. "I would never do that."

His head tips up, and our eyes lock. "Not consciously, Nessa. But I don't want or need complications."

"So, that's all I am to you? A complication?" I snap as anger rears its head.

"You know I don't mean that."

I fold my arms around myself protectively. "Has this summer meant so little to you?"

"Of course not." His eyes plead for understanding that is in limited supply. "I've loved hanging out with you, but we are going in different directions, and we want different things from life."

"No, we don't," I shout. "I want the same things as you. To

enjoy college life. To pursue my passions. To leave the past in the past. To finally live now that I'm free to make decisions for myself. To make something of myself!" My heart races as pain slams into me on all sides. "But I don't get to live that life. I'm trying to make the best of the hand I've been dealt, so don't tell me we want different things because that is not the fucking truth!" I roar, fully giving in to the anger that is buried deep inside me. This isn't all attributable to him, but he's lowered my defenses, my walls are down, and all the pain is flooding through.

Remorse flashes momentarily across his face. Or maybe, it's pity. The emotion is gone so fast I didn't have time to dissect it. "I didn't stop to think about how disappointing that is for you, and I'm sorry, Nessa. You deserve to have all that, but it changes nothing. It's best we end this now. For both our sakes."

He's clearly made up his mind, and how easy it seems for him to toss me aside.

He doesn't look like his beating heart has been yanked from his chest. Like he's struggling to breathe or his legs are about to go out from under him. Whatever emotion I thought I saw on his face is gone, replaced with gritty resolution. This is barely a blip on his radar. He has already moved on. "Did you care for me at all?" I whisper.

His eyes meet mine, and I catch a tiny glimpse of humanity. "Of course, I care for you. I do. I wish it could be different, but it can't."

"If you truly cared for me, this wouldn't be so easy for you."

He opens his mouth to speak before clamping his lips shut, clearly thinking better of it. He shrugs, but the movement is stiff, like he's forcing himself to appear detached. He's emitting conflicting vibes I can't figure out. Or perhaps, it's that delusional part of my personality seeing things that don't exist. Clinging to stupid hope long after it's evaporated into thin air.

"I'm doing what's necessary," he quietly says. "When you calm down, you'll realize I'm right."

"Don't try to tell me what I'm feeling," I hiss. "You have no clue how I feel."

He shrugs again, and it irritates me to no end. "I don't know what else to say here, Vanessa. We had fun, but it's come to an end. I'd like to part ways as friends, but that's up to you."

"I don't want to be friends, Jackson." I reach toward him, and pain stabs me in the gut when he sidesteps me, shaking his head. "I want more. Please reconsider." Anger has given way to panic again.

Jackson is all I have.

Without him, my life is empty.

I can't lose him.

I love him, and I know he loves me too.

He's just too afraid to admit it to himself.

A muscle pops in his jaw as he stares at me. "I'm sorry, Nessa, but I'm not changing my mind. I don't want to hurt you any more than I already have."

His mask comes down again, and I wonder if he is even human behind that gorgeous façade. I know there is no point pleading. He has shut himself off completely. Anything I say will bounce off those walls he's erected. I'll only make myself look even more pathetic than I am.

I laid my heart on the line, hoping it would be enough, but I completely misjudged him and the situation.

He doesn't love me.

How could he? I am unlovable.

He doesn't even care.

Why would anyone? It's not like I've got anything to offer.

I am expendable, and I doubt he'll even remember me in a week.

Why should he? It's not like I'm special or in any way memorable.

Inside, I'm empty. Hollowed out. Until this painful, dark entity springs to life in my stomach. It's a writhing mass of tangible pain that feeds off my distress and the agony of his rejection. Growing at an exponential rate, it sucks all the good stuff into its orbit, swirling and churning until it has consumed every part of me. I shiver as cold, dark tentacles claw at my insides, invading every muscle and sinew, erasing the light, like death snuffing out life.

"Get out." I point at the door. "I never want to see you again."

"I don't want to leave it like this." He steps toward me carefully.

"I've said all I want to say. You know where the door is."

He swoops in, pressing a lingering kiss to my forehead. I should push him away, but I'm working too hard on not breaking down in front of him. "You are far too good for me, Nessa," he whispers. "You deserve someone who can give you their whole heart, and that will never be me." He eases back. "I'm sorry." He tries to make eye contact, but I stare through him.

I can't look at him.

I want him gone.

I need him to leave before I fall apart.

"Goodbye." He walks out the door, and I slump against the counter, gripping it for dear life, holding my tears in until I hear the front door closing downstairs.

Then, I give in to my grief. Sobs rip from my soul as I bend over the counter, crying like I haven't cried in a long time. My shoulders heave, and my breaths are erratic as I struggle to draw enough air into my lungs. Painful cries bounce off the silent walls, and it truly feels like I'm dying. I'm in agony. Pain has a vise grip on every part of me, and I'm suffocating under dark emotions I've worked so hard to suppress. My heart is torn to shreds behind my rib cage, and pain is the only substance flowing through my veins.

A hand fists my hair, and my cries instantly die out as I'm yanked back from the counter and viciously thrown across the small kitchen area. The side of my head hits the corner of the counter, and I scream as piercing pain lances across my skull. I'm shoved with force, and I lose my balance, swaying on my feet. My spine slams into a cupboard, and my shoes fly in different directions as I slither to the ground, my body contorting in pain.

"You pathetic bitch," Aaron sneers, looming over me. Horror engulfs me as I stare up at him while pressing two fingers to my head. My fingertips come away bloody, and I wonder if I have a concussion. "It's no surprise he's dumped the trash." He kicks me in the stomach, and I double over as bile travels up my throat.

My head is spinning, and black spots mar my vision.

Crouching down in front of me, he grips my chin painfully. "I warned you not to interfere."

My head whips back as he slaps me hard, and my vision blurs out for a few seconds.

"You fucking dare to report me to social services?" He slaps me again, and I force myself to focus, blinking my eyes repeatedly, refusing to give in to the darkness beckoning me. A ripping sound echoes through the air, and a light breeze blows across my legs.

Terror punches me in the gut as I stare at my torn dress.

"I had a choice," he continues, standing as he glares at me, bloody and bruised at his feet. "I thought of taking it out on your sister. I knew that would inflict the most pain, but it hardly seemed fair." He unbuckles his belt, and my stomach lurches as fear ransacks my body, heightening my senses and invoking my fight-or-flight response. "It seems you need a reminder of what's at stake."

The sound of his zipper spurs me into action. I sit forward, push his pant leg up, and bury my teeth in his shin, biting down hard.

He roars, and the unexpected pain has him stumbling back. I seize the opportunity, staggering to my feet. Ignoring the rush of blood to my head and the pain searing through my body, I grab the first thing my hand lands on. I swing the skillet at him, but he ducks down in time, so it only glances off the side of his head.

He roars again, lunging at me.

I shriek, darting around the other side of the counter, racing toward the door as he chases me. "Help!" I scream although I know it's futile. Unless someone happens to be passing by on the sidewalk, there is no one to hear my pleas.

His hand clasps my ankle, and I go down, landing hard on my face. The skillet skates across the floor out of my reach. Pain charges through my body, and I whimper as I'm flipped over. Weight presses down on my hips as he sits on me. I'm fighting to maintain consciousness while he tears the rest of my dress off, leaving me exposed to him in my underwear. "Help!" I scream again, but my voice is weaker.

"Scream all you like." He shoves his pants and boxers down, freeing his disgusting cock. "There is no one to hear you."

My eyes dart manically around, and although my vision is still a little blurry, I spot one of my shoes lying off to the side. I reach for it, my fingers curling around the soft velvet material. He's too busy stroking his cock and salivating over my body to notice until it's too late. This time, I get a good hit in, slamming my wedge heel into the side of his head.

172

Jackson

What a pity I hadn't worn stilettos tonight.

He shouts out as he falls sideward, clutching his head while he crashes into the small lamp table. The lamp wobbles before falling, smashing into a gazillion pieces on the floor.

A pounding at the door downstairs pricks my ears. "Nessa!"

"Jackson! Help!" I scream, crawling toward the door to my apartment.

A foot presses on my spine, flattening me to the floor, holding me in place. I cry out, screaming at Jackson to hurry.

"You tell him anything, and I will rape her repeatedly until I'm fully acquainted with her pretty little body. Then, I'll let my friends take turns," he warns in my ear. His finger presses against the crack in my ass, penetrating me through my lace panties. Tears pour from my eyes, and I silently urge Jackson to hurry up. "Interfere again, and your sister will pay the price next time."

A loud crash echoes from downstairs as he tugs on my hair. He slams my head down into the floor, and my world turns dark.

Chapter Nineteen
Jackson

"Here." Hunt hands me a cup of ass masquerading as coffee when he reenters the private hospital room.

"Thanks. I think." I take a sip, grimacing.

"Whoever did this worked her over good." Hunt sinks into the chair beside me, glancing at Nessa.

She's still out cold. Hooked up to a machine with a drip in her arm. I stare at the cuts and bruises covering her gorgeous face with a massive lump in my throat. "I want to rip the fucker limb from limb."

"Thank fuck you went back."

I dread to think what would've happened if I hadn't changed my mind and returned.

"Why did you?" Hunt asks, eyeballing me with curiosity.

Things have been better between us these past couple weeks. We agreed to call a truce for the wedding, because neither of us wanted to draw attention to the fact we've been arguing or the reason why. We have kept our friends out of my revenge plan for a reason. The truce helped to ease the tension.

As did my promise to break things off with Nessa when I returned.

"I was coming back to tell her I'd changed my mind. That I didn't want to break up. That I would try the long-distance shit."

Hunt frowns, but it lacks malice. "Why?"

That's the million-dollar question. I fucked everything up tonight. Kissing her before breaking it off was cruel, and it only tortured both of us. But I let my emotions get to me. The truth is, when it came to crunch time, I didn't want to end things. The thought of not seeing her, not holding her or touching her, has me tied into knots.

It's official—I'm a hot mess.

My feelings are an epic clusterfuck when it comes to this girl, and that was *not* supposed to happen. I have a goal. I need to avenge Dani's death. Falling for Nessa wasn't part of the plan.

These thoughts were bouncing through my brain, but I forced myself to stick with the program, and I ended things with her. I felt like the biggest prick leaving her apartment. Picturing her heartbroken face with the pain of my rejection clearly shimmering in her eyes gutted me, and I was already second-guessing myself.

Then, I had a light bulb moment that changed the entire course of events.

"I realized something as I pulled away from her place," I tell Hunt, running a hand over my prickly jaw. This is the only part of the truth I'm prepared to admit. "Someone is watching her."

Hunt's eyes widen, encouraging me to continue.

"I've spotted a silver Honda Accord outside her place before. I didn't pay it much attention, assuming it belonged to someone who worked in the area. I noticed it again when I was leaving her place earlier, and it triggered a memory. I saw that same car in The Hamptons. It followed us when we left East Avenue. I wasn't focused enough to make the connection then, but it clicked for me today."

"You think it's Christian?"

I nod. "Who else could it be?"

He leans forward on his elbows. "It could be someone her stepdad employed to keep tabs on her, or it could be any elite member. If others know she is Christian Montgomery's only surviving heir, they could be after her. We can't jump to conclusions and assume it's that bastard."

I hate he could be right. "Whoever it is, it means this isn't over." I pick her hand up, lacing my fingers through hers, feeling a surge of remorse and protectiveness I'm struggling to contain.

"I agree," Hunt says, surprising me. "But for different reasons."

"I want to keep her safe too." I reply to the unspoken part of his statement. "I meant it when I said I cared for her. I felt like shit hurting her earlier." The whole time Nessa and I were talking, I was tempted to backtrack, but I stuck to the script because it was what I'd promised Hunt and I believed she wasn't my connection to Christian.

If he has someone watching her that changes everything.

"Could he be responsible for this?" I ask the question that's been playing on my mind.

Hunt exhales heavily. "We both know what he's capable of, but if he's watching her, it means he wants to keep her safe. And if he isn't the one watching her, I struggle to see how he'd benefit from attacking her."

"He could use it to manipulate her," I say, thinking aloud. "You're not safe there. I can protect you etcetera. And then, he gets her wherever he needs her to be, makes her feel indebted to him, so she does what he wants her to do."

"There are a lot of anomalies," Hunt supplies. "And we could be completely wrong."

"Whoever it is, why the fuck didn't he do anything?" I drag my free hand through my hair. "He was sitting right outside her apartment while she was being attacked. I know because the car was there and I was tempted to accost the fucker, but I thought better of it. We don't want to scare him off. He could be our only lead to Montgomery."

"I agree, and unless he's bugging her place, he probably wasn't aware she was being attacked," Hunt surmises. "I'll go over tomorrow and run a check," he adds.

I pause for a second before voicing my suggestion because I know Hunt won't like it, and I know it's crossing a line. "We should install a bug in her place."

His nose scrunches up while he contemplates it. "Ordinarily, I'd say no, but I think it's warranted now. You didn't remove that tracker from her cell, right?"

"I didn't, and the bug is our best option. We can make sure she's safe and watch out for contact from that asshole." So far, there is zip. No email or cell contact, and I scoured her apartment and searched her bag for a burner cell, finding none.

The door creaks as an older nurse with gray hair tied up in a bun enters the room. She treads quietly across the floor, smiling softly. "She hasn't woken yet?" she asks, and I shake my head. Removing the chart at the end of Nessa's bed, she quickly reads over it. "She was heavily sedated when she arrived, so she won't wake for a couple of hours yet. I'll check back." She walks off, pausing at the door to glance over her shoulder. "Oh, I almost forgot, the police are here. They are asking to speak to whoever found her."

"That would be me. I'll be right out," I confirm.

"You want me to call your lawyer?" Hunt asks, pulling out his cell.

"Nah." I pull Nessa's hand to my mouth, kissing her knuckles. "It's good. I'll see what they want first." Bending down over her bed, I kiss her forehead. "I'll be right back, babe."

Hunt eyes me curiously but says nothing, sipping his coffee as I exit the room.

I talk to the male and female detective in a small office at the end of the hallway.

"And you didn't see the perp?" the guy asks while the woman takes notes.

"No, but I was only in her apartment for a few minutes. The guy must've been hiding on her balcony or in the bathroom as the rest is an open plan."

"What made you return?" the woman asks.

"I had said some things I didn't mean. I was coming back to apologize. I heard strange noises coming from her apartment, and then, I heard her call out for help."

"Why didn't you call nine-one-one then?" the man asks.

"Because I was fucking worried about my girlfriend! I wanted to get into her apartment to help her. Those were the only thoughts in my head." I force myself to calm down, pushing my agitation aside. I fucking hate that I left her defenseless. That I didn't suspect anything untoward.

"What did you find when you broke into her apartment?"

Pain spreads across my chest as the visual resurrects in my mind's eye. "Nessa was unconscious on the floor, facedown. Her dress had been torn off. There were signs of struggle."

I legit almost died when I found her like that. The fear was real. In that second, nothing else mattered but her.

"And you didn't see the perp?"

I shake my head. "I called nine-one-one while I checked her vitals to ensure she was breathing. When I ended the call, and I confirmed she had a pulse, I noticed the door to the balcony was open. I looked out, but whoever he is, he was long gone. He must've used the fire escape."

"We have a team over at Ms. Breen's apartment now, but that is the initial conclusion our colleagues have reached," the woman confirms.

"Can you think of anyone who would want to hurt Vanessa?" the man asks.

I shake my head even though I have theories. I wouldn't put it past that bitch Melania to arrange something like this, but after I sent her evidence confirming I know she's having an affair with a married man, I doubt it's her. That scandal would ruin her reputation and her father would disown her, so I'm pretty confident she wouldn't make a move against Nessa.

I have my suspicions about Aaron Breen, so it could've been him. Or it could be Christian or any of the asshole elite.

But I'm fucked if I'm admitting any of that to the police.

We'll conduct our own investigation and exact our own punishment.

"She's a sweetheart. I can't think of anyone who would do this to her," I lie.

"Very well, Mr. Lauder." The man stands as the woman closes her notepad. "We have your contact details, and we'll be in touch if there is anything else. We'll return in the morning to speak with Ms. Breen."

I get up, accepting the card he hands me. "If you think of anything else, please call me."

"Thank you, Detective." I almost puke at my polite bullshit.

"Well?" Hunt asks when I reenter the room. I hand him a fresh coffee from the machine in the hallway.

"Standard questioning. Nothing I couldn't handle." I retake my seat, claiming her hand again. "I presume there's been no change."

"Nope." Hunt sips the coffee, making a face. "And the coffee's still shit."

Hunt is snoring softly in the chair when Nessa wakes up three hours later. It's the middle of the night, but I haven't been able to sleep.

She's disorientated at first, so I call the nurse. I watch her prop Nessa up in the bed, helping her to take a few sips of water before she checks her vitals, and administers more pain medication.

When we are alone again, I scoot my chair closer. "How are you feeling?"

"Sore, but I'm still breathing, so there's that."

I don't know how she can joke at a time like this. "I'm so sorry, Nessa. I should have been there. If I had stayed, you never would've been attacked."

"It's not your fault." She gently squeezes my hand. "He would've just come back."

I brush stray strands of hair off her face. "Do you feel up to telling me about it? Do you know who did this?"

She wets her dry lips, gulping. She doesn't say anything for a few minutes, but I wait her out. "He crept up on me and threw me across the kitchen. I hit my head and fell to the floor." Her eyes lower to the bed, and she rubs her finger back and forth across the place where the drip is inserted in her hand. "He wanted the keys and alarm code to the diner. When I refused to tell him, he ripped my dress and started unbuckling his belt."

Acid crawls up my throat, and I clench the hand resting on my thigh. "Did he—" She shakes her head, cutting me off mid-sentence. I almost collapse in relief. The thought of someone doing that to Nessa twists me into knots and inflames the murderous rage that lingers in my tissues.

"I bit him and got away," she continues explaining. "I hit

him with the skillet but not hard enough. I was crawling away when he grabbed me again. He was preparing to rape me when you started banging on the door. I hit him with my shoe, and then, he knocked me out. That's all I remember."

I lean in and kiss her cheek. "Thank fuck, you fought him."

"He still overpowered me." She shivers. "If you hadn't arrived, he would've raped me. Maybe even murdered me." A tear creeps out of the corner of her eye.

"Hey. I did get there in time." I brush her tear away.

"Why did you come back?" she asks as a different form of pain materializes in her eye.

"I came back to apologize and to take it back."

"What?" Her eyes probe mine. "What do you mean?"

"I'll try the long-distance thing. I don't want to break up with you. We'll try to make a go of it."

A smile lights up her face, and I swallow back my self-loathing. "What changed your mind?"

"I felt like shit when I walked off, and I was already fucking missing you." That's not a lie, but it's not the full truth either. "I knew I'd made a mistake." I should try to warn her though. "But you shouldn't get your hopes up too high. You know I'm new to all this. I don't know if I can do it, but I'll try."

"That's all I ask," she says. "I don't want to lose you, Jackson. You're ... important to me."

I peck her lips, offering her another truth that is only half the story. "You're important to me too."

Chapter Twenty
Vanessa

The hospital releases me into Jackson's care the following morning after the paperwork has been completed and after I have finished speaking to the cops. Jackson stayed with me during the interview, listening as I fed them the same half-truth I'd fed him. They seemed to buy it, promising they would be in touch as the investigation progressed.

Jackson helps me into his SUV while Sawyer heads off in his car. "Where are we going?" I ask when it's apparent we're not going to my place.

"To the penthouse," Jackson replies, stabbing me with a frown through the mirror. "You didn't think I was letting you stay at home by yourself?"

"I don't want to be a burden." I shift position on the back seat, gritting my teeth as my stomach protests at the motion. Already, I have a large bruise forming on my belly as well as matching bruises on my back. My face is a mess, and I have a lump the size of a golf ball on my temple.

But it could've been a lot worse.

I almost puke as the memory of him stroking his cock returns to haunt me. There would be no coming back from it if he'd raped me again. That would be the final nail in my coffin. The point where I jumped off the ledge and drowned.

"You're not a burden," Jackson says, turning on to the road that leads to Hunt's place. "You're my girlfriend, and I want to take care of you."

I know he's carrying guilt for my attack. He believes if he'd stayed the attack wouldn't have happened, but he's only partially right. He would have staved off the attack, but there is nothing Jackson could have done to prevent it. Aaron would have attacked as soon as I was alone.

"You are not responsible for what happened to me, Jackson. Please tell me you know that."

"I should have protected you."

I force myself to sit more upright, biting the inside of my cheek to resist crying out as pain slams into me. "You saved me, Jackson. You're my hero."

A look of sheer disgust washes over his face. "I'm the anti-hero, Nessa. Please don't paint me as anything but that."

"Why would you say that?" I ask, thoroughly confused.

His features even out as he pulls into the assigned parking space, cutting the engine. He smiles as he turns to me. "Ignore me. I'm in a weird mood. Worrying about you and lack of sleep has messed with my wiring." He flashes me one of his trade-mark grins.

Jackson carries me in the elevator, cradling me close as we travel to the penthouse. As soon as we are inside, he carries me straight to his bedroom.

He is the most attentive caregiver ever, and I fall a little more in love with him. After helping me to shower, he dresses me in clean pajamas before administering my pain meds and falling into bed beside me. We sleep the afternoon away before staying in bed watching TV and talking.

Hunt returns from my apartment confirming the police have finished their forensic analysis. I have a momentary bout of panic that the asshole left prints until I remember he wore gloves.

Jackson cooks dinner, serving it to me in bed. He props me up on pillows and puts *The English Patient* on when he leaves to go for a run. Hunt keeps me company for a while, reminding me I need to take more pain pills. It doesn't take long until I nod off again.

I wake suddenly, sometime in the middle of night. Jackson is out cold beside me, his fingers entwined in mine. My heart surges to life, and I swallow over the messy ball of emotion clogging my throat. I came so close to losing him, and I hated how it made me feel. I never want to experience pain like that again, so I vow to do everything in my power to make our relationship work.

My thoughts return to last night, and fear for Kayleigh is at the forefront of my mind. I don't trust Aaron not to take this out on her because he didn't get to punish me. Terror consumes me again, and I mull over my options as I lie awake, unable to sleep. My choices are limited, because I'm under a time constraint, and I've got to take action now.

As daylight filters into the room, I know what I must do.

I have to fess up to Jackson and Sawyer.

About the attack and the sexual, physical, and emotional abuse I suffered at Aaron's hands as a kid. I'm terrified it will color how Jackson sees me, but I must put my own selfish needs aside for my sister.

I cannot protect her alone.

I need money and a team of kickass attorneys.

I don't have those kinds of resources, but the guys do.

I need their help, and that means telling them everything.

However, fate intervenes, making that unnecessary.

Mom calls at three p.m., and this time, I pick up. My hands are shaking as I answer her call, wondering what she has to say.

"He's dead," she blurts without even saying hello. "Aaron is dead."

I don't respond for a couple seconds, totally shocked. "What?" I splutter.

"The police were just here. He didn't come home last night, but I assumed he was with one of his whores." She doesn't sound surprised or annoyed. I guess I'm not the only one who knew their marriage was a sham. "He wrapped his car around a tree sometime in the early hours of the morning. He was drunk, and there was evidence of narcotics in his system. He died upon impact."

"He's really dead?" This feels surreal.

"He is. I have to go to the morgue to formally identify him, but his ID was in his wallet, and the police said it's definitely him."

I burst out crying. Words filter down the line, but I can't hear them, and she eventually hangs up. Wave after wave of relief floods my system as I purge some deep-seated pain.

Thank you, dark fairy godmother, or karma, or whoever the fuck up there is finally looking out for me.

However this happened, I am so grateful.

I'm so fucking happy he's dead.

Good riddance.

I don't care how that makes me sound. That man was a monster who abused me and my mother for years. I still don't know what he has done to my little sister, but I'm confident it hadn't been going on long, and I'm hopeful this won't destroy her in the same way it destroyed me.

Jackson

"Babe?" Jackson crashes into the room, his eyes wide with terror. "What's wrong?"

He sits on the edge of the bed, and I collapse against him, sobbing into his shirt. "Nothing's wrong. Everything is okay. It's going to be okay."

I stay at the penthouse for the next week, and Jackson and Sawyer prove they meant every word when they said they were here for me now. They attend the stepmonster's funeral with me, escorting me to the house afterward where Mom and I play our roles to perfection. I stay the night with Jackson by my side, and the following morning, I have a brief talk with Mom.

There is a lot we need to say, but now isn't the right time. I need to let the dust settle a little before I broach the subject of therapy for Kayleigh. However, I get her agreement that I can see Kayleigh and Hunter whenever I like, and we make tentative plans for next week.

I am hoping to develop a stronger relationship with Hunter now Aaron is out of the picture. He always kept us apart, and his close relationship with his son meant I couldn't arrange sneaky weekly visits with him like I did with Kayleigh. It's not Hunter's fault, but I know I couldn't have trusted him to keep the visits secret in the way Kayleigh did.

Aaron dying fixes a lot of things, but nothing can fix the damage done to my relationship with my mother. She failed to protect me. She knew what kind of hell I was enduring, and she sought solace in a pill bottle instead of saving me. I know she was a victim too. I know he hit her, and I'm sure that's not the extent of it, but she's an adult. She had the power to stop it, and she did nothing. I will never forgive her for that, but I want to have an amicable relationship with her for the sake of the twins.

They need me now more than ever.

Unlike Mom and me, they are genuinely grieving the loss of their father. Kayleigh is every bit as upset as Hunter, but I don't know if she's confused and struggling to understand her emotions or if it's all genuine grief. Until I get to the bottom of what he did to her, it's too hard to guess what she's feeling.

I hope for her sake that it hadn't really begun. That she can forget it and remember her dad how he was before, because that means she won't live with the knowledge about who he really was. It's better for the twins if they can mourn the man they thought he was and grow up without the type of pain I will continue to hide deep inside.

I hope Mom seizes this opportunity to turn her life around. That she can be a parent to the twins and give them the mother I was denied.

I guess time will tell.

I return to my apartment the day before Jackson and Sawyer are due to leave for Rydeville. Physically, I'm feeling a lot better. The bruises are fading, and I don't ache as much. Emotionally, I'm not doing so hot. I'm going to miss Jackson so much when he leaves.

I got excited a few days ago when Mom deposited a large sum of money in my account. I have enough cash to pay for RU now, but enrollment is closed for the semester. I was so disappointed when I got off the phone with the administration department of the private university. However, they have emailed me the relevant forms for January, and I'm hopeful I'll be accepted then.

The silver lining is I'm no longer stuck in the city. I have money now, which gives me options. So, I'm reverting to Plan

B: I'm going to move to Rydeville and find temporary work there until the new year. That way, I'll be around to see Jackson every day, giving our relationship every chance to flourish. It's the next best compromise and a hell of a lot better than the long-distance relationship we had planned.

I handed in my notice to Paul, but it will be a couple of weeks before I can move. I need to find a place to live and pack up my stuff, and I don't want to leave until Paul has found a replacement.

I'm sitting on my couch, listening to music as I rifle through the mountain of piled-up mail when I come across an interesting, large, shiny silver envelope. I flip it over, but it has no return address on it. Opening it, I remove a few bundles of paper with mounting curiosity.

I'm blown away by the contents, and I have to reread it several times before it's sunk in.

Holy shit.

I turn on my laptop, copying the link from the letter, flipping through the photos with a disbelieving smile on my face. I flop down on my bed, laughing hysterically, excitement bubbling in my veins. I scream into my pillow, beyond exhilarated.

I cannot believe this.

I don't know how Jackson has done this, but I'm giddy he went to so much trouble. This proves his feelings are real, and if I was harboring any doubts, this has eliminated all of them.

I don't get why he wants to remain anonymous. Probably because he knows I wouldn't accept it from him otherwise.

I'm going to pay him back as soon as he comes clean about what he's done.

But, for now, I'll play along.

"You didn't have to go to this much trouble," Jackson says the following afternoon as we are enjoying a final meal together. Sawyer is supervising the removal of the last few boxes while Jackson and I are enjoying the warm sunshine up on the roof.

"I got everything from the diner," I explain. "It wasn't too much trouble, and with my staff discount, it didn't even cost much." I scoop up another serving of lasagna. "I brought containers for the leftovers so you can take them with you to reheat later. I also baked more of those brownies you like," I add, removing the box from my bag. I slide it across to him, smiling. "Oh, and I picked up some of that aromatherapy sports massage oil I mentioned. It works great on tight calf muscles." I hand him the silver bottle.

"You're spoiling me." Jackson winks.

"Consider it a thank-you gift for taking such good care of me last week." I put my silverware down, trying to contain my grin, but it's been permanent on my face since I opened that envelope yesterday.

"You seem ... happy." He looks and sounds perplexed. "Can't wait to see the back of me, huh?"

I giggle, and he stares at me like I've grown an extra head or ten. He leans his elbows on the table, shooting me an inquisitive look.

Fine. He wants to maintain the charade. I'll play along.

"That's not why I'm so happy I could burst," I exclaim.

"Put a man out of his misery." He gives me a goofy smile.

"I was going through my mail last night, and I made a very important discovery." Butterflies are going crazy in the pit of my stomach, like they have been since yesterday, and I'm smiling so hard my face is actually paining me.

"What kind of discovery?" he asks, and I have to hand it to him. He's got the unsuspecting, dumb role down pat. I'm practically bouncing in my seat, and he chuckles. "What did you take because I'm thinking I want me some of that," he teases.

"Oh my God, Jackson." I jump up, rounding the table and throwing myself on his lap. "I'm so high on life right now," I squeal.

He makes an "oomph" sound when I land in his lap, laughing as his arms securely wrap around my back. "Okay, crazy girl." He tweaks my nose. "Spit it out."

"I've been awarded this amazing scholarship from an anonymous fund."

"What?" His brows knit together, and he looks completely caught off guard. If I didn't know better, I'd say he is completely in the dark.

Give that man an Oscar!

I peck his lips. "We can be together now! I have a place in RU, and an apartment, and everything. Isn't it awesome?"

Shock splays across his face, and he really should consider taking drama classes.

I kiss him again. "Now, we don't have to do the long-distance thing. We can be together for real." I clap my hands. "This is going to be the best year ever."

Part Two

Rydeville University – Freshman Year

Chapter Twenty-One

Jackson

I'm drunk by the time Hunt arrives at my house in Rydeville. It's a miracle I made it here in one piece, because I was so fucking pissed as I drove from New York that I barely registered the journey.

I pop the cap on another beer, guzzling it like its water as I pace the room, my brain churning with thoughts.

"What the actual fuck?" Hunt asks, dumping his duffel bag on the floor in the living room, surveying the mess I've created.

Empty beer bottles litter the coffee table and papers are scattered across the hardwood floor. I scoured the files I've collected over the past six months, looking for clues, because there's got to be something we missed.

"Are you drunk?" he asks, scrutinizing my face.

"Why the fuck does that matter?" I hiss, swallowing another mouthful of beer.

"What's happened now?" He folds his arms, a hint of concern crossing his face.

"She fucking played me." I shake my head, barking out a laugh. I jab my finger in the air, ignoring how the ground sways under my feet. "I thought I was in control, but it's been her all along."

"You're not making any sense." He clears papers off the couch, dropping onto it. He yawns, clawing a hand through his hair.

I grind my teeth to the molars. "She fucking knows, Hunt. Nessa *knows!*"

"You'll have to be more specific than that."

"She is in cahoots with that murdering bastard!" I yell, clutching the arm of the couch as the room tilts. "This was a setup." I flop down beside him. "A ploy to get to me. I'm surprised she hasn't knifed me in my sleep already."

Hunt exhales heavily. "What am I missing?"

"He wants me dead," I slur, gulping back more beer. "I killed his precious son, and now, he wants to take me out."

"If that was true, he would've tried before now," Hunt calmly replies. "He might be overseas, but he still has friends and resources. If he wanted you dead, you'd be dead."

"Thanks for that reassurance," I snarl, flipping him off.

Hunt stands. "I can't talk to you when you're like this."

I tug on his jeans, pulling him back down. "She's coming here," I explain. "Nessa's enrolled in RU, and he set her up with an apartment. It's all arranged."

"She told you that?" Disbelief blares in his tone.

"Yep."

"She told you it was Christian?" He quirks a brow.

"Of course, she didn't," I scoff. "It was an 'anonymous' special scholarship." I make air quotes with my fingers. "She must think I'm an idiot if she expects me to believe that horseshit."

Hunt's brow puckers as he thinks about it. I slurp more of my beer. "Maybe, she doesn't know. Maybe, he's done it like this to keep the truth from her."

"Then, what's the fucking point of it? He can hardly get her to do his dirty work if she's not in the know." Anger pumps through my veins, and I clench my fist. "I know you want to see the good in her, Hunt, but it's all been an act." I eyeball him, venom flying from my mouth. "She's changed but not in the way we thought. He got to her. He set the whole thing up. He told her to reel me in, and when I'd fallen for her, when my defenses were lowered, they were going to strike."

I throw my bottle at the wall, and it shatters upon impact. Climbing to my feet, I pace again. Rage is like an inferno inside me, building and building, needing an outlet. I clench and unclench my fists as I walk back and forth across the room. My head spins from a combination of alcohol and confusion, and I'm so fucked up. I recall the past couple months and how things were between us, and there's a part of my brain that refuses to accept she was faking. It seemed so real. *She* seemed so real. But none of it was.

To think all those displays of emotion were an act.

She really is a piece of work.

"She's a nutjob," I murmur to myself as I pace, forgetting Hunt is in the room. "Of course, she is. She's his offspring. Her mission was to make me fall in love with her, and I'm the stupid fuck who did." I grab fistfuls of my hair, pulling tight, enjoying the stinging pain racing across my scalp.

"So, you admit you're in love with her," Hunt states.

"What?" I stop pacing, glaring at him. "Of course, I'm not."

"But you just said—"

"I didn't fucking say that, all right!" I slam my fist into the wall, cracking the plaster and leaving a hole. "I don't fucking love her. It was fake. It was all fake. On my side. On her side. The whole fucking thing is a sham. It's all part of the game." I plop my butt on the coffee table, leaning toward my buddy. "That's why we haven't been able to find anything. Why we couldn't place Dani on that island owned by Gerald Allen Junior, why we couldn't connect him to Christian and the elite, why we can't locate that fucker's hiding place, why I couldn't find any evidence that he's been in contact with Nessa, and why Nessa has a bodyguard."

I throw up my hands. I think I've made my point clear.

"Christian is protecting his investment and waiting for the right time to make a move. He is one step ahead of us, Hunt." I shake my head, disgusted with myself for being so clueless and ignorant of what was under my nose.

"This is all conjecture, man." Hunt leans forward, placing his hand on my shoulder. "I know you're pissed, but you're drunk, and your feelings for her are clouding your judgment. The only way you'll know for sure is to ask her. Sit Nessa down and ask her."

I snort out a laugh of incredulity. "Are you fucking kidding me right now? I can't ask her!" I roar. "That will play straight into his hands. He can't know that we know. That is the only way we can get ahead now. She has promised him something, and I'm gonna find out what." I bite the inside of my mouth, drawing blood. "All the shit I've done to protect her, and she was probably laughing behind my back. I am such a fucking idiot." I slam my palm into my forehead.

"I think you're wrong, Lauder."

"Are you in love with her or something? Because I don't understand why you keep jumping to her defense."

"C'mon, man. That's the easiest part in all this."

I stare him down, and he rolls his eyes. "I've known her since we were kids. We lost our virginity to one another, and I've been a shitty friend to her these past few years. I barely gave her a passing thought. If I had, I would've realized something was going on with her. Why don't you see that?"

"You're delusional, man. I know what I see, and it's not

some meek, innocent girl needing protection. She's harnessed her craziness and perfected her acting skills, and that makes her lethal."

"I don't agree. Your feelings for her mean you aren't seeing it clearly."

"Don't fucking tell me what I feel!" I shout, hopping up. "That has nothing to do with this. You didn't see the look on her face when she was telling me. No one accepts an anonymous donation with such glee. She wasn't even curious about her benefactor. She was looking at me with this knowing look, and she could barely contain herself the whole time. She knows where the money came from, Hunt. She fucking knows." I bury my head in my hands, so fucking annoyed at my stupidity. When I lift my eyes, I meet Hunt's conflicted gaze. "She might as well have planted a 'sucker' sticker on my brow she was that fucking obvious!"

He sighs again. "Okay. Calm down before you give yourself an aneurysm."

I flip him the bird, my mind processing options, because I need a new plan. She's not getting away with this. The game is still on; it's just moved to a new level.

"Let me talk to her," Hunt offers.

"Like fuck you will. That'll ruin everything, or haven't you been listening?"

"I—"

"He wants me dead, Hunt." I cut him off. "I killed Trent, and he won't rest until he kills me. Think I'm delusional all you want, but you know the way that sick fuck's mind works. You talk to Nessa, and you might as well write my death warrant."

He rubs at his temples, considering it for a few minutes, before he sighs in resignation. "Okay. What's the plan?"

"She thinks she can mess with my head? I'll give her a taste of her own medicine. I'm gonna fuck her up so bad she's incapable of doing anything that asshole asks her to do."

"Lauder."

"Don't use that fucking tone with me, Hunt." I glare at my best buddy. "The only way to get to him right now is through her."

"I can't stand by and watch you hurt her. This feels wrong."

"What they did to Dani was wrong!" I scream. "Or is Nessa more important than my tortured, dead sister?"

Hunt's anger sharpens, and his eyes narrow. "I can't believe you said that."

"You've got to choose. Nessa or Dani. You can't pick both sides."

"Jesus Christ, Lauder." Hunt hops up. "You've lost your fucking mind. Do you even hear yourself? How fucking crazy you sound? This is not some twisted competition, and Nessa had nothing to do with what happened to Dani," he shouts.

I stand, shoving his chest. "How do you know?" Blood turns to ice in my veins as the thought pops in my head. "Nessa was around Dani every summer. How do we know she didn't help Christian kidnap her? That she hasn't been in on this all along?" I grab hold of that train of thought and run with it. "Maybe, that's why she was so fucking trashed all the time. She needed to blot out the truth of what she'd done."

"You need help, Jackson." Hunt's expression softens. "You never dealt with Dani's death. You buried your grief with booze and weed. And this fixation with revenge is changing you. It's destroying you, and you can't even see it." He waves his hands in front of me. "You've lost yourself, man, and I'm worried. You need to let it go. Make amends with your dad, and move forward with your life."

"You don't know shit, Hunt."

"I know this man in front of me, spouting crazy ridiculous shit about the woman he loves, is not who you are."

I open my mouth to protest, but he cuts me off.

"Deny it all you fucking want, but I know you are in love with her like she is in love with you. This can be resolved if you just sit down and *talk* to her."

"Fuck me." My lips pull into a sneer. "You're like a broken record, and I don't feel like repeating myself. That's not gonna happen."

"I can't do this anymore."

"Three minutes ago, you said okay!"

"I've changed my mind. I trust my gut, and my gut says she's innocent in all this. I don't want any harm to come to you *or* her. The only way we can achieve that is by working together."

"I disagree, and there's no way I'm opening up that conversation with her."

He pinches the bridge of his nose, pinning me with a weary look as he says, "Then, you're on your own."

"Fine. I'll manage it myself." I step up to him, nostrils flaring. "But you don't breathe a word to Nessa or tell any of the others. You agree you won't interfere, and I won't tell Xavier about Sydney."

His face pales, and his lips pull into a tight line. "How the fuck do you know about that?"

"You think I haven't sensed your reluctance from the very start? That I haven't hired my own people?" It's rare I ever surprise Hunt, but I sure as fuck have shocked him now. "You're not the only one with secrets to protect. You keep mine, and I'll keep yours."

"This is an asshole move, Lauder."

"So is telling me you'd help and then bailing on me for a girl who is playing you for a fool."

"That isn't the only reason. Now, who's not listening?"

I shrug. "Do we have a deal?"

His nostrils flare, and I can tell he wants to punch my lights out. "I won't end my friendship with Van."

"Play the martyr. See if I care." I step up to him, thinking this might work to my advantage. "Be her friend if it's so fucking important to you, but you promise right now that you won't get involved, you won't ask her about Christian, or get in my way."

He contemplates it for a few tense beats, before nodding. "I don't like it, but I agree." His Adam's apple bobs in his throat. "And you won't tell anyone about Sydney. Especially not Xavier."

"I'll keep my end of the bargain as long as you do the same." The room spins again, and I've depleted my energy reserves. I need to sleep so I can get up tomorrow and map out my revenge. "The others can't know about this, so we'll have to pretend you haven't switched sides."

Tomorrow, when the alcohol has fled my system, I know this will hurt.

Hunt is my best friend, and I never wanted it to come to this, but he's left me with little choice.

"For fuck's sake, Lauder." Hunt stares at me with the saddest look. "This isn't the schoolyard, and I haven't switched allegiances. I'm trying to be a friend to both of you. I am so fucking pissed at you right now. I know you're making a mistake, but you're my best friend, and that hasn't changed just because you have your head stuck up your ass."

He clamps his hand down on my shoulder. "I don't like any of this, and I won't play an active part, but I'm not abandoning your stupid ass, so there will be zero pretending on my side." I can tell he means that. "I'll be here to help pick up the pieces when it all comes crashing down on you."

Chapter Twenty-Two
Vanessa

I check the time on the dash of my brand-spanking-new Range Rover Evoque, calculating I'm about ten minutes outside Rydeville. Thank God, I managed to arrange everything this past week, because classes start tomorrow and I'd hate to miss the first day.

Chloe's cousin June is covering my shifts at the diner until Paul can find a permanent replacement. Paul has decided to relocate from New Jersey, so he'll be moving into the apartment. Ensuring I wasn't leaving him in the lurch was important to me. He's done so much to help me, and I could never do that to him.

Jackson hasn't returned any of my calls or texts, which is odd, and it has me a little anxious, but I'm still really excited to start this new chapter in my life. It finally feels like everything is coming together, and I've never been happier.

Jackson is probably busy catching up with his friends and getting settled into his house, and I'm overreacting, reading more into it, as usual. Sawyer said he'd help me move in, and

I'm quietly optimistic my boyfriend will show up with him tonight.

Saying goodbye to Mara, Paul, and Chloe was tough. I will miss them so much. I had to wrench myself away from Kayleigh and Hunter too, but I promised my little princess I'll visit some weekends and during school breaks.

When I met Mom during the week, she agreed to bring Kayleigh to the therapist's appointment I set up for her. The nice lady I met with specializes in dealing with children, and I'm hopeful she can help Kayleigh to deal with her trauma. I thought I would have to convince Mom, but she put up no resistance. That, combined with her admission she's weaning herself off the pills and booze and attending an outpatient rehab program gives me hope she'll pull through for the twins.

Driving past the sign welcoming me to Rydeville is a memorable moment, and I can't hold back my goofy smile. I'm a little early, so I drive around acquainting myself with the place. The town is even more beautiful than I expected. The clean streets, pretty floral displays on the sidewalks, expensive storefronts, gorgeous promenade surrounding a stunning beach, and bustling bars and restaurants confirm its status as one of the best places to live in Massachusetts.

My new penthouse apartment is just off the main town square and only a ten-minute drive from the state-of-the-art university campus. Staying in one of the dorms on campus would have been ideal, but it would be ungrateful to decline the accommodation that came with my scholarship. Perhaps, I can move to the dorms at a later stage.

I pull up in front of my apartment building a few minutes later, getting out and hurrying into the office to pick up my keys and the codes for the parking garage and the elevator. The smiley woman behind the counter hands me a welcome pack, explaining about the pool, gym, concierge, and laundry services. Of course, I've already checked all this out online, so I shove the info in my bag and say goodbye. I'm dying to get up to the penthouse and make myself at home.

Sawyer is parked at the curb when I walk outside. He opens his door and stalks toward me with a big smile on his face. The passenger door slams shut, and I inwardly swoon. Butterflies run amok in my chest, and I can't contain my grin as I wait for Jackson to make himself known. My smile slips momentarily when Xavier's green spiky hair rounds the hood of Sawyer's SUV, but I quickly recover.

"You made it." Sawyer bundles me into a hug. "I'm so happy you're here."

"*We're* happy you're here," Xavier says, pulling me out of Sawyer's arms. He lifts me up, spinning me around. "I'm really happy for you, Van. I'm glad everything is working out."

"I wasn't expecting to see you," I truthfully admit when he puts my feet back on the ground. "But I'm glad you're here."

"I hung around later than usual because I wanted to help get you settled, but I'm heading back to Boston tonight."

Xavier has an important position with Techxet, the company Sawyer's father owns. They recently opened a new branch in Boston, and Xavier was one of their key hires. He tried to explain what he does the weekend we first met, but IT is not my forte, and it all went over my head. I know enough to understand he's passionate about his job, and I imagine he's a very dedicated employee.

"I really appreciate that. You're a good friend."

He kisses the top of my head. "I consider you a friend too, and I wouldn't be here unless I wanted to be."

I pluck up the courage to ask the question. "Where's Jackson?" My gaze bounces between Sawyer and Xavier.

"Out somewhere," Sawyer says, shooting me a sympathetic look. Xavier lowers his eyes to the ground, avoiding eye contact.

"Oh." Their reactions are weird. Something is off, but I can't put my finger on it. Everything was great when we parted ways last weekend. Jackson was shocked over my news, but he didn't seem unhappy about it. *I mean, why would he be?* He went to all this trouble to keep me close to him, so I don't understand what's going on. *What if he's changed his mind?* I almost puke as that thought lands in my head.

I don't share my concerns with Sawyer and Xavier or admit Jackson hasn't contacted me at all this week, because he's their friend, and they shouldn't be caught in the middle. Instead of probing further—because it's clear the guys are uncomfortable—I drop the subject, forcing a smile on my face. "I'm sure I'll catch up with him tomorrow."

Sawyer drives behind me as I pull into the basement parking garage, and then, the guys help me carry my boxes up to the penthouse apartment. We stack them up against the wall in the hallway outside my door, making a couple of trips to get everything, before I venture into my new living quarters.

Pushing my disappointment at Jackson's no-show from my mind, I open the door to my new place, sucking in a gasp as tears of joy prick my eyes. Oh my, wow. It's even more gorgeous than the pics I viewed online.

The main door opens directly on to a wide open-plan living area. On the left is a closet for coats, and on the right is a huge modern kitchen with glossy white and gray cupboards, stainless-steel appliances, and a marble countertop. The island unit houses four stools on one side for casual dining. Behind it is an elegant, long dining table, with seating for eight, of a more formal nature.

The whole length of the room at the back, facing the floor-to-ceiling windows, is the main living space. There are three long white leather sectionals, grouped around a rectangular walnut coffee table. A giant TV is mounted on one wall. Behind that is another seated area, composed of a few large recliner chairs centered around a circular glass coffee table. The wall behind that area holds a large bookcase, crammed full of books.

The walled balcony that wraps around the front and side of the penthouse houses an array of seating areas, and I spy a small grill in the corner. The balcony faces the front of the building, overlooking the street down below, but it's high enough to afford privacy. I can definitely see myself making good use of the space.

"Wow. This is amazing," Xavier says, whistling under his breath as he drops a couple of boxes on the floor. I hadn't realized I'd just walked off, leaving the guys to carry my things in.

"I can't believe it." I'm sure my face showcases my disbelief. This is the stuff of dreams, and it's not something that usually happens to me.

"You must've really impressed this anonymous sponsor," Sawyer says, depositing a few more boxes.

"I hope so," I blurt, smiling shyly, because I'm not sure if Sawyer is in the know. "I hope he hasn't changed his mind. That I haven't displeased him."

Sawyer frowns. "Why would you think that?"

I shrug, biting on my lip. "Call it intuition? I don't know."

"I thought it was anonymous?" Xavier says, huffing as he slams another couple of boxes down on the ground.

"It is. I'm speaking in general terms. Good stuff doesn't normally happen to me, and I've a habit of messing things up. I don't want to fuck this up."

Xavier slings his arm around my shoulders, kissing my temple. "Keep the faith, girl. You won't fuck it up."

There are stairs leading off both sides of the living area, so I leave the guys downstairs to explore the upper level. The upstairs is every bit as impressive as the first level, and I cannot believe this gorgeous place is all mine. The left stairway leads to my master suite with adjoining bathroom and private balcony facing the back of the building, overlooking a small well-maintained courtyard. The right-hand stairs lead to two guest bedrooms with a shared bathroom. All the rooms are well proportioned and expensively furnished. It's clear an interior designer decorated the place, and it's tasteful even if a little monochrome and cold. Once I add my own bits and pieces, I'm sure it will feel more homey.

Sawyer orders takeout, and conversation flows naturally while we eat. I thank them profusely for their help, promising to text Sawyer when I arrive on campus in the morning. Xavier gives me a bone-crushing hug before they leave, wishing me good luck for tomorrow.

I spend the rest of the night unpacking my things, using it to distract my errant thoughts. I tried calling Jackson again, and when he didn't pick up, I sent him a message, letting him know I'm here.

But there was no response, and I can't shake the feeling something is gravely wrong.

He's ignoring me on purpose. I just can't figure out why.

I'm so exhausted by the time I crawl into bed at one a.m. that I fall asleep immediately, and I'm grateful my brain is too tired to obsess over Jackson anymore.

Hauling my weary butt out of the bed at seven, I shower and get dressed in shorts and a cute shirt. Grabbing my cardigan, I slip on my ballet flats and leave the apartment, snatching an apple for later. My stomach is tied into knots, and I couldn't force any breakfast down. My nerves are stretched thin as first-day worry competes with anxiety over Jackson.

Jackson

I give myself a little pep talk as I drive through the impressive wrought-iron gates at the entrance to Rydeville University.

Although I have checked the campus out online, nothing compares to the up-close-and-personal experience. The campus is stunning with traditional tall red-brick buildings that have been meticulously maintained and updated since they were built in the nineteenth century. Manicured lawns and leafy trees line the paths intersecting across campus. The large glass building in my rearview mirror is the specialist sports center, complete with pool. The newer buildings dotted around the expansive campus house various food courts. The dorms are a half mile from the main campus, accessible by a private campus-run bus service. Bicycles are also available to rent by the hour.

I drive around for a few minutes, nerves jangling in my gut, commingling with fledgling excitement, until I find a vacant space. As I pull into it and cut the engine, I vow to get here even earlier tomorrow.

Pulling up the digital map on my cell, I memorize my route, grab my bag, and get out of the car before I talk myself out of it. Nerves slam into me from all corners, and I take successive deep breaths to calm down.

I hurry across campus, and the gentle warm breeze lifts strands of my hair, drying any remaining dampness. I had only given it a cursory blow-dry this morning, content to let my natural soft waves cascade down my back. It's a glorious day, which is a good sign, and I silently remind myself this is my dream come true and that nerves are normal.

Sawyer is waiting outside Manning Hall for me with a smile on his handsome face. Manning Hall is home to the business school and department of psychology, and it is where most of my classes will take place.

"Good morning." He greets me warmly, handing me a coffee.

"Morning. Thank you." I take the coffee, inhaling the bitter, nutty aroma, hoping I can drink it without throwing up.

"How did you sleep?" he asks, holding another paper cup.

I anxiously look around, but there's no sign of my boyfriend. "Like the dead," I joke. My stomach churns with nerves, and I'm only capable of sipping my coffee.

"Sorry I'm late." A girl with piercing green eyes and long, soft dark-brown curls materializes beside us. "It took ages to find a parking spot."

Sawyer hands her the cup. "It's cool." He turns to me. "Van, meet Shandra. She's also a freshman, and she has a few classes in this building."

"Hi." I smile, ignoring the fluttering feeling in my chest. "Nice to meet you."

"You too. Sawyer has been telling me all about you. Welcome to Rydeville." She tosses hair over her shoulder, catching the light, and I notice gorgeous red undertones that contrast beautifully with her green eyes.

"Are you from here?" I inquire.

She nods, her soft curls bouncing around her face, and one would have to be blind to ignore how striking she is with those almond-shaped green eyes, that lustrous hair, and gorgeous olive skin. She's of average height and slim with a similar figure to me. The most engaging thing about her is her genuine friendly smile. Although she is extremely pretty, I can already tell she's not one of those girls who flaunts her looks, using it to her advantage. I feel an instant connection, just like I did when I met Chloe for the first time. I think Shandra and I could be good friends. I really hope so.

"So, you know Jackson too?"

"Yep. I know the cheeky charmer. Then again, most

women do." She grins until she notices the expression on my face. "I'm sorry." She looks over at Sawyer, her brow furrowing. "Did I say something wrong?"

"No. It's fine," I rush to reassure her. "I know Jackson has a past. I'll just have to get over myself." She still looks confused, glancing between me and Sawyer. "He hasn't mentioned me, has he?" Acid crawls up my throat.

She shakes her head. "He hasn't been around this summer. The only time I've seen him was at the wedding in Alabama."

"Shandra is good friends with Abby," Sawyer explains.

Oh. I hadn't thought about meeting Kai's wife. I hope things aren't awkward. Shandra is looking to me for an explanation. "Jackson and I have been dating over the summer," I say.

Her eyes blink wide, and she stares at me for a few silent beats. "Oh, wow. Sorry, that was rude of me. I'm just a little shocked. I didn't think he dated, and I wasn't aware." She recovers, smiling broadly again. "But that's great. He's a good guy. And you're a knockout, so he clearly has good taste." She loops her arm through mine. "We should probably head in."

"You good, Van?" Sawyer asks.

"I'm fine. Thanks." I kiss his cheek. "I appreciate all you've done for me."

That you've been here for me when my boyfriend has gone AWOL. I think that, but I don't articulate it.

"Have a great first day." I plaster a cheery smile on my face, pretending like I'm not a bag of nerves on the inside.

"You too," he says. I turn around, but he lightly takes my arm. "Call me anytime if you need me. I'm here for you." His sincere eyes bore into mine.

"I will, and thanks, Sawyer. You're a great friend." As the words leave my mouth, I wonder if my outburst at The Hamptons is behind his sudden desire to be there for me. If he is trying to make up for the past. Whatever it is, I'm grateful to call him a friend again. I have always liked Sawyer, and it would be nice to rekindle the close friendship we had when we were young kids.

"So, you and Jackson, huh?" Shandra says as we join the throngs entering Manning Hall.

I gulp back a mouthful of coffee. "Yep. And believe me, no one was more surprised than me."

"I'm sensing a story." She grins at me, still holding on to my arm.

"We've known each other for years. Our families have vacation homes together. We didn't have much time for one another in the past, so it's funny how things have turned out."

"Do you know Kai too?" she asks, and I nod.

"What about you? Are you dating anyone?"

Her smile fades. "I was dating Abby's twin brother Drew for a while. Actually, I was engaged to him for a few months."

"Wow." To get engaged at a young age is not unheard of in the wealthy circles we mix in, and I read some stuff back in the spring when that Parkhurst organization was raided by the FBI. It was connected to some elite group, and I know the guys were somehow involved, but I don't know the specifics, and I never thought to ask Jackson.

"Drew is a great guy," Shandra says as we advance along the crowded hallway, past rows of lockers. "But we're not together anymore, and things are ... complicated." She looks so sad, and I feel an uncharacteristic urge to hug her.

"I'm sorry."

"Oh!" Shandra glances over my head. "Speak of the devil. There's Jackson."

I strain my head in the direction of her finger, spotting the back of his head and his broad shoulders as he leans sideways against a locker. His head is lowered, and his stance gives the impression he is talking to someone. Mobs of students stream past him so I can't see who.

"Let's go say hi." She stays with me as I maneuver my way across the hallway. My heart is beating frantically, and butterflies are careening around my chest. My stomach dips, and I genuinely think I might puke. I'm on edge as I approach him because I don't know what to expect.

I come up behind him, placing my hand on his back. "Jackson."

Initially, he stiffens under my touch before relaxing. When he turns around, it all happens as if in slow motion. His cocky smirk disarms me, and I'm bowled over by gorgeous blue eyes I know so well. So, I don't notice *her* at first—the girl he has his arm around.

She's beautiful with big brown eyes and masses of sleek, long dark hair. She's slim but much curvier than me with big boobs, shapely hips, and a flat stomach.

Her arm slides around his back, and she snuggles into his side, draping herself all over him.

"What's going on Jackson?" I ask, hating how my voice trembles.

"Was my lack of communication too subtle for you?" he snarls, clamping his hand possessively on her hip. His eyes scour me in obvious disgust, making his loathing clear.

Nausea twists my stomach into knots, and intense pain presses down on my chest. "I don't understand," I blurt, because I don't have a clue what's going on.

"Let me make it clear for you." He grins at the girl on his arm before turning another hostile glare on me. "Your needy, clingy ass is dumped." He leans into my face, and I cower under the intensity of his hateful stare. "It was all *fake*. Every single moment. And you fell for it so easily." He barks out a bitter laugh. "As if I would ever be interested in someone like you." He eyes me from head to toe again, and my stomach flips at the derisory expression on his face. "It meant nothing. *You're* nothing. Now fuck off. I've found someone worthy of my time."

I'm conscious of Shandra tugging on my arm, whispering something in my ear, but all I can see is Jackson smirking as he lowers his head to kiss a woman who isn't me.

Chapter Twenty-Three
Vanessa

I race off, grateful the crowd has died down so I can make a quick escape. It also helps there are less people around to witness my humiliation. I have no clue where I'm running, but I keep going until I find a bathroom, slamming through the door, thankful it's empty. I rush into a stall, bend over the toilet bowl, and vomit the scant contents of my stomach.

Footsteps race into the bathroom, halting behind me.

"Let me help," Shandra says, holding back my hair as I heave again.

Tears stream from my eyes, and the crushing pain in my chest makes it difficult to breathe.

I can't stop seeing it—Jackson kissing another girl.

Or hearing his cruel words.

It meant nothing. You're nothing. It was all fake.

I dry retch, hugging the porcelain god, with more silent tears rolling down my face. When the nausea passes, I scramble to my feet, instantly embarrassed Shandra was witness to that.

"Are you okay?" she softly asks, passing me a couple tissues.

I use one to clean my mouth and the other to wipe my tears away. "No," I honestly admit. She can see what a mess I am, so there's little point lying.

"I take it back." Her eyes glint with righteous indignation. "He's not a good guy. He's a fucking asshole. I can't believe the things he said to you back there."

"Where's the fire?" a female voice says as more footsteps thud on the tile floor. "Oh."

I look over at the new arrival, sucking in a breath. I know who she is from pictures in the paper, and Xavier showed me some photos from her wedding on his cell last night.

It's Abby. Kaiden's wife.

Wow, she's even more beautiful in person with her big brown eyes, flawless skin, full mouth, and wavy dark hair. She's more petite than she looks in her photos, but she has this fierceness about her that practically exudes from her pores.

She looks from Shandra to me, her eyes instantly filling with compassion. "Are you okay?"

"I will be." I force out a small laugh, sniffling. God, this is so humiliating and not the way I wanted to meet Kai's wife.

"This is Vanessa. She's the girl Sawyer told us about last night," Shandra explains.

"Yes. Of course." Abby nods. "You're an old friend of Sawyer's, right?"

"She's also Jackson's *girlfriend*." Shandra speaks up before I can. "Or at least she was until five minutes ago when the jackass cruelly broke things off with her in the hallway before locking lips with some other girl."

"What the what?" Abby looks completely shell-shocked. "You were dating *Jackson*? As in, Jackson Lauder?" Her voice elevates a few notches, and her eyes almost bug out of her head.

"It seems I was his dirty little secret," I admit. My heart hurts with a fresh wave of pain. He was so ashamed of me he didn't even tell his friends we were dating. Except... "Didn't Xavier mention me?"

Her brows knit together, and a fierce expression lights up her eyes. "Are you telling me Xavier, *my* Xavier, knew you and Jackson were together?"

I bob my head. "I met him when he stayed with Sawyer one weekend in New York, and they both helped me move in last night."

Shandra and Abby stare at me like I've just told them I bumped into Stephen James in Rydeville. "Wait? You didn't know that?"

Abby shakes her head, pulling out her cell. "No wonder Xavier didn't mention you to me. That would've required telling me he spent the weekend fucking Sawyer." Her fingers fly across the keypad of her phone. "I'm going to kick his ass. Then, I'm going to kick Sawyer's ass." She slips her cell back into her purse. "Wanna go tag team on Jackson's ass? Because he deserves the biggest ass-kicking of all." She waggles her brows, and I know she's trying to lighten the mood, which I'm grateful for, even if there is nothing she or Shandra can do or say to lift my spirits.

"I'm down with that plan. Nothing like an ass-kicking first thing Monday morning," Shandra quips.

More tears pool in my eyes. These girls have only just met me, yet they are ready to wade into battle on my behalf. I've never had that before. "Why would you do that for me? You don't know me, and you're friends with these guys."

Shandra hands me a new tissue.

"Us girls have got to stick together," Abby says. "And I know how it feels to bear the brunt of Jackson's cruelty," she adds, surprising me. "Although Kai was the worst."

"Cam is cruel to you?" I blurt.

She startles, and she and Shandra share a look.

"You know who I am," Abby says.

I nod. "I know Sawyer and Jackson from The Hamptons. We've been friends since we were kids through our parents. I knew Kai as Cam, because he hung around with us a few summers." Perhaps I should say something—about sleeping with her husband—but it'd be a bit weird to blurt that out when we've only just met. Plus, what happened between us was in the past, and it honestly meant nothing. Kai probably doesn't even remember. The last thing I want to do is hurt Abby, so I decide not to mention it.

"Ah, that makes more sense, and no, Kai isn't cruel to me. He's an amazing husband, and I love him to death. But they were total assholes to me when they first arrived in Rydeville."

"Sounds like someone hasn't eradicated that asshole gene," Shandra supplies.

I walk toward the sink, conscious time is ticking by and we have to get to class. "Jackson has been the sweetest, most attentive boyfriend all summer. That asshole out there is *not* the guy I was dating," I say over my shoulder as I rinse my mouth and wash and dry my hands.

"We'll get to the bottom of it," Abby says. "But right now, we should get to class." She turns to me. "Sawyer said you're studying psychology like me."

"I am."

She smiles. "Great. It's good to have a partner in crime already."

God, I fucking love her. No wonder Kaiden married her. Abby is as genuine and welcoming as Shandra, and it feels good to have someone in my corner.

"Let's get our butts to Introduction to Psychological Science before we get booted out on day one." Abby jerks her shoulder in the direction of the door.

"I've got business management," Shandra says, tossing her

empty coffee cup in the trash. I have no idea what happened to mine. I guess I discarded it at some point when I was fleeing. "Catch you both at lunch."

"Absolutely." Abby leans in, hugging her. "We're claiming a table, and everyone will be there." Some silent communication passes between them.

"Good luck convincing Kai to accept Charlie." Shandra grins.

"This bullshit is stopping," Abby says, looping her arm in mine. "I have Kai wrapped around my pinkie. He'll do what I say, or I'll deny him sex until he relents."

Shandra bursts out laughing.

My mouth hangs open a little. "Would you really do that?"

"No." She grins. "I love sex with my husband far too much to deny myself, but he doesn't need to know that."

We find our way to the correct auditorium, slipping into a row at the back a couple of minutes after the lecture has started. It's a large class, and we're not the only ones running late, so we get away with it.

I try to concentrate and take notes like Abby, but my mind keeps wandering. I honestly think, if it wasn't for Shandra and Abby, I would've left by now. My heart hurts. Like it physically pains me. It feels like I could die. I want to curl into a ball, close my eyes, and never wake up. My lower lip wobbles, and I warn myself not to break down in here. It's embarrassing enough that countless strangers witnessed my humiliation in the hallway.

I don't want to be defined as the broken girl anymore. This was supposed to be a fresh start, and already, it feels like I'm back in the same place. Everything I thought I knew has turned upside down. All my plans lie in tatters at my feet. I'm not sure I have the strength to fight back this time. Not when I'll see Jackson all over campus, reminding me of his rejection. Every time I see him, I'll know I'm unlovable, gullible, and so desperate for attention I continue to fall prey to assholes who only want to use me for my body.

None of the men in my life have ever cared for me. I thought Sawyer was my friend, but he clearly knew this was coming, and he said nothing. He made no mention of the fact I was Jackson's girlfriend when he contacted the girls last night to talk about me. He did nothing to prepare me for this, so he's on my shit list too.

Another thought lands in my brain, and my spine turns rigid. Bile pools at the base of my throat.

Jackson isn't my anonymous sponsor.

He *couldn't* be.

It's obvious he doesn't want me here, so why the fuck would he pay for me to attend RU and provide me with a top-notch penthouse apartment?

Truth is, he wouldn't. He *didn't*.

That is why he looked so shocked last week. He wasn't acting. He genuinely had no idea. He had no intention of pursuing a long-distance relationship with me, and my admission threw a wrench in the works. I don't know why he came back to my apartment the night I was attacked, but it wasn't to rescind his breakup. When he saw what happened, guilt got to him, so he cared for me to assuage his conscience, presuming he wouldn't see me again once we parted ways in New York.

Except my anonymous sponsor altered my future, forcing him to face me one final time.

I shiver as ice tiptoes up my spine. *If Jackson isn't my anonymous sponsor, who the hell is?* Apprehension causes goose bumps to sprout on my arms as I think of who it could be, but I draw a blank. I make a mental note to check with the administration. Although, if it's anonymous, I doubt they will divulge anything.

My fear subsides, giving way to thoughts of Jackson again. Pain charges through me like an invading army, and I can scarcely breathe over the lump in my throat.

I still don't understand why he had to be so cruel. *He tried to let me down gently the first time, so how is this different?* The disgust and loathing in his eyes can't be faked though. He legit hates me, and there will be no rescinding anything this time.

Agony twists my gut into knots and pummels my heart. The image of Jackson kissing that girl surges to the forefront of my mind, and I squeeze my eyes shut to ward off tears. Inside, that swirling black void gains momentum, churning and churning until it's a violent burst of dark energy swallowing me whole.

"Hey." Abby clutches my arm as she whispers. "You're going to be all right."

I open my eyes, staring at her through blurry vision. "How could he do this to me?" My voice breaks, and I swipe at the errant tear sneaking out of my eye.

Sympathy washes over her face. "You love him."

I nod slowly. "I'm pathetic." I wonder how long it'll take her to ditch me when she realizes I'm not cool to be around.

"You're not pathetic. Love isn't pathetic," she adds.

All around us, people stand as the professor brings the class to a close. We stay in our seats as students stream out of the auditorium.

"In my limited experience, love is complex and painful and full of obstacles to overcome," she continues. "Some external. Some we put in our own path. But once you get past those, love is the most exhilarating, blissful, rewarding thing. And it's worth all the pain to get to that point."

"It's one-sided, Abby. He doesn't love me."

"You don't know that for sure." She chews on her lip. "Jackson doesn't give many people his time, yet he spent the summer with you. That means something." She eyeballs me. "I won't give you false hope, but if he lashed out, it means he's *feeling*, and Jackson works hard to suppress his emotions. I wouldn't be too quick to write him off."

"You didn't see the way he looked at me." A shudder works its way through me. "He hates me. He said I meant nothing, that it was all fake, and the look on his face confirmed it."

"We need a girls' night," she says, surprising me. "I'll fill you in on my story. It might help put things in perspective. And in the meantime, we're here for you." She stands, and I gather up my stuff, shoving my iPad and notepad in my bookbag.

"Thank you. I'd be a basket case if it wasn't for you and Shandra."

We walk out side by side. "You don't need to thank me. Any friend of Sawyer's is a friend of mine, and Xavier says you're a sweetheart. That guy has a built-in bullshit detector. If they both vouch for you, that's good enough for me."

Chapter Twenty-Four
Vanessa

"How are you holding up?" Shandra asks as we stand in line for the register at the food court.

"I'm okay." I've numbed my thoughts and emotions, shoving them behind those steel bars I've resurrected. I just want to survive this day. Then, I'll go home and rage at the world. "How were your classes?"

"Good. It was a productive morning."

"Okay." Abby appears in front of me as I hand my card to the girl behind the register. "Don't freak out, but Jackson will be at our table."

"What?" I squeak, almost dropping my card when the girl hands it back to me.

"We're all sitting together. There are enough of us that you can avoid talking to him."

I shake my head. "I can't do that. I can't sit at the same table as him and watch him all over some other girl."

Abby grabs my tray, handing it off to a dark-haired guy passing by. "Chad, do me a favor and take that over to Kai." It's said less like a question and more like a demand.

"Hey, Abby." He kisses her cheek, readily taking my tray. "Of course. You know I'd do anything for you."

She points over my shoulder. "We're sitting over there, and I expect you to join us."

She's super bossy, but I love it. I can see why Kai fell in love with her. She's beautiful, smart, confident, and outspoken.

Everything I am not.

"Come over here." She takes my hand, pulling me over to the corner, just inside the door. Shandra trails us. "I know you love him, and he's taken a machete to your heart. We'll make him pay for that." Shandra nods in agreement. "But you are *not* leaving. You have every right to be here, and you are going to hold your head up high and show him that *he* means nothing."

"Abby is right. Make it an Oscar-worthy performance," Shandra says. "Sit with us, and ignore him. Laugh and look like you haven't a care in the world. It will seriously piss him off."

"Flirt with Sawyer," Abby adds. "That will really annoy him."

Their fighting spirit bolsters my fragile ego, and I find myself nodding. "Okay."

"That's it." Abby grins. "I see that fire in your eyes. Use that. Remember how angry you are, and use that to fuel your performance. I'm not saying it's easy, but you'll feel so much better if you do this. You can't avoid him forever, so it's better to get this over and done with now."

"And you have us," Shandra adds. "We have your back."

"I'm so glad I met you both. You have no idea how much this means to me."

"You're one of us now, Van," Shandra says.

"Call me Nessa," I say, and my lips twitch. "It's what Jackson calls me."

"Hell yeah." Shandra grins, nudging my shoulder. "Let's play him at his own game."

We push off the wall, and I follow Shandra's lead with Abby behind me. My heart is pumping furiously, and blood rushes to my ears the closer we get to the table. I wipe my clammy hands along the side of my shorts. Abby tugs on my elbow, and I stop, turning to face her. "Don't flirt with my brother Drew," she whispers.

"I wouldn't dream of it," I whisper back. "I know he has history with Shandra."

Her eyes pop wide. "She told you?"

"She mentioned it."

"I don't know what's going on, just that things are awkward as fuck. She doesn't want to talk to me because he's my brother, and I respect that. Having you here is good. Maybe, she will open up to you. Keeping this shit locked up inside is never good."

Tell me about it. I have years of pent-up emotions stored inside me, waiting to explode.

"Oh God." My stomach dips to my toes as I spot the back of Jackson's head. I slam to a halt at the sight of the same girl sitting on his lap.

"You can do this," Abby says, snarling in Jackson's direction. "Get angry and stay angry. And don't look at him."

It feels like the entire food court can sense how badly I'm shaking as I approach the table. I follow Shandra to the opposite end of the table to Jackson, claiming an empty seat beside Sawyer. Shandra sits on my other side, and Abby drops into the seat beside her, which also happens to be right beside Kai. She drops a kiss on his lips, and they share a moment as their eyes meet. It reminds me of similar moments I shared with Jackson, and I have to look away before I lose the tenuous control on my emotions.

I turn away as Sawyer slides my tray to me. "Are you okay?" he whispers.

"A heads-up would've been nice," I murmur.

A loud giggle emanates from the top of the table, and it takes colossal willpower not to look up. I dig my nails into my thighs, cursing that stupid bitch. *How can she want to be with him after the way he spoke to me this morning?*

"Let's talk this evening," Sawyer says.

Kai's fork drops on the table, clanging noisily. "Vanessa?" He gawks at me, like he's just seen a ghost.

"Hey, Cam." Shit. Nerves have me on edge. I clear my throat. "Sorry, Kai." Wow, he's gotten even hotter since the last time I saw him. And he's lost that air of aggression that used to follow him everywhere. Marriage clearly suits him.

"What are you doing here?" he asks, sliding his arm along the back of Abby's chair.

I glare at Sawyer. "Why didn't you tell him?"

"I was waiting for someone else to," he mumbles, and I almost jerk my head in Jackson's direction, but I stop myself in time.

"I'm Chad." The guy sitting across from me, the one who took my tray, extends his arm, and I shake his hand.

"Nessa. Thanks for carrying my tray."

"You're welcome. This is my boyfriend, Vic." He gestures at the guy sitting beside him.

He's tall with a lean build and cute wireframes. He nods politely at me while smiling. "Good to meet you."

"Might as well get all the introductions out of the way," a guy with a deep voice says, and I turn my head slightly to look at the guy sitting on Sawyer's other side.

I catch a glimpse of Jackson out of the corner of my eye, and pain spears through my heart. The brunette is still on his lap, her arms wrapped around his neck, and he's running his hand up and down her back.

Shandra discreetly pinches my knee under the table, and I

snap out of it, giving the good-looking guy with the dark hair and eyes my full attention. "You must be Drew," I say, because the resemblance to Abby is strong.

"Welcome to Rydeville." His entire face comes to life when he smiles, and I can see why Shandra is interested in him. "Are you staying on campus?"

"No, I'm—"

"I don't think we've finished with the introductions," Jackson bellows, commanding everyone's attention.

"I already know who you are," I say without looking at him. I grip the edge of my chair, bracing myself for the onslaught I know is coming.

"But you haven't met the beautiful Belinda," he mocks.

"I don't care that we're in public, Jackson," Abby retorts, standing abruptly. Her chair scrapes along the floor, drawing the attention of the students at adjoining tables. "I will still kick your ass."

"This should be interesting," Sawyer murmurs, pursing his lips.

I ignore him, because it's not funny, and I'm reminded I'm mad at him too.

Jackson chuckles. "You seem to be laboring under some misapprehension, Abby darling. I'd be happy to clear it up for you."

"I'm pretty sure I have all the facts." Abby stabs her finger in his direction. "You're an asshole, and we'll be having words."

"Babe." Kai takes Abby's hand, pulling her back down. "What's going on?"

Abby's eyes meet mine. "Jackson has disrespected Nessa, and that shit is not happening on my watch."

Jackson chuckles, like it's the funniest thing he's ever heard. "That wasn't the misapprehension I was talking about."

"Lauder." Kai's tone carries considerable warning. His eyes flicker to mine briefly.

Fuck. He remembers.

All my muscles lock up tight as an ominous sense of dread washes over me. My head whips around of its own volition, and I pin terrified eyes on Jackson, my distress over the fawning girl on his lap paling in comparison to what he's about to do. My eyes beg him not to do this, and the asshole smirks.

"What are you insinuating?" Abby asks, suspicion creeping into her tone.

"Ask Kai how he knows Vanessa." Jackson waggles his brows.

Abby's gaze bounces between me and her husband.

"Shit." Sawyer groans, dragging a hand through his hair.

"Shut your mouth, Lauder," Kai warns, but Jackson ignores him, hell-bent on staying the course.

"Better yet, ask Vanessa how intimately she knows your husband," Jackson continues, oblivious to all those he hurts with his words, because he's not just ruining my friendship with Abby before it's even begun; he's damaging his friendship with her and one of his best friends.

Abby's frozen stare pins me in place, and I want the ground to open and swallow me.

"You're fucking dead," Kai roars, jumping up, fists clenched, ready to kill his friend.

Sawyer moves fast, grabbing Kai before he pounces on Jackson.

"You slept with Kai?" Abby asks, shock splayed across her face.

"It was one time, years ago. We were both trashed, and I barely even remember it," I explain, gulping over the painful lump in my throat. She stares at me, and I hang my head in shame. I've officially reached my limit, and I need to get out of here. Grabbing my bag, I stand.

Shandra shoots me a sympathetic look as she circles her arm around Abby. Kai glares at Jackson, but the asshole just sits there smirking with the bimbo on his lap giggling like she hasn't just witnessed devastation.

"I'm sorry, Abby," I say, clasping the strap of my bag and walking off.

Jackson is grinning like the cat that got the cream as Belinda paws at him. Anger blisters under the surface of my skin, and I stop, glaring down at him. "I don't know how I ever saw any good in you. You're poison, and you infect every person you touch. That was a shitty thing to do to your friends. I hope you're proud of yourself."

I walk off, holding my head up high, but it's all a façade.

I can't stay here any longer. *How can I face Abby now she knows I had sex with her husband?* She'll hate me and want nothing to do with me.

In a few hours, Jackson has succeeded in obliterating my heart, destroying my burgeoning friendships, and shattering my dream.

I virtually sprint out of the building and across campus to my car, ignoring the vibration of my cell in my jeans pocket. I need to get out of my head and lick my wounds away from here.

The second I reach my penthouse apartment, I take the bottle of vodka I just bought out of my bag and retreat to my bed to numb my pain and block out reality.

Chapter Twenty-Five
Jackson

"Where is he?" Anderson's furious voice filters into the kitchen from my hallway, and I brace myself for an ass-kicking. I deserve it. It was a low blow, and I didn't stop to consider how it would hurt Kai and Abby. I was too fucking pissed that Nessa has somehow already gotten Abby and Shandra on her side, that she was sitting at our fucking table, whispering cozily with Sawyer, and that she had the nerve to ignore me.

I can't ruin her if she pretends like I don't exist. So, I took action to force her to confront me, pissing my best friend and his wife off in the process.

Angry footsteps thud down the hallway and enter the kitchen.

I turn around just as he thrusts his fist in my face. My head whips back as pain glances along one side of my jaw, up over my cheekbone, rattling my skull. "Aw, fuck." I straighten up, just as Abby comes at me, slapping the other side of my face with more force than I'd expect of her.

Now, I've got matching soreness in both cheeks, but I

deserve it.

"You motherfucking asshole," Anderson says, reeling Abby into his arms. "What the fuck is your problem?"

"How long do you have, and where do you want to begin?" Hunt drawls, propping his butt against the edge of the kitchen table.

"Fuck you, man." I flip him the bird.

"I want answers, and I want them now," Abby says, glaring at me.

"It was a shitty move, and I shouldn't have pulled it. I apologize if I hurt you. That wasn't my intention."

She prods her finger in my chest. "We all know your intention was to hurt Nessa, and that is not acceptable to me. She's the one you owe the biggest apology to."

My eyes pop wide. "You're fucking defending her?" I throw my hands in the air. "She slept with your husband, and you still want to play nice?!"

Abby smirks, extracting herself from Anderson's embrace, putting her face all up in mine. "Kai has explained the circumstances. It's part of his past. One I knew he had when I married him. It was a shock hearing it like that, but I'm not angry with Nessa." She jabs me in the chest with her long nail. "I'm angry with you!"

"This is priceless." I tug at my ears because they're obviously malfunctioning. "Someone hand me a syringe. My ears are clearly blocked because you did *not* just say what I think you did."

She grins, and there's a wicked glint in her eye I've seen before. "News flash, asshole. If you thought your little stunt would ruin my friendship with Nessa, you are sorely mistaken. If anything, you've just made me more determined to make her my new best friend."

"*Our* new best friend," Shandra says, arriving in the

kitchen with Drew in tow.

Great. Just what I need. Abby's annoying twin sticking his nose where it's not wanted.

"Have you all gone mad?" My gaze jumps around them.

"The only crazy person in this room is you," Hunt supplies.

"Everyone, sit down," Abby demands, pointing at the kitchen table. "We're talking this out."

"Like hell we are." I fold my arms and pout. "This is nothing to do with any of you, and I'm not discussing it." I shoot Hunt a warning look, silently reminding him of our deal.

"You made this about us the second you dragged us into this," Anderson says, still glaring at me like he wants to slice my head off my body. "You hurt my wife, dickhead, and you'll give us fucking answers, or the next time, I won't just throw a punch. I won't stop until you're lying in a pool of blood at my feet."

"It's time," Hunt says, eyeballing me.

Wait? What! He better not be saying what I think he's saying. "We have a deal," I hiss in his ear as he moves to go past me.

He barks out a harsh laugh. "If you think Abby isn't going to get the truth out of you, you clearly don't know her as well as you think." He slaps me on the back. "Fess up, man. They'll be on your side. It's the only way you'll repair the damage you did today."

My shoulders slump in resignation. I knew returning to Rydeville would increase the chances they'd find out, but I wasn't expecting it to happen so soon.

Hunt and Shandra make coffee while I grab a beer from the refrigerator. I definitely need alcohol for this conversation.

When everyone has a drink, and we are all seated around the table, I wait for the interrogation to begin.

Anderson looks at Abby, nodding, and I can't help the

cocky smirk that crosses my mouth or the words that leave my lips. "You are so pussywhipped."

"Abby's the boss," he calmly replies, not rising to the bait.

My grin disappears at the expression on Abby's face. Fuck. She's like a piranha, sharpening her teeth, preparing to rip through my flesh, and I'm ready to shit my pants.

"What is going on with you and Nessa?"

I flinch at her use of that name, because only Kayleigh and I call Vanessa that, but I'm guessing that's the point. "Nothing is going on. We're done. She was a hole to fuck when I was bored." I shrug, smirking like the words didn't feel like poison spewing from my mouth.

"You're disgusting." Shandra shakes her head, her look full of loathing.

"Agreed," Abby says, and the look of disappointment on her face guts me. Abby is more than just Anderson's wife. We have a connection. A special friendship. What she thinks of me matters, which is why this entire situation is a complete clusterfuck, because I can't stick to my plan with Nessa and maintain Abby's respect.

"We'll be here all night if you're going to act like an idiot," she adds, letting me know she's not buying the bullshit I'm peddling. "Tell the fucking truth, or I'll let Kai have at you. I won't hold him back."

Anderson is a legend in the underground fighting scene in New York, and I've watched him destroy guys with lethal precision, barely breaking a sweat. That was just for sport. None of them had done anything to deserve a beating, so Abby's threat is no idle threat, and I know Anderson is pissed enough he'd do it.

No one hurts Abby without paying the price. Dude is tits over ass crazy about her, and he'd kill for her without even blinking an eye.

I sigh, rubbing my sore jaw, wondering if I should do this. I catch Sawyer's eye, and he nods. Guess I'm doing it.

Air whooshes out of my mouth as I prepare to spill my guts. "I'll tell you about Nessa, but I need to go further back to properly explain it."

"We're listening." Abby leans forward, propping her elbows on the table, granting me her full attention.

"Christian Montgomery is the one who kidnapped, tortured, and raped Dani." Fuck, it's harder to say that than I thought.

Shocked silence greets my statement, and I force myself to continue. "Your father knew," I tell Anderson. The vein in his neck throbs as he clenches his fists on top of the table. "He told me last year when we visited your place to make plans."

"That's why you were like a zombie before we moved to Rydeville," Anderson surmises.

I bob my head. "It threw me for a loop for a number of reasons."

"Why didn't you tell us?" He looks at Hunt. "Or have you known all along?"

Hunt shakes his head. "I only found out after everything went down at Parkhurst."

"I'll get to that," I say, clamping my hand on my thigh to stop my leg from shaking.

"Atticus told me to keep it a secret. Promised we would go after Christian as soon as we had dealt with Michael Hearst. He kept drumming the bigger picture into me, so I agreed to set my personal agenda aside to help you take him down and avenge your mom."

"He had no right to ask that of you," Anderson says. "Your need for revenge was no less than mine."

"That doesn't matter now."

"It fucking does!" Anderson shouts, thumping his fist on

the table, rattling the wood. His eyes are blazing with hatred for the father he now despises. "We had countless opportunities to take Montgomery down, and now, the bastard is on the run. I'm sorry."

"Don't apologize. This isn't your fault, and it wasn't just your father. Mine didn't want me to do anything either."

"Wait?" Drew angles his head, staring at me. "Are you saying your dad knows it was Christian too?"

"He knows, and he doesn't fucking care." I dig my nails into my thigh as anger scorches a path through my body.

"That's not exactly true," Hunt interjects.

"That's why you're barely talking to him," Anderson surmises.

"That and the fact he's the reason Dani was taken in the first place."

"Why?" Abby asks in a soothing tone. "What did he do?"

"Dad and Ethan Hunt had partnered on this high-tech project they were devising to revolutionize Formula 1 racing, but they needed a robotics partner on board." Abby's eyes widen in recognition. "Montgomery's company was the foremost expert on robotics, so they approached him to see if he was interested. Dad said they didn't know anything about the elite or Christian's role in it when they first reached out to him. Christian expressed interest in the project, so Hunt's dad did the usual background checks and unearthed shit they didn't like. They pulled out, but Christian got wind of what they'd discovered, and he kidnapped Dani as a warning to them to keep their mouths shut."

"Oh my God." Shandra squeezes my hand. "I'm so sorry, Jackson."

"Dad's terrified he'll come after me or Mom, so he refuses to do anything. He said Christian made it clear they were to forget what they knew and he'd accept Dani's punishment as payment in full."

I understand his fear. I do. Especially where Mom's concerned. I know what the elite is capable of. But Dad's loaded, and he has the resources to keep us safe. Plus, Christian is already gunning for my ass, so I say we take the fight to him first. I don't understand why Dad is still reluctant to go after him, and that's the crux of our issues.

"You only found this out last year?" Abby asks.

"Yeah. After Atticus told me it was Christian, I went to Dad. I couldn't believe he'd known all along. He refuses to go after him, because he's scared of retaliation, but I can't accept that." I eye everyone around the table. "I spent years blotting it out, and last year was the worst because those revelations killed me." A lump wedges in my throat, and I swallow hard. "Being around that prick and not being able to do anything nearly destroyed me."

"I don't know how you did that," Anderson quietly says.

"I was here for you and then for Abby. That was what was most important." I glance at both my friends, suddenly very ashamed of my behavior today. "And I shit all over that today. I'm fucking sorry."

"How does Nessa fit into all this?" Abby asks again.

"After everything went down at Parkhurst, I switched my focus to Dani. Your strength encouraged me to get my act together," I tell her. "As soon as my head was clear, I knew I wanted revenge. No, I *needed* it." I stare at the painting over Abby's head because that's the only way I'll be able to admit this. "It hurts so fucking much. Dani suffered and I did nothing to prevent it. She came back broken and like a shell of herself. I couldn't help her, and she killed herself because she couldn't get over what had been done to her. It's that bastard's fault, and I won't stop until he pays."

Chapter Twenty-Six
Jackson

"Why were you doing this alone?" Anderson asks. I drop my gaze to his. "You and Abby had been through hell, man, and you'd only come out the other side. You needed time to heal and to be together. I didn't want to drag you into this." I look at Drew and Shandra. "I didn't want to drag any of you into this, but I couldn't do it alone, so I approached Hunt, and he agreed to help."

"My father was involved with the project that was the catalyst," Hunt says. "I feel a responsibility, and Dani was like a big sister to me too. I want that bastard to pay as much as Lauder does, and I agreed we would leave you guys out of it for the time being."

"I forgive you," Abby blurts, stretching across the table to take my hand in hers. "For your shitty behavior today." She squeezes my fingers. "And we appreciate that you gave us time, but you are not shutting us out of this anymore."

"Agreed," Anderson says, sliding his arm around his wife's back. "Tell us everything else we need to know."

"We have a few guys digging through stuff, trying to find a link between Montgomery and Gerald Allen Junior."

Shandra frowns. "You think there's a link between the Florida politician who was jailed for sex trafficking minors and the elite?"

"Dani was kept on an island, and, to the best of our knowledge, the elite don't have any islands. The description fit, and we were able to place Allen with some other elite members, but we can't place Dani there or tie him to Montgomery."

"I wonder if Selena Kennedy was there the same time Dani was missing," Abby muses out loud. "Perhaps, she might recognize a picture of her?"

"Perhaps," I say, drumming my fingers on the table, trying not to remember the interview Selena gave about her time as a sex slave on that island. The thoughts of Dani going through any of that is more than I can bear. "But we think Keven Kennedy might be more useful. The FBI is conducting a huge investigation, and they might know something."

"We didn't reach out to him," Hunt confirms to Anderson. "Because he's your contact, not ours. We were afraid he might mention something to you, but if you could do that now, it would help."

"Consider it done," Anderson says. "I'll call Rick when I'm back home and get him to set that in motion."

"What's your motivation?" Drew asks. "What's the end goal here?"

Imbecile. *Hasn't he been paying attention?*

"I want to torture and murder that bastard Montgomery. That good enough for you?" I hiss.

"How does confirming whether Dani was on that island help?" Shandra asks, jumping in before words get heated.

"Someone is hiding that bastard, and we've checked all his elite contacts, their associates, and sent a couple PIs overseas to locations we've uncovered, but they have turned up zilch. Someone else is helping him, and I think it's Allen or someone in that circle."

"Has Xavier been helping you?" Abby asks, turning steely eyes in Hunt's direction.

"Xavier is in the dark because we couldn't trust him not to blab to you," Hunt admits.

Abby grins.

"But we'll be bringing him into the loop now," I add, because Xavier is the fucking best at this stuff, and we need his help. I'll leave it up to Hunt to smooth the waters there.

"What about Charlie?" Abby asks, and Anderson groans.

"This needs to be kept close, and Charlie is still on the fringes. I want him kept out of this." I drill her with a cautionary look.

Abby will struggle with this because she's been fighting in Charlie's corner, wanting him back in the crew. I get it. He took a bullet for her. Proved his loyalty in the end, but he's still done a lot of shady shit, and I understand why Anderson is wary. I share his concerns. "Until I know Charlie can be trusted, I want him nowhere near this."

Abby opens her mouth, about to object, but Anderson shakes his head, and some silent communication filters between them. She closes her mouth, pulls back her hand, and sits back in her chair. "Fine. For now."

"We have to be careful," Hunt says. "Jackson killed Trent, and Christian isn't letting that slide."

Abby goes deathly pale. "Has someone tried to kill you?" She chokes out.

"No, but that only means he's biding his time to strike when I least expect it."

"You shouldn't have been managing this yourselves."

Anderson glares at me. "We're a fucking team. Don't ever forget that again."

Hunt gets up to make a fresh pot of coffee.

"You still haven't explained how Nessa fits into this," Abby says. She's like a dog with a bone, and she won't drop it until she knows everything.

"She's Christian's daughter," I say, and every jaw drops to the floor.

"Holy shit." Abby shakes her head in disbelief. "I should've guessed from the resemblance. I was wondering why she looked so familiar to me."

Hunt refills everyone's mugs, handing me a cold beer, while I update them on what we discovered, what I had planned, and what went down with Nessa over the summer, including my suspicions over her involvement. Hunt adds his two cents' worth, explaining how his gut tells him she's innocent and Christian is manipulating her for some aim. We argue back and forth a bit as the others take it all in.

"I'm not buying that. No fucking way." Shandra glances between me and Hunt. "You didn't see her this morning after you spewed all that horrid shit in the hallway. She was destroyed. There's no way that's an act."

"I agree," Abby says. "But it's more than that. What happened to that girl?"

"What do you mean?" I ask.

"Didn't you see it in her eyes? In her whole demeanor and the way she carries herself?"

"See what?" There's an edge to my tone because I don't like the vibes I'm picking up. Either they are on my side or they're not.

"Someone broke her, and I'm not talking about you although I'm sure you've added damage." Abby leans her head on Anderson's shoulder, and his arm tightens around her.

242

"Maybe, it's because I know what it's like, but I saw it in her eyes. She's in a world of pain, Jackson."

"You're imagining things because you want to see the good in her when there really isn't any," I retort, unable to hide the bitterness from my tone.

Kai snarls, his eyes narrowing and fists flexing as he glares at me, sending me a silent warning to back the fuck down. He's like an overprotective grizzly bear when it comes to Abby. Anyone even looks funny at her, and he's ready to tear them limb from limb.

It's hysterical.

Except when I'm on the receiving end of it.

"Don't try reasoning with him," Hunt says in a clipped tone. "He's in love with her, and he has himself all tied up into knots."

"For the last fucking time," I growl, "I am not in love with her! I fucking hate her." My jaw aches I'm clenching my teeth so hard.

"Sure, you do." He smirks, and I want to ram my fist into his face.

"Watch it," I snap.

"You're fucking terrified of facing your feelings, so you'd rather believe she's the enemy instead of an innocent victim."

I snort out a laugh. "You're such a fucking hypocrite. Why don't we talk about your feelings for Xavier or how you've been hiding your own shit?"

Hunt's face darkens like thunder, and his eyes warn me not to go there.

"Why don't we keep this conversation focused on where it needs to be?" Anderson says. "What are we going to do about Vanessa?" He glances between me and Hunt. "I've got to admit her being here makes me uneasy."

"Babe." Abby lifts her head, cupping Anderson's face. "I

told you I'm cool with it, and if she's a pawn like Sawyer believes, then she's in as much danger as Jackson. We can't walk away from her."

"I planted a couple bugs and cameras in her place last night," Hunt admits.

I stare at him in shock. He had walked away. Said he wouldn't get involved or interfere, yet he does that. Guy's baffling as fuck.

"Don't look at me like that," he says, pointing at Abby. "It's to keep her safe. A guy already broke into her apartment in New York a couple weeks ago and attacked her."

Abby and Shandra send daggers at me.

"I take it back," Abby snaps. "I don't forgive you. I want to slap you again."

"How could you treat her like you did this morning knowing she's just gone through that?" Shandra asks.

"I told you my reasons, and I'm not fucking repeating myself. You're all giving me a fucking headache." I rub at the tense spot between my brows.

"If you're going to continue with this obnoxious plan of yours," Abby says, drilling her finger in my face, "you and I will have a problem, because I told her she could count on me, and I'm not taking that back."

"Babe." Anderson faces Abby. "I know you have a big heart, and you want to take her under your wing, but you don't know her, and none of us know whether she is or isn't involved. Hanging out with her is dangerous no matter which way you look at it. The smart thing is to distance yourself from her."

"You want me to slap you too?" She turns her hostile lens on her husband, and I'm glad I'm not on the receiving end of it anymore.

"We can't leave her defenseless," Hunt argues. "Even if she

does know about him or they've been in contact, she still has no clue who he is or what he's capable of."

"Hang on here a sec." I swivel in my chair to face him. "You believe me now?"

Hunt rubs the back of his neck. "I still don't think she's working with Montgomery, but she made a weird comment today about her anonymous sponsor."

"Ha. Told you."

"Don't look so pleased. I haven't changed my mind. Van has changed, and if she's caught up with Montgomery, she still deserves our protection."

"I don't know," Anderson scrubs a hand over his prickly jaw. "She's reckless and prone to wild behavior."

"Not anymore," Hunt says.

Anderson arches a brow, his disbelief clearly written on his face. And I get why he's wary. Nessa was especially clingy with Anderson, chasing after him like a lovesick puppy, hanging off his every word. Pain slices across my chest as that thought pings in my head, but I force it aside, because I. Don't. Care. She's a lying, deceiving cunt, and I hope Anderson gives her hell.

"Why is it so hard to believe she's changed?" Hunt asks, eyeballing Anderson. "We've all changed too. You should cut her some slack."

"I don't trust her," Anderson replies, shrugging unapologetically.

"You don't have to," Abby says, fixing him with a fake sugary smile. "Shandra and I will hang out with her. We'll keep her safe."

"See, that there. That's what I have an issue with." Anderson grips her chin in his fingers. "I won't have you hurt because of her."

Abby slaps his hand away. "You're almost as bad as him now." She jerks her head at me for a nanosecond before turning back to her husband. "You don't get to tell me what to do or who to hang out with. How can you turn your back on a girl in danger? I know that's not who you are. I need you to be okay with this, Kai, because I'm not backing down. Nessa needs a friend, and there's no way in hell I'm stepping aside if that bastard Montgomery has her in his sights."

Fire burns in her eyes, and it's familiar. There is no point trying to reason with Abigail Anderson when she gets something into her head. This is a foregone conclusion. She's not walking away, and that makes things much more difficult for me.

"We should go check on her," Abby says to Shandra. "Make sure she's okay." She glances at her watch, looking up at Anderson. "We can squeeze in a quick visit before dinner."

"I don't think that's wise," Hunt pipes up. "I checked the camera feed when I got home. She's not in a good place. She'll be embarrassed if you see her like that." He glances at me, conveying everything he's not saying with the disgusted expression on his face.

Good. I'm glad she's hurting. Bitch fucking deserves it. No one gets to treat me like an idiot without suffering the consequences. And I've barely even begun. By the time I'm through with her, she'll wish she'd never been born.

"I'm going to grab some food and head over there in a while. I'll look after her, I promise," Hunt reassures Abby.

I flip him off 'cause I'm immature like that.

The piranha's teeth sharpen. "Fuck you, Jackson," Abby hisses. "This is all your Goddamned fault."

"She brought it on herself," I snap back, tamping down the guilt churning in my gut. Anderson growls again, but I ignore him. "She's been lying to me as much as I've been lying to her. She deserves everything coming her way."

Shandra places her hand on my arm, much to Drew's

obvious displeasure. Shit is bad between them right now, but there was a time they seemed pretty loved up. I suspect Jane Ford is the reason Drew has backed off. Stupid, weak fucker. Those two women have him by the balls, and he's letting them.

I smirk as he eyes Shandra's hand like it's an explosive. His gaze narrows on mine, silently warning me. If I thought Shandra would be up for a roll in the sack, I'd be all over that shit. Pissing Nessa and Drew off would be like scoring the ultimate two for one. But Shandra's not that type of girl, and I wouldn't even waste my time trying. Guess I'll have to find other ways to wind Drew up.

Dude really gets under my skin these days. Things had been okay between us, and it was Hunt who had an issue with Abby's twin until the douche brought up the night Anderson and Abby let me into their bedroom. It was a onetime thing, the night of the anniversary of Dani's death. I was in a bad place, and my friend recognized that. I didn't touch Abby. No way in hell would Anderson allow that, but I did jerk off watching them fuck from a chair by their bed. Hands down, it was one of the hottest nights of my life, and I didn't even get laid.

Anderson is a lucky man.

Anyway, I won't go into all the details, but Drew was aware of that night, and it must've been brewing in his head, because he verbally attacked me one night last May, warning me to butt out of their relationship and to back off his sister. I didn't appreciate his tone or his condemnation, and things have been frosty between us since.

Now, I get my rocks off riling the dude up any chance I get. Case in point.

"Please don't do this," Shandra pleads, dragging me back into the conversation. "You don't have to do it."

I move her hand off my arm. "Butt out, Shandra. Haven't

you got enough problems of your own to worry about?" I purposely stare at Drew.

"Fuck off, Lauder," Drew snaps. "Don't try to deflect from the mess you've created by throwing shade elsewhere."

I flip him the bird. "Why are you even here? Let's not pretend we like one another."

"Shut. Up. Jackson." Abby's gaze dances between me and her brother. "You're both giving me a headache. Sort your shit out because we've got bigger problems to deal with. Like this issue with Nessa and the impending elite vote to elect a new president."

Anderson frowns. "Can we not talk about that. I'm already in a foul fucking mood, and that will turn me psychotic."

I know Kai and Rick are worried about their younger brothers, Joaquin and Harley. They have done everything to keep them protected and away from all the elite shit. Pressure is mounting now that the organization is restructuring, and a new president is close to being elected. None of us know what will happen or how it will impact us, so to say things are a little tense is an understatement.

I also know this new elite shit is the reason why Kai and Rick have stopped actively searching for their missing brothers. Atticus Anderson put their two youngest brothers up for adoption after their mom passed, and no one knows where they are. Anderson is desperate to find them, but he's holding back now out of fear they'll fall into the elite's clutches if they reconnect.

He's walking a tightrope, and the strain is obvious on his face.

It's another reason I didn't want to pull him into this shit.

Abby kisses Anderson softly before turning her attention to me. "We've got to go. Mom's expecting us for dinner. I have one thing left to say." Her brows knit together. "Actually, two."

I roll my eyes and cross my arms, preparing for whatever

misguided wisdom she's about to unleash on me. She fixes me with a stern, disapproving look that has me slumping a little in my chair. I feel the oppressive weight of her displeasure sitting on my chest like it's a tangible thing.

"First. Belinda is not welcome at our table. Don't invite her again."

I smirk. My plan worked. She got to Nessa. To Abby and Shandra too if I'm reading the vibes correct. Awesome. And I know just how to up the ante, so I nod, as if it's no biggie. If that's how she wants to play it, fine. I'm gonna have fun with this. "What else?" I ask, ignoring the daggers Anderson is sending my way.

"I know you feel something for Nessa. You can deny it till the cows come home, and I still won't believe you." She drops the glare, compassion filling her eyes as she leans across the table at me. "How will you feel if he hurts her? If he kidnaps her and takes her away from you? If he tortures her, abuses her, ra—"

"Enough!" I jump up, knocking my chair over in the process. I can't think about that shit. "You've made your point."

"At least this way, Abby and Shandra will know if anything is going on," Hunt supplies, doing his best to defuse the tension in the air.

"We're not spying for you," Shandra huffs. "You can get that idea out of your head."

"We're going to be her friend," Abby says, glancing at me again. "Because we want to be, and because I will not sit back and watch anyone hurt another woman. Not Christian Montgomery. Not those bastard elite." She pokes her finger at me. "And especially not you."

Chapter Twenty-Seven
Vanessa

As I stare at the pic on my cell that Jackson sent me last night, I'm hoping if I look at it enough times it will numb me to all emotions. I can make out his arm and the side of his head, but most of the image is centered on the blonde sleeping in his bed. She's lying on her stomach, hair spread across her face, so I can't tell if she was awake or asleep when he took the photo. Sheets are draped casually at her waist, confirming she's naked.

Pain rips through me, making a mockery of my stupid hope. I seriously contemplate getting back into bed and sleeping my hangover off, but fuck Jackson Lauder. Chloe is right—he isn't worthy of my time or my headspace, and he's certainly not worth tossing my dream aside for. I'm glad I called my bestie last night for advice. She was fuming when I told her what'd gone down, and she helped set me straight.

Fuck him to the high heavens. He is not ruining this opportunity for me.

Sometime during the night, when my overwrought brain dissected everything, I realized I have the control here. Jackson wants to hurt me. That much is evident, but he can only hurt me if I let him. And I'm done letting men destroy me. I'm not convinced I'm strong enough to do this, but I'm going to try. Compared to what Aaron did to me, this is a cakewalk. If I could pull myself back from the brink that time, I can do it again.

Walking into my bathroom, I switch on the shower, chanting a silent battle cry in my head as I step under the warm water. I will show that asshole that he meant as little to me as I meant to him. Doesn't matter that it's all lies. He won't know that. Tipping my head back, I close my eyes as water cascades down my face, mapping out a strategy in my head.

I spent years wearing a mask to disguise the things happening in my bedroom at night. Now, I'll just wear a different mask to hide my heartbreak and pretend like I'm a fully functioning member of society. I need to shut off my emotions again, but I need to do it without relying on alcohol or drugs because that's a one-way ticket to hell, and it's a destination I've got no desire to revisit. It won't be easy, especially if I've lost Abby and Shandra's friendship, but I owe it to myself to fight for my future.

No man is going to hold me back.

Especially not Jackson Lauder.

"How's the head?" Hunt asks, handing me a bottle of water when I reach Manning Hall.

"Not good. It's like someone has taken a hammer to my skull, but I'll survive."

"These will help." Hunt offers me some pain pills, but I shake my head.

"No thanks. I try not to use medication if I can help it." I open the water, greedily drinking it.

"I'm glad you're here," he adds.

"You were expecting me to be a no-show," I surmise.

He nods. "I'm happy I was wrong. For what it's worth, I don't approve of how Jackson is treating you."

"Jackson who?" I attempt a lighthearted tone, but I'm not sure I've quite pulled it off.

"You're going to be fine." Leaning in, he kisses my cheek, surprising me. "You are stronger than you think."

"Thank you." My nose scrunches. "I think."

"I meant what I said last night. I'm still your friend, and I'm here if you need anything."

"Thank you, and you're forgiven. I appreciate you stopping by last night to check up on me. No one usually cares."

"I'm not the only one who cares." Looking over my shoulder, he smiles, relief blatant on his face. "The cavalry has arrived. My work here is done." He winks at me. "Try to stay out of trouble." He brushes past me as all the tiny hairs rise on my arms. "Ladies," he says behind me.

"Sawyer," Abby says, and panic bubbles up my throat. "See you at lunch."

Forcing my panic to one side, I slowly turn around, ready to face the music.

"Hey, Nessa." Shandra darts in, giving me a quick hug. "How are you feeling today?"

"Like I have a jackhammer in my head," I blurt the truth.

"That jackass is not worth a hangover," Abby says, looping her arm in mine. "But I get it."

"I owe you an apology," I blurt again because I have zero filter. It's even worse at times when I'm drunk where I literally spew the thoughts in my head like I'm thinking them out loud. "I'm so sorry I didn't say anything. I didn't know how."

"No apology is necessary, Nessa," Abby says, as we walk up the steps. "I'm not going to hold something that happened between you and my husband years ago, before I was even on the scene, over your head or let it ruin our friendship. Although, I'd prefer you keep the deets to yourself."

My cheeks flare up. "I would never say anything like that! God, I'd be happy if we never ever mentioned it again." Especially the part where I pathetically followed his ass around, desperately craving his attention.

Shandra opens the door, and we step into the building.

"Sounds perfect to me." Abby smiles, and there's no hint of ill will on her face. A layer of stress lifts from my shoulders and I let out a shuddering breath. "Jackson is the biggest jerk for blabbing that."

"Boy's got issues," Shandra murmurs.

"I honestly didn't think you'd speak to me again," I admit as we make our way along the hallway. It's busy again, and noisy chatter swirls around us.

"I have had enough of men's interference to last me a lifetime," Abby replies. "I make decisions for myself, and no man is going to take away that control. We're here for you. That hasn't changed."

"So, you better get used to us," Shandra jokes. "Because we're going nowhere."

"I feel sick," I blurt as we line up to pay for our lunch in the food court after our morning classes have ended.

"I've banned Belinda from our table, and I doubt Jackson will risk being nasty to you in front of us, so don't worry. It will be fine," Abby reassures me.

Except it's not fine.

"You have got to be kidding me." Abby shoots daggers at the back of Jackson's head as we approach our table.

Belinda is gone, all right. But she's already been replaced by a skinny blonde with an unnatural rack. Barbie is on his lap, arms wrapped around him, fake tits smushed into his face, and I want to yank her up by her bleached head and drag my nails down her face. The image of the photo he sent me flashes unhelpfully across my retinas. Obviously, she's the blonde who shared his bed last night. Agony slams into me at the thought of her having sex with my boyfriend.

Not your boyfriend, you sap. Ex-boyfriend. Get with the program.

Thanking my snarly inner voice for reminding me of my agenda, I tug my steel walls up, securing them around me as I rally my resolve. I don't care. He's a petty, juvenile prick and someone who is completely undeserving of my love and my attention.

Ignoring him and his latest fuck buddy, I sink onto the empty chair beside Sawyer. I press a kiss to his cheek. "How's your day been?" I inquire.

"Better now you're here."

I laugh, nudging his shoulder. "Liar."

Snaking his arm around my shoulder, he presses a soft kiss to my temple. "I'm not lying." Placing his mouth by my ear, keeping me under his arm, he adds, "I'm offering my services if you want to use me to rile him up."

"Why would you do that?" I ask, peering into his earnest hazel eyes. "He's your best friend."

Grinning, he shrugs. "Take your pick. He's acting like an ass. I want to prove a point. And I owe him payback. He's been pissing me off for weeks."

I think about it, seriously considering it for a few seconds before I dismiss it. I wriggle out from under his arm. "Thanks for the offer, and I might take you up on it down the road, but, for now, I'm taking the moral high ground."

His eyes shine with pride. "You are way too good for him, Van. Don't ever sell yourself short."

A throat clearing on my other side claims my attention. Turning my head, I come face to face with Kaiden Anderson, and my stomach dips to my toes. Shandra is seated in between us, and Abby is on Kai's other side.

"I want to apologize if I was less than welcoming yesterday," Kaiden says, startling me. I was ready for him to rip me a new one. It's what the old Camden would've done.

"You don't have anything to apologize for, but I appreciate it." If anything, I'm the one who should be apologizing to him for my past behavior, but I promised Abby I wouldn't bring it up again, so I don't broach the subject.

Abby elbows her husband none too subtly, and Sawyer chuckles.

"I have no issue with you being here," Kaiden adds, glancing between me and Abby. "Or being friends with my wife. You're welcome at our house anytime."

"Pussywhipped." Sawyer coughs, murmuring under his breath, and Kai flips him off.

I pretend I haven't heard. "Thank you. And congratulations on your marriage. I wholeheartedly approve of your choice. Abby is amazing, and one of the kindest people I've ever met."

His features soften as he slides his arm around her waist. "She is. My wife is all kinds of wonderful."

Jackson makes a gagging sound from the top of the table, accompanied by more female titters.

"Where does he find these women?" I mumble. "And can any of them think for themselves?"

"You don't want to know," Sawyer replies. "And doubtful."

"You look like shit, Nessa," Jackson hollers. "Rough night?"

"What makes you think I want to talk to you?" I ask, purposely looking at him, working hard to keep my features cold and impassive. I'm not cowering anymore.

His eyes skim my face while his hand glides to the blonde's hip. She runs her fingers through his hair, and I want to rip her hands off him.

I don't care. He means nothing. He's a prick. She's welcome to him. I bolster my walls, promising myself I'm strong enough to do this and survive.

"You might want to start using makeup, sweetheart," Jackson says, smirking at me as he rubs circles on the blonde's hip with his fingers. "Unless you were going for the washed-out junkie-whore look on purpose."

"Eat shit and die, asshole," I reply, pleased when my voice comes out level even though my stomach has dropped to my toes and my left leg has started shaking of its own volition.

Blondie sticks her tongue in his ear, grinding on his lap, and I look away before my mask drops, revealing my hurt. I'm aware how easily women fall into Jackson's lap; otherwise, I'd think he paid her to act as obnoxious as possible. *Has she no pride?* We're in the middle of a packed food court. No one wants to see that when they're trying to eat.

"I never thought I'd say this," Abby cuts in, glowering at Jackson. "But I think I preferred you when you were stoned. At least, you were funny and charming. Now, you're just spiteful and mean, and that shit's never attractive."

"Control your woman, Anderson," Jackson coolly replies, her words just flying over his head. "Or you won't like what I'm about to say."

"Shut your fucking mouth, or I'll shut it for you," Kaiden snarls, flexing his arms and balling his fists. I recognize the dark expression on his face, having been on the receiving end of it

more times than I can count. Kaiden looks two seconds away
from tearing strips off his best friend. "Take your slut, and sit
someplace else, Lauder."

Anger rolls off Jackson in waves. "You seem to have
forgotten how you treated Abby when we first showed up in
Rydeville, and if Nessa can't handle that I've moved on, she can
sit someplace else. No skin off my back."

"If anyone is leaving, it's you," Drew cuts in. His icy tone
and cold, harsh stare surprises me, and I shiver at the lingering
menace simmering at the back of his eyes. Drew has hidden,
dark layers, and I don't think I'd like to get on his wrong side.
"Or can't you work out when you're not wanted, Lauder?"

"Jackson, please." Abby's tortured expression and
emotional tone claims everyone's attention. "You don't need to
do this. We need to stick together, now more than ever."

Jackson slides the blonde off his lap and stands. Blondie
instantly suctions herself to his side, pinning me with a smug
expression as her hand lands on his butt. "This is fucking bullshit." Jackson jabs his finger at Abby and Kai, and I've never
seen him so mad. "I put my own shit aside to be there for both
of you last year, and this is how you repay me? You pick her
side just like that? What the fuck, man?" He glares at Kai.
"Abby thinks for you now? You can't stand her!" He points at
me, raising his voice, ensuring those in the vicinity are well
aware of what's going down.

"She is still the same pathetic, clingy hot mess who used to
follow you around begging for scraps. The same girl who would
fuck anyone for attention. The same girl who told you nothing
was off-limits and you could do whatever you wanted to her."

"I'll happily fuck her," some asshat behind me pipes up.

"We can tag team!" another douche adds.

Kaiden swivels in his chair. "Shut the fuck up, or I'll have
you expelled," he warns, and that thankfully mutes the idiots. I

know Kai is a descendant of one of the founding fathers—something I read online about Rydeville—but I don't know if he has that kind of authority.

"You know I'm right, Anderson," Jackson continues, because he likes to have the last word.

I have no recollection of saying that to Kai, but I can't rule out the possibility I probably did. Embarrassment crawls over my skin, and I hang my head in shame. Heat creeps up my neck and over my cheeks. *What was I thinking?* I can't be friends with these people. Jackson is never going to accept it.

As soon as the warmth has left my cheeks, and I'm confident I don't look like a withered tomato, I lift my head and push my chair back, ready to leave. Sawyer clamps his hand on my thigh, stalling me. He shakes his head. "Let the toddler have his temper tantrum." He speaks loud enough for Jackson to hear.

"Oh, whatever." Jackson throws his hands in the air, proving Sawyer's assertion. "Choose *her* over our friendship. See if I fucking care." He slams his lips down on the blonde's, and I avert my eyes as pain crashes into me, knocking all the air from my lungs. "C'mon, babe," he murmurs in that sexy voice of his. "Let's screw in the bathroom. It beats sitting here with these boring fucks."

He knocks his chair to the ground before walking off like he's the one who's been wronged. I don't understand him or why he feels the need to inflict further pain on me. He publicly dumped me, humiliating me in the process, and he's irreparably shattered my heart. *Isn't that enough?*

"Please tell me I was never that pathetic," Kaiden says to no one in particular.

"You were almost as bad," Abby says, and my eyes lift in surprise. "But Jackson's definitely going for gold." Her sympathetic gaze lands on my face. "I'm sorry he's being such a dick."

"Please stop apologizing for him. And I'm the one who's

sorry." I stand, grabbing my tray. "I know he wants to hurt me. I don't understand why, but I can handle it. Me sitting here is causing problems for all of you, so I think it's best I sit some-place else."

Abby opens her mouth to speak, but I hold up my hand, halting her. "It's better this way, and there's nothing you can say that'll change my mind. I need to stop by the bursar's office anyway. I'll catch you in class."

I walk off before anyone can say anything else, feeling proud I've done the right thing. I'm hopeful I can survive this even if my dickhead ex is determined to do everything to drag me down.

Chapter Twenty-Eight

Vanessa

"The record is sealed? What does that mean?" I ask the kind lady with the enviable red hair behind the counter in the bursar's office.

"That someone in a position of power or with considerable clout has requested the matter be kept confidential. That's usually the way it works with anonymous sponsors, although this does seem a little unusual because there was no scholarship fund established or application process documented."

"Is there anyplace else I can go for more information?"

She shakes her head. "I'm afraid not. I suggest you count your good fortune and make the best of the opportunity that's been afforded to you. There are very few scholarships handed out for RU, and admittance is high. You're extremely lucky."

I guess I must be. However, it's still a puzzle I want to figure out. In my experience, nothing is given without something being expected in return. Prickles of apprehension coat my skin whenever I think about my anonymous sponsor. *Who is he or she, and why pick me?*

I thank the woman and make my way back to Manning Hall.

I keep myself busy the next couple of weeks, on purpose, to distract myself from thinking about the jackass or how my heart still beats out of control for him. I throw myself into my class-work and my assignments, spending my evenings in the library most nights except when I'm meeting Abby for a run on the beach or attending a yoga class with Shandra. I still refuse to sit at their table in the food court, much to Abby's chagrin, but it's easier for me this way, and that's the only reason she backs down.

I try to sit as far from their table as possible so I don't have to watch Jackson flirting with whatever girl has caught his eye that day.

There's an apparently endless stream of willing girls ready to drop everything for him. You'd think I'd be numb to it by now, but it still hurts whenever I see him with a girl draped around him like an accessory.

Which is why I agreed to attend my first college party tomorrow night. Abby and Shandra are coming here to get ready. Hence why I've been out grocery shopping, stocking up on snacks and drinks. Stepping into the elevator, I hug the bags to my chest, resting my head against the wall and closing my eyes. I'm determined to flush that asshole from my system, and the only way I'll get over him is to move on.

So, tomorrow's the night. I'm going to find a hot guy to get lost in. Sex with someone else will help me forget him, and I need that so bad.

Every morning, Jackson messages me with a new picture of his latest bed buddy, crushing my heart all over again. When I blocked his number, he started messaging me from a different cell, and thus, the pattern began. Now, I just delete them without looking because my fragile heart can't take any more blows.

I thought when I stopped sitting at their table that I could avoid him, but he's determined to make my life miserable, showing up before some of my classes to either hurl abuse, paw at the current girl on his arm, or remind me my time with his friends has an expiration date, because once I revert to form, they'll dump my ass and forget I ever existed.

His words, not mine.

But they're sharp and pointed, and they hit the intended target, smashing my walls and piercing my heart.

Funny thing is, his behavior only makes me more determined to stand my ground. In a weird way, he's helping me. I'd be lying if I said he wasn't getting to me, because he is. I've lost count of the nights I've cried myself to sleep, but I only resorted to drowning my sorrows in a vodka bottle one night this week, so that's progress.

Exiting the elevator, I walk to my door and open it. My foot hits something on the floor as I step into my place, and I almost trip over the package before my sneaker sends it flying across the room. I dump my groceries on the island unit in the kitchen and move to retrieve the mystery item sitting on the middle of the floor.

I crouch down to pick it up, my heart racing as I recognize the envelope with the same printed font on the label. I open it as I walk to the living area, plonking my butt on one of the couches. Depositing the contents of the envelope on my lap, I frown as a slim silver cell phone slides out, along with a folded piece of paper. I open the note first, and my heart falters in my chest when my gaze rests on the enclosed photograph.

The picture shows two men, dressed in expensive suits, side by side, smiling at the camera. They are both of similar height, but the man on the left is much older. With his dark-blond hair, slim physique, and classic good looks, he cuts a dashing figure for an older dude. The younger blond guy on his right is seriously hot. Not quite in Jackson's league but not far off it either.

I scowl at my own thought, wishing I could remove all trace of Jackson Lauder from my lovesick brain.

Returning my attention to the stranger in the photo, I inspect him in more detail. Broad shoulders give way to muscular arms the dress jacket can't hide, and it's clear this guy works out. The cocky grin on his face is a little off-putting, but he has gorgeous features, and I haven't met any good-looking guy my age who isn't at least a little arrogant about his looks. His hair is more of a golden-blond color whereas the older guy's hair is a darker, dirtier shade of blond and his eyes are bluer, but there's no mistaking the resemblance—they are obviously father and son.

I have no idea who they are. I've never seen them before, and I don't know why someone would send me their picture. Unfolding the letter with shaky fingers, I have a strong sixth sense this letter is going to fundamentally change me.

My dearest Vanessa,

I'm sorry it has taken years to write this letter, but your mother and her husband concealed your existence, denying me the opportunity to be a father to you. I don't know what they have told you, or if they have told you anything at all, but my strongest desire is to connect with my daughter and to make up for lost time.

If I had known I had a daughter, I would

have been an active part of your life. I cannot fathom why your mother would keep you from me, or my son, your brother, Trenton.

I imagine this has come as a shock, but I hope it is a pleasant one. It is my greatest wish to meet with you. To finally get to know you. To love you like you deserve to be loved.

I presently reside overseas, and my business interests are such that I cannot travel to visit you, but I hope you will consider coming to visit me? I will make all the necessary arrangements, and I will send someone to collect you when the time is right.

You most likely have questions. Concerns. That is only natural. I hope this photograph of me with my son will help to put your mind at ease. As you can see, the resemblance between all of us is unmistakable. I knew you were my flesh and blood the minute I found you.

I hope you are settling into my alma mater and that you like your new home. I have established a trust fund for you and set up a bank account in your name. The details have been input to your new cell phone. I ask that you reserve this phone for communication with me. It's imperative that you don't mention we are in contact with one another.

Your mother and her husband kept you a secret from me for a reason, and I'm worried for your safety should anyone discover we are communicating.

I hope we can meet in the very near future. I think it's about time you got some answers. In the meantime, should you need me, please contact the number stored in the phone.

Yours lovingly,
C.M.

I clutch the letter in my fingers as I slump back on the couch, shocked and speechless. *What the ever-loving fuck?* My brain is fried, shooting conflicting thoughts around my skull. *Is this for real?* I pick the photo up again, examining it in more detail, and there is no doubt I share a strong resemblance to both men. *But is that enough to prove it?* I only have his word he's my father, and he didn't even sign it personally. Alarm bells are ringing in my head, but I'm intrigued too. Plus, there's everything he's done for me already. *Why would he go to such trouble and expense if he was lying?*

Mom spoke about my father one time and one time only. I was twelve, and Aaron had just taken my virginity. I lay in bed at night trembling in fear, praying for someone to rescue me. I remember begging God to send my real father to save me. I asked Mom about him the next day. I'd always known I had a different dad, because Aaron reminded me regularly that I wasn't his biological daughter. If he'd had a conscience, I'd say he did it to try to justify his actions, but that bastard had no moral compass, and the only reason he mentioned it was to put me in my place. To remind me I was lesser than him and to taunt me that my own father had abandoned me.

So, I asked Mom. I'm sure I asked when I was younger too, but I have no earlier recollection. However, I remember every word Mom said when I was twelve and I plucked up the courage to ask her who he was and where he was.

"Your father is dead, and there is to be no more mention of him in this house." She had gripped my arms hard, leaving more bruises. "Especially to Aaron." She made me promise not to breathe a word about him again, and I didn't.

Any notions I'd entertained of my real dad riding to the rescue evaporated that day. I have thought of him on occasions. Wondering what my life would have been like if he hadn't died. If I had grown up with him instead of that monster Aaron Breen.

Could it be true? Could this C.M. really be my dad? And why did Mom lie? I know he said not to talk to anyone, but that doesn't give me a warm and fuzzy feeling. I won't fly overseas to meet a man I've never met before just because he's thrown money at me and told me I'm his daughter.

He could be some sick stalker for all I know.

There's only one way to be sure.

I need to talk to Mom.

"Vanessa. This is a surprise," Mom says when she opens the door, not looking all that shocked to see me despite her words. She steps aside to let me in, glancing over my head, and biting her lip.

I look behind me before she closes the door. "What is it?"

"Nothing." She plasters a fake smile on her face. "I saw lights out on the road, and I was curious."

She slurs the last sentence, and I narrow my eyes at her. "Are you drunk?"

I trail her as she walks into the living room. "It's Friday night. I'm enjoying a few glasses of wine. There's no crime in that."

I'm about to open my mouth to criticize her for falling off the wagon when I remember my own recent descent from grace, so I purse my lips and push the criticism back down. I'll worry about that another time. Right now, I have more urgent questions.

"Would you like one?" She points at the half-empty bottle of white wine.

I shake my head. "I'm driving."

"Suit yourself." She proceeds to top her glass up, almost to the brim.

"Are the twins asleep?"

"They're not here. Kayleigh is at a sleepover at Ashley Stevens' house and Hunter is staying with Benjamin Peters this weekend."

"Since when are they allowed sleepovers?" I ask, perching on the edge of the couch.

"Since that bastard died," she snaps, downing a large mouthful of wine.

"Fair enough." Aaron was anal about not letting the twins out of his sight, and he never permitted sleepovers. I've always assumed it was because he was a control freak, but now, I think it was because he knew there were other monsters like him out there.

"I'm sure you didn't come here this late at night to discuss the twins' sleepovers. What do you want?"

"Wow. Nice to see you too, Mother," I hiss. "Can't I just be visiting?"

"Are you?" She arches a brow.

I sigh. "No. There is a reason for my visit."

I ignore her irritating condescending look and narrowly avoid flipping her the bird. Jackson is rubbing off on me.

Ugh. *Shut up, stupid brain.* I shake the asshole from my thoughts, remembering why I'm here.

Retrieving the photo from my purse, I silently hand it to her. She clutches it with trembling fingers, staring at it for so long I begin to suspect she's stopped breathing.

"I wondered how long it would take him to reach out to you now that Aaron is dead."

I grind my teeth to the molars. "So, you don't deny it? That you lied to me?"

"I did what I could to protect you."

I bark out a laugh. "Are you fucking kidding me?" I yell. Her words are like waving a red flag in front of my face. "You have never protected me! You knew your husband was raping me, and you let him climb into my bed night after night!" I screech.

She gulps back wine, flinching from my words and my tone. "I can't do this right now, Vanessa."

"No," I harrumph. "Of course, you can't. I don't know why I'm even bothering."

Silence engulfs us, and the air is heavy with years of unspoken questions and futile answers.

"Is it true? Is that man my father?" I ask when I've sufficiently calmed down.

There's a pregnant pause before she answers. "Yes. He's your father." Judging from the pained expression on her face, it hurt her to admit that.

"Why? Why did you tell me he was dead? How come he didn't know about me?"

I'm not really expecting her to answer, because Mom runs screaming from serious conversations that require her to be honest, but she shocks me by opening up a little. "I was only seventeen when I had you. I was so young. So naïve." She stares off into space as she talks. "Chris wanted to get married, but I didn't want to be tied down. He was older than me and getting pregnant was a ... mistake."

Just when I think she can't hurt me anymore, she says that. Squeezing my eyes shut, I fight tears. I shouldn't be surprised I was unwanted. It's not like she's done anything to make me feel I was. It's different hearing it spelled out so bluntly though.

I am ice. I am snow. I am made of stone.

I tug my walls up, banishing feeling, reminding myself I am numb to words that can hurt me.

"If I was such a mistake, why didn't you tell him? Let him take me?" My voice is so cold I almost don't sound like myself.

"I was going to give you up for adoption," she admits, turning to face me. "But the second you were born, I changed my mind. I took one look at your gorgeous little face, stared into your trusting eyes, and I knew I couldn't give you away."

If I hadn't bolstered my walls, I'd almost believe the emotion shimmering in her gaze and the tears spilling from her eyes are real.

"Why didn't you tell Chris about me then?"

She averts her gaze again. "I didn't want to be forced into marriage with a man I didn't love."

Oh, wow. This just keeps getting better and better.

"I got a job that came with a small studio apartment, and I found a daycare for you. I was determined to look after you. Then, I met Aaron, fell head over heels in love with him, and we were married one week before your first birthday. He

270

became your father then, and I didn't give Chris another thought."

"Fantastic choice by the way," I sneer. "You couldn't have picked a worse father for me."

I snatch the photo from her hand, slipping it back in my purse. I've heard enough. I had other questions, but I can't stay in her company a minute longer; otherwise, I'll be up on a murder charge. I got the confirmation I needed, and now, I want to get the fuck away from this bitch.

"I thought I was doing the right thing." Her pleading eyes don't work on me, because I'm immune.

"Why did you tell me he was dead?"

"Because he was in all the ways that mattered." She drains the last of her wine, grabbing the bottle and dumping the rest of it in her glass. "Aaron was a very jealous man. When he asked me who your father was, I lied. I needed you to protect that lie."

"How do you sleep at night?" I hiss. "You should never have been a mother because you don't know the meaning of that word."

"I know," she whispers, and that's the last thing I hear before I flee the house.

I pause at my car, bending over as delayed pain rips through my body, crippling me. I clutch my car, squeezing my eyes shut to ward off the tears.

Fuck her. I hate her and the choices she made that brought me to this point.

She doesn't want me. She never has.

No one ever does.

Aaron despised me, hurting me repeatedly, in so many ways.

Jackson used me, and now, he taunts me at every corner, reminding me how pathetic and weak I am.

It's only a matter of time before Sawyer gets fed up with me again, and I doubt Abby and Shandra will stick around once they know the real me.

No one wants me.

I'm an abomination that should never have existed.

That's not entirely true, that inner voice whispers in my ear. Someone does want me. Someone who would've loved me if he'd known. Someone who has already done more for me than anyone in my life, and we haven't even met.

Drying my tears, I remove the silver cell from my purse and pull up the only number stored there.

I tap out my first message to my father.

Me: I got your letter. I'd like to meet too. Love, Vanessa.

Chapter Twenty-Nine
Jackson

"Oh. My. Gawd!" Elle squeals so loud, my eardrums riot. She jumps on the seat beside me, her blonde curls bouncing around her shoulders, as she stares at the Rothwelds' mansion when it comes into view. Our driver maneuvers the limo around the water feature, gradually slowing down. Elle's eyes are out on stalks, and her mouth hangs open in a most unattractive manner. Honestly, it's like she's never seen a house before.

Hunt peers down his nose, hitting me with the full extent of his disapproval.

Get in line, dude.

I face this every single day. All my friends are disgusted with me, and though I am sick of arguing with everyone, it's not enough to derail my plans. Nessa is proving tougher to crack than expected. Begrudging admiration festers under my skin, but I shove that emotion aside. Admiration and Nessa no longer belong together. I cling to the last vestiges of my anger, reminding myself of what she's done, but it's getting harder to hold on to my hate. Harder to deny myself.

"I think I just died." Elle claps her hands, jumping around like a kindergartener let loose in a toy store. Her movement lifts the hem of her cheap, illuminous-pink dress even higher up her thighs, offering a glimpse of her equally gaudy, pink lace panties.

A shudder works its way up my spine, and I avert my gaze.

"Pity you didn't," Hunt says, doing nothing to hide his comment.

She's so tongue-tied over Edward's impressive red-brick traditional family home, with stately pillars and vine-covered walls, that she doesn't even hear him insulting her.

I sigh. It's going to be a long night.

Different women have adorned my arm every day for the past two weeks, and each one has annoyed the fuck out of me. I thought it was worth it to see the crestfallen look on Nessa's face, but I'm beginning to think the price *I'm* paying is too high, and Nessa's expression has gone from devastated to disgusted, so I'm not convinced this approach is working anymore. Their nonsensical chatter and those high-pitched giggles are irritating the fuck out of me. I'm worried my brain has stopped functioning with the lack of intelligent conversation.

Don't even get me started on my dick. That sucker hasn't risen his head for any of them. Not even when I've got a chick planted on my lap at lunchtime. Shocker, I know. It would be easier if my cock showed some life, but nope, he has zero interest in even attempting to get any of them in bed.

Chuckling to myself, I imagine Nessa's reaction to the daily texts I've been sending her. I had the biggest smile on my face the time she blocked me. That's how I knew I was getting to her, so I've continued to send her daily pictures. First pic was some chick I slept with from my West Lorian days, but all the others have been photos I've downloaded from the web. Let her think I'm sleeping with the women I parade around RU when the truth is I haven't even locked lips with most of them.

I have forced myself to kiss a couple of girls in front of her, purely to piss her off, yet I fear I've pissed myself off worse. Fooling around with these girls is sucking the life out of me, and I can't do it any longer. I will find more creative ways to ruin Nessa instead.

"No way!" Elle screeches at the top of her lungs, and my ears protest again.

If looks could kill, Hunt would've just buried me six feet under.

"They have those servant people carrying floats of champagne."

"Do you purposely go out of your way to find lobotomized females, or is it purely accidental?" Hunt inquires as the driver opens the limo door.

"Their IQ score is generally not on my list of requirements."

"I've noticed," Hunt drawls, as we climb out behind my date. "Fake tits and annoying hyena laughs appear to be essential traits though. Can't say I'm fond of either."

"Nor me," I mutter before I think better of it.

Hunt tugs on my elbow, holding me back. Elle skips toward the front door like a kangaroo on speed. "Quit this shit already. You're dividing the group and pissing everyone off. Keep this up, and you'll be lucky to have any friends left."

"Can we skip the lecture for one fucking night, Hunt? I'm not the only one pissing people off."

"Just drop the animosity toward Van. We don't have an issue with her. Hate her in silence, from a distance, if you must, but give the rest of us a break. We're not in high school anymore," he adds as we walk toward the door. "Unless you didn't get the memo."

"I'll think about it," I huff, purely to get the fucker off my back before he annoys me again.

"About fucking time." He thumps me on the back, and I swing for him. Ducking down, he laughs when my fist meets empty air. He saunters into the house, accepting two glasses of champagne from the haughty-looking waiter standing in the hallway.

I trail after him, cursing him under my breath.

"Hey, Elle," he calls out, and my date stops in front of us, turning around way too fast in those skyscraper heels. She manages to stay upright, but only just. Her eyes are as big as saucers as she takes in the plush surroundings.

"Picked you up another *float*." Hunt raises a glass of champagne, and she instantly downs the one in her hand. Looking around, she dumps her empty flute on a lamp table beside an ornate vase that looks old as shit. In her haste to reach Hunt, her hip collides with the corner of the table, and it wobbles precariously. I react fast, jumping forward and catching the vase before it falls. I'm less lucky with the empty glass though. It shatters into tiny pieces on the porcelain floor, capturing the attention of every person in the hallway.

I'll need to get totally wasted if I'm to survive this party with my sanity intact.

"Oops." Elle giggles, sipping on her new glass of champagne like she hasn't just embarrassed herself and me.

"Elle." Hunt's sly tone suggests he's up to no good. "You wouldn't happen to be named after Elle Woods by any chance?"

"Huh?" Elle's face scrunches up, and she's looking less and less attractive by the second.

"She was a character played by Reese Witherspoon in a movie called *Legally Blonde*," Hunt explains.

I chuckle. Xavier's influence is showing.

"I don't think so," Elle replies, looking thoroughly confused by this conversation, and that makes two of us.

"She had the same first name. She loved the color pink." Hunt gestures toward Elle's dress. "She was ditzy as fuck and … oh, that's where the comparison ends because she was actually intelligent behind the cutesy exterior and you." He bores a hole in her skull, and I almost feel sorry for her. "You're every bit as dumb and annoying as you look."

"Sawyer!" Abby's chastising tone echoes off the high ceiling as she stomps toward us, her heels clicking off the floor as she approaches. "Don't tell me *you've* resurrected your mean gene too!" She thumps Hunt in the arm.

"He *is* mean," Elle agrees, slurping her champagne like it's soda.

Like I said, it's going to be a long night.

"I commiserate," a familiar voice says, raising all the hairs on the back of my neck. "I used to have shit taste in men too until the last asshole helped me see sense," Nessa adds, ghosting past me like I'm the one who doesn't exist. Musky, sweet, vanilla scents tickle my nostrils as her hypnotic perfume swirls around me, sending me back to nights when she was wrapped in my arms and everything felt right with the world.

I've never felt more…me than when I was with Vanessa. Her presence in my life soothed my frayed edges, and, for the first time in years, I was happy.

It was all a lie. The tetchy devil on my shoulder reminds me of what's important.

It's not how fucking hot she looks in that figure-hugging short red strapless dress. Or how long her legs appear encased in gorgeous gold strappy sandals. Or how silky smooth her hair looks falling down her back in sleek sheets. I can't see her face from this angle, because she's refusing to acknowledge me, but I know what I'd find if I could.

Perfection personified.

A goddess sculpted with the finest hand. A temptress plucked straight from my dreams.

She's the enemy.

She betrayed you.

Played you.

Made you fall for her and look like a fool.

That is the only truth that matters, and I hate that I constantly need to remind myself.

Of course, my dick refuses to cooperate, stirring to life for the first time since I jerked off this morning to thoughts of *her*. It's as if Nessa has cast a spell on my cock, meaning it only gets hard for her.

She walks ahead with Abby and Shandra, turning the corner like a graceful gazelle, granting me a perfect side view, and God-fucking-damn it, she's sensational. Hands down, the most beautiful woman I've ever seen. My cock hardens painfully behind my zipper, and I silently curse my stupid hormones for not getting with the program. Discreetly, I adjust myself in my dark jeans, cautioning my dick to calm the fuck down.

She's only a pussy. Nothing special about her. At all.

"You look like you need a drink or ten," Anderson says, clamping his hand on my shoulder. I hadn't seen or heard him come in, but as soon as Abby appeared, I knew he wasn't far behind.

"You'll need the same once you meet Elle," Hunt drawls.

"Elle?" Anderson lifts his brows. "Do I even want to ask?"

"Jack-sun!" As if on cue, my date materializes in front of me, clutching another glass of champagne, collapsing into my arms.

"Is she drunk already?" Anderson asks, his lips curving at the corners.

"Yup," Hunt replies. "Fun times." He yanks Anderson by the elbow, pulling him away from us. "Enjoy your night, Lauder. Nice knowing you." Hunt grins, stalking off with Anderson, both chuckling as they leave me to my fate.

Assholes.

Taking Elle's hand, I follow the others into the belly of the house in the direction of the music.

I've got to hand it to Edward Rothweld—dude knows how to throw a party.

Beats pulse through various speakers mounted around the large ballroom. A celebrity DJ spins tunes from the stage at the top of the room. Waiters carry canapes and glasses of champagne as they move around the space. Partygoers swamp the free bar at the right-hand side of the room. No red cups of warm beer or cheap vodka shots are available tonight. Only premium brands, craft beers, lush cocktails, and expensive champagne will do for the eldest son of one of Rydeville's most prominent politicians.

The Rothwelds aren't one of the founding families, like Abby's, Anderson's, or Barron's families, but they are in the upper echelons of elite society.

Although this isn't an official elite event—there's no dress code, no old perverts in sight, and it's a mixed college crowd of elite and non-elite—appearances clearly still matter to Edward.

Elle clings to my arm as we take a quick tour so I can get my bearings.

Dancers throw shapes on the large dance floor in the center of the room. Circular tables surround the space on all sides. A door at the top of the room leads to another spacious area with a separate bar and more casual seating. Low couches are dotted around the room, mixed with high tables and stools.

Open French doors lead outside to an impressive patio with more seated areas, bordered by manicured lawns housing an array of colorful shrubs and flowers. The pool is covered, and all the lights are off in the adjoining pool house. It's clear Roth-weld runs a tight ship, keeping revelers away from family heirlooms or places he doesn't want them exploring.

Heading back inside, I let my gaze roam the room, looking for an exquisite creature in an eye-catching red dress. Elle wanders toward the bar while I search the crowd because I clearly love punishing myself.

It doesn't take long to locate Nessa, and I'm not that surprised to discover she's the center of attention on the dance floor. A muscle ticks in my jaw as I watch the predators circling the girls as they dance, seemingly oblivious to the attention they're garnering. The flashy diamond on Abby's ring finger lets them know she's off-limits. Most everyone at this party knows who she is, who Anderson is, and that Shandra Farrell may no longer be engaged to Drew Manning, but that doesn't mean she's fair game either.

Which leaves Nessa.

The mystery woman in the stunning red dress, commanding the floor as she sways her hips in time to the music, tossing her long dark-blonde locks over her shoulders, dancing like she hasn't a care in the world.

The vultures are salivating as they vie for her attention, and I'm primed and ready to go to war.

Chapter Thirty
Jackson

"Still denying you love her?" Hunt asks, appearing at my side. He hands me a beer, and I momentarily consider dumping it over his head.

"Enough already." I drain half the beer in one go.

"You're going to lose her if you don't retrieve your head from your ass," Anderson adds, coming up on the other side of me. His eyes lock on Abby, and from his tense stance, I know he's ready to go to war too. One stray hand. One flirty smile. One wrong move, and Anderson will wade into the crowd to defend Abby's honor. Doesn't matter she's damn capable of defending her own honor. That's just the way he rolls.

"Would you both stop talking like you know how I feel. It's irritating as fuck."

"You think I haven't been where you are?" Anderson asks, briefly ungluing his eyes from Abby. "I understand more than you realize."

"How come you can trust Nessa just like that?" I snap my fingers, finishing my beer, and dumping it on a tray as a waiter walks by. I snag a glass of champagne even though it's not my drink of choice, but I need to get drunk and fast.

"I agree with Hunt. She *has* changed, and everyone deserves a second chance. Even Vanessa."

"Have you forgotten the package she received yesterday?" I glance between them. "Wake the fuck up. He just sent her a burner cell. It's hardly so he can read her bedtime stories."

"All that proves is he's reached out to her. You can tell she's shocked by the expression on her face in the footage." Hunt jumps to her defense again. Shocker.

"It's a pity you couldn't read the contents of the letter," Anderson adds. "That would help clarify things."

"We've zoomed in, but it's too blurry," Hunt says. "Xavier knows a dude who might be able to clean it up so it's legible."

"Or you can ask Abby to find the letter and take a picture of it," I suggest.

Anderson swings around on me, his dark eyes flashing with warning. "Abby is her friend, not your fucking spy. She's dropping hints, hoping Nessa will open up to her, but that's for her benefit, not yours. Abby is worried about her."

"So am I," Hunt adds just as Elle returns. "I don't like it."

Neither do I, but for different reasons. It's why I sicced a PI on Nessa this week, something I haven't told the others. They would go apeshit on my ass. Especially the girls, spouting invasion of privacy, etcetera. Fuck that shit. If Montgomery is in contact, it's only a matter of time before he makes himself known. Either she'll do his bidding or she'll go to him or maybe both. I want to know, and I want to be there. It might be the only opportunity I get.

"I wanna dance," Elle slurs, pouting as she drapes herself all over me.

Why the fuck did I bring her? Oh yeah, to annoy Nessa,

only she couldn't care less. She hasn't once looked in my direction tonight. I should have attended solo with Hunt.

"Oh shit." Hunt almost chokes on his beer, and my head whips back around to Nessa, all the blood slowly draining from my face.

She's dancing with some dude I've never seen before. Pressed up against one another, they are face to face, and she has her arms around his neck while his hands are on her waist as he bends down, whispering in her ear.

"Who is that fucker?" I blurt before I can stop myself.

"What fucker?" Elle slurs, her eyes following my line of sight. "Wow. He's one hot tatted sexy beast." Irritation crawls over my skin, and I grind down on my teeth before tuning her out.

"No idea," Anderson says. "I've never seen him before."

"He looks shady as fuck," Hunt adds, extracting his cell.

"No shit, Sherlock," I hiss, eyeing the guy with suspicion as Hunt taps away on his phone. A deep scar trails from his left eye across his temple and into his shorn dark hairline. Tats cover his arms, disappearing under his black T-shirt, emerging at both sides of his neck. He's tall, built, and wearing ripped jeans and scuffed boots to an exclusive party, which means he's clearly not from around here. He sticks out like a sore thumb, and he knows it. But he clearly has zero fucks to give. Dude exudes vibes that suggest he's not to be messed with. "What the fuck is she doing dancing with him?" I snap.

"Nessa always liked living on the edge," Hunt replies, looking up from his cell. "Looks like that part of her personality hasn't changed."

"How the hell did he get in here anyway?" I glance around, looking for Rothweld so I can get him to throw this punk out on his ass.

Of course, he's nowhere in the vicinity, because that would be too convenient. I could look for him, but I don't want to leave Nessa alone with that guy. My eyes home in on his hands as they move lower, landing on her ass, and I growl, cursing under my breath.

Elle wraps her arm around my waist, and I instantly remove it, stepping sideways to create space between us. I can't stand her touching me, and I need to get rid of her fast.

Nessa and the asshole are dirty dancing now, grinding their hips and pawing at one another, and rage infiltrates my system, sweeping through me like a river overflowing its banks. "What the fuck does she see in him?" I seethe. "He looks like he just walked off the set of *Sons of Anarchy*."

"Oh my God. I love that show," Elle unhelpfully mumbles, reaching out for me again. "Jax Teller is so fucking hot."

I push her away, swiping another glass of champagne and handing it to her. "Knock yourself out, sweetheart."

"Lauder." Hunt's tone carries warning.

"Relax, Dad. She's my date. I'll look out for her and make sure she gets home."

I'm not a total prick.

Removing my cell from my jeans pocket, I tap out a message to the driver to return. I'll send Elle on her merry way so I can focus on protecting Nessa from creeper dude, because that shit will not end well.

Nausea climbs up my throat when I lock eyes on Nessa again. Pinpricks puncture my aching heart as I watch her kissing him in the middle of the dance floor. Hands clench at my side, my muscles lock tight, and every inch of my being demands I storm over there and reclaim what's mine.

"Easy, tiger," Hunt says, noticing my reaction because that dude misses nothing.

"I don't like him," I hiss.

"Who?" Elle frowns, a dazed look in her eyes as she glances

around, stumbling a little. I grab her elbow to steady her before letting go.

"Course, you don't." Anderson smirks. "Payback's a bitch."

"Whose fucking side are you on?"

"The side where you fucking open your eyes and see what's staring you in the face."

"Come on." I grab Elle's arm, not taking my eyes off Nessa as she makes her way through the crowd on the dance floor, hand in hand with the asshole.

"Dude."

"Fuck off, Hunt."

"Leave it, Lauder." Anderson shakes his head. "You'll piss her off, along with Abby and Shandra, if you interfere."

"Like you wouldn't do the same," I scoff.

He shrugs, fighting a smirk, because he knows I'm right. "Your funeral."

Leaving my friends, I tow an inebriated Elle along with me while I stalk after Nessa and the asshole.

They stop just behind the door to the other room, and I pull Elle over into the corner. It's quieter and darker here, which makes it perfect for spying. The asshole has his back to the wall, and Nessa is pressed up against him, her hands resting on his broad chest. I want to rip them off him before laying into the prick for even daring to breathe on her.

She's mine.

A territorial growl gurgles up my throat, and it's taking every ounce of self-control not to smash the guy's face into the wall. How fucking *dare* he touch her.

"Bryant," Nessa purrs in that sultry sexy voice I love. "I like it. A sexy name for a sexy guy."

I cough-laugh; I can't help it. That is cheesy as fuck. Not that you'd know it from the guy's expression. He's peering at her with an amused-slash-lust-filled gaze I know all too well.

Nessa's head whips around, and I yank Elle in front of me, pulling us farther into the corner, burying my head in her shoulder so it looks like we're making out.

"I'm glad I came here tonight," the asshole says. "Was planning on ditching, but I changed my mind at the last minute."

"You're not from around here either, are you?" Nessa asks.

Elle palms my dick as her lips suction on my neck, making a slurping sound. Slapping her hand away, I grab her champagne flute, placing it against her lips. "Not now, babe," I whisper. "I just want to hold you." *Gag.* She falls for it though, holding on to me with a dreamy expression on her face. "I think I already love you," she slurs.

Gee, lucky me.

Okay, I am a bona fide prick. I'll own that shit, but she's driving me mad, getting in the way of my stalking. I purposely zone her out, refocusing on Nessa and the jerk, subtly lifting my head and watching them over Elle's shoulder.

"Prestwick?" Nessa says. "That's California, right?"

"Yeah."

"How come you're here? Who do you know?"

"A dude I know from way back is friends with the guy who's throwing the party," he says. "We are visiting for a few days and that's how I scored an invite."

He runs his fingers through her hair, and I bite the inside of my mouth so hard I taste blood.

Fuck, I need a drink.

Snatching my half-empty glass of champagne from the ledge I left it on, I swallow it in one go.

"How about you?" he asks, palming her ass and pulling her in flush against his dick.

I tighten my arms around Elle's waist because I need to hold on to something to stop myself from going over there and landing a punch on his smug face.

"Friends from college know Edward Rothweld. I piggy-backed on their invitation."

"You go to college around here?"

"Yeah. RU. What about you?"

"I think that's enough small talk, don't you?" His flirty statement is a clear deflection. One look at the guy, and you know he's not a student. Doubt the punk even got his high school diploma. It's not like he can admit he sells drugs or guns because, let's face it, it's got to be one or the other.

Screw me if I sound judgmental. I couldn't give two shits. That asshole has his hands all over *my woman*, and I'm two seconds away from going postal on his ass.

My cell vibrates in my pocket, and I pull it out, reading the message confirming our driver is here. I'm conflicted. I really don't want to leave Nessa. Especially now that the asshole has his tongue shoved down her throat. But I need to send Elle on her merry way before I sort that fucker out, and she's far too drunk to leave to her own devices.

So, I do the decent thing and escort my date outside, placing her protesting ass in the car before handing the driver her address, telling him to return as soon as he's done.

When I return to the ballroom, Nessa and the punk are gone, and my blood pressure rockets into coronary-inducing levels.

I race to where Anderson and Hunt are still standing guard at the side of the dance floor. Abby and Shandra are oblivious to the fact their new friend has gone AWOL with some degenerate. I grip Hunt's shoulders. "Where did Nessa go?"

He glances at the door, where I last saw them, confirming he had eyeballs on her for some of the time. "She was there a few minutes ago."

"Well she's not fucking there now!" I'm aware I'm

screeching like an overwrought female on her period. Zero fucks to give.

"Relax." Hunt shoves my hands off his shoulders. "She's a grown-ass woman. She knows what she's doing."

"Hunt." I thump him in the arm. "She's probably drunk, and he's taking advantage right now."

"She's been drinking water all night. She's completely sober," Hunt confirms. "If she's gone off with that dude, it's consensual."

"Did you not see him? He's a fucking delinquent!"

"Rothweld vouched for him," Hunt coolly replies.

"That makes me feel so much better," I retort, sarcasm thick in my tone.

"Then you probably don't want to know he's a member of The Arrows, a notorious gang from Prestwick in Cali," he adds on purpose to piss me off.

I thump him in the arm. "How could you let her go off with him? Ugh." I drag my hands repeatedly through my hair, debating whether to stay and punch my best friend or chase after my girl.

Anderson cracks up laughing. "Oh, how the mighty have fallen. This is too funny."

"This isn't fucking funny, fucker." I grab fistfuls of my hair, pacing in front of them. "I need to find her right now. I need to make sure she's okay."

"Sure, you do." Anderson's smug grin makes me want to punch him. "Admit you're jealous, and we'll help you find her."

"Fuck you and your juvenile ass."

"You are in no position to throw stones," Hunt says. "You've been acting like a five-year-old whose puppy was kicked for weeks."

"Fine, I'm jealous." I give in without further argument,

because three bodies searching this vast house is better than one. "Now will you help me find her?"

We split up, taking different parts of the mansion. It helps that most of the house has been cordoned off to partygoers. I sprint along the back corridor that intersects the ballroom from the main living section, frantically opening and closing doors, my heart beating out of control at the thought of what could be happening right this fucking second.

It doesn't matter whether it's consensual or not.

If that dude has laid his hands on any part of her naked flesh, I will fucking kill him with my bare hands.

Moans filter from a room on my left, and I slam to a halt, blood rushing to my head. I tug at the door handle, but it's locked. I curse under my breath, panic welling inside me until it feels like I might explode.

"Go away!" a man with a deep, rumbling voice says, and I recognize the asshole instantly.

"Nessa! Open this fucking door right now!" I hammer my fists on the wood.

"Fuck off, Jackson," she yells before adding, "Ignore him. He'll go away."

The moaning starts again, and it could be my imagination, but it seems even louder this time. A red haze coats my eyes as anger shuttles through me like a tornado hell-bent on destruction. I slam my shoulder into the door repeatedly, my anger mounting to dangerous levels, but it barely budges.

"Get lost, Jackson!" Nessa screeches. "I fucking hate you! Go back to Bottle-blonde Barbie and get her to suck your dick." She's pissed, but she doesn't know me at all if she thinks that'll make me leave. Clearly, she wasn't as oblivious as she pretended to be, and that spurs me on too.

Hushed conversation ensues behind the door, but I can't

make out the words. A minute later, the moaning restarts, and I'm officially all out of patience.

My eyes dart wildly around the hallway, looking for something I can use to attack the door, but there isn't anything suitable in sight.

Walking back the way I came, I quickly open and shut doors until I discover a wall-mounted fire extinguisher in a small utility room. Unclipping it from the brackets, I race out into the hallway and over to the door where Nessa and that asshole are hiding out. Using the extinguisher to hammer at the door handle, I aggressively swing it over and over until the handle gives way and the door pops open.

I crash into the large bathroom, blood pounding in my head and fists clenching. Bile floods my mouth when I take in the scene before me.

The dickhead has Nessa pinned against the wall, and his hand is moving underneath her dress. A primal growl travels up my throat, and I let it loose as something snaps inside me. I lose all sense of reality. Red-hot possessive rage courses through my veins, and I lunge at the guy just as he moves Nessa to the side.

She's screaming. He's shouting, cracking his knuckles, and swinging at me, but I barely hear it, barely register anything over the rage consuming me from the inside.

We fight. Throwing multiple punches and jabs. Clothes rip. Blood flies. Glass shatters. Pain ricochets in my skull and shoots across my torn knuckles, but it only encourages me to fight harder to protect what's mine.

This dude is more ripped than me, but what I lack in muscle power, I make up for in sheer aggression. It's pouring out of me like a river overflowing its banks. I hardly feel his hits. I just keep lashing out, matching him punch for punch, swinging and diving, thumping and kicking.

It only stops when we're forcibly dragged away from one another.

"Jesus Christ, Lauder." Anderson has a vise grip on my arms, pulling me off to one side of the room while I thrash about. Wet warmth trickles over my lips, dripping down on to my shirt. "Calm the fuck down," he hisses in my ear. "You're barely even human right now, and you're scaring Nessa."

That is possibly the only thing he could say that would work.

Gradually, my pulse slows, my heartbeat steadies, and my surroundings come into focus.

The bathroom is trashed. Toilet lid broken. Tiles splintered. Jagged cracks mar the old-fashioned tub that has probably been in the family for generations. The mirror lies shattered in pieces. Blood splatters mix with torn shirts and pieces of glass, scattered around the floor.

The asshole glares at me with naked hatred in his eyes. Blood leaks from his nose, his lip is split, and he has a few other facial cuts. His shirt is ripped, exposing a chest mottled from my punches. I have no doubt if I had a mirror it would confirm I'm in a similar state.

I sag against Anderson as all the fight leaves my body. My eyes find Nessa's, and terror shoots up my spine. She's huddled against Hunt, wrapped in his arms, staring at me with disbelieving eyes. Her expression is a combination of fear, disgust, and loathing, and something inherent dies inside me with the realization I have majorly, epically, fucked up.

"Nessa," I croak, wriggling in Anderson's grip, urging him to let me go.

"Don't make it any worse than it already is," Anderson pleads in a low tone. I force my body to relax, nodding, and he releases me, seemingly satisfied I'm not going to go apeshit on the dude's ass again.

I take a step toward the girl who holds my heart in the palm of her hand. The only girl to ever bring me to my knees.

There's no point denying it anymore.

I am so fucked when it comes to Vanessa Breen.

I am completely and utterly under her spell.

It doesn't matter that she's betrayed me.

I fucking want her so much. I miss her so much.

"Babe." I take a step toward her.

Her eyes immediately narrow to slits. "Don't call me that. I'm not your babe. I'm not your anything." Revulsion is evident on her face, because she's doing nothing to shield it from me. She wants me to see that I disgust her. That I've crossed a line. I have pushed her too far.

Stepping out of Hunt's protective embrace, she squares up to me. "You make me sick. I don't know what I ever saw in you. Stay the hell away from me, Jackson. I want nothing more to do with you."

Chapter Thirty-One
Jackson

"D oes it hurt?" Hunt asks, watching me gently prod my nose. We're at Abby and Kai's house, having Sunday dinner with the whole crew. Olivia—Abby and Drew's mom—and her friend Sylvia are also here.

Sylvia used to be married to that bastard Christian Montgomery, and Trent was her son. I killed Trent during the shootout at the Parkhurst vote, so it's fair to say I'm not on her list of favorite people. The last time we attended dinner here, she pulled me aside to tell me she has forgiven me, because she understands it was self-defense. It took a lot of balls to say that, and I respect her for it, but things are still strained, as I suspect they always will be.

Hunt is staring at me with concern, waiting for a reply.

"Hurts like a bitch," I quietly admit, not wanting Barron to hear. Charlie punched me earlier when I made a rude comment to his new girlfriend, Demi. I deserved it, because I was way out of line, but I'm in a permanent bad mood these days, lashing out at everyone and everything.

It's been three weeks since the disastrous party at the Rothwelds', but it feels more like three years. Nessa is ghosting me, completely shutting me out of her life, and I'm a hot mess. She wouldn't even come for dinner; persistently refusing Abby's invitation when she discovered I'd be here, and she only hangs around with the others when I'm not involved.

She hates my guts now. Not that I can really blame her. I have treated her like shit, and now, I'm paying the ultimate price.

My emotions are out of whack, and I flip-flop between love and hatred in the blink of an eye. One part of me pines for the sweet girl I fell for over the summer, lamenting her loss, and missing the feel of her in my arms. The other part is still convinced she betrayed me, that she has earned my wrath, reminding me it's better this way. The intensity of my erratic emotions has me ping-ponging all over the place, and I'm going to give myself a brain aneurysm if I can't quiet the turmoil in my head. The purple shadows under my eyes attest to my many sleepless nights, and I'm seriously losing my mind over this girl.

"Serves you right," Hunt adds. "You've turned into a raging asshole. You need to fix shit with Nessa before you drive us all insane with your crazy mood swings."

I flip him the bird. "I apologized to Charlie and Demi, and I've been on my best behavior since."

It's been a strange-ass day. Xavier discovered evidence confirming Demi is cousins with Abby and Drew. Their grandmothers were sisters, apparently. It certainly helps explain the striking similarity between the two girls that had everyone freaking out.

At one time, I harbored notions of finding my own Abby clone. Now, Charlie has found one, but all I can think about is a certain blonde beauty who has messed with my internal wiring. I can't get Nessa out of my head, and I'm driving myself loopy.

I secretly watch Charlie and Demi across the table, envying their obvious closeness.

Abby has been dogged in her determination to bring Charlie back into the fold, and it looks like she's succeeding. He's certainly easier to be around now that he has the lovely Demi by his side. He appears to be in a better place, looking more relaxed and content than I've ever seen him. I don't begrudge the dude his happiness although I'm still wary of him.

A pang of longing bites me in the ass, and I wish Nessa were here. It would be seamless. My friends already like her, and she'd fit right into the gang with zero effort. But I think that ship has sailed. I'll be lucky if she ever speaks to me again, let alone anything else. I purposely adjust my train of thought, refocusing on the discussion around the table, before I sink into depression again.

The topic of conversation has switched to the elite and the recent appointment of William Hamilton as the new president of the order has incited lively discussion. Drew, Charlie, Kai, and Rick are all expected to be initiated as full members soon because they are the descendants of founding elite fathers. It's not something any of us are comfortable with because the organization is composed of leaders and members who are sick bastards with their hands in several cookie jars.

"What do we know about the new president?" Drew asks Xavier.

"William Hamilton is the eldest son of a founding father from Texas. Family comes from oil. He's married with two daughters. He was one of the men swindled by Christian and one of the very few who publicly opposed Michael Hearst for president. He has spoken out about the archaic rules and asserted his desire to modernize the elite."

"Sounds squeaky clean," I cut in. "I'm not buying it." While Hunt, Xavier and I don't have anything official to do with the elite, we support our friends, so the latest developments are just as concerning to us. I also know whatever Christian has planned for Nessa is tied up in this, so I've more than a vested interest in what goes down.

"Neither did we," Hunt says, putting his glass down. "So, we did some investigating on the darknet—"

"And this guy makes Michael Hearst look like the fairy fucking godmother," Xavier finishes.

"Do you have to cut across me every time?" Hunt's lips pull into a thin line as he glares at Xavier. I've still no idea what is happening with them. I haven't asked, because my own messy love life is torturous enough, but I've spied Xavier sneaking in and out of the house on several occasions, so I know they're still fucking.

"No need to get your panties in a bunch. We play for the same team, remember?" Xavier flashes him a cheeky grin.

"Just tell us what you discovered," Abby says, exasperation lacing her tone. "And keep your foreplay confined to the bedroom."

Hunt fixes Abby with a withering look, and Anderson, predictably, glares at him.

Charlie whispers something in Demi's ear, and when she smiles, she looks so much like Abby it knocks the air out of my lungs again. Freaky as fuck, those two.

Xavier clears his throat. "It's the usual elite bullshit. Professional businessman with legit businesses that are all a front for a host of illegal activities, but this guy is into everything."

"And we mean *everything*." Hunt cuts off his lover this time, but Xavier just smiles, further incensing him. Hunt clenches his jaw as he speaks, looking like he's about to explode. "Drugs, guns, sex, and it's a global operation worth *billions*."

"This is like déjà vu," Abby says, leaning back into Anderson's chest.

"Round two is due to begin," Drew agrees. "And we need to get battle ready."

The conversation moves to the FBI investigation now winding down. Keven Kennedy believes the elite has some powerful authority figures on their payroll and that a few scapegoats paid the price in return for making it all blow over. It fucking sickens me that these people get away with kidnapping, rape, murder, and all the illegal activities they hide behind respectable fronts.

We met with Keven last week to discuss our belief that Dani may have been held on Gerald Allen Junior's sex island, and he's going to see what he can dig up and whether he can find any link between him and Montgomery.

The guy is a fucking diamond. One of the nicest guys I've met, and we owe him so much already. He's also intelligent, with sharp instincts, so if there is dirt to be discovered, I'm confident Keven is the man to locate it.

Tension erupts when Abby suggests Charlie needs to bring Demi up to speed, because the world we mix in is a dangerous one, where family members and loved ones are used as pawns as commonly as sneezing.

The thought makes me uneasy. If Hunt and the others are correct, and Nessa isn't in cahoots with her bio dad, then she is in grave danger. Especially with the elite ball scheduled for next month.

The new board and structure will be unveiled by Hamilton, and it's going to be a huge deal with every elite member across the state in attendance. The fate of my friends will most likely be revealed then, so we're all on edge waiting to find out what he has in store for them.

By now, Hamilton knows the full extent of what we did back in Wyoming—we almost succeeded in bringing the elite to their knees. There is no way he'll let that go unpunished.

The guys and I clear up after dinner while the ladies talk in the living room. After a few photos are taken, Demi and Charlie say their goodbyes. Olivia and Sylvia are next to go, leaving the usual gang.

We sip beers at the table while Anderson tries to get Rick on the phone. Rick is Anderson's eldest brother. He lives in Boston, and he's studying to be a doctor at Harvard. One of his best friends is Kyler Kennedy—Keven's brother. Their friendship has proven rewarding in several ways. The Kennedys have gotten us out of more than one tight spot over the past year, and they're great friends to have.

Rick was supposed to be here today, but he went to meet with a senior elite member who is on the reorganizing committee. Apparently, this guy is a decent dude—one of the few within the elite world—and we're hoping he might be of some help.

"Sup, dude?" Anderson says, answering the phone when Rick returns his call. "I'm putting you on speaker."

"Hi, Rick," Shandra purrs, smiling flirtatiously even though Rick can't see her. Drew scowls, but I'm guessing that's the point.

"Hey, pretty lady," Rick replies, knowing he's winding Manning up.

I smirk while Anderson snorts, and Drew's scowl deepens.

"How did your meeting go?" Abby asks, focusing the conversation before it turns into a bloodbath.

"Good, I think."

"That sounds hopeful. Not," Hunt drawls, earning a thump to the arm from Abby.

"Let the man speak, for God's sake." She rolls her eyes, and Anderson preens like a peacock. He loves when she gets all feisty and bossy.

"Robert Huss seems like a solid guy," Rick starts explaining.

"One of the few good ones, but it's obvious he's already frustrated at the direction the reorganizing committee is heading in. He shares our concerns. The most alarming thing to come out of the conversation was confirmation that Denton Mathers is a close confidante of William Hamilton. Hamilton, as we know, was defrauded by Montgomery."

"And Mathers was tight with Montgomery," Shandra butts in. "Which makes little sense."

"That doesn't matter to these assholes," Drew says. "Loyalty is transient and negotiable for the right price. Hamilton is from Texas. Mathers is from Bama. They run in the same business and social circles, and I bet they share similar beliefs, posing as devout Catholics every Sunday while they conduct illegal shit and acts of depravity every other day of the week. It doesn't matter if Mathers was or is close to Montgomery if Hamilton needs him."

"Huss said the presidential vote was close and Hamilton did what was necessary to secure the votes needed," Rick says, confirming Drew's point.

"That's reassuring," I deadpan, cricking my neck from side to side.

"We've got to assume Mathers had something to bargain with," Anderson says.

"Or he is playing both sides," Abby suggests.

"That sounds just like him," Xavier agrees.

"Huss thinks it's definitely connected to Montgomery, in part," Rick adds.

All the hairs on the back of my neck bristle, and I brace myself, because I know something's coming that I won't like.

"Hamilton must hate Montgomery after his company was overcharged by Christian's," Xavier surmises.

"Undoubtedly, but Montgomery is a founding father, and he carries clout," Rick supplies.

"But he's MIA and there's an international warrant out for his arrest," Hunt says. His troubled eyes meet mine, and I know he's picking up the same vibes I am.

"Huss believes Montgomery has done some deal with Hamilton with Mathers as conduit. Montgomery has lost a lot of influence, but there are those who still owe him a few favors. Huss thinks he called in those favors to help Hamilton get elected."

"What does Montgomery get in return?" I ask, gripping the edge of my chair tight.

"Huss thinks Montgomery wants Hamilton's help in getting the warrant squashed so he can come back to the US." Rick pauses for a couple beats.

"Just spit it out, Rick," I hiss. My knee taps off the floor, and anxiety has corded the muscles in my shoulders into knots.

"They know about Vanessa," Rick says in a quieter tone. Anderson has been filling him in, so he's aware Nessa is in Rydeville. He knows what has gone down between us, and he understands the danger she's in whether she's a willing participant in this game or not.

"Christian has signed his elite rights over to her temporarily by proxy," he adds, confirming something we've suspected. "Huss said he believes they are already grooming her for this world so she'll do his bidding until he's in a position to return. It's a win-win for Montgomery and Hamilton. Hamilton has Mather's and Montgomery's other supporters on his side, plus he gets Montgomery's vote for each of the initiatives he wants to bring in, and Montgomery is given a get-out-of-jail-free card."

I jump up, and my chair falls to the floor with a loud thud. "Over my dead fucking body!" I yell.

I know they can make this happen. The scandal has blown

over. They've handed over a few scapegoats, paving the way for that prick to return to the US.

Around the table, everyone trades concerned looks, but it's telling that no one speaks. No one offers platitudes or words of encouragement because we all know there are no words that can instill confidence.

Christian is still one step ahead of us, and we all know it.

"Van is the key to this," Hunt says, fixing my chair and pushing me back down into it. "I think we have to take our chances and ask her outright what she knows."

"I'm with Hunt," Anderson agrees.

"Me too," Rick adds.

Abby clears her throat, claiming my undivided attention. "I know what you believe, Jackson." She leans forward on her elbows so she's looking me straight in the eye. "But I don't think Nessa has any idea of what's going on. I've briefly mentioned elite stuff, and all she seems to know is what's in the public domain."

"If she does," Xavier adds, "she's the best fucking actress on the planet."

"What if you're wrong?" I ask, eyeballing Abby. "You've dropped hints, tried to get her to talk about her family, and she clams up."

"Because she doesn't trust easily," Abby replies.

"And your behavior hasn't helped either," Drew says.

Abby glares at him. "Not helpful, Drew, and I'm sure I speak for everyone when I say we are all sick of the two of you bickering. Get over yourselves already."

I bite back my retort, working hard to restrain my frustration. "If we're wrong, and we ask her outright if she is helping Christian, then she'll run straight back to him and tell him we know. Then Hamilton, Mathers, and whoever the fuck else they have in their corner will know we're onto them. More than that, they will know we care about her, and it will only place her in worse danger."

"But if we're right," Shandra says. "We can bring her up to speed. Let her know the exact kind of monster he is and keep her safe."

"We know you don't want her to get hurt," Abby adds.

"He's already hurt her," Drew interjects, and I can't hold back this time, lunging for him across the table. I grab a handful of his shirt before Hunt pulls me back.

I growl at Drew, flexing my fists, longing to punch him until that smug grin is wiped off his face.

"I don't want her to get hurt," I confirm in a gritted tone. "Even if she's been lying, I don't want her mixed up with those assholes."

"I vote we ask her," Shandra says.

"If we're right, we can use this to our advantage," Hunt adds. "Let her take Montgomery's vote, but she can use it for good."

"Only if she agrees," Abby says. "No one at this table is manipulating her."

"I'm not sure that'd work," Rick says, and he's been silent so long I forgot he was listening on the other end of the line. "If Christian wants her to vote a certain way, and she votes the opposite way, he'll know we are on to him."

"And that will only place her in more danger. Fuck." Abby slumps in her seat.

We are going around in circles, and no matter which way we look at it, it all ends up with Nessa in a precarious position.

My resolve strengthens, and it's a major breakthrough. I don't care about the how or the why anymore. I just care about protecting her from those perverts. Even if there is no future for her and me, I want to keep her safe and out of their clutches.

"This is a fucking nightmare," Anderson says, pulling Abby into his arms and kissing the top of her head.

"It is," Rick agrees. "And we've got to make our minds up soon, because Huss also confirmed something else."

"What is it?" I ask.

"An invitation was issued to Vanessa. She will be at the elite ball next month."

Chapter Thirty-Two
Vanessa

I glance out the window of the small private jet, peering into the dark night sky, wondering where the plane is taking me. My father has been very circumspect with the arrangements, and I could be flying to Timbuktu for all I know.

Nerves jangle in my stomach. I hope I'm doing the right thing. I haven't told anyone where I'm going because Chris, *my dad*, said it was imperative this was kept between us. Apparently, he's this hotshot businessman, and privacy is a luxury he's rarely afforded. When he explained he wanted the opportunity to get to know me away from the intrusive lens of the world's media, it made sense. Still, I had reservations, because it's not exactly normal.

I remind myself that he's *my father*. My mother confirmed it and the fact he has only recently discovered I exist.

Since then, Chris has looked after me. Setting me up in a gorgeous apartment, organizing it so I get to go to RU, lodging an obscene amount of money into a bank account for me, and establishing a trust fund. Between this and the money Mom gave me after that asshole Aaron Breen died, I will never

305

again have any money worries. While I'm not materialistic like some of the girls I know, I *am* a survivalist, and it's a relief not to have to worry about having enough money to pay my bills.

My father has gone to great lengths to take care of me, and I can't deny how good it feels to have someone looking after me. Flying me out to meet him shows he wants me in his life, and that speaks volumes. Yes, there's a teeny-tiny niggling worry at the back of my mind. It's only natural. I've never met him, and this is all a bit cloak-and-dagger. But I trust him.

I was tempted to tell Abby and Shandra, because they are great friends, but Dad asked me not to tell anyone, and their connection with Jackson means I have to hold some stuff back. I want to trust them completely. Genuinely, I do, but I've only known them a few weeks, and while they are still friends with that prick, I must keep some walls up.

They have tried to coax me into talking about Jackson, on several occasions, but I don't want to even think about him, let alone discuss him. Jackson doesn't deserve to occupy any of my headspace after the shit he's pulled, so anytime Abby tries to talk to me about guys, I clam up like an oyster.

Abby begged me to attend dinner at her place today, but hell will freeze over before I willingly attend an event with my asshole ex. After that stunt he pulled at the party last month, it is easier to hate the cockblocking asshat now.

I was enjoying making out with Bryant before Jackson fucked up my plans. I'd been doing so well that night. I'd barely even looked at my ex and his latest arm candy. I knew I looked like a million dollars, and I was enjoying the attention on the dance floor. I didn't touch a drop of booze or take anything illegal.

I was high on possibility and determined to fuck Jackson right out of my head.

I would've succeeded too if the asshole hadn't lost his shit and started a fight with Bryant.

I've never seen Jackson so out of control. Honestly, it was as if he'd shed his skin and inhabited some feral beast's body. He was enraged. Barely human.

Bryant gave as good as he got, but it was the dark rage blazing in Jackson's eyes that separated them. I never saw that side of him when we were together, but watching him unleash a torrent of aggression on Bryant was eye-opening. Jackson is hiding some deep-seated pain, and it's no wonder he lost it so spectacularly. His reaction intrigued me as much as it scared me and turned me on, and I wonder what that says about *me*.

Still, it doesn't excuse his behavior. He ruined my night, robbed me of some much-needed payback, and I won't forget that in a hurry.

Bryant was hot and surprisingly sweet for such an obvious bad boy. From the expert ways his fingers massaged my pussy, I know he would've been a great lay. Now, I'm stuck with the equivalent of lady blue balls, thanks to Jackson fucking Lauder.

Oh, it's okay for him to sleep around, but the minute I try to get some, he's all up in my business.

Fucking asshole.

I fucking hate his smug, gorgeous face.

I've done everything in my power to avoid him these past few weeks, and not having a physical reminder helps. I wish I could say I've managed to successfully evict him from my mind, but I can't. The asshole still corrals my thoughts more often than I'd like, but at least, I've stopped mooning over him.

Now, I'm plain ol' mad, so I cling to my anger, using it to mask my confusing feelings over the blond-haired, blue-eyed devil.

And now, I've let him hijack my mind again. Ugh. I slam my palm into my brow a few times as if that will shake him free from my thoughts. Sighing, I close my eyes, urging my brain to toss the jerk aside.

The plane tilts to the left, dragging me out of my head and back into the moment. Lowering the window blind, I accept a blanket from the flight attendant, recline my chair, and attempt to sleep.

I don't want to show up yawning and with big bags under my eyes.

Making a good first impression is important to me.

So, I close my eyes and focus on muting my troubling thoughts. The gentle purring of the engine lulls me into unconsciousness, and the last thought I have before I fall asleep is whether my brother Trenton will be there with Chris or not.

"Where are we?" I ask from the back seat as the driver exits the small airport, heading out onto the highway. Although, calling it a highway is a bit of a joke. It's only got two lanes on either side of the road, so it's more like a mini highway.

All I've managed to observe thus far is that I've been traveling for more than twenty hours—including the two stopovers to refuel—which means we're a long way from home. The airport we just left is named Arrecife Airport, and the climate is warm and humid. It feels like it's pushing eighty outside, and my dress is already clinging to my back. Thank God, this car has an air conditioner, because turning up like a hot sweaty mess is not in my plans.

The guy sitting in the passenger seat narrows his beady eyes in warning at me through the mirror. He's ginormous with boulders for shoulders, massive thighs squeezed into black pants, and sly, untrustworthy eyes. His thickset mustache infringes his top lip, and his mouth is pulled tight with disapproval. He looks like he eats children for breakfast, and a shiver works its way through me. Tendrils of fear crawl over my skin, and for the first time, I'm regretting my decision to come here without telling a soul.

I don't even know what country I'm in! *What the fuck was I thinking?!*

The scary guy turns his attention back to the road, and I release the breath I was holding, rummaging in my bag for my cell. Using the bag to shield my movements, I power up my normal cell, grateful when it switches on and automatically connects to a local network. I leave it on, slipping it into the top zip pocket of the bag, where I can reach it fast should I need to.

Next, I power up the cell phone Chris sent me, opening the new message.

Chris: I'm glad you landed safely. I'll see you soon. Love, your father.

A layer of stress lifts from my shoulders. He knows where I am, and he is waiting for me. I'm worrying for nothing. Still, I don't turn my regular cell off. Just in case.

The driver switches the radio on, and I'm startled to hear songs I know because the blue and white road signs are in a foreign language. I studied German and French at school, so I know it's not that. *Maybe Spanish or Portuguese?* We drive by industrial buildings and large storefronts, and I'm relieved to see some familiar brands, which hints at a certain level of civilization. Large palm trees line the side of this strip of road, their branches swaying in the wind as cars zip by.

The farther we travel, the more we appear to leave civilization behind and the steeper we climb.

Pressing my nose to the window when we leave the highway, I marvel at the crystal-clear blue ocean on our left. There is barely a ripple in the water and hardly a cloud in the azure sky. I study the landscape as we continue our journey, climbing higher and higher, past small, quaint towns dotted along the coast, overhanging sandy beaches, and that stunning shoreline. The land is a weird mishmash of dry, brown, barren rocky terrain interspersed with green shrubs and pockets of foliage growing out of weird gray earth. Craggy cliffs emerge on both sides, and I can honestly say I have never been to any place like this.

We come to a stop ten minutes later outside high black iron gates. The property is bordered by tall stone walls on both sides. Barbed wire and wall-mounted cameras scan the road outside as the driver speaks into the keypad.

Anxiety flares in my gut, twisting my insides into knots, as the gates open slowly, granting us entry. I'm jostled from side to side as the car bumps along the rough gravel-lined driveway. Unusual flowerbeds line both sides of the driveway, housing several large trees mixed with smaller green shrubs and large cacti with red-fringed tips, planted into the same weird gray earth I spotted previously.

My eyes are out on stalks as we draw up in front of the stylish Mediterranean-type bungalow. Sandstone contrasts with pristine white-painted walls and the floor-to-ceiling-length windows that appear to wrap all the way around the house, making it look bright and airy.

But it's the handsome older man in loafers, khaki shorts, and a crisp white polo shirt, waiting at the front door, who invokes the biggest reaction.

My heart is galloping around my chest like an uncontrollable spinning top, and my palms are suddenly clammy. Wiping them down the front of my pale-pink dress, I swallow back the panicked knot clogging my throat, urging my body to calm down.

The driver opens my door, and I swing my trembling legs out, grateful I chose to wear black ballet flats instead of the stilettos I was considering. I have made an effort with my attire because I want to look nice the first time I meet my father.

The scary-looking dude exits the passenger seat, and he retrieves my suitcase from the trunk before slamming it shut. I jump a little, standing rooted to the spot, terrified and unable to move.

The man, my father, *Chris*, moves toward me with a smile. He's wearing sunglasses so I can't see his eyes, but his smile is warm and inviting, and it helps to settle my nerves.

Forcing my limbs to move, I walk toward him.

"Vanessa." His voice is deep and masculine. "I'm so happy you're here."

"I'm happy to be here too," I croak, hating how my voice quakes with nerves.

"Don't be nervous," he says, still smiling at me. "I don't bite." He flashes me a set of dazzling pearly whites, almost blinding me.

Prickles of apprehension snake up my spine, but I force them aside, staring at my father as a whole host of emotions threatens to drown me.

"This has been a long time coming," he says. "I wish I had known about you sooner, but better late than never. Now, we have all the time in the world to get to know one another." He stops, looking a little unsure. "Could I?" He pauses momentarily, and his Adam's apple bobs in his throat. "Could I have a hug?"

I find myself nodding, because it's not a strange request. *Most fathers hug their daughters, right?*

Very gently, he wraps his arms around me, and I rest my

head on his chest. He holds me tighter, pressing kisses into my hair, and it feels ... strange, uncomfortable. I'm not used to affection from a parental figure, and I'm unaccustomed to such loving gestures in general. This entire trip is stretching me out of my comfort zone, and I'm trying to be brave, but I can't deny I'm grateful when he doesn't prolong the hug for too long.

"I imagine you are tired after your long trip. It's the afternoon here, so I thought you might like to freshen up in your room and then we could enjoy a drink on the terrace before an early dinner."

"That sounds lovely."

"Very well." He snaps his fingers at the scary-looking dude, and it's only then I realize the driver has disappeared with the car. "Ivan. Take my daughter's suitcase to her room."

He nods, taking my suitcase and disappearing inside the house. My gaze scans several cameras mounted on top of the house, along with a couple of men walking the perimeter of the grounds. "Are they bodyguards?" I inquire. It's not unusual for high-powered businessmen to have bodyguards, but it seems a bit over the top considering the idyllic setting.

"Yes," Chris confirms, sweeping his arm to the side and ushering me into the house. "I know you were brought up in similar social circles, so I'm assuming you are familiar with the need for important men to hire security details to protect them and their families. Every successful man attracts enemies. It's par for the course."

"I understand," I say, instantly cooling down when we step into the air-conditioned villa.

He escorts me into a large open-plan living area with a sophisticated modern kitchen and a comfortable living room. The windows open out to an exquisite view of the cliffs and the sparkling ocean in the distance. "Where are we?" I ask again, hoping my father will give me an answer this time.

"We are on Lanzarote. It's one of the Canary Islands. Just off the coast of Africa, although it's part of Spanish jurisdiction," he confirms, opening the refrigerator door. "Have you ever been here before?"

I shake my head. "I've visited Cannes and Paris in France, and we took a family vacation to Greece one year, but most of my summers were spent in The Hamptons."

"Of course. I know Aaron was into that scene."

I turn away from the view, arching a brow as Chris approaches. "You knew him?"

He hands me a glass of water, shaking his head. "Only after the fact," he cryptically replies.

He steers me out of the living area to the back of the property where the bedrooms are. "I've put your things in there," he says, opening the door to a large airy white bedroom. It opens out onto the outside space, and the double doors are open a smidgeon. The soft breeze flowing into the room lifts the light gossamer curtains, tossing them around. "You have an en suite bath to yourself." Chris points at the closed door. "Take whatever time you need, and join me outside when you are ready."

"Okay. Thanks." I shuffle anxiously on my feet. It's all so awkward.

He walks off, stopping with one foot out in the hallway. Slowly, he turns around. "I'm very glad you're here." His voice drops a few decibels. Shoving his shades on his head, he stabs me with piercing blue eyes. "You look like her, you know. Your mom," he adds. "Only more beautiful."

"Thank you." To me, that's not actually a compliment, because I don't want to be compared to that woman in any shape or form, but I accept it as one so as not to appear rude.

When he slips out of the room, carefully closing the door behind him, I flop down on the big bed, smiling to myself like a goober as I contemplate the strange turn my life has taken.

Chapter Thirty-Three
Vanessa

"I was hoping Trenton might be here," I admit as we eat dinner outside on the gorgeous terrace. We are under a large canopy with an impressive pool on one side and an exotic garden on the other. In the distance, a few boats bob on the placid blue-green expanse of the Atlantic Ocean.

We've spent a couple of hours chatting over wine, just getting to know one another. I allowed myself one glass, to help settle my nerves, but I've been careful to pace myself because I don't want to lose control or embarrass myself. Chris has been peppering me with questions about my life, and I can't remember the last time someone took this much interest in me.

Contemplating my question, he lowers his head but not before I spot the pain flaring in his eyes. Setting his silverware down, he dabs the corners of his mouth with a napkin, exhaling heavily. His chest heaves, and his hands shake. Silence engulfs us, and I fear I've said something wrong. I chew my chicken slowly, debating whether I should ask him what's wrong or wait for him to explain. I decide to keep my mouth shut in case I fuck up again.

Clearing his throat, he lifts his head. "I was hoping to avoid this topic of conversation until tomorrow." The tormented expression on his face, and the tears welling in his eyes, sends panic flooding through me.

"We don't have to talk about it," I whisper, inherently knowing this isn't going to be a happy story.

"Your brother is dead, Vanessa. He was murdered a few months ago."

My fork drops to the table with a loud clang. "Oh my God. I'm so sorry." I clasp my hand over my mouth, struggling to process the conflicting emotions tearing through me. I'm sad that I never got the chance to know my brother, and I want to ask Chris what happened, but I don't want to be insensitive either, because it's obvious he's grieving.

"He would have loved you," Chris says with a sad smile. "He always wanted a sibling, and he was a fan of all pretty things." He reaches out, tucking a piece of hair behind my ear. "You share similar features. He had blond hair and blue eyes too. I'm sorry you never got to meet. That's something else you can blame your parents for. They have taken so much from you. It's so wrong."

I bob my head, agreeing with him, and he doesn't even know the half of it. "You don't have any other children?" I ask even though I'm pretty sure I already know the answer.

"You're my only surviving heir."

It's an odd way of putting it. "What was he like?" I inquire, pushing my half-eaten plate away.

A woman appears from behind us, clearing our plates away. It's the same lady who brought me extra towels and cooked our gorgeous dinner, so I'm guessing she's the housekeeper.

Chris smiles up at her, and her pretty cheeks flush with color.

"Trent was a good boy," Chris says, starting off into space

while sipping his sangria. "He knew his place in this world, and he always made me proud. He had a bright future ahead of him. A future snuffed out by that degenerate L—" He stops mid-sentence. "Forgive me, my dear." He takes my hand in his much larger one, and I fight the urge to flinch. I'm not used to adults being touchy-feely in a purely platonic way, and it's going to take a while to get used to it. "It's still hurts too much to speak about it."

"That's okay," I assure him. "I understand."

"I know you'll make me proud too, Vanessa. I can already tell you're a good girl and that you have a bright future ahead of you too." His eyes bore into mine as he squeezes my hand before releasing me.

"Thank you for everything, Chris. I'm very appreciative of all you have done for me."

He scowls briefly, but the look is gone so fast I'm not sure I didn't imagine it. "It's my pleasure, and, please, call me Christian. No one calls me Chris. My name is Christian Montgomery."

He pins me with a funny look, peering into my eyes, as if he can break into my thoughts. I think I may have offended him. He's only ever referred to himself in his messages as C.M. or Father, so this is the first time I'm hearing his full name.

Why does it sound familiar?

"I apologize for any offense," I say. "Mom called you Chris, so I just assumed that was your name."

A blinding smile is back on his face. "It's not a big deal. Just my name." He chuckles, eyeing me as if he's expecting a reaction. Relaxing a little in his chair, he beams at me, and his smile seems more genuine this time. "And if you would prefer to call me Father, nothing would make me happier."

I peek my head out into the hallway the next morning, checking the coast is clear before I slip out of my room. Fighting a yawn, I pad to the kitchen, slamming to a halt when I spot the housekeeper humming to herself as she stands over the stove, stirring eggs in the skillet.

She whips her head around, her cheeks flushing when she notices me standing there. *You should be embarrassed,* I think, fake smiling at her as I walk to the counter and pour myself a glass of orange juice.

She's the reason I'm smothering yawns this morning. At least, I presume it was her tangoing with Christian between the sheets last night. My stomach twists up as I remember the screams and moans coming from his room. It has left a nasty taste in my mouth.

Why would he fuck the housekeeper knowing I'm in the room next door?

And isn't she a little young for him? She can't be more than a few years older than me. It makes me uncomfortable, and I'm not sure what to do with that.

Swallowing my distaste, I accept a plate of eggs and bacon from her, taking it outside to enjoy the beautiful morning.

I'm halfway through my eggs when Christian makes an appearance.

"Good morning." He leans down, kissing my cheek, and I have a sudden urge to scrub at my skin and wipe his saliva from it.

"Good morning." My smile is tight-lipped, but if he notices, he doesn't mention it.

"Did you sleep well?" he asks, and I almost choke on my scrambled eggs.

"Oh dear." He flashes me a dazzling smile, and I'm beginning to think he's doing that on purpose. "Were we a little too loud last night?"

Lord, please open the ground and swallow me. I do *not* want to be having this conversation right now. "A little," I mumble, shoveling more eggs in my mouth so he takes the hint and ends this Godawful discussion.

"Lucia is enthusiastic, but I'll try and keep her quiet tonight." He waggles his brows suggestively.

My cheeks burn with embarrassment, and I almost spit my eggs out all over the table.

"I apologize for oversharing," he says, handing me a fresh glass of juice. His smile holds amusement. "Trent and I used to trade war stories." He winks again, and it grosses me out. "I'll try to remember you're a lady and that it's not polite conversation."

Eh, yeah.

"What about Trent's mother?" I ask. "Where is she?" He's not wearing a wedding ring, I've noticed, and he hasn't mentioned a wife, but it'd be odd if he wasn't married to someone at some point. He's handsome, rich, and successful, and you can't tell me he didn't find someone to put a ring on.

"We're divorced," he says through gritted teeth. "She was a drunk for most of our marriage."

"You have a type," I blurt before I can think better of it.

His eyes probe mine, his angry look fading away. "Your mother too?"

I nod.

He's quiet for a moment while he tops up his coffee from the pot. "I'm sorry you experienced that. No child should grow up in an environment like that."

I shrug, not wanting to get into it. This conversation is already weird as fuck, and something is a little off with him this morning. I went to bed happy last night, and now, well, I'm not sure what to make of things.

"I thought we'd take my boat out today," he says. "Lucia

will fix us a picnic basket for lunch. There are some pretty caves we can explore, so make sure to wear a bathing suit and bring sunscreen."

I'm sitting in my room, holding my cell in my hand, chewing on my lip as I contemplate whether to send this text to Abby or not. She's been trying to reach me. I have several missed calls and texts asking me to contact her. She's probably worried because I'm skipping classes. I could reply and tell her I'm out of town for a few days and not to worry, or I could let her know exactly where I am, and whom I'm with, just in case anything should happen to me.

Maybe, it's the lack of sleep, but my nerves are on edge, and something just doesn't feel right today. I can't put my finger on it, but my instinct is screaming at me, and I'm not usually one to ignore a gut feeling. Perhaps, coming here was a mistake, but there's nothing I can do to fix that without a time machine. Coming here without telling anyone was a mistake too, but that's something I *can* fix, so I tap out a quick message before I overthink it.

Me: I'm okay. I'm in Lanzarote with my dad, Christian Montgomery. I'll be home in a few days.

"Vanessa." Christian raps on my door. "Are you ready?" he calls out.

"I'll be right there."

I pop my cell into my makeup case where I stowed it last night. Just before I headed to bed last night, Christian asked me if I had brought my other cell with me, which struck me as odd. *Why would that matter?* My gut encouraged me to lie, so I told him I only brought the cell he sent me, and that seemed to appease him. My sixth sense prompted me to hide it, so I did.

Maybe, I should take it with me so I can respond when Abby replies. I take it from my makeup bag and drop it into the inside zipped pocket of my bag. Standing, I grab my bag and my towel, conducting a mental checklist to ensure I haven't forgotten anything, before I skip out of the room to join my father.

Christian drives us to the small marina in an open-top BMW. It reminds me of the journey from New York to The Hamptons that I took with Jackson. My heart squeezes in my chest, like someone has a hand around it, whenever I think of that weekend. It didn't end the best, but it had started out so promising. I squirm a little on my seat as I recall how hot it was riding Jackson on the lounge chair outside the bedroom. It feels like a lifetime ago.

How did it go so wrong?

Why did it go so wrong?

I still don't have answers to my questions or understand why he turned on me or why he was playing with me in the first place.

Maybe, Abby is right. Perhaps, I should talk to him when I return. To clear the air and get some closure. Shandra and Abby have been great friends, and I owe it to them to try to smooth things over between me and my ex. If they're going to be a part of my life, I have to accept he's a part of their lives too. I need to find some middle ground where I can tolerate him.

"We're here," Christian says, startling me. I barely even registered the journey. A car pulls up behind us, and two men get out. One of them is the scary dude from the airport ride, and I recognize the other guy from prowling around the house last night. Goose bumps sprout on my arms, and I fight a shiver as I climb out of the car, wondering if this level of protection is really necessary on an unassuming island like this.

Christian approaches Ivan, the scary dude. "You can both stay here. I'd like some alone time with my daughter." Christian takes the wicker picnic basket from the man's hands.

Ivan just nods, and I wonder if he ever speaks.

I traipse alongside Christian as we walk past a row of boats harbored at the pretty marina. He's in a great mood, pointing out various things as we walk, regaling me with stories about the history of this fishing village.

"This is mine," Christian says when we reach the end of the path, stopping in front of a glistening silver luxury sailing yacht.

It's not huge-huge, but it has a semi-open top deck and an enclosed bottom deck. Access on and off the boat is via the lower level, so I hop over onto the flat, unenclosed section at the back, before opening the door which grants entry to the cabin area. A set of stairs on the right-hand side leads to the upper level, which is where the control panel is and the open area for sunbathing.

I explore the enclosed space while Christian goes upstairs to start the engine.

I trail my hand over the circular cream-colored leather seating area, surrounding a glossy walnut-topped table, imagining how glorious it would be to eat meals here with the sun streaming through the window, watching the world racing by. Up ahead is a small galley kitchen. It's perfectly equipped with everything one would need to entertain. At the rear of the space is a bedroom with a large king-sized bed occupying most of the room, and on the other side is a small bathroom with a shower.

Finishing my exploration, I walk up the steps to the next level just as the yacht slowly moves forward, leaving the marina. "Do you like it?" Christian asks, glancing over my shoulder, pinning me with one of those dazzling smiles of his. I guess he only has to flash that grin at women, and they drop their panties for him. I'd prefer if he didn't use it on me, but I'm probably being overly sensitive.

"It's great. I love it," I truthfully admit, taking a seat on one of the leather-backed benches that line both sides of the upper deck.

Putting my sunglasses on, I fix my hair into a casual high bun, watching the land disappear behind us as Christian picks up speed, maneuvering the boat out into the open ocean, quickly eating up the miles.

I apply sunscreen to all areas of exposed skin, but I keep my light, sleeveless cotton minidress on, uncomfortable stripping to my bathing suit in front of him.

Tilting my head up, I angle my face, welcoming the warm sunshine on my skin.

"There's a lounge chair over there," Christian says. "Lie down and make yourself comfortable."

I hesitate for a moment before getting up and lying down on it, facing it away from him. I doze off for a few minutes, coming to when I feel a finger trail up my arm. I jerk awake, pulling my legs up to my chest and wrapping my arms around my knees in a familiar protective pose. I blink furiously as my eyes adjust to the bright light, and I re-center myself.

"Relax," Christian says, pulling over a lounge chair beside me. "I didn't mean to startle you. I think you're getting burned. You should apply more sunscreen." He hands me a bottle of water, and I loosen my tense muscles, stretching my legs back out.

"Thanks." My mouth is parched, so I greedily glug the water while he takes sips from a glass of white wine. His shirt has disappeared and his feet are bare, so he's only wearing black swim shorts, hanging rather low on his hips. He's in good shape for an old dude though. It's clear he takes care of himself.

I notice we are stationary, the boat bobbing gently on the ocean, and I cast a glance around to check out our surroundings. In front of us is miles and miles of open ocean, and a few hundred feet behind us is the cliff face. Several openings are visible under the gray rock, leading to dark, hidden chambers. "Are those the caves you mentioned?" I ask.

"Yes. We can explore them after lunch. If you like." He fights a smirk.

Weird.

"Sounds fun," I agree.

"You must be melting in that dress," Christian says a couple of beats later. "You should take it off."

Alarm bells ring in my ears even though it's not that unusual of a request.

It's more the way he said it.

"I'm good." I shoot him a quick smile before drinking more of my water, purely to avoid talking about it anymore. But he's like a dog with a bone.

"You don't have anything I haven't seen before," he drawls. "Go ahead. Don't make yourself uncomfortable on my account."

Nerves shoot across my gut, and fear creeps over my skin, one inch at a time. I'm uneasy, and I'm not altogether sure why except my instinct is screaming in my ear again. I lower my gaze to my bag, double-checking to ensure it is still beside me. "Honestly, I'm good," I repeat when he continues staring at me expectantly. "I'm not even that hot," I lie. "I've been feeling a little unwell since breakfast. I hope I'm not coming down with something."

"Let me check." He swings his legs around, placing his hand on my brow before I can stop him. "You do feel a little clammy. I have a first aid kit in the bathroom. Let me grab some pills for you. I have just the thing to settle your stomach." He rises, shooting me that grin again, and I'm really starting to dislike it and him.

"No!" I blurt. "I don't take pills. I don't like the way they make me feel."

He eyes me strangely for a couple seconds before reclaiming his seat. "Suit yourself. If you change your mind, let me know." He reaches behind me, pulling another bottle of water from the mini refrigerator. "You should drink lots of water. You don't want to get dehydrated. It can happen quickly in the sun."

"Okay, thanks."

Silence descends, but it's not a comfortable silence. It's the awkward silence that exists between two strangers.

"So," he says, after about ten minutes has passed, cutting through the silence. "There was something I wanted to discuss with you."

"Okay." I draw the word out, suddenly apprehensive. Little beads of sweat dot my brow, and I'm so hot it feels like my clothes are stuck to my body, and I'm seconds away from self-combustion. My heart is racing fast, skipping to a quicker beat, almost like it's trying to flee my chest. I was lying a few minutes ago when I said I was feeling a little unwell, and now, I'm wondering if I've jinxed myself, because I genuinely do feel ill now.

"I'm a little unhappy with you."

Fear races through me at his words, and the less than friendly look on his face.

"Me?" I squeak. "What did I do?" Oh my God. I bet he found out about my arrest for shoplifting when I was fourteen. My face heats even more at the prospect of having to explain myself. If he's gone digging in my past, he'll know I nearly got expelled from school, had to skip a year, and I came close to a full-blown nervous breakdown. If he starts questioning me about it, he might discover the reason why, and I don't want him to know. I don't want anyone to know.

"I hear you've been dating Jackson Lauder. This displeases me greatly."

"Wait. What?" I splutter. *Did he just ask me about Jackson? What the hell has he got to do with anything?"*

"You're to stay away from him. That's an order."

"An order?"

"Yes," he snaps, turning the full extent of his cold glare on me.

I cower in my chair, pulling my knees up to my chest, as my heart thumps wildly behind my rib cage. Fear bathes me from head to toe, and I've a real bad feeling about this. I wipe my arm across my sweaty brow, blinking profusely as my eyes turn blurry.

"I know you're a good girl underneath that naughty reputation you've obviously worked hard for," he adds.

Oh fuck. He does know. Removing my sunglasses, I rub at my eyes, wondering why my vision is out of focus. "What's Jackson got to do with anything?"

"Everything." Darting forward, he grips my chin painfully. His face is close, *too* close, and as his eyes drill into mine, he shields nothing from me, boldly showing me his true colors.

Panic charges up my throat as I see the truth he's been skillfully hiding. I'd know that dark glint anywhere. I spent years staring into the eyes of a monster who shared the same predatory gaze.

What have I done? Traded one monster for another?

"Jackson Lauder murdered your brother, Trent, and you're going to help me exact my revenge."

Chapter Thirty-Four
Vanessa

"Wʜat?! No! No way." I shake my head. "Jackson is a lot of things, but he's not a murderer."

"You stupid naïve cunt!" he hisses, slapping my face. "You dare to call me a liar?"

My head is fuzzy, my cheek hurts, and my heart is trying to beat a path out of my body as crippling fear lays siege to my insides. But I've been here before, and I know how to appease the beast. "No, Father. I'm sorry," I say in my meekest voice. "If you say he did that, I believe you."

Christian stares into my eyes for a few moments, his shoulders relaxing as a relieved smile graces his ugly mouth. He rubs his thumb along my lower lip. "Aaron taught you well. I guess I can thank him for training you."

I stare at him horror-struck as his words register in my muddled brain, and he starts laughing. The asshole laughs, like it's the funniest thing he's ever seen.

"What? You think I don't know everything there is to know about you?" he sneers. "I needed to find out if you were capable enough to do my bidding." His hand leaves my face, trailing down my neck.

I move to slap him away, but my arm is all floppy, and it won't cooperate. Another layer of horror sweeps over me as realization dawns. "What did you do to me?"

"I put a little something in your water that will make you more amenable. Not enough to make you unconscious, because I want you awake, but enough that you're cooperative."

"You twisted bastard," I slur. "I'm your daughter. Your flesh and blood!" A thought stops me. Maybe I'm not. Maybe it's all been a lie. Maybe—

My head whips back as he slaps me across the face again, and I cry out.

"You *are* my flesh and blood, darling. You are a Montgomery, and you are going to prove that to me." He arches a brow, his lips curving up at the corners. "Ask me how."

"Fuck you!" I slur, attempting to slap his hand away when it lands on my chest. But whatever he's drugged me with has done an effective job. I'm losing control of my faculties, and I can't make my body do what I want it to do; however, I'm still alert enough that I'll remember everything he subjects me to.

"That's not very ladylike. You've been spending too much time with that cunt Abigail. She's on my shit list too, and you'll help me handle her. It's been a long time coming." The look in his eye can only be described as sheer evil.

Tears roll down my face as he tears my dress off me, licking his lips as his gaze roams my body. He straddles my waist, cupping my breasts through my suit, kneading them roughly. "Could be a bit bigger, but we can fix that."

"I'm your daughter, you sick fuck!" I shout, attempting to bump him off me, but I can barely make my body move.

He slaps me across the face again. "You say that like it would turn me off." He palms the bulge in his shorts, and my stomach lurches as nausea punches me in the gut. "When all it does is turn me on. In the elite world, daughters learn to pleasure their fathers from an early age." He leans down, licking a path between my breasts, and I cry out, more terrified than I've been in years. "Don't worry, we can have fun catching up."

My sobs come thick and fast, and I'm glad my tear ducts still work, because I won't lie back and pretend this is *fun*.

"But it can't be all fun and games," he adds, his hands wandering lower on my body as he sits up straighter. "You have an important job to do. You will act as my spokesperson in all elite matters, voting as I instruct. In public, you will be the perfect elite princess." He grips my chin roughly again. "You will not do anything to embarrass me. You represent the Montgomery name now, and that comes with responsibilities. We are descendants from one of the Rydeville founding fathers."

His hands roam my body, touching me all over, and nausea swims up my throat.

"My contact will touch base with you when you return to the US, and your training will begin immediately." His tongue darts out, licking the salty tears dribbling over my lips and down my chin, and he pins me with that monstrous grin again. "In case of confusion, that also means you will spread your legs for him whenever he desires it. You will let him use your body any way he sees fit. And should he need you to pleasure any other elite male, you will do so willingly and give them the ride of their lives."

"You're insane," I slur. "I will never do that! And I won't help you hurt Jackson or Abby."

Fuck acting obedient.

He's rendered me powerless, and after he's raped me, I will not walk out of here intact. I can't survive this again. I know I can't. My head spins, and my fighting spirit peters out.

I need to die.

Want to die.

It's the only escape from this hell.

Perhaps, if I antagonize him enough, he'll snap and strangle me. Or dump my uncooperative body in the ocean.

He slaps me harder this time, and a feeble scream escapes my mouth. "Listen here, you ungrateful little cunt." He cups my pussy. "This belongs to me. *You* belong to me. In every sense of the word. And you will do what I say, because if you don't, this time, there won't be anyone there to save Kayleigh."

All the blood drains from my useless body. "What? No!"

"This is the part where you thank me," he drawls, sliding his hand underneath my suit and palming my bare pussy.

I stare at him, horror and disgust and a million other thoughts fighting for space in my head.

He barks out a laugh as he slides two fingers inside me, pumping them roughly.

I sob as my hazy mind struggles to decipher his meaning while my body protests the unwanted intrusion.

"You didn't honestly think Aaron's death was an accident, did you?" My eyes pop wide, and he chuckles again as he rubs my clit with his thumb. "I know he fucked you for years. Took your precious virginity." His tone mocks me. "At least he helped break you in." Removing his fingers, he pushes them into his mouth, sucking loudly.

I heave, my stomach lurching violently, getting ready to expel my breakfast.

"Hmm. So sweet," he murmurs as his eyes glint with wicked intent. His hands return to my breasts, and he pulls the top of my suit down, exposing my bare chest. He tweaks my nipples with his fingers, hurting me, and I sob. "Where were we? Ah, yes. Aaron. Let's finish our discussion so we can get the party started."

His devilish eyes devour me, and I'm such a fool I didn't see the truth before now. I've been so blind. So stupid. So naïve. I should have trusted my friends and told them about him or at least let them know where I was going and why. I have no one to blame for the mess I'm in but myself.

"Aaron should never have touched what belonged to me, but I decided to excuse him for his earlier actions. After all, you are quite the little slut, aren't you, Vanessa?" He pinches my nipples, and I cry out. "You'll be punished for fucking Lauder, Anderson, and Hunt. But we'll get to that in due course. Aaron signed his own death warrant when he broke into your apartment and attempted to enjoy you again. How fucking dare he!" He swipes his hand out, sending his wine flying. Glass shatters, raining down on the upper deck as the glass and the bottle break into smithereens upon impact. "He'd been warned to stay away from you, but he just couldn't help himself."

"What did you do?" I slur. My head is swimming, and my eyelids are growing heavy.

"Bribed one of his whores into drugging his whiskey. Then, I had my guy follow him home, waiting for the perfect place to run him off the road."

"Silver Honda," I murmur, piecing it together.

"Top marks for observational skills, darling." He leans down, sucking my nipple into his mouth, and more silent tears roll down my face.

"It worked like a charm," he says, straightening up again. "Aaron crashed into the tree, and his neck broke instantly. He was dead within minutes. It was the perfect murder. No one even suspected foul play with the level of alcohol and narcotics in his system." He fondles my breast with one hand, using his other hand to push down the front of his shorts, freeing his gross erection. He moans as he strokes his cock, kneading my breast with demanding fingers. "You don't seem upset."

"Because I'm not. I hated that prick."

"Me too." He winks, as if we're coconspirators in this. "You don't need to worry about him. I took care of it. I despise loose ends." He picks up his pace, pumping his shaft faster.

"You're disgusting," I slur, watching him jerk himself off with growing revulsion and potent fear.

"I'll take that as a compliment, darling. And I'm done with this conversation. You are going to do as I say, Vanessa, because I make Aaron Breen look like Prince Charming. If you disobey me, if you *deny* me, deny any of the elite, I will take Kayleigh, and I will ruin her far worse than you've been ruined. Trust me, it will make what happened to you look like a fairy tale."

Tears stream down my face as I acknowledge he's won. I don't care about my life, but I care about hers. I will do whatever he wants if it's the only way I can protect my little sister and keep her away from this sick bastard and his pervert friends.

"Do we have an understanding?" he asks. I nod. "Good girl." He thrusts his cock against my crotch, and only the thin layer of my swimsuit separates us.

I'm going to puke. Preferably all over him.

"I knew you could be obedient with the right incentive." He climbs off me. "So, this is what's going to happen next. I'm going to take you downstairs to my bed and fuck every hole in your gorgeous, young body until you bleed. Tomorrow, after you've recovered, we will sit down and run through the plan. The following day, you'll be returned to the US. You can't be gone too long, or those meddling offspring you're friends with will start to suspect something."

He pulls his shorts up, adjusting his hard-on. Lifting me up, he throws me over his shoulder. "Sound good?" he asks, laughing when I don't reply. He slaps my ass, laughing louder, and the sound is pure evil. "I thought so."

Chapter Thirty-Five
Jackson

"Steady," Hunt whispers, grabbing my arm like he's done a hundred times in the past five minutes. I know we need to time this perfectly so that sick pervert doesn't murder Nessa, but it's killing me hiding down here while he's up there hurting the woman I love. The three of us tread water as we lurk at the rear of the lower level of Montgomery's luxury yacht—the only way on and off this boat— waiting for the right opportunity to strike. Anderson looks at me, and his expression conveys everything I need to know. He understands my frustration, acknowledges we're doing this the right way, reassuring me we'll save my girl.

Montgomery appears at the top of the stairs, and I stop breathing. Nessa is flung over his shoulder, her limbs flopping like limp noodles. He's grinning like he's the king of the world, and I can't wait to wipe that condescending smirk off his face. His loud voice carried over the breeze, so we heard every word he said. I have never felt more helpless—forced to stand by while he did and said disgusting things to her. These past few minutes have aged me. That bastard destroyed my sister, and hell will freeze over before I let him destroy Nessa.

Thank fuck, the time for action has arrived, because I'm consumed with dark rage, and it needs an outlet *now*. Years of pent-up frustration and fury whip through me, and I'm struggling to keep a leash on it. I wanted to charge up there and ride to the rescue the second we got here, but the guys held me back. He would've heard us coming and reacted accordingly. Despite the plans he has in mind, Montgomery wouldn't lose any sleep over killing Nessa in front of me, purely to goad me, to watch me unravel.

Waiting him out was the right course of action even if it tested my self-control. This way, we have the element of surprise. And with three against one, he doesn't stand a chance. That'll serve the arrogant prick right for leaving his bodyguards at the marina. No doubt, it was a calculated move to get Nessa alone so he could sate his twisted desire.

When Montgomery's foot hits the last step, I get ready. Anderson passes me the Glock he had strapped to his thigh, mouthing that the safety is off. The instant Montgomery turns right, heading through the lower level, I haul myself up onto the boat, rip the door open, and charge toward him with Anderson and Hunt at my back.

The asshole is so fixated on what he's going to do to my girl he doesn't react until it's too late. As he turns around, I press the gun into the side of his skull. "Hand Nessa to Anderson."

Nessa mumbles something, but her words are slurred and indecipherable. She doesn't move. Not even a twitch, and panic bubbles up my throat. I had almost lost my mind when he confirmed he'd drugged her. My friends had to physically restrain me that time.

We don't know what he's poisoned her with, but if I discover it's caused any permanent damage or it forces her into a dark spiral, I will dig his lifeless body up and kill him all over again. I grind my teeth to the molars, wanting to tear the bastard limb from limb right this fucking second, but I remind myself patience is a virtue and all good things come to those who wait. Yeah, I'm a walking cliché, but I'm barely keeping my shit together, so screw me if I'm unoriginal.

The veins in my neck and my arms throb, and my fingers twitch with the effort involved in holding myself back. I'm ready to rain hell on his perverted ass, but Nessa needs to be safely away from him before I go at this asshole.

Montgomery's harsh laugh grates on my nerves, but I remind myself of all that's at stake. Every second Nessa is around him, she's in danger. I'm not letting him manipulate me or bait me into attacking him until I'm ready, because I can't risk her getting caught in the crossfire. "Well, well, this is a surprise." He grins like he doesn't have a gun pressed into his head. As if we pose no threat.

Good. Let him underestimate us, like most of the elite has.

Anderson glares at Christian while lifting Nessa off him. The top of her bathing suit is undone, revealing her bare breasts as Anderson gently hands her to Hunt. Hunt is under strict instructions to stay with her while Anderson and I take our time torturing the bastard who hurt the women we love.

A red haze washes over me, and I lose all control, slamming my fist into Montgomery's nose. A satisfying crunching sound confirms I've broken it, and it's music to my ears. His head jerks back, and he roars, bringing one hand to his nose, which is now gushing blood. He grabs the top of the leather-filled circular booth with his other hand to stop himself from falling. In an unexpected move, he snatches a cup from the table, slamming it into the side of my head.

Pain rattles around my skull, and I almost drop the gun, but my fingers curl around it at the last second. Anderson throws a couple of powerful punches, pushing Montgomery back a few steps. Anderson's next punch knocks him to the ground, and I jump on top of Montgomery, thrusting my fist into his solar plexus.

Moving his head to one side, Montgomery spits out blood on the floor, attempting to laugh. "You're fucking pathetic. Boys pretending to be men," he says, rearing up and swinging at Anderson.

Old dude's got more stamina than I gave him credit for. Those elite bastards sure train them well, but no amount of skill can match the lethal fury fueling Anderson and me.

Anderson ducks, dodging Montgomery's fist, just as I land a punch to the asshole's rib cage. "Fuck," he hisses through gritted teeth as the sound of bones cracking tickles my eardrums.

"Hunt," I call over my shoulder, handing the gun to him. This will be much more satisfactory using my bare hands.

Anderson and I take turns going at him, kicking and punching him, until there isn't one part of his body we haven't bruised, broken, or bloodied. He gives up fighting after the first few minutes, which is a little disappointing. When he's stopped moving, and his face is swollen beyond recognition, we stop. Anderson checks his pulse. "He's still breathing."

"Good." I climb to my feet, pushing wet hair back out of my eyes. "Hunt." I keep my eyes on Montgomery as I call out for two reasons. One, I don't trust Montgomery not to find a second wind.

In the movies, the bad guys *always* get up when you think they're down.

And, two, I can't look at Nessa right now, because I'll want to go to her, and I must end this first.

Anderson and I both have legit reasons to want this asshole dead, but he agreed I get the kill shot.

Hunt offers me the gun, but I shake my head. "I want the Stryker." Concern flashes in Anderson's eyes as he scrutinizes my face, and I can only imagine what he sees staring back at him.

Beating the bastard has barely taken the edge off my murderous rage, and putting a bullet in his skull will not sate my inner monster. Shooting the fucker would be cleaner but far too easy for a bastard like him.

Montgomery deserves to die slowly and painfully, to be gutted from the inside out like the monster he is. I owe it to my sister, to Nessa, to Abby, to Olivia and Sylvia, and all the other women he's kidnapped, tortured, and raped over the years to ensure he suffers.

Hunt places the knife in my hand, holding my gaze. "Do what you need to, but don't lose yourself."

Anderson squeezes my shoulder. "Make him pay, brother."

I stand over Montgomery's body, staring at him for a few minutes. I kick at his leg repeatedly until he groans. I want to ensure he's awake for this. "Not so powerful now, huh, Montgomery. You sick fuck." I kneel, cutting his swim shorts away. "I killed your sick bastard of a son, and now, I'm going to kill you too." I poke the knife into his pubes, and a strangled sound travels up his throat. "This is for my sister." I move the knife lower, shoving the blade into his balls repeatedly before slicing his dick off. Inhuman sounds gurgle from his throat, and he coughs up blood. "This is for daring to hurt the woman I love." I drag the knife from his pubes up through his stomach and over his chest. "This is for sexually assaulting Abby." I run the knife horizontally across his chest, pulling it down along his right side. "And this is for the years you inflicted torture on Sylvia and Olivia." I drag the knife up his left side.

The gargled howls leaving his mouth only spur me on. Perhaps, I should worry about the sick satisfaction mixing with adrenaline flowing through my veins, but I don't. This asshole has had this coming to him for years. "Join your perverted son in hell, Montgomery. You will never hurt another woman again."

Then, I lose it. Slashing at him, over and over, tearing through skin, muscle, and bone. Ripping through his legs and his arms, I savage his torso until it's a bloody mess of butchered organs and tissue. Still, I don't stop, bringing the knife down, again and again, venting my anger and aggression with every slice of my knife.

"Enough, Jackson." Anderson pulls me off him. "He's dead, man. He can't hurt anyone anymore."

Slowly, I emerge from my fugue state, staring at the mangled body of Christian Montgomery with detached eyes. Casting a glance at myself, I realize I'm covered in his blood. More blood pools around his body, flowing in rivulets down the floor.

I push Anderson off. "I need to clean up."

I don't look at Nessa or Hunt as I walk past them out the door, taking a running leap off the end of the boat, submerging myself in the cool ocean. When my head pops up, I scrub at my skin quickly, removing all traces of that bastard's blood and DNA from my body.

"I wouldn't stay too long out there," Anderson says, poking his head over the edge. "There could be sharks around."

"There *are* sharks in these waters," Hunt hollers. "I Googled it on the way here."

I've got zero desire to become shark nom-nom, so I haul ass back onto the boat, taking a moment to compose myself before facing Nessa.

"Here." Anderson hands me a towel.

"Is she okay?" I whisper as I dry off.

"She's barely coherent." A muscle flexes in his jaw. "There

are no apparent physical injuries, but we still need to get her to a doctor."

I nod, pushing past Anderson, heading into the cabin, making a beeline for Hunt. Nessa is cradled in his arms, her eyes darting wildly around, and I wonder how much of it she was aware of. I hope I didn't frighten her. That she isn't scared of me.

I sit down, opening my arms, and Hunt wordlessly passes her to me. Contentment sinks bone deep as I embrace her for the first time in months, and it's a welcome emotion because I'm feeling weirdly numb. "It's okay, babe." I press a kiss to her temple, peering into her eyes, trying to hold my alarm at bay when I spot her pupils darting wildly around. "You're safe now."

Her mouth moves, and she spews a jumble of words, but nothing that is distinguishable. Holding her closer, I shut my eyes, using the feel of her body against mine to keep me grounded.

I've got to make things right with her, because almost losing her today has woken me the fuck up. She means everything to me, and I'm done denying it. Done hurting both of us.

I press my mouth to her ear even though Hunt and Anderson are standing over the dead body, talking in hushed tones, not paying attention to us. "I love you, Nessa," I whisper, hoping it registers. "And I'm going to make everything right as soon as I know you're okay." I kiss her temple. "Try to sleep it off, baby. I've got you." I rock her in my arms until her eyes shutter closed and her breathing evens out. Placing my fingers at the pulse point on her neck, I breathe a sigh of relief at the gentle thrumming under my skin.

"She okay?" Anderson asks, dropping down beside me.

"I think so. She's sleeping."

"It must've been GHB," Hunt says. "And based on the fact she didn't pass out until now, I'd say he gave her a low dose."

"It's still dangerous, and we need to get her checked out." Gently, I brush hair back off her brow.

"Agreed, but what are we going to do about him?" Anderson asks.

I wish there had been more time to plan this, but there wasn't. We had to react fast.

I was just about to leave Anderson's place after Sunday dinner when I noticed multiple missed calls and texts from the PI I hired to watch over Nessa. I called him immediately, losing my shit when he confirmed she'd been picked up by a private car and driven to the private airfield at Logan International. I knew she was going to Montgomery, and I went into complete panic mode. Right then, whether she played me or not didn't matter. All I cared about was that she was going to meet that prick, and I was terrified.

I ran back inside and blurted everything to my friends. We cobbled a plan together, leaving quickly to chase after her. The girls weren't happy about staying behind, but we had no idea what we were walking into and it was too dangerous. Besides, Christian probably has eyes on us, and if everyone disappeared, it might've tipped him off.

Thank fuck, Nessa had her cell with her and Hunt had had the wherewithal to plant trackers in all her bags too. Drew managed to get us out on the Manning Motors private jet a few hours later, and from there, with Xavier's remote help, we followed Nessa to Lanzarote. Then, we had to bide our time and wait for an opportunity to present itself.

The last twenty-four hours have been the longest of my life, and I didn't sleep a wink last night, worrying about what he was doing to her in that fortress up on the cliff.

"That's the million-dollar question," Hunt replies, dragging a hand through his hair, looking uncharacteristically ruffled. "I doubt we can bribe that local guy to get rid of his remains as easily as we bribed him to take us out to the caves."

"No shit, Sherlock." Anderson rubs at his temples.

"Calling or emailing for help is too risky. We can't leave any trails," I say.

"The obvious solution is to dump his body in the ocean and let the sharks take care of it," Anderson supplies. "Then we clean this shit up, chart a course to someplace safe and catch a plane home from there."

"Sounds like a viable plan. Lauder?" Hunt eyes me. "It's your call."

I nod just as the rumble of an engine pricks my ears. Our heads whip up at the same time.

"What fresh hell is this?" Anderson asks, eyeing the black speedboat chopping through the water, making a beeline for us, with trepidation.

There isn't time to clean up the mess in the boat or to dispose of the body, so we'll just have to face the music. Laying Nessa down flat on the seat, I kiss her cheek before standing beside my friends. I grab the Glock and open the door. "I guess we're about to find out."

Chapter Thirty-Six
Jackson

The speedboat pulls up alongside the back of the yacht, cutting the engine and laying anchor. We stand as a united front at the back of Montgomery's boat, arms folded, waiting for them to make themselves known. The Glock is tucked into the back waistband of my shorts, close at hand if we should need it. Two guys with jet-black hair and serious expressions walk to the side of their boat, facing us. "Mr. Lauder," the slightly taller one on the left speaks. "We're employed by your father. He sent us to follow you."

Hunt, Anderson, and I exchange wary expressions.

"He's been trying to reach you," he adds.

Our clothes, cells, wallets, and other personal belongings are back on the boat we used to get here. A local guy we met at the marina received a handsome sum to drop everything and bring us out here. We promised him we'd double the money if he waited for us and took us back to shore, but that plan is scrapped now.

"I don't have it on me."

The other guy extracts his cell, punching in some buttons. A couple of minutes later, he passes the cell to me.

"Hello."

"Jackson. Thank God." My father's relieved voice filters down the line.

"What's going on, Dad?"

"I'll explain everything when I see you. I promise. You can trust my men." There's a pregnant pause. "Did you get to him?" He doesn't need to name him, or ask the question he really wants to ask, for both of us to know who and what he's referring to.

"It's over."

Dad bursts out crying, and I swallow over the massive lump in my throat. The only other time I've seen or heard my father cry is when Dani died. He was inconsolable for days. I shuffle awkwardly on my feet, my gaze landing on Anderson's. He clamps a hand on my shoulder in support.

"It was supposed to be me." Dad sniffles. "I didn't want you carrying that responsibility, Jackson."

"It was always going to be me, Dad."

Silence engulfs us for a minute. He clears his throat, and when he speaks again, he's the formidable businessman I know. "Here's what's going to happen. My men will handle the scene and get you to safety. I'll send a plane for you."

"We have a plane," I cut across him. "The Mannings' private jet is waiting for us."

"I'll contact Drew and get it rerouted. Your mother and I are in London, so it will only take a few hours to get here. Stay sharp. See you soon." He hangs up before I can argue, but that's okay, because I won't be arguing with him today. It's easier with his help, and it sounds like he wants to have a serious conversation, which is something I've desired for the past year.

I hand the cell back to his guy, as the other dude's cell rings.

"What's going on?" Hunt asks.

"Dad's guys will clean up here and get us to the plane. We're visiting my parents in London, but it'll be a quick visit." I glance at Anderson. "See if you can find Nessa's bag. We know she brought one." I jerk my head at the stairs to the upper level. "I'm guessing it's up there."

Anderson heads off to investigate.

The taller guy ends his call and jumps from his boat to ours. "You can go with my colleague. He will arrange your transportation."

"We need to pick up our clothes," I explain. "And my girl-friend needs medical attention."

"I will organize it," he says.

Twenty minutes later, we are on our way. The local dude has been paid off. We have our clothes and shit, and Anderson updated Abby while Hunt spoke to Xavier. I'm holding Sleeping Beauty in my arms, and I can't wait to get the fuck away from this island.

We arrive on the neighboring island of Fuerteventura thirty minutes later to discover an ambulance and a blacked-out Land Rover waiting for us. Nessa is still out cold, but the EMT, a man I guess to be in his early thirties with very good English, checks all her vitals while I do my best to answer his questions. He tells us there isn't much we can do but wait for the effects to leave her system. He says all trace of GHB is usually gone within twelve hours, which is one of the reasons why it's so popular as a date-rape drug.

Nessa needs rest, sleep, food, and water. We thank him and get settled in the car. Anderson sits up front with my dad's guy who doesn't say very much, but that's okay because Nessa is sleeping and we're all exhausted.

The private jet has a bedroom which I commandeer when we climb on board. Not that the guys would ever protest.

The girls come first.

Always.

Which is something I should never have forgotten.

I place Nessa under the covers, tucking them up under her chin, before crawling on the outside, lying down beside her. I don't remember falling asleep, but I must have because I wake with a start when I feel the bed moving.

Nessa is sitting up on the side of the bed. Her legs are planted on the floor, her shoulders are hunched, and she has her head in her hands.

"Nessa." My sleep-laden tone bounces off the quiet walls. "Are you okay?"

She moves her body slowly, as if she's carrying a heavy weight, turning to face me. Beautiful blue eyes, that star in my dreams, lock on mine. Although her eyes are bloodshot and red-rimmed, her face is a shade paler than usual, and her hair is a mess of tangles, she's still the most beautiful girl I've ever seen. "My head hurts. I feel nauseous, and I'm a bit confused," she admits in a hoarse voice.

Sitting up, I yawn, rubbing sleep from my eyes. "I can help with the confusion, unless you'd rather not know."

She considers that for a minute, shaking her head. "I'd prefer to know."

Swinging my legs around, I stand. "Okay. But let me get you some water first."

Her lower lip trembles, and tears pool in her eyes. "He spiked my water, Jackson. I'm so stupid. I knew it tasted off. Salty. If I hadn't drank it, I could've fought him off."

Walking around the bed, I sit down beside her, careful to keep some distance between us even though I want to hold her in my arms and kiss her fears away. But I don't want to crowd her. She's been through an ordeal, and I don't know if my touch will comfort or frighten her.

"This isn't your fault. He was a sick bastard who loved to hurt women."

"Was?" she whispers. I watch as her expression transforms from confusion to panic to relief. "You ... you killed him."

I nod. My throat is as dry as the Sahara Desert when I speak. "I had hoped you didn't see that." I know I was out of control. I'm not going to apologize for that, but I hate the thought my savagery might have frightened her again.

"I did, but it's hazy. All of it's hazy because my vision was so messed up."

"We think he gave you GHB. That's one of the known side effects."

"Is he really dead?" Her eyes examine mine.

"He is. We couldn't let him live. *I* couldn't let him live."

"Good," she whispers, and my heart hurts when tears pool in her eyes again. "He ... he was going to rape me. He ... he touched me." Sobs burst from her chest, and we move toward one another at the same time. My arms open in invitation, and she falls into me.

"I'm so sorry, Nessa." I hate I had to listen while that was happening, but the plan worked. We got the bastard, and he's not here to hurt her ever again.

"Don't say that," she says in between sobs. She lifts her head, pinning me with glassy eyes. "You saved me from a fate worse than death. He was going to make me do hideous things." A violent shudder wracks her slim frame.

"I know, babe." I press a kiss to her head, thinking of all the things that bastard said. Several revelations were made, and I want to ask Nessa about a few things but not now. She's too fragile, and she needs to sleep and heal.

"Thank you, Jackson. I don't know how you were there, or why, but you saved me. You saved Kayleigh."

My eyes burn with fierce determination. "I will always save

you, Nessa. No one will ever hurt you again, and that includes me." Gently, I cup her gorgeous face. "I'll explain it all later after you have rested. I will tell you everything, but there is one thing I need you to know now."

My heart swells in my chest, and a rush of butterflies swoops into my stomach. I hope she can't tell how nervous I am. I'm not sure if she heard me earlier, and I need to ensure she knows this. "I love you. I have for months now. I was too afraid to admit it to myself, let alone to you, but I can't hold it inside anymore."

Tears cascade over the gentle slopes of her cheeks, and I hate that I've hurt her. I want to punt kick myself in the head for being such an ass. It's obvious from the conversation on the boat that Nessa wasn't aware of what Christian had planned. That she's an innocent in all this.

"I know I have fucked up so bad, and I'm sorry for every cruel word and action. I was a prick, and I'm so unworthy of you, I know that." I brush her tears away, kissing her flushed cheeks. "I wish I had a do-over so I could do it right this time, but I want to make it up to you if you'll let me. I want to prove I mean what I say."

She opens her mouth to speak, but I press a finger to her lips. "I don't want you to say anything. I want you to hear the truth in my words, to hold them close, and to think about it. To think about a future for us." I kiss her forehead, my lips lingering there for a few beats as I savor the feel of her in my arms and the taste of her skin against my mouth. I ease back, releasing her. "There's a small bathroom through there." I point at the door at the side of the bedroom before leaning back and grabbing the pile of clothes I removed from my bag earlier for her. "Sweats and a shirt. I know it's not ideal but—"

"Thanks. They are clean and *not* this bathing suit." She offers me a shaky smile as I place them on the bed beside her.

348

"I'll be right back. I'm going to get you some toast and a drink." Something hydrating that isn't water. I glance at my watch. "We should be landing in London soon."

"London?" she croaks.

"We'll be staying the night at my parents' home in London. I hope that's okay."

Panic races across her face, and I take her hands in mine. "It'll be fine. They have an idea of what went down. They'll just be relieved to know we're all unhurt." I want to tell her to trust me, but I know I've got a lot to do before we're in that space. "And we'll be flying back to the US tomorrow."

"Don't leave me," she whispers, gripping my hand close. "Please."

"Nessa." I peer deep into her eyes. "I'm going nowhere. I'm never leaving you again."

Chapter Thirty-Seven
Jackson

"**M**y baby!" Mom rushes out the door of our eight-bedroom detached Kensington home, flinging herself into my arms.

"Hey, Mom." I bundle her lithe, dancer-slash-model's figure into a bear hug. "It's good to see you."

She grabs my cheeks, peppering me with kisses.

I think she missed me.

She holds me at arm's length, her troubled gaze roaming me from head to toe. "Are you okay?" She inspects the lump at my temple that's already bruising before lifting my busted knuckles to her face, muttering in Czech under her breath as she inspects my torn, bloodied skin.

"Mom, I'm fine," I say as Anderson and Hunt climb out of the car.

While Mom's diverted welcoming them with boisterous hugs and kisses on the cheek, I lean back into the car, holding out my arms to the vulnerable, scared girl cowering on the back seat. "I told you I'd look after you, and I won't leave your side. I promise." Cautiously, she scoots along the seat, taking my hand.

The second her soft flesh meets mine, warmth treks up my arm, spreading throughout my body, soothing me all over. I help her out of the car, circling my arm around her shoulder.

"Vanessa!" Mom approaches. "How wonderful to see you after all this time although I wish the circumstances were more pleasant." She examines Nessa from head to toe, like she did with me. "Jackson. Don't be rude." She swats at my arm. "I need my hug."

"Mom." My tone warns her to back off, but Mom is not one to be told no. She comes from a large family in Prague, and they are super close and super touchy-feely.

"It's okay." Nessa's voice is quiet as she shucks out of my arms. She's visibly trembling, but it doesn't deter Mom.

She wraps Nessa up in her arms like she's cotton wool, holding her tenderly and dotting kisses into her hair. "*Můj drahý*. It's going to be okay."

Dad can't know exactly what went down, but he knows the type of man Montgomery was and that Nessa needed medical care, so he knows she's traumatized. He's clearly prepped Mom so she's aware to be extra careful around Vanessa.

Tears glisten in Nessa's eyes, and I can't take it any longer. "Mom." My gaze dances between Mom and Nessa.

Mom's eyes light up as she scrutinizes the expression on my face. "*Miluješ ji.*"

I only ever picked up a few of her Czech sayings, but I'm pretty sure that means you love her. "Yes. Now hand her back." I open my arms, and she releases Nessa with a squeal. I place protective arms around Nessa. "Sorry. She's probably going to fuss over you like crazy," I whisper.

"I'm so happy my boy is in love. This is wonderful." Mom claps her hands.

Behind me, Anderson cough-laughs, and I just know Hunt has the smarmiest grin on his face. They love to see me suffer.

Pricks.

Thank fuck, we're only staying one night. Don't get me wrong. I *adore* my mother, but Nessa and I have a lot of shit to work through, and Mom is likely to put her foot in it before I've had a chance to fix things.

"Come in, come in, and I'll show you to your rooms." Mom flaps her hands about, ushering us inside.

We follow her into the high-ceilinged entrance hall, and Nessa smiles up at me as she glances around. Mom has a real flair for interior décor, and she's decorated the UK house in a combination of modern and traditional styles, paying homage to the existing Victorian architecture.

"I kept dinner for you all, and you can eat after you freshen up," she says, as we follow her up the sweeping staircase to the second level where the guest bedrooms are. "Boys, you can take these rooms." She points to two rooms on the left. "I assume Vanessa will be sleeping with you, Jackson, so I put her things in your room."

Vanessa's eyes pop wide while Anderson coughs again to disguise his laughter.

"Thank you, Laurena," Hunt says, ever the suck-up.

"We'll meet you downstairs in a few," Anderson says before they slip into their respective rooms.

"Things?" Vanessa asks as we follow Mom up to the next level. The upper level houses the family bedrooms including the master suite my parents sleep in, along with my room, and what used to be Dani's room.

"I know you had to leave the Canary Islands in a hurry," Mom explains. "So, I went shopping to get you a few things." She gently touches Nessa's hand. "Any excuse, am I right?"

"That was very generous and thoughtful," Nessa says. "Thank you so much."

Yeah, thanks, Mom. I like seeing Nessa in my clothes, and I had zero issue if she had to wear them until we returned to Rydeville, but I can't be mad Mom went to so much trouble to care for my girl. She's a mom in a million, and I know I'm lucky to have her.

I open the door to my bedroom and burst out laughing. "A few things?" I arch a brow at Mom. My room is covered with bags. They are all over the bed and lining the floor.

Mom smooths a hand over her long blonde hair. "I might have gotten a little carried away." She shrugs, smiling as she takes Nessa's hand, pulling her into the room. "You don't need to take all of them with you. You can leave some here for when you next come to visit. I called your mom to get your sizes, so hopefully everything fits." She leans in close to my girl. "Don't worry, I didn't explain you were here or the circumstances."

Holy fuck. Mom really went all out. She must want me to settle down pretty bad. Where she's from, it's not unusual to settle down at an early age, and I know she wouldn't bat an eyelash if I told her Nessa and I were getting married.

Warmth spreads across my chest at the thought, and I'm not freaking out at the idea. Quite the opposite. Huh.

"This is amazing, Mrs. Lauder," Nessa says, surveying the bags with wide eyes. "You really didn't have to go to this much trouble."

"Nonsense. A girl can never have too many clothes. Especially one as beautiful as you. And call me Laurena. Mrs. Lauder sounds ancient!" She squeezes Nessa's hand. "You really have blossomed into a stunning beauty." She smiles. "My son is a lucky man."

Fuck, this is awkward. Nessa and I aren't even together, and if Mom keeps this up, we never will be. She'll send Nessa running for the hills before the night is out.

"You two are going to make beautiful babies," she adds, proving my point.

Nessa gulps, looking blankly into space as she turns to me for help.

"Oh my God. Mom!" I grab her hand, escorting her to the door. "Stop! You're going to scare Nessa away." I kiss her cheek. "You're the best, Mom. I love you, but you need to leave."

She laughs, and her green eyes sparkle with mirth. "You know I need some grandchildren, Jackson."

"Goodbye." I close the door in her face, and her tinkling laughter follows her as she walks down the hallway. I press my brow to the door before turning around and grinning. "Sorry. She tends to get carried away."

"I'll say." Nessa laughs, and it's the first time all day that her brow is free of worry lines, so I guess that's something else I can thank Mom for. "But she's amazing," she continues. "I'd forgotten how full of life your mom is."

"Never a dull moment, but I wouldn't change her for the world." I shove my hands in the pockets of my jeans, glancing around. "Do you need a hand unpacking all this?"

She shakes her head. "I'll manage."

"Do you want something to eat now? You only had toast on the plane."

"I'm not sure I can eat much," she admits. "And I'd rather take a shower and get changed."

"How about I run you a bath, and then I'll leave you to freshen up?"

"That sounds lovely."

I walk to her, gently reeling her into my arms. "You doing okay?"

She looks up at me with big trusting eyes. "Did you mean what you said on the plane, Jackson?"

"I did. Every word. I'm done fighting my feelings. Done acting like a heartless prick. I can't live without you, Nessa. I mean that. You're it for me." I don't want to say too much or push her before she's ready, and we still have so much to talk about. "I hope I haven't blown it between us, but even if I have, know that I will always be here for you. I'm making it my mission to ensure no one ever hurts you again, and that is one promise you can count on."

Chapter Thirty-Eight
Jackson

I leave Nessa to her own devices after running her a bath. While I was filling the tub, Mom left a pitcher of water, a glass, and some fresh fruit for her. Grabbing a quick shower in the main bathroom, I towel dry my hair before pulling on a clean pair of jeans and a sweater. October in London is cold, and my balls are already freezing. I toe on my Chucks and head downstairs to find Dad, but he finds me first.

"Son." He's waiting at the bottom of the stairs for me. "I'm so glad you are okay." Without hesitation, he pulls me into a hug, and for the first time in a year, I return his embrace. We cling to one another for a couple minutes, before breaking apart. "Let's talk in my study."

I follow him into the grand room with high ceilings and bay windows. Heavy patterned curtains frame the glass panels, creating an old-world feel. The whole room has that vibe, but it works. Both for the room and my old man. Instead of sitting behind his wide mahogany desk, he motions for me to sit with him in the high-backed leather chairs in front of the roaring fire.

He pours two whiskeys, adding ice and a thin layer of

water, before handing one to me. "I think we'll need alcohol for this conversation."

I take a sip of the liquid, welcoming the fiery, bitter sting as it glides down my throat.

"Tell me everything that happened," he says when he's seated in front of me, one leg casually draped over his knee.

I could demand he talk first, but something has shifted today. Within me, and in my relationship with my father. A certain sort of peace has descended on me since I avenged Dani's death although I'm sure that's only temporary. I'm guessing the next few months will be the challenge, because now I've dealt with that murdering prick, I will finally have time to grieve, and I know that's going to be painful.

Things have altered in our father-son dynamic too. I felt it on the phone when he cried. He's been holding out on me. It's clear he had his own plans, and I'm embarrassed for jumping to obvious conclusions, for the things I've said to him, and how I've treated him this past year, for not trusting him more, and for not realizing the obvious truth—my father would die for his family, and there's no way he would ever have let Christian Montgomery get away with what he did to his daughter.

I misjudged him and the situation, but grief can do that to a person. We have both suffered in different ways as we've struggled in the aftermath of Dani's death.

All of it ends now.

He listens attentively as I update him fully on everything that went down today with Montgomery and the things leading up to it. He refills our glasses, without interrupting me, and by the time I'm finished, I'm drained.

"I meant what I said on the phone, Jackson. I never wanted you to take this burden on. To carry this truth with you for the rest of your life. I'm an old man. Dani was my daughter, and she was only taken because Hunt and I made a terrible business decision."

"You didn't do any of those things to her, Dad. That bastard is the only one responsible. And I don't feel burdened. I feel lighter, freer. Dani was my sister, and that man also hurt Anderson's wife and mother-in-law, and he hurt Nessa today. It would have been a lot worse if we hadn't been there, so if that's your way of asking if I'm troubled over what I've done, the answer is no."

"It feels a little inappropriate to say this, but I'm going to say it anyway." He puts his drink down, leaning forward in his chair. "I'm proud of you, Jackson. I'm proud of the man you're becoming."

"Thanks, Dad." A messy ball of emotion wedges in my throat. "It means a lot that you'd say that especially after the horrible way I've treated you recently. I misjudged the situation and you. I'm sorry."

He waves his hands about. "I've already forgiven you for that. You were justified in your anger, and I wish I could've told you the truth, but I was trying to protect you. To keep you out of it. I knew letting you move to Rydeville was a mistake, but you were adamant about supporting Kaiden, and we thought we could trust Atticus." He shakes his head. "He played Hunt and me for a fool. Using our resources to further his own aims when he knew our interest lay with Montgomery."

"Atticus has paid the price for his treachery, and it couldn't have happened to a more deserving man."

"I agree, but I'd still like the bastard found and taken to task for his sins."

"It will happen, Dad. Kai and Rick won't stop looking for him. He needs to make this right."

"It's a miracle those boys turned out as solid as they did. They must have more of their mother in them."

"They do."

We stare into the fire as a comfortable silence envelops us. Flames lick the top of the open fireplace, wafting and weaving, sending blasts of heat in our direction, warming my chilled bones.

"I have wanted that man to pay from the moment he took Dani," Dad admits, staring into the flames as he begins opening up. "I was frantic with worry. I hired a ton of different private investigators to scour the world looking for her, only for them to turn up empty-handed."

His Adam's apple bobs in his throat. "I even went to Montgomery's office, got down on my knees, and begged him to return her." A muscle clenches in his jaw. "The sick bastard got off on that, and he taunted me about..." He grabs his whiskey, draining the rest of the amber liquid in one go. "I was broken, son." He glances at me. "A shell of a man. The only way I managed to drag my ass out of bed every day was my fear of anything happening to you and your mom. He threatened you both too."

"Why did he come after you and not Hunt?"

"Oh, he threatened Hunt too, but that's something for Ethan to discuss with Sawyer." He stands, pouring more whiskey into his glass. I place my hand over my drink, declining more. I don't want to get drunk. Nessa's had a horrific day, and she needs me—I can't support her properly if I'm drunk.

"He went after me first because I had a daughter. Those perverts get off on hurting women and children. I'm sure you've seen that by now." I nod, because I have. "He took Dani, and it destroyed all of us. It almost ruined my marriage, and you almost threw away your future."

"Is that why you were insisting I attend RU?"

"In part," he admits, swirling the amber liquid in his glass. "You were already going off the rails, and I needed to try to keep you on the right path. But I also believe it's important to get a strong education. I would like you to take over from me at some point, but I won't force you, Jackson. Either to stay at RU or to take over the reins with the business. It's your life. Your future. Your choice."

Wow. This is huge. If he'd said this to me a couple of months ago, I would've bailed on RU instantly. Without a second thought.

Now, things are different.

"I'd like to think it over, but I have no plans to drop out of college."

A genuine smile graces his lips. "Would this have anything to do with the beautiful young lady up in your room?"

I tilt my head to the side, smirking. "It has everything to do with Nessa."

"Ah, I see." His smile grows wider. "You have found your soul mate."

"I have."

"I'm happy for you son, and I hope you both are as happy as your mother and me."

My skepticism shows on my face.

"Out with it. There will be no more secrets in this family."

"How can you say she's your soul mate when you asked her for an open marriage?"

His features soften as he stares at me for a few beats. His silence tells me he's contemplating admitting something. He clears his throat, eyeballing me. "It's because she is my soul mate that I agreed when she asked me."

"Wait! What?" I splutter. "Are you saying Mom is the one who asked for an open marriage?"

His answering smile holds a tinge of amusement. "Is it really any surprise, Jackson? Your mother is a free spirit. A beautiful, vibrant, energetic butterfly who needs to spread her wings. I never want to clip those." He sips his whiskey, looking thoughtful as I slump in my chair, flabbergasted. "I will admit it took some time for me to come around to the idea because sharing her didn't appeal to me."

"So why did you agree?"

"It was share her or lose her," he quietly says. "And existing in a world without your mother is not existing."

"I don't know what to say," I blurt.

"When you get married, and you start a family, you will realize that rarely are things black-and-white. It's only when you are in that situation you fully appreciate what it means to truly love someone. To properly compromise. Don't feel bad for me, son. I am happy. I love your mother, and I've never wanted any other woman. I've had the odd fleeting dalliance, but I have done nothing to earn the reputation the media presents of me. Your mother is discreet in her affairs and respectful to me. I always know who she's seeing and where she's going. They never last long, and it's been a lot less frequent than I expected. We've made it work."

I imagine a scenario where Nessa asks me for an open marriage, and my stupid brain instantly flashes back to the night of the party and the rage I felt watching her with another man. "I could never do that. I could never share Nessa."

"I don't think you will have to. Something tells me that woman will cherish you for life."

"Well," I admit, rubbing the back of my neck. "I have a lot of groveling to do before we get to the cherishing part, but I'm determined."

Dad cracks up laughing, and I join him. It's been a long time since we've just sat down and talked without harsh words or angry looks.

"I just ask one thing, Jackson. Please don't treat your

mother any differently. She adores you, and it would break her heart if you thought ill of her."

"I'm not gonna lie, Dad. It freaks me out a little, and I'll need to process it, but I don't want to hurt Mom."

"Good boy." He slaps my shoulder. "Is there anything else you need to know?"

"Why didn't you retaliate? What were you waiting for?"

"When Montgomery let Dani go, he did so on one condition. That we never disclosed what we had discovered about him, his company, and the elite and that we never reported what had happened to her. He promised to kill you and your mother if I made one move against him. I couldn't risk it, Jackson. You saw how broken your sister was. I couldn't risk anything happening to you or Laurena. And Montgomery was watching. He had people shadowing us. He sent spies into my businesses."

"That's why you went crazy with a new security system and additional bodyguards." I run my hands along the arms of the chair, seeing a lot of things in a new light.

"Yes, and it's also why I didn't openly retaliate after Dani died. The threat against you and your mom was still very real. As much as I wanted that bastard dead, I wouldn't jeopardize your safety. It's why we let Atticus and Wes go after Hearst while we stayed in the shadows. The plan was to take down Hearst and then take Montgomery down next, but everything changed after things went to shit at Parkhurst."

"Me killing Trent changed things."

He nods. "He renewed his threat, and he has made several attempts in the past few months on your life and your mother's life."

"What?!" I roar, jumping up. "What do you mean?"

Dad stands, and he's remarkably cool considering the bomb he just dropped. "Calm down, son. Sit." He pushes me into the chair. "I've had a team of men protecting you and your mother. I didn't want to worry you, so I said nothing. It also worked better that you weren't aware. Christian tried several times, but I hired a group of ex-mercenaries this time, and these men know what they are doing. None of the thugs he sent got close to you or your mom. Then word got out that his hitmen were turning up in body bags, and no one wanted to take the gig. While this was happening, I sent PIs out around the world, trying to find him. My guy followed you to Lanzarote and reported that Christian was there. I had a PI on the ground in Europe, so I reassigned him. The plan was for them to take Christian out, but you beat them to it."

I drop to my knees on the floor in front of him. "I'm so sorry, Dad. For not believing you. For not trusting you."

"Stand up, son."

I climb to my feet. "I appreciate your apology, but it's not necessary. Like I said, I have already forgiven you." He places his empty glass down, wrapping his arm around my shoulder. "Now, what do you say we join your friends and your lady love for dinner? I think it's high time we celebrated."

Chapter Thirty-Nine
Vanessa

I have always been fond of Jackson's parents, and their warm welcome today reinforces that sentiment. Laurena has gone out of her way to ensure I'm comfortable and I have everything I need. Travis has been charming and friendly over dinner, politely inquiring into my wellbeing without intruding. It's clear Kaiden and Sawyer are comfortable around Jackson's parents, laughing and joking and appearing relaxed.

I wish I could do the same, but I'm exhausted, and quite frankly, it's an effort to smile. I eat, purely because I don't want to offend Laurena. The spicy chicken and couscous dish is delicious, but my stomach revolts at each swallowed mouthful, still tender after being drugged.

Jackson squeezes my hand under the table. "You okay?" he whispers. He's asked me a bunch of times already, and it's obvious his concern is genuine. So were his heartfelt words earlier, but there is much I don't know and a lot to forgive him for.

I nod, feebly squeezing his hand in return, but he's not buying it. Jackson knows me well enough to see the truth I'm desperately trying to disguise from his family and friends. Despite the front I'm wearing, I am broken inside and so mad at myself. It seems I'm destined to run headfirst into the worst kind of trouble, making one bad decision upon another that all end up with me getting hurt.

I'm grateful to be here with Jackson, because right now, I need him to remind me of who I am, and I need his strength and support to get through this day. I'm beyond grateful he cared enough to follow me halfway around the world. He saved me from that bastard, they all did, and I will forever be in their debt.

I hang my head as a familiar blanket of shame ghosts over me. *How could I have been so gullible? So naïve? So utterly ignorant of the warning signs that were right under my nose?* You'd think having survived one monster I would learn to recognize another. But nope. Instead of using my brain, I had blinders on, running straight into the arms of another predator.

My entire body shakes and shivers at the thought of what he had planned for me. Memories of his hands on me, in me, return to haunt me, and I squeeze my eyes shut, needing it to stop. I'm aware I'm visibly trembling, and I probably look like a basket case, but I can't halt my body's natural reaction.

I need something to take the edge off, but there's no way I'm touching alcohol or drugs after what my body has been put through today, so that only leaves...

Jackson's arm wraps around me as he pulls me in closer to his side. "It's okay. I'm here. I've got you."

Tears glisten in my eyes as I look up at him. I don't want to be this weak, pathetic, naïve creature any longer. This stupid, vulnerable girl who willingly jets off to meet a stranger purely because he made me feel wanted, because he said and did all the right things to make me trust him when I never should have.

"I need you," I whisper, low enough so only he can hear.

He nods, pressing a kiss to the top of my head. "I'm here, babe. Whatever you need is yours."

He has misinterpreted my statement, and I need to make my intentions clearer. "Can we go upstairs?" I whisper.

His eyes skim my face, frowning a little with whatever he finds. Then, his loving smile returns, and he kisses my brow, squeezing my hand again. "Of course."

He releases his hold on me, pushing his chair back and standing. "We're going to call it a night."

"Do you need anything, Vanessa?" Laurena asks in that soft, lyrical voice of hers, one that still bears a slight accent in homage to her heritage. She rounds the table, sliding her arms around my shoulders and kissing my cheek.

"No, thank you. You have already ensured I have everything I need." I smile shyly at her, and she kisses my cheek one final time before returning to her seat.

Jackson pulls out my chair, helping me to stand.

Travis rises, kissing both my cheeks. "Sleep well, my dear."

"You too," I mumble, my skin heating in a blush, unaccustomed to such blatant displays of affection.

Sawyer hugs me next. "It's going to be okay, Van."

"Thank you," I blurt, realizing I haven't thanked him or Kaiden. I glance over Sawyer's shoulder at Kai. "Thank you both for helping Jackson to rescue me."

"You're one of us, Nessa," Kai confirms.

Sawyer eases me out of his embrace.

"Abby, Shandra, and the others wanted to be there too," Kai explains. "They told me to tell you they love you and everyone is glad you're okay."

Jackson reels me into the side of his body, wrapping his protective arm around me.

"Tell them I'll call them tomorrow when we get home."

"Goodnight, everyone," Jackson says, speaking for both of us, guiding me out the door and up the stairs to his room.

He closes the door quietly behind us, locking it as I walk to the bed and lie down. I cleared away all the purchases Laurena made earlier, but I didn't have the time to go through everything, so some of the clothes are hanging up in Jackson's extensive walk-in closet, and the rest are still in the bags lining one side of the wall. I unpacked all the cosmetics and toiletries, placing them in one of the cabinets in the bathroom.

It felt a little weird putting my possessions away in Jackson's space, alongside his things, but in another way, it felt completely natural.

"Talk to me," he says, kicking off his Chucks as he sits on the edge of the bed beside me. "What's going through your mind?"

I reach my hand out, palming his gorgeous face. He hasn't shaved in a couple of days, and there's a light layer of sexy dark-blond stubble lining his jawline. My fingers rub across the fine, prickly hairs as he stares at me with those spellbinding blue eyes. "My head is a mess," I truthfully admit. "I feel so stupid, Jackson. I *was* stupid."

"Shush." He weaves his fingers through my wavy hair. "None of this is your fault. That prick manipulated you because that's the way the elite do things."

"I don't want to talk about that," I spit out. I sit upright, leaning in closer and holding both sides of his face. "I know we need to. But not tonight. I can't face that yet."

He clasps the nape of my neck gently. "What do you need?"

"You," I whisper, feeling heat creep up my neck. "I need you to help distract me. To push these thoughts from my head."

"Nessa." His eyes flood with love and sympathy. "I would

love nothing more than to bury myself inside you, but, baby, you've been to hell and back today, I don't want—"

Tears stream out of my eyes. "Jackson, please." I scoot in closer until there is barely any space between us. "Please don't say no. I need you. I need you to replace the memory of his touch. I need to feel your hands on my body. I need to feel you moving inside me to know I'm still alive. That he hasn't ruined me like he threatened."

He brushes my tears away. "Nessa." His voice cracks, and a single tear rolls down his cheek. "You have no idea how hard it was to hold back while he was doing those things to you." He collapses against me, pulling me into his arms. I nuzzle his shoulder as he wraps his warm, strong, protective arms around me. "I want to go back and kill him all over again for hurting you." His chest heaves as he sobs, and I cling to him while I cry. It's no surprise our emotion needs an outlet. It's been a stressful couple of days for both of us. "If anything had happened to you, Nessa. God." His voice cracks at the end, and he holds me closer, his sobs intensifying.

We stay like that for a few minutes, expunging our emotions in a much-needed therapeutic cleansing as we cling to one another, crying.

"Jackson." I run my fingers through the silky strands of his hair. "I love you so much, and I know we have a lot of things to discuss, but right now, I need you to make love to me. Please don't make me beg."

He lifts his head, sniffling. "Are you sure this is what you want?" I nod. "Then, you don't have to beg. I told you that before. Never again with me."

He stands, yanking his sweater over his head with one hand. Crouching in front of me, he takes my hands in his. "Just promise me you'll tell me if I do anything you don't like or if you want me to stop."

"I promise," I readily agree, leaning down and pressing my lips to his. It feels like forever since we last kissed, but my mouth remembers his, my lips tracing every familiar curve of his lips, my tongue exploring his hungry mouth. We kiss for ages, letting our lips do all the talking this time.

When we break apart, we are both flushed and panting. But there are no hideous thoughts racing through my mind. No distressful images burning the back of my retinas. There is only a gentle, soothing warmth building inside me, spreading out, healing me from the inside.

Slowly, we undress, watching one another as we shed clothing until we are both naked. Jackson pulls back the covers, crawling in after me, pulling my body flush against his until we're pressed together, skin to skin. He threads his fingers through my hair while dusting feather-soft kisses all over my face. "I love you, Nessa. It will only ever be you."

"I love you too," I reply, arching my neck as his lips trail lower. His tongue licks that sensitive spot just under my ear, and I moan, pressing my hips against his, thrusting against his hard-on. Carefully, his hands roam my body, tenderly caressing my skin, igniting an outbreak of fiery tremors in their wake.

Jackson rolls me on to my back, climbing over me, using his elbows to prop himself up. Waves of messy blond hair tumble over his brow when he bends down to kiss me. Our mouths collide in the most loving kiss, and every soft brush of his lips unknots the ball of anxiety in my chest, chasing away my fears and my insecurities.

This side of Jackson is not one I'm hugely familiar with. Usually, he prefers a rougher approach, a more demanding kiss, a firmer claiming of my body, but he instinctively knows what I need now, and he's delivering in spades.

His lips and his hands are worshipful as he showers affection on my body, invoking the most incredible sensations inside me. My touches are equally reverential as I explore every inch of skin on his body, and with every loving stroke, every adoring kiss, I'm melting into the bed and drowning in him.

I experience a moment of panic when he slides a finger inside me, and he notices, stalling over me and breaking our kiss to examine my eyes.

"I'm okay," I reassure him, stretching up to kiss the corner of his mouth. "More than okay. Please don't stop."

Keeping his eyes trained on mine, he slowly pumps his finger in and out of me, drawing the most delicious tremors of bliss from my body. He removes his finger, sliding down my body, and I spread my legs for him, arching my back and grabbing the bottom sheet of the bed, whimpering when his tongue licks a path along my slit, lavishing my overheated skin with attention.

Closing my eyes, I forget about everything but the careful, slow, adoring way he's enjoying my body. Using his fingers, his tongue, and his lips, he brings me to a heavenly climax, one I feel in every part of my body.

"God, I love you," I whisper, swiping my tears away as he climbs back over me.

"I love you, too, babe. So fucking much." He kisses me softly. "You still want to do this?" he asks, lining our bodies up.

"More than I've ever wanted anything."

He threads his fingers in mine, keeping his eyes locked on me as he slowly inches inside me. The incredible fullness fills every empty part of me, warming me from the inside out. We move together in slow, sensual strokes, our bodies perfectly in sync, our hearts aligned, and it's the most loving, sweet, tender, exquisite moment of my life.

We kiss over and over again, taking our time as our bodies flow and ebb, neither of us in our usual hurry to reach the finish line. Every touch, every whisper, every kiss, and every caress are healing me, and from somewhere deep inside, my strength returns, bolstering me with confidence, reassuring me I can do this.

We arrive in Boston at three o'clock the next day, climbing into the waiting Land Rover, grateful to be back on home soil.

"Abby and Shandra wanted to pick us up," Kai explains, glancing into the back seat. Spotting me snuggled against Jackson, he fixes me with his warm, brown gaze and smiles. Sawyer and Kai have been treating me with kid gloves, watching me when they think I don't notice, waiting for me to break, most likely. "But I thought you might need some space."

"I do." I need to fess up to my friends, but that can wait until tomorrow, because the conversation Jackson and I need to have takes precedence. "Tell Abby I'll see her in class tomorrow and we can catch up then."

"You're not taking the rest of the week off?" Jackson asks, his brows knitting together.

"I've missed enough classes as it is."

"Are you sure you're up to returning so soon?" he adds, rubbing soothing circles on my side with his thumb.

"I'm not going to crawl into bed and lick my wounds, no matter how tempting that is," I admit. "Because then that bastard has won. He hasn't ruined me. He didn't win. *I* did. *We* did." My gaze jumps between Jackson, Sawyer, and Kaiden, because I want them to hear what I'm saying.

I mean every word of it, but I also know it's fighting talk and I might have days where I feel the complete opposite, where I might struggle to get out of bed, but I'm determined, and I truly believe that is half the battle.

I have survived worse and come out the other side. I can

handle this. What he did, what he tried to do, will not unravel my hard work.

I figure I can continue to beat myself up over my failure to read the obvious signs, and my poor judgment, or I can learn from it, dust myself off, and get back on the saddle. I prefer the latter, and I'm strong enough to do this, because I pulled myself back from the brink before.

I don't think I've given myself enough credit, and I need to cut myself some slack.

Focusing on all the negative, stupid shit I've done isn't helpful. Prioritizing the good in my life and remembering how I've clawed my way out of a dark hole need to remain my focus, because those bastards may have claimed my past, but the only person owning my future is me.

Chapter Forty
Vanessa

"**I** don't think this is a good idea," Jackson says when we pull up to the front of my apartment building. "You could still be in danger."

"From the contact Montgomery mentioned?" I refuse to call him by anything else now.

Sawyer nods. "We haven't been able to identify who was helping him. We don't know what this person's instructions are. I agree with Lauder. You should move in with us. It's safer there."

"I know you all mean well, but I need to do this for me." They look at me like I'm swinging from the insanity tree. I clasp Jackson's hand, looking directly at him, although my words are for all of them. "I know you want to protect me, and I love you for that, but I can't hide behind you. I need to do this myself. To prove that I'm strong enough to come through this on my own."

"But you're not on your own, babe," Jackson pleads. "And this is too risky. Please, I'm begging you. Come back to my place. Let me keep you safe."

I understand his logic, and I can see where he's coming from. I'd be lying to myself if I said I wasn't petrified of returning to my penthouse alone, but that's exactly why I have to do this.

I can't let Jackson fight all my battles for me.

I can't crumple at the first sign of danger.

I will be smart this time. I will be observant and vigilant. And I'll be prepared.

"Can't you keep me safe here?" I ask. "You can help me to install the best security systems, and maybe, I should get a bodyguard."

Sawyer purses his lips, looking out the window, while Jackson rubs the back of his neck in an awkward tell.

"What don't I know?" I ask, reading their signs.

"A lot," Jackson reluctantly agrees. "And I really think we need to talk today." He glances out the window, up at the building, sighing. "I don't like this. Not one little bit, but if you're determined to do it, let me stay here for a couple nights until we have protective measures in place."

That's not an unreasonable request.

"I can sleep on the couch," he adds. "I'm not expecting anything."

Kaiden snort-laughs from the passenger seat, and Jackson flips him the bird.

"I have guest bedrooms. You don't need to sleep on the couch."

Hurt darts over his face, but he composes himself quickly. "Okay. It's settled." He looks at Sawyer. "I'll talk to Nessa about options, and we'll call you later to put some plans in place.

"Cool." Sawyer pulls me into a hug. "Stay safe."

"I will."

376

We get out, saying goodbye to Kaiden before making our way inside.

When we step out of the elevator on the penthouse level, Jackson pushes me behind him, snatching the key from my hand. "Stay here. I want to check the place first. Xavier said it's okay, but I want to be sure."

He leaves me scratching my head in confusion as he slips into my apartment, gun in hand, wondering what Xavier has to do with anything.

"It's clear," he says, opening the door for me. I step inside while he brushes past me to grab our bags.

"What did you mean by Xavier said it's okay?"

"That's part of what I need to tell you," he admits, looking sheepish again.

"Okay." I glance around my place, but everything looks just how I left it. "Let me make us something to eat, and we can talk in the living room."

Jackson wanders around the apartment, running his hands through his hair as I make us some wraps. I pour juice into two glasses instead of grabbing water from the refrigerator. I'm not sure I'll ever be able to drink a bottle of water again without wondering if it's been spiked. Grabbing a bag of chips from the cupboard, I load everything on a tray and carry it out of the kitchen.

Jackson rushes forward, taking the tray from my hands and carrying it to the coffee table.

I sit on one side of the couch while he takes the other. "I'm not even sure where to start," Jackson says as we munch on our late lunch.

"From the beginning. Why did you date me?"

"I need to go further back to explain," he says, and I urge him to continue with my eyes. "This is about Dani," he adds even though

I've got no idea why his sister committing suicide has anything to do with me or our situation. "Two years before Dani killed herself, she was kidnapped, tortured, and raped repeatedly by Christian Montgomery and other men at some island she was imprisoned on."

My glass slips out of my fingers, juice spilling all over me, the couch, and the floor.

"Shit. I'm sorry for just dropping that on you, but there's no way of softening this," Jackson says, jumping up and racing to the kitchen.

My heart is thumping behind my rib cage as I process his words, staring off into space, contemplating unimaginable horrors.

Jackson returns, handing me a wad of paper towels, helping me to mop up the spillage.

"Oh my God, Jackson." My voice quakes, and my lips tremble. "I can't believe that monster did those things to Dani! Why didn't your dad press charges? Why wasn't that sick fuck locked up?"

"It's complicated, but the CliffsNotes version is he was blackmailing my father and Hunt's father. He threatened to kill me and my mother if Dad went to the police. He made several attempts on our lives these past few months."

"What?" I can hardly see through my blurry vision. Jackson moves beside me, taking my hands. "He tried to kill you?" Montgomery's words flit through my mind, and I didn't believe him when he said this, but after witnessing the lethal way Jackson took care of him back on the boat, I know it's the truth. "Because you killed Trent."

"He told you about that."

I nod. "He made out like Trent was this angel, but I know you wouldn't have killed him without good reason, and if he was anything like his father, he was the devil incarnate."

"He was his Mini-Me," Jackson confirms. "He wasn't a

good guy. Abby was forced into an engagement with him, and he was a prick to her. She can fill you in on the deets. I killed him in self-defense." Jackson explains about the elite, their depraved, illegal activities, what Atticus—Kai's father—tried to do, the things that went down at Parkhurst six months ago, and how Trent tried to kill Abby and then tried to kill Jackson.

"Jesus Christ. I'd really love a drink right now, but I'm trying to abstain," I blurt, rubbing a tense spot between my brows. This is total brain overload. To some, talk of sex slaves, sex dungeons, and other nefarious deeds might seem far-fetched, but after my upbringing, I have no trouble believing it. "Why didn't I know any of this? The news reports I read barely mentioned this stuff."

"Because they covered it up. The elite have powerful contacts in the world of business and politics, and it's in a lot of people's interests to see the organization continue."

"This is what Montgomery meant when he said I would do his bidding."

He bobs his head. "There are four founding elite members from Rydeville. Anderson. Manning. Barron. And Montgomery."

"What exactly does that mean?"

"It means you are a descendant of a founding family, which is not something to celebrate. Now Montgomery is dead, you are arguably in worse danger."

"Why?"

"They elected a new president recently, and he's restructuring the organization. It looks PC until you dig beneath the layers. They have no intention of changing their ways. Did you receive an invitation to that elite ball happening in a few weeks?"

"I did, but I wasn't going to go. I assumed it was an error."

"It's not. They know who you are, Nessa, and now that Christian is dead, his place will automatically go to you."

"Well, I'll pass. I don't want anything to do with such a disgusting organization."

"Unfortunately, it doesn't work like that. You'll have to attend, but most of us will be there. We'll keep you safe, and we'll bring you up to speed before then."

"Okay, so how does this link to you wanting to date me?"

Jackson sighs, leaning back against the couch. "I was only twelve when Dani was returned home, so my parents didn't tell me what had happened to her then, but I knew something terrible had gone down because she wasn't the same sister. I tried to help her, but I didn't know how."

He pulls at a loose thread on his sweatpants. "She tried to kill herself the first time two months after she came home," he quietly admits. "She overdosed on prescription meds. I found her passed out in her room. My parents got her to the hospital in time, and then, she spent some time in a rehabilitation program."

He turns his head so he's facing me directly as he speaks. He looks so tormented, and my heart aches for him. "My parents did everything to help her, but the damage was too great." Tears leak from his eyes, and I wrap my arms around him. "We were devastated when she jumped off that roof. I lost myself to booze, weed, and women for a few years because I couldn't deal with the pain especially after Atticus told me he knew Montgomery was behind Dani's ordeal and that my father had known too."

He explains about the discord with his father over the past year and how they've patched things up.

"I sobered up after everything went down at Parkhurst, and all I could think about was murdering that bastard, but he had fled overseas, and we couldn't find him. Hunt and I were working together, trying to find him when your name popped up."

"You knew I was his daughter. That's why you did it," I surmise.

He runs his hand up and down my back. "I wanted to get close to you to find out if he'd been in contact with you."

"He hadn't. At least not yet."

"I know that now."

"What was your plan?" I'm deliberately keeping calm, but the storm is building inside me.

I was a means to an end. That is all.

He winces, but he doesn't look away, keeping his eyes glued to mine as he admits the disgusting truth. "My plan was to make you fall in love with me, to trust me, so you'd tell me where he was."

"But I didn't know anything about him then."

"I had no way of knowing that."

"You could've asked me outright!" My outrage is climbing.

"I wanted to, but it was too risky. If you were working with him, it would ruin everything."

The memory of our last lunch at Sawyer's penthouse swims before my eyes, and all the puzzle pieces slot into place. "You knew he was behind my scholarship." My eyes pop wide. "You thought I knew! That I was lying to you!" His jaw pulls taut as he nods. I thump him in the arm. "I thought it was *you*! I thought you'd done all that and kept it anonymous because you knew I wouldn't accept charity. I stupidly thought you loved me so much you did it to avoid the pain of separation. I was going to pay you back when you fessed up, but then, I turned up at school and you were horrible to me!"

I jump up, and tears prick my eyes, only they're angry tears this time. I pace the floor as remembered humiliation slashes across my chest.

"Nessa." He stands, coming toward me, but I hold my palm up to keep him back. "I was in love with you, and I thought you'd betrayed me. That you were playing me the whole time. I was destroyed."

"Hah! The irony." I prod his chest with my finger. "I didn't betray you, you fucking asshole! I was honest with you. I opened my heart and let you in and you ... you shit all over me."

"I know, and I'm sorry. I was so confused. I tried everything to evict you from my head, but you wouldn't fucking leave."

I plant my hands on my hips. "What? Your endless stream of bed buddies couldn't help you forget?"

Oh my God, how did I forget that? How could I have let him make love to me last night? I probably have the clap or crabs now.

I am clearly insane.

"I didn't sleep with any of them," he rushes to reassure me. "I haven't slept with anyone else but you since before the summer. I swear."

I snort. "As if I believe a word that comes out of your mouth. You betrayed me, Jackson. You made me fall in love with you, and it was all a lie."

He rushes me, putting his face all up in mine. "It started out like that, but it was real, Nessa." He takes my hand, placing it on his chest, right in the spot where his heart is currently thumping like crazy. "I fucking swear it was all real. I fell for you, hook, line, and sinker. How could I not? You're smart, sweet, caring, beautiful. Everything I never knew I needed. Everything I hadn't realized I was looking for. These past couple months have been agony. I can hardly breathe without you, baby. I need you. I—"

I clamp my hand over his mouth, unable to hear any more.

I'm so confused, and I don't know what to think. I'm furious at his betrayal. He tricked me. Played me for a fool, and

I was the idiot who fell for his seductive charm. Yet, he saved me from that bastard and a life that would not have been worth living.

But that was for Dani.

He did that for his sister.

He wanted his revenge, and his plan worked in the end because I was the one who led him to Montgomery.

It was never about me.

"What else don't I know?" I snap, because I know there's more. Removing my hand from his mouth, I step back, purposely creating distance between us, folding my arms protectively across my chest.

Jackson's shoulders slump in defeat, and his voice sounds resigned when he hammers the final nail. "I hired a guy to watch you. That's how I knew you'd left to go meet him. I placed a tracker in your cell, and Hunt placed cameras in here and in your bags. We used those to follow you to the Canaries."

My heart ruptures, splintering into broken pieces. I genuinely thought Sawyer was my friend, but he was only playing the game too.

"Hunt did it to protect you," Jackson adds as if he's read my mind. "The reason we were arguing all the time was because he didn't agree with my plan. He never wanted to see you hurt, and he never believed it. Hate me all you want, but Hunt's motives were pure. It was always about protecting you from Montgomery and the elite."

"And the others?" I ask, almost choking over the lump in my throat.

"Knew nothing until we moved back here. Abby is disgusted with me, and she refused to get involved."

"Why did no one ask me?" I roar. "This all could've been cleared up if someone had had the decency to talk to me. You all knew he was my father and that he was a manipulative, depraved bastard, yet you sat back and let it happen!"

I turn around, chest heaving, barely able to breathe over the heavy betrayal pressing down on me, constricting my lungs to the point of pain.

"We knew he was plotting to kill me, and asking you outright could've backfired," he quietly admits.

"Not one of you trusted me," I sob.

"That's not it, Nessa. It was complicated as fuck." He walks in front of me, lifting his hand to wipe my tears.

"Don't touch me," I screech, moving away from him.

Pain slams into him, radiating from his tortured eyes. "Don't blame Abby or Shandra. They have had your back from day one. They've been worried sick. The reason they didn't ask you was because of me, but you didn't trust them either, Nessa. You went running off to meet that monster without telling anyone. You'd been in contact with him for weeks, and you said nothing."

I cannot believe he is trying to turn this around on me. Perhaps, there's a kernel of truth to his statement, but it doesn't mean what he did, what they *all* did, was justified. I understand their loyalty is to Jackson. He's their friend, and they barely know me. Of course, they would choose him over me, but I can't get over the fact they knew how dangerous he was, and no one dropped any hints. I'd no idea they knew C.M. If I did, this might have played out differently.

I have officially reached my breaking point.

The good news is, I'm no longer mad at myself. Oh no, all my rage is now firmly channeled in one direction—the blond-haired blue-eyed devil in front of me.

I jerk my chin up, spitting venom from my eyes. "Get out!" I yell. "Get the fuck out, Jackson, and don't ever come back. I hate you."

Chapter Forty-One
Jackson

S tanding in front of the mirror, I scowl at my reflection. The clean-cut guy in the fitted Prada tuxedo looks like the quintessential all-American male, but appearances *are* deceiving.

Underneath that charming exterior lies a coward and a fraud.

My treatment of Nessa has been so wrong. I manipulated her to serve my own agenda, proving I'm no better than the elite. I despise myself for the things I've done, not just to her but to my friends too. I'm lucky they are still standing by my side after the shit I've pulled.

I have failed Nessa time and time again, and I don't blame her for giving me the silent treatment these past three weeks. I have hurt her so much, and it was pointless in the end. She was wholly innocent, like Hunt speculated, and if I'd had the balls to open up to her, things would be very different right now.

Hindsight is a cruel bitch, casting new insights that seem so obvious now it's almost laughable. I was such a tool not to see what was right in front of me, *who* was right in front of me. I misjudged her and the entire situation, and it would serve me right if she never spoke to me again.

Except I refuse to give up, because I love her, and I won't stop fighting until she believes me.

"You sure about this?" Hunt asks, lounging against the doorway of my bedroom.

"Yes." I grab my keys and slide my wallet into the pocket of my pants. "No other man is escorting my girl. Ever," I add, my tone bursting with determination.

"She could go postal on your ass," Hunt warns.

"That's a risk I'm willing to take. She's entering the snake pit, and hell will freeze over before I'll let her go in there without me. Besides," I say, slapping him on the back. "We need you and Xavier manning things remotely." We both know Xavier could handle it alone, but I was never letting Hunt go as Nessa's date to the elite ball tonight—it was always going to be me.

"You have your equipment?" he asks.

I nod, pressing my fingers to my ear to ensure the tiny bud is still in place. The small microphone chip is adhered to the inside of my breast pocket. All that's needed to activate it is to press in on it. Then, it'll transmit to Xavier and Hunt, and my friends will be privy to my conversation if they have their devices switched on. The rest of the gang will be there, and everyone is wearing the same monitoring equipment.

Hunt's dad's company, Techxet, has developed a whole range of new monitoring and security equipment on the QT. It's a secret project, managed by a secret division in the company, and it's all very covert. While it's still in the prototype phase and undergoing continuous research and development, we have found numerous opportunities to test out the various products.

Jackson

"Be careful," Xavier adds, popping up behind Hunt. "And mind our girl."

"Always," I promise, leaving my house and jumping into my Maserati.

"What the hell are *you* doing here?" Nessa snaps, pouting when she sees it's me and not Hunt behind the door.

"Taking Cinderella to the ball." I waggle my brows, flashing her an award-worthy smile as I whip the bouquet of red roses from behind my back, hoping it will help to soften her up.

Don't get me wrong—Nessa is perfectly entitled to her rage, but she's got to forgive me sometime. *Right?*

"You look stunning," I truthfully admit, admiring how sophisticated she looks in the deep-blue satin gown. It's classically elegant with off-the-shoulder lace straps, a beaded corset top, and a flowing skirt. A simple silver diamante necklace and bracelet compliment her choice of gown, and her hair is styled in a glamorous chignon. While it's not low cut, or daring, and most likely chosen not to draw attention, there is no way she'll avoid it looking like that. "I don't think you realize how beautiful you are, Nessa. You take my breath away."

"You expect me to believe that crap?" she hisses, but it's lacking heat.

"It's the truth." I shield nothing from her, granting her my full honesty, hoping she can see how sincere I am.

She snatches the flowers from my hands. "I'll put them in water." She pauses briefly. "Thanks." It looks like it physically pains her to say that, but Nessa was never one of those ungrateful, rich bitches who didn't appreciate token gestures.

"You're welcome." I flash her another grin, moving to follow her inside, when she slams the door shut in my face.

"Ouch," I murmur to myself, flattening my back to the wall, reminding myself it's still a victory because she hasn't sent me away.

The door swings open five minutes later, and she steps outside, wearing a silver cashmere pashmina and carrying a glittery blue purse. "You can tell Sawyer he's back on my shit list for this," she says, striding toward the elevator, ignoring my offered hand.

"He won't be pleased. You've only just taken him off it." Nessa hasn't just kept me at arm's length; she's been avoiding everyone. She's understandably pissed.

Abby, Shandra, and Hunt managed to get her to talk to them this week, explaining how we'd agreed to open up to her that fateful Sunday and how much everyone regrets leaving it too late. Whatever they said worked, and she's forgiven them.

Not me though.

I'm still at the top of her shit list, but I'm determined to break her reservations down and win her back.

"Maybe he should have considered that before he betrayed me again," she huffs.

"You could tell me no," I jest.

She pins me with a glare the White Witch would be proud of. "If I thought that'd work, I would." The elevator pings, and she steps inside, her gown swishing around her legs as she walks.

"You know me well." I step into the elevator beside her, fighting another grin.

"I've seen a different side to you these past couple of weeks. I know you'd just pester me to death until I agreed."

Truth. I've been relentless since the day we returned from London and she kicked me out of her place.

Every day, I greet her in the parking lot at RU with a latte, fresh fruit, and yogurt. Every evening, she returns to find a rose waiting for her at her car. Every night, she receives a goodnight text from me, reconfirming my love.

Abby helped me choose some photo frames, and I printed out the few photos I have of us together, keeping one by my bed while sending Nessa a matching one. She hasn't let me inside her place to know whether she kept it or threw it in the trash.

I'm trying to find little ways to show her I care, hoping in time she'll give me the opportunity to prove it in other ways too. However, right now, her safety is of most concern to me, and that trumps everything else.

She can stay mad at me for eternity as long as she's protected.

I stayed up all night that night with Hunt coming up with a plan. We knew she'd never hear us out, so we emailed her full details of the plan, letting her know she could amend anything if she didn't like it. I was only reasonably confident she'd reply, but I was happy to be proven wrong. Nessa is taking the elite threat seriously, and she agreed to never leave the penthouse without at least two items with tracking devices on her.

We supplied her with a ton of the Techxet tracking chips for her personal use and for adding to her siblings' cells. Xavier uploaded the tracking software app to her cell and her laptop, demonstrating how to access it and how to pull up the camera feeds for her penthouse.

She asked us to install a high-tech security system at her mom's house, and that was taken care of along with assigning bodyguards for her, her mom, and the twins. I'm using the company Dad recommended. They are made up of ex-mercenaries who are used to covert ops, and you would hardly know they are there.

Nessa also agreed to the transformation of one of her

bedrooms into a panic room. Xavier knew a guy who got it done within a few days, and now, she has a safe place to retreat to should anyone get past her security detail and the new alarm system we've installed.

Also, on our list of priorities was checking if her name, not that bastard Montgomery's name, was on the deeds. It was a huge relief to confirm it's all hers along with the bank account and trust fund he established for her.

Of course, Nessa won't let me pay for a fucking thing. She's insisting that all the invoices are sent to her for payment.

There's a certain poetic justice in the fact Montgomery's money is now being used to protect his daughter from the very monsters he planned on handing her over to.

I didn't argue with her on anything. I understand she's trying to reclaim her independence, and it's important to her that she stands on her own two feet. She's a lot stronger than she's given herself credit for, and I respect her enormously, but I still lie awake at night, worrying about her living alone despite everything we have in place now.

"Earth to Jackson." Nessa snaps her fingers in my face, and I realize we've reached the basement parking lot.

"Sorry." I wait for her to exit the elevator first before following her. "I'm over here." I gesture to where my sleek, black Maserati Quattroporte GTS awaits us. "How are Kayleigh and Hunter?" I ask as I unlock my car, opening the passenger door for her.

Her face lights up, and a genuine smile crosses her face. "They're doing good. We had a fun weekend."

I know, because I spent the weekend in New York too, but she isn't aware. She has twenty-four-seven bodyguard protection, so it's not necessary, but I can't bear to let her out of my sight in case something happens.

"I'm glad." I help fold her skirt into the car before closing the door.

"How many cars do you own?" she asks, admiring the plush leather interiors.

"This, the BMW convertible, my SUV, and my Mustang," I admit, reversing the car out of the parking space. "But Dad has over thirty cars I have access to as well. He's been collecting them for years."

I steer the car out of the garage, and it's an effort to drive slowly. "Did you give any more consideration to that Lexus I recommended?" I know Nessa loves her Evoque, but there are safer cars on the market that are bulletproof, fireproof, and virtually elite-proof, and I'd really prefer her to drive one of them. I was going to just buy her one and leave it outside her building, but the chances are high she'd return it, so I proposed she purchase one instead.

"Do you really think it's necessary?"

I glance at her briefly as I head out of Rydeville. "Yes. I thought Abby explained about the elite?"

Nessa looks out the window as the town whizzes by. "She did."

"Then, you understand the danger." I deliberately soften my tone. I don't want to freak her out, but she needs to be aware of the risk. Everything is on the table now, and I want her to be fully aware so she can make her own informed decisions.

"Why do you think I agreed to let you escort me?" She swivels in her chair so she's facing me.

"Because I'm handsome as fuck and make the best arm candy," I tease before adding, "And we already covered the fact I'm a persistent fucker." I'm being lighthearted on purpose, hoping it will help her to relax. Her hands are clasped in an anxious knot in her lap, tremors shake her arms, and the slightly panicked look in her eyes is a dead giveaway. She's nervous and with due cause.

"I'm scared," she admits in a whisper. "What if they find out what we did to Montgomery?"

Without overthinking it, I pull over to the side of the road and kill the engine. "You mean what *I* did, Nessa." I take her trembling hands in mine, relieved when she doesn't push me away. "We don't know who he was in contact with. It's been over three weeks since he died, so I'm guessing someone probably suspects. For now, you stick to the story we concocted. You only recently discovered your biological father, and you look forward to meeting him in the future. You're honored to represent him in elite matters."

"They'll really believe that?" Her voice quakes.

"They're all pretentious assholes playing parts. If they don't believe it, they'll never let it show. Remember what Abby and Hunt discussed. You don't leave my side tonight. When you need to use the restroom, I'll escort you. If I'm called away, you stick with Anderson, Drew, Rick, or Charlie." Charlie is back in the fold now, and he's in the know about everything that's happened.

She nods, blowing air out her mouth. "Okay. I can do this." Steely determination glints in her eyes.

"I'm so proud of you."

Her eyes narrow in suspicion, and I hate that she doubts everything that comes out of my mouth.

"It's the truth. You're so incredibly strong and brave." I haven't forgotten the words I overheard on the boat that day. I know there's more she hasn't told me, but I haven't asked because she hasn't been speaking to me. We've spoken more tonight than we have in the past three weeks.

She stares at me, like she wishes she could delve into my

skull and verify it herself. "That's debatable," she finally says, shrugging.

I open my mouth to protest, but she cuts me off.

"We should get moving. I don't want to be late, and Abby and Shandra are almost there."

Ignoring the tightness in my chest and the painful lump in my throat, I nod, starting the engine, and hightail it out of there.

Chapter Forty-Two
Vanessa

"This is my brother-in-law Rick," Abby says, introducing me to the tall good-looking guy with dark hair and blue eyes who could pass for Kaiden's doppelgänger. He's seated on her left at the table while Kaiden is on her right. Jackson and I are seated across from them, but my date is currently at the bar getting drinks.

Abby and Drew's mom is seated at the table next to us with some older guests. Abby explained earlier this week that her mom's best friend, Sylvia, was married to Montgomery and both women suffered at his hands. She suggested I meet her, but I'm not sure I'm up to that yet.

Everything I've learned from Abby, Shandra, and Sawyer this week has been a bit overwhelming. Now, I understand the grave threat the elite poses and the precarious situation I'm in, it's easier to let go of my anger at their betrayal. Of course, my greatest anger has been reserved for Jackson, because his betrayal cuts the deepest, but as the weeks go by and his persistence to prove he cares shows no sign of wavering, I'm finding it harder and harder not to let it go.

Underneath all the hurt, anger, and pain, there is love, and I'll have to confront it some time.

"This is Rebecca," Rick says, sliding his arm around the stunning redhead seated beside him, his words dragging me out of my inner monologue.

Rebecca smiles, nodding at me. "Nice to meet you."

"You too." I have no idea who she is, and I'm fairly certain Abby never mentioned her, so I don't know if she's his girlfriend, an acquaintance, or just his date for the night.

"I remember you from West Lorian," Rick says, gracing me with a wide smile.

"Well that can't be good," I joke, swiping my clammy palms down the front of my dress. Rick was a few years ahead of us in school, so that means he was there when I almost got expelled during freshman year and had to repeat. Between that and the shit he must've heard about me from his brother and his friends over the years, I can only imagine the impression he has of me.

He chuckles good-humoredly. "I form my own opinions. And any woman who has tamed the legendary Jackson Lauder has got to be someone special."

"Thanks for that, dude," Jackson says, coming up alongside me. "Love you too."

Jackson hands me a Coke before sitting down on my left. I notice he's not drinking either. In fact, as I glance around our table, I see no one is drinking, and that's telling.

"Is it safe to drink?" I whisper, gulping as I look around the opulent ballroom.

Circular tables are beautifully laid out underneath glistening chandeliers, dotted spaciously around the large room. A long bar runs the length of the room on one side while doors to the hallway and bathrooms are on the other side. The rear of the room is enclosed, and a raised dais faces us at the top of the space. The room buzzes with loud chatter and vibrant laughter, and anyone poking their head in would assume this is a normal high-society event.

We know better.

Jackson rests his arm along the back of my chair, leaning in to my ear. "If this was an elite event being held at one of their locations, I'd say you're right to be suspicious, but the Boston Merrion Hotel is one of the most prestigious hotels in town, and this is the first of six formal elite balls being held in different states over the next two months, so they'll be on their best behavior." His eyes soften. "Your drink is safe, but if you want me to taste it first, I will."

I shake my head. "It's fine. I'm overreacting." I pin him with a shaky smile. Truth is, I'm scared shitless. It would be easier if I knew the man or men Montgomery was communicating with so I'd know what to expect.

"He might not even be here," Jackson whispers, instinctively knowing what I'm apprehensive about. But I don't believe for one second that he isn't worried about the same thing. "We have no clue how the invitation process worked. We were expecting a lot more than two hundred guests to be in attendance tonight."

My eyes roam the crowd again as I sip my Coke. At the top of the room, the large stage has been set up with a screen and a podium for the after-dinner speeches and presentation.

I've already been introduced to William Hamilton and his wife because he made the rounds when everyone first piled into the room. I followed the others' cue, acting polite and friendly, even laughing at his stupid attempt at humor, while my heart was careening around my chest like crazy.

"Are you doing okay?" Shandra whispers in my other ear. She's seated on my right-hand side, beside Drew.

"I'm okay. How about you?" I deliberately eye Drew. Shandra believes he only invited her because you don't turn up to these things without a date, but I think there's more to it. She's told me a little of what's been going on between them, and it sounds like he has feelings for her but he's trying to avoid confronting them.

She shrugs, but I see the hurt in her eyes. "He's barely talking to me, and he hardly even looked at me when he came to collect me. Abby and I did most of the talking in the car on the way here."

"Men are dicks," I say, probably a little too loud. Jackson's head whips around, and he frowns. He's currently stretching across the empty chair, talking to Kaiden.

"There you are!" Abby says, looking up and over our shoulders. "I was beginning to worry." Her brows knit together in confusion as she glances around. Shandra and I swivel in our chairs, watching as a knockout guy with piercing green eyes reaches our table. "Where is Demi?" Abby asks, and I deduce this is the infamous Charlie I've heard about.

"She's not coming," Charlie says, claiming the empty seat beside Drew.

"What do you mean she's not coming?" Abby narrows her eyes on Charlie, and all conversation mutes around the table.

"If you must know, we broke up," he mutters, avoiding eye contact.

"What!" Abby shrieks, glaring at Charlie.

Abby and Drew discovered Demi was a distant cousin a few weeks ago, and Abby really likes her. Only a few days ago, Abby was talking about setting up a girls' night out with the four of us.

"Wow," Jackson says in my ear. "Seems I don't own the monopoly on epic fuck-ups."

"It would appear so." I take a tentative sip of my Coke as waiters and waitresses move around the room, delivering our appetizers.

Jackson

We talk among ourselves as the various courses are served. I manage to force some food down, which is a miracle because my stomach is still tied into knots. This part isn't bad, but I know it's later, when the dinner and the presentation are over and the party really gets going, that I need to watch myself. After dessert has been cleared away, the presentation begins, and everyone gives the new president, William Hamilton, their full attention as he explains about the restructuring of the organization and the work of the reorganizing committee.

"Every voice counts, and we want to hear from you," he says, his loud, confident voice projecting around the room.

Jackson coughs. "Bullshit."

"Questionnaires will be sent out next week, and we value your input." Hamilton clears his throat, drinking from his glass of water before he continues. "New blood is vital to the development and growth of our community, so particular emphasis is being given on developing our young people through invigorated new initiation programs. The first group program will be held in January at our new private facility in Virginia. Male descendants of founding families who are next in line for ascension to full membership will be invited in this round, and for the first time ever, we will be including eligible female descendants to join our ranks."

Hushed conversation sweeps the room.

"What the actual fuck?" Kaiden hisses, a muscle clenching in his jaw.

Abby looks over at me. "Does this mean what I think it means? That Nessa and I will be expected to participate?"

"Over my dead fucking body," Jackson snaps. "That will not be happening."

"Agreed." Kaiden and Jackson share a knowing look.

"They can't force you to attend," Drew says, looking at his sister. "I'm the descendant on the Manning side."

"He was vague on the details," Abby says. "I'm married to a descendant and from a founding family myself. I bet he makes up some bullshit to get me to initiation. He's determined to make us pay." I don't know how she can look and sound so calm as she says this.

"What happens at initiation?" I whisper to Jackson.

He takes my hand under the table. "Nothing good, but you won't have to deal with it. I promise."

I want to believe him, but after everything I now know about the elite, I know that's a promise he isn't qualified to make.

"Dance with me?" Jackson asks a short while later after the presentation and speeches have concluded.

I've been in a bit of a daze since the whole initiation program was mentioned, and I didn't even realize the stage had been cleared to make way for a jazz band.

"Babe." Jackson's hands land on my shoulders, squeezing gently. "You up for it?"

"I'm not your babe," I mumble, but it lacks bite. I'm struggling to hold on to my hatred, especially when he seduces me with his legendary charm, and Jackson knows it.

"I apologize. *Baby*."

I roll my eyes, letting him pull my chair back and help me out of my seat. "You're incorrigible."

He pins me with a blinding smile that knocks the air from my lungs. "But you still love me."

I fold my arms and glare at him. There is no way I'm confirming he is still the owner of my heart.

He chuckles, taking my hand and slowly reeling me into his chest. "It's okay. You want to make me suffer, and I deserve it. I can grovel some more, but you should know by now that I'm going nowhere." A naughty glint flashes in his eye. "I will be

Jackson

your faithful puppy, nipping at your heels, craving your affection, waiting for the day you give in."

I roll my eyes again. He's ridiculous.

His expression softens, and he gazes at me adoringly. "I love you, Nessa. I love you more than I ever thought possible. There are no words in the English language to describe how much you mean to me."

"Please put him out of his misery," Drew says, poking his head in between us. "I can't take much more of his pathetic pining."

"Back off, Manning," Jackson grits out. "You're hardly in any position to throw shade. I fucked things up with one woman. You've managed to do it with two." Jackson's smug grin is going to earn him a punch in the face if he doesn't shut up. "Dat's true skill. Take the crown. You can have it."

"Oh my God." I grab Jackson's arm, pulling him away from the table before Drew knocks him flat on his ass. "Do you have a death wish? Or you love acting like you're five?"

"He started it." He pouts.

I shake my head in exasperation. "I rest my case." I walk off.

"Babe." He wraps his arms around me from behind.

"Jackson!" I shove his arms away, turning to glare at him.

"I'm sorry. I just miss you, and it makes me snarkier and needier than usual." He pins me with these puppy-dog eyes, and my resolve is faltering fast.

I hold out my hand. "You promised me a dance. Let's see if you've got any moves."

Jackson has *all* the moves, and it's even more impressive considering we're dancing to a traditional jazz number. I am putty in his hands, letting him spin me and duck me and twirl me around. "Where did you learn to dance like this?" I rasp when the music alters, slowing down, and he pulls me into his arms.

More couples get up, joining us on the busy dance floor.

"Mom's a dancer, remember?" He tweaks my nose. "Dani and I took dance lessons for years. Mom bribed me into doing it because Dad has two left feet and she needed someone to practice with."

I grin. "That is very sweet."

"It's hell. Now, every event we attend, she drags me up to dance with her. It's cringing."

"I never realized you were such a momma's boy," I tease.

"Guilty as charged," he admits, reeling me in closer. His hands hold me firmly at the waist as his eyes drift to my lips. "I want to kiss you so badly right now." His voice deepens, and his pupils dilate with unconcealed desire.

"Jackson," I warn, "you can't push me."

"I never would." He brings his gaze back up, peering deep into my eyes. "Guess I'll just have to lie in bed later imagining your lips on my mouth."

I'm expecting him to add something dirty, but he doesn't. I arch a brow.

"What?"

"That's it?"

He pins me with a shit-eating grin. "I was going to add how I'd jerk off to thoughts of you riding my cock. You know like you did in The Hamptons? So fucking hot. But I thought better of it, because I'm trying to woo you and Mom says I need to be romantic and keep my filthy thoughts to myself."

I stare at him flabbergasted.

He chuckles. "I've rendered you speechless. I'll consider that a win."

"You've talked to your mom about me? And you talk to her about your *sex life*?" I lower my voice, glancing around, conscious of our surroundings.

"I asked Mom for advice, and I guess she knows the male mind." He shrugs.

"I love your mom," I blurt.

"She loves you." Tentatively, he cups one side of my face. "It was thoughtful of you to send her the card and gift. You made her day."

"She went out of her way for me. Both your parents did. It was just a little token of appreciation."

"You do know she's already planning our wedding." He grins, and I stare at him dumbfounded.

"I thought you went to her for advice, so that implies she knows we're not together anymore. Why on Earth would she be planning our wedding?"

"Because she has faith in me," he says, moving his hand to the nape of my neck. "And she has faith in you," he whispers over my mouth, moving in closer.

"Jackson." I take a step back even though it pains me to do it.

He holds up his hands. "I'm sorry. It's just so hard to keep my hands and my lips off you."

"You're not going to give up, are you?"

He vehemently shakes his head. "Never. You're it for me, babe." He tweaks my nose, and it's so damn hard to stay mad at him. His expression sobers up. "If you give me another chance, I promise I'll never let you down again."

"I'll think about it," I murmur, and he picks me up, grinning like a little boy in a candy shop as he swings me around.

My cheeks are on fire, and I swat at his arms when he puts me down on the ground. "We're not supposed to be drawing attention," I hiss.

"You're right. Sorry," he says, not looking in the least bit sorry.

I roll my eyes. "I need to go to the ladies' room."

He offers me his arm. "Lead the way."

Jackson waits out in the hallway while I step into the restroom. It's not too busy with only a few stalls occupied. I attend to business, and I'm washing my hands at the sink, looking at the renewed glow in my cheeks, when the door locks with a distinct click.

All the hairs rise on the back of my neck, and my spine stiffens as I feel the ominous presence filling every nook and cranny in the room. My eyes flit to the stalls behind me, but they are all empty.

I'm alone. Trapped in here with this dark entity. The urge to squeeze my eyes shut and pretend like nothing is happening rides me hard, but I ignore it. I'm not a terrified little girl anymore, and I'm not going to let anything happen without a fight.

I whip around just as *he* reaches me.

My eyes pop wide in horror as I stare at a face that regularly features in my nightmares.

"Hello, Vanessa," he says, stopping right in front of me, leaving barely any space between us. "I've been looking forward to seeing you again." He's wearing the same arrogant smile I'm familiar with.

Memories return, threatening to derail me, but I jerk my chin up and lift my shoulders, determined not to give in to them or to cower from this monster.

"I'd like to say the same, but I'd be lying." I'm proud my voice doesn't shake even though I'm quaking like a leaf inside. Pressing a hand across my chest, I move my pinkie, activating the audio recording chip. "What do you want?"

"That's a loaded question if ever I heard one," he says, smirking. Strands of dark hair fall across his brow, and while he's still aesthetically handsome, to me, he will always be ugly on the outside and the inside.

"I'm coming," Jackson whispers in my ear.

"My boyfriend is outside," I blurt as nerves get the better of me.

"I'm counting on it. Mr. Lauder has been so attentive all night." A shiver crawls up my spine at the thought he's been watching me and I didn't notice.

"Tell me, Vanessa," he says, grabbing my throat as the door rattles. "Did you enjoy your time in Lanzarote?"

Panic jumps up and bites me when his fingers squeeze my throat. His breath is stale and warm on my face as he leans in close, pressing his disgusting lips to mine. He grinds his hips against me, but the layers of my skirt shield me from feeling his arousal. Tears leak from my eyes as memories I'm trying to forget surge to the forefront of my mind.

I freeze, every muscle locking up tight, my brain checking out as I give in to the inevitable. Darkness infiltrates every part of me, swallowing up the light, and I'm back there, in the past, frightened and alone, at his mercy.

The door groans with successive shakes as Jackson roars in my ear, shouting at the others for help, but I barely hear it in my frozen state.

"I might know if I could find my dear friend Christian, but he appears to be missing," the monster says. "You wouldn't know anything about that, now would you?"

Chapter Forty-Three
Jackson

Kai, Charlie, Rick, and Drew race toward me as I shove my shoulder at the door again, but the fucking thing won't budge.

"Step aside," Anderson demands, producing a fire extinguisher and smashing it into the door. He moves his arm back, ready to slam it into the wood again, when the door suddenly swings open.

"Mathers!" I snarl, lunging at him. "You fucking bastard!" I ram my fist into his face, hitting him square in the nose as I push him back into the bathroom. Shoving him out of the way, I run to where Vanessa is trembling and crying by the sink.

"Nessa." I deliberately soften my tone, lifting my hand carefully to touch her face. "It's okay. I'm here." I brush my thumb along her cheek, urging her to look at me.

"Jackson," she whispers, pinning me with terrified eyes. Her lip wobbles, and she collapses against me, clinging to me as she sobs. My heart breaks all over again, and Denton Mathers is lucky my girl needs me, because otherwise, I'd be over there making mincemeat of him.

"What the fuck did you do to her?" I snarl, holding Nessa close as I glare at Mathers over my shoulder. Kai has him pinned to the wall, the others forming a circle around him.

"Not enough," he coolly replies, smirking, and Kai punches him in the gut.

Mathers doubles over before straightening up, fixing us with an evil grimace. "I really wouldn't do that, gentlemen. I think you'll find the new president a lot more focused on discipline than the previous one. You have initiation coming up in a couple of months. Take my advice. Don't piss him off in the meantime."

"What is going on here?"

Speak of the devil. William Hamilton forces his way into the bathroom, his gaze bouncing astutely around the room. His eyes land on Nessa, and then, he turns his attention to that slimeball Mathers.

"What did you do?" His voice drops a few octaves.

"Nothing." Mathers holds up his hands. "I was just having a friendly word in Vanessa Montgomery's ear. It's not my fault the kids overreacted." He dabs at the beads of blood trickling from his nose.

Hamilton stares at us, and I maintain eye contact, challenging him with a warning look. He breaks our stare down, addressing everyone in the room. "We are hosting these events in public places for a reason. To assure the public at large they have nothing to fear, and you idiots decide to destroy hotel property and attack a senior elite member."

"He locked himself in here with my girlfriend to threaten her and to incite us. How about you reprimand him for that," I hiss.

"And you are?" Hamilton eyes me like I'm scum on the bottom of his shoe.

"None of your fucking business," I retort, because fuck

him. I'm not an elite. I don't have to act civil to him, and I sure as fuck don't answer to him.

"Kindly leave." Hamilton glares at me before swinging his gaze on the others. "All of you. You are no longer welcome here." He points his finger at my friends. "I know who you are, and this is the exact type of behavior that must be stamped out. I expect you to generously compensate the hotel for the damage, and I'll make sure this little incident disappears."

Nessa has her face pressed into my chest, but she has stopped crying. I smooth my hand up and down her back, hating how badly her entire body is trembling.

"Touch her again, asshole, and you're dead," I warn Denton as we move past him.

"Was killing both Montgomerys not satisfying enough, Lauder?" he baits. "I think you fit right in around here, and you know it."

"Enough." Hamilton barks, glowering at Denton.

I fix both men with dark glares as I leave the room, holding Nessa at my side, her head buried in my chest.

Anderson looks Nessa over, and his troubled eyes meet mine. He can tell she's hanging on by a thread, and we need to get out of here.

"Can someone drive us?" I ask, because there's no way I'm prying myself from Nessa in this state.

"I will," Abby says, storming up the hallway, closely followed by Shandra.

"I'm coming too," Anderson adds, throwing his car keys to Drew.

"Where's Rebecca?" Rick asks, alarm lacing his tone.

"Mom has her," Abby confirms, and his shoulders relax.

"Everyone, meet back at my place," I say, walking toward Abby with Anderson at my side.

"Nessa." Abby places her hand on Nessa's back, but she still won't lift her head from my chest.

I shake my head at Abby. "Can you grab her purse and meet me at the car? I'll text you the location in the garage." I just want to get Nessa the fuck out of here now. Anderson slides his arm around his wife, and they exit the hallway into the ballroom.

"There's a back stairwell this way," Drew says, pointing to the corridor on my left. "Take the left at the end, and you'll see the door."

I nod my thanks and take off.

I'm in the back seat, cradling Nessa to me, when Abby and Kai show up a few minutes later. "Thanks for this," I say when she slides behind the wheel. Anderson takes shotgun.

"No thanks necessary." *Is she okay?* Abby mouths, and I shake my head.

I hold Nessa close, my arms wrapped firmly around her, while I dot kisses into her hair. She isn't crying anymore, but she's shaking uncontrollably, and I wish I could ingest her pain and free her from hurting.

Mathers acted like he knew her, and I'm dying to find out what's going on, but she's falling apart in front of me, and I don't want to do or say anything to make it worse.

Abby drives us out of the city in silence, her worried gaze locking with mine through the mirror on several occasions. Anderson holds his hand over hers from time to time, and I can tell being back in this world has heightened his protective instincts.

We are about halfway back to Rydeville when Nessa stirs, straightening up and easing out of my arms. When she looks at me, it's like she's looking through me. She has a dazed expression in her eyes that troubles me. "You know him," she whispers.

I nod, wetting my dry lips as I risk asking my question. "You know him too?"

She bobs her head, and a strangled noise crawls out of her mouth. It's the type of anguished, baleful sound I imagine I'd hear if I found an animal in pain, dying at the side of the road.

My helpless eyes meet Abby's and Kai's in the mirror. Tears stream down Abby's cheeks, and I wonder if she's remembering her own ordeal at the hands of Christian, Trent, and Denton.

"He raped me when I was fourteen," Nessa whispers, and my helplessness turns to horror and rage. "It was the summer before I started high school. Mom had gone out with the twins for the afternoon, and he showed up with Aaron at the house. He'd visited before, and I never liked the way he looked at me."

She shivers all over, and I clasp her hand as Abby pulls over to the side of the road, putting the car in park. Very gently, I move my hand to the top of Nessa's dress, pressing down on the chip adhered to the swell of her breast, deactivating the audio device. I don't think she wants to broadcast this to everyone.

Anderson pulls Abby over into his lap, circling his arms around her as his worried eyes meet mine.

Nessa's hand is cold in mine, her fingers just limply lying there, and when she speaks, it's in a monotone voice. She's staring straight ahead as she talks, but it's like she's not here. Abby shoots me another concerned look as she turns around in Anderson's lap, giving Nessa her full attention.

"They took turns all afternoon," Nessa says. "It felt like it lasted days. Everywhere hurt."

I squeeze my eyes shut, forcing my tears to subside.

"Aaron had been climbing into my bed since I was ten," she continues, and a fresh wave of horror accosts me. I'd suspected as much when I heard what Montgomery said to her on the boat, but this is even worse than I'd imagined. "He raped me for the first time when I was twelve. Mom knew, but she didn't care. It meant he stopped raping her."

Abby is openly crying now, and Anderson is visibly distressed. I know both have compassion for Nessa, but it's also resurrecting the stuff that happened to Abby this past year, and those memories are not pleasant.

"I went crazy after those bastards tag teamed me," Nessa admits. "I did a ton of crazy shit. Got arrested for shoplifting. Skipped school. When I showed up at West Lorian, I was belligerent and rude. I got in fights with other girls. I—"

She doubles over, clutching her stomach. I wrap my arms around Nessa again. "It's okay. You don't have to continue."

"I want to," she cries, lifting her eye, stabbing me with red-rimmed swollen eyes. "I want to purge this now, because if I don't, it will fester inside me until my insides turn rotten. And then, he's won. They've all won."

My beautiful, brave warrior. Still battling. Still surviving.

Abby reaches out, twining her fingers with Nessa. "Survivors," she says, letting her know she understands.

"I thought it was behind me," Nessa continues, sniffling. "I was proud of me, because I got away from Aaron and I built a new life. I worried about Kayleigh though." She turns to me. "It was Aaron who attacked me at my apartment, because I'd reported him to social services after I spotted bruises on my sister."

I had guessed some of it from what Montgomery said on the boat, but everything slots into place now.

"He warned me if I told you that he'd rape her and let his friends rape her too. I had to lie."

"I understand." I rub a hand up and down her back. "You were protecting your sister."

"When he died, I was so happy. So hopeful for the future," she sobs.

Jackson

Until I fucked with her head. God, I have so much to answer for.

"You know what's really fucked up?" she asks us, her gaze flitting between me, Anderson, and Abby. "Montgomery staged his murder so it'd look like a car accident. He murdered him because he had the nerve to come after me again. He said he'd no right to touch what was his." She shakes her head, and wild laughter bursts from her mouth. "What the fuck is wrong with these people?!" she shouts.

"They have no conscience," Abby says. "And they think we were born to spread our legs for them. They legit believe that."

"I thought it ended with Montgomery, but it's never going to end, is it?" Nessa pins doleful eyes on me, and I want to bundle her up and run away. To find some idyllic island oasis where no monsters exist, and no one can find us. Only I'm not naïve enough to believe such a place exists.

"Let me protect you. Let me love you." I kiss her cheek. "You don't have to do this by yourself anymore."

"I'm so tired, Jackson." She slumps against me, resting her head on my shoulder. "How many times do I have to go into battle?"

"I don't know, babe." I kiss her temple. "But you're no longer going into battle alone. You have an army beside you, and we'd die before we let anyone hurt you again."

"Is she okay?" I ask Abby when she materializes in my kitchen a couple of hours later. The mood is somber since we all arrived back at my place. Abby wanted to talk to Nessa, woman to woman, and the only reason I left them alone was because Nessa asked me to.

Abby jerks her head to the side, and I join her in the corner.

413

"She's asleep and doing as well as can be expected, but she's been through so much, Jackson. More trauma than one person can endure. Denton didn't hurt her in the bathroom, but he didn't need to. His threats have sent her spiraling into the past. She needs to talk to someone. The only time she ever attended therapy was after that happened at fourteen," Abby confirms through gritted teeth. "But that bastard Breen warned her not to say a word or he'd bring Denton back for a repeat performance."

"I'm glad he's dead because it saves me the job." I shake my head, feeling so helpless. "How do we help her? Tell me what to do?" I plead.

"She needs time to heal, and you need to be gentle with her. Let her direct the course of your relationship. She has agreed to speak to Mom and Sylvia," Abby adds.

"Is that wise?"

"They are the perfect women to speak to. Montgomery abused and raped them too, and look at everything they suffered at the hands of the elite." Her chest heaves. "But they survived. They are both living their best lives now. They have found a way to deal with it and move on. Nessa needs to hear that because she's lost hope. Mom has contacts, and I'm hoping Nessa will agree to talk to a therapist. It would be good if you encouraged that too."

"Of course. I'll do anything I can to help her."

"I know you will." Abby rests her head on my shoulder, and I hug her to me.

Anderson is watching us like a hawk, but it's not like before. There is no suspicion or wariness in his gaze these days. He's just concerned for his wife. He hates to see her upset, and I fucking get it now. The thought of Nessa hurting so much is killing me.

"Go hug your man," I whisper. "He needs to see you're okay."

"Jackson." Abby shucks out of my arms, looking up at me. "I love her, and I admire her so fucking much. The things she's gone through. It guts me." Her voice chokes, and her eyes pool with unshed tears. "I know you guys have gone through hell, but please tell me this is real for you, because she can't suffer any more pain."

Anderson comes up behind Abby, pulling her into his arms as a sob leaves her mouth.

"I love her, Abby. I cannot stand the thought of anyone hurting her, least of all me. Which is why I will do everything, and I mean everything, to protect her and keep her safe. No one is hurting my woman again. Especially not Mathers and those other elite bastards."

"You can't stop that train wreck," Hunt says, his voice grave.

I walk to the table and flop down beside Xavier. He slides me a whiskey, and I take it. Everyone is here with the exception of brooding Barron and Rick and Rebecca, because Charlie is sulking over his breakup and the other two live in Boston.

"You heard what Hamilton said tonight. Women are being initiated now, and that's probably thanks to us," Drew's tone is scathing. "We've just made everything ten times worse."

"We don't know that," Abby says over a yawn, as Anderson pulls her down onto his lap.

"The other problem is Mathers knows we killed Montgomery," Anderson adds. "That places Nessa in even greater danger because Montgomery's official elite membership will now be transferred to Nessa. She will have to attend official meetings, events, and votes. Either way, she'll be expected to attend initiation too."

There is no way I'm allowing that to happen, and I know

how to stop it. I know how anal the elite are about traditions and rules. "He didn't change the rules though. He just added to them, right?"

Anderson frowns. "What are you getting at?"

"If Nessa marries, the responsibility passes to her husband, so it's simple. We'll get married, and I'll take her place."

Chapter Forty-Four
Jackson

A deathly silence descends upon the table. Shock splays on most faces except for Hunt's. He grins at me. "That would work. And it means we have another voice around the elite table."

"You sure you want to get involved, man. You're outside this bullshit now. Whatever hell they plan to unleash won't be pleasant," Anderson says.

"He's already involved," Drew says. "There is no such thing as being on the outside."

"I was involved the minute Montgomery stole my sister from me," I agree.

"You're all forgetting one important thing here," Abby says.

"You're assuming Nessa wants to marry you," Shandra cuts in, for the first time, lifting her head up from the table.

"And you're assuming she'll agree to let you do this," Abby adds.

"She loves him," Hunt says. "She won't turn him down." I love his confidence, but I don't fully share it. My girl is fragile and hurting, and a lot of that is down to me. If I had all the time in the world, I know I'd win her over, but time is a luxury we don't have. This needs to happen before the new year, and that only gives me a couple of months to prove I'm marriage-worthy.

"You agreed when Anderson posed a similar scenario," I remind Abby.

"She refused at first," Anderson pipes up. "Until I made her see sense." His lips curve into a smirk.

Abby, predictably, slaps her husband's chest. "It wasn't until you made me see sense, dumbass. It was when you convinced me you were doing it because you loved me and not just to protect me."

I scratch the back of my head. "Isn't that the same thing?"

"Now who's the dumbass." Anderson's smirk grows, but I'm too tired to flip him the bird.

"No, Jackson. It is not the same thing." Abby jabs her finger in the air at me. "Nessa has fought like crazy to take back control of her life and stand on her own two feet. If she thinks you're doing this just to protect her from occupying a seat around the elite table, she'll turn you down flat. She needs to know you are doing it because you love her and can't live without her."

"But I can't!" I cry out. "And it's because I love her that I want to protect her."

Shandra hits her head on the wooden tabletop. "No. You stupid man. If you say that, she'll never agree." Drew lifts her head up, rubbing at the red mark on her brow, pulling her over onto his lap, and that's something I haven't seen in a long time. She curls around him, clinging to him like a limpet.

Women are so fucking complicated to figure out.

"So, what do I say?"

Anderson clamps a hand down on my shoulder, lifting his tired wife in his arms. "That's one you've got to work out for yourself man."

Jackson

"I'll help," Xavier says, lifting his head from his laptop. I don't know what he's doing, but it must be important because he hasn't looked up once, and I didn't even think he was following our conversation.

"Eh. Yeah, thanks, but no thanks." I am *not* taking proposal advice from Xavier Daniels.

"Ouch. Dagger straight through the heart," he quips, palming a hand over his chest.

"It's late." Hunt closes the lid on Xavier's laptop, pressing a kiss to the top of his head. "Let's go to bed."

"Is it okay if we crash here too?" Drew asks, and I'm not mean enough to tell him to fuck off. Shandra is already fast asleep, her arms wrapped firmly around him like she's afraid he'll disappear if she doesn't hold on tight.

"Sure. You can take the bedroom at the very end of the hallway on the right." Anderson and Hunt have their own rooms here, so everyone knows where they are sleeping.

I creep into my darkened bedroom, shedding my clothes as I walk across the carpet to the bed. Nessa is still asleep, thank fuck. Carefully, I crawl under the covers and spoon her from behind, pleased when she mumbles my name and grabs my hand, holding it against her stomach.

The next couple of weeks are some of the most painstaking of my life. I wake up every morning, dying to propose to Nessa, but I hold back because she needs time to heal. Abby took her to speak to Olivia and Sylvia, and it seems to have helped. Olivia helped Nessa find a therapist, and I drive my girlfriend there every day after classes end. We haven't had any formal discussion of our relationship, but Nessa is more or less living here now, and she's stopped pushing me away.

At night, we make love until she falls asleep in my arms. I hold her sobbing form against my chest when she wakes up during the night, screaming and crying, and I hate how routine her nightmares have become and how little I can do to help.

But, gradually, it gets better, and the nightmares occur every few nights instead of nightly, and I'm coaxing more smiles from her during the day. We drive to college together, and Nessa is a permanent fixture at our lunch table too. Apart from classes, and her therapy, we spend every spare second together, and I've never been happier.

The only blip on the radar is the elite threat hovering overhead like a nasty thundercloud, and my desire to make this woman mine. The second the idea occurred to me, my brain ran with it, and now, I'm obsessed about sealing the deal. I already have the ring, thanks to a shopping expedition to William Goldberg's in New York. Mom helped me choose it, and I can't wait to see it glistening on Nessa's finger.

On Friday night, we take a run along the beach, like we usually do, and I decide to throw caution to the wind.

It's now or never.

I'm done waiting to have this conversation.

It's going down now.

When we've finished our run, I take her hand, pulling her over to the dunes that line this stretch of beach, flopping down on the grass and patting the space beside me. It's not exactly warm this time of year, but it's dry, and the wind isn't too strong. We're both still panting from our run, our body temps elevated. "Come sit with me. I have something I need to say."

"This sounds serious," she jokes, dropping down beside me, stretching those gorgeous, long legs out in front of her. My cock, predictably, thickens behind my shorts, but I urge the snake to simmer down.

"It is." Our knees brush as I turn my body toward her,

taking her hands in mine. I peer earnestly into her eyes, ignoring the butterflies dancing a jig in my stomach, the bile coating the back of my throat, and the nervous adrenaline shooting through my veins, concentrating on the words I have memorized. This speech is too important to get wrong, and I've had weeks to think about what I want to say.

"Prepare yourself," I half-joke, smiling. "I've got a lot to say, and all I ask is that you hear me out before you say anything."

"Okay." Her big eyes do nothing to hide her fear.

I press a soft kiss to her lips, and it takes colossal willpower not to turn it into something more because I love kissing her so much, and I could do it all day long. "This isn't anything to be afraid of. Quite the opposite."

I hope.

"Just spit it out. Please."

"I love you. I love you so much, and I hope you've seen that these past few weeks, because I know you need more than just words. But today, today, I need you to listen to my words and really hear what I'm saying." She nods, and I peck her lips again. When I pull back, I peer deep into her eyes, willing her to hear me, see me, and feel me.

"When I followed you to Lanzarote, all I thought about was you. It was all about getting to you in time to stop him hurting you. Fuck, I was so scared of what I'd find, and I couldn't sleep, couldn't eat, could barely breathe until I knew you were okay. Nothing else mattered. I was there for *you*."

Yes, I killed him for all the women he'd wronged, but as we were chasing halfway around the world after Nessa, I didn't once think about my revenge plan. It was all about saving her.

She swipes an errant tear away, and I kiss her cheek. "You have given me a purpose, Nessa, given me a reason to live. Before you, I was barely even existing. Those months I spent without you were the worst months of my entire life, because I was missing you so much, and I knew I was fucking everything up, but I didn't know how to make it right. I couldn't see it then, but I see it now."

I pause for a breath, because this is the risky part. I promised myself I wouldn't hold anything back. That I would let it all out, because there is no prospect of a future without complete and utter transparency.

"I was no better than those bastard elite. I hurt you and betrayed you and lied to you, and I swear that isn't who I am. I will *never* do that to you again. The thought of hurting you makes me ill, and it's my life's mission to ensure that never happens."

I raise our conjoined hands to my lips, pressing kisses on her knuckles. "You are the only woman for me, Nessa. I've known it all along, but it took me some time to admit it even to myself. But there is no doubt in my mind. You are my person, my soul mate, the other half of my heart, my future wife, the mother of my children, and the woman I will grow old and die with."

I kneel, keeping our hands linked. "Marry me, Nessa." She gasps as a steady flow of tears rolls down her face. "I have a whole romantic proposal worked out, and I have a ring, but I wanted to sit and talk to you first because I wanted you to understand how much I love you and whether we marry now or in a year, two years, ten years, shouldn't matter because my love is eternal. It's going nowhere. Just like me."

I bolster my courage, praying she takes this the way it's intended.

"But I want to get married now because I don't want to wait. I already know I love you and that's not changing, but I'm scared of what these bastards have planned for you. No one is ever hurting you again, Nessa, and it's my job as your soul mate to protect you and keep you safe. You haven't been protected or loved or cherished as you should have been, but that all ends now, because that is what I'm offering. It's part of what comes with my heart and a place in my life as my wife."

"What exactly are you saying, Jackson?" Her voice is choked with emotion.

"Marry me now, and let your elite responsibility pass to me. Let me shield you from those who want to hurt you. Let me protect you so our married life is a normal married life without elite interference."

I swipe at her tears with my thumbs while my heart pounds in my chest like it's about to take flight. "So, what do you say, babe? Will you share your life with me? Will you make me the happiest man alive by agreeing to marry me?"

Silence engulfs us, and the next few seconds add years to my life. *Years.*

"Yes," she blurts, and a sob bursts from her mouth as the most beautiful smile graces her lips. "Yes, I'll marry you, Jackson." She flings her arms around my neck. "Nothing would make me happier."

Chapter Forty-Five
Vanessa

I'm humming to myself as I set the table for ten, running through the mental checklist in my head to see if I've remembered everything. This is the first time we are hosting all our friends for dinner since we got married in Las Vegas two weeks ago.

Jackson and I eloped, marrying in a cute little chapel, before celebrating our wedding with a stay in the Damien-Hirst-designed penthouse suite of the Palms Casino Resort. It was magical, and I loved that it was just the two of us. We plan on holding a proper wedding next year—Laurena will throw a fit if we don't, and Kayleigh is dying to be a bridesmaid—once we get through the forthcoming elite shit heading our way.

It's been a hectic time, what with our wedding, Kai and Abby's wedding anniversary, and the fifth anniversary of Dani's death. That was a tough day for my husband. I think Jackson thought it would get easier after avenging his sister's death. He's only now realizing how much grieving he has to do and that the pain of her loss will always be with him although it may fade.

We made love for hours that night, clinging to one another, remembering all the things we have to look forward to and the fact we're both still alive, still surviving after the blows life has dealt us.

I'm glad I was the one holding him that night, the one supporting him through his pain, and that he let go and leaned on me, letting me be there for him in the way he's been there for me.

Light catches the ten-carat pear-shaped blue-diamond ring on my finger, reflecting colorful rays against the walls, and I still pinch myself every day because I can't believe I'm Mrs. Jackson Lauder. Jackson's heartfelt speech that day on the beach cemented everything for me, his words sinking soul deep and embedding in my heart, confirming the rightness of everything.

Perhaps, we're crazy. We're still young, we've been through so much shit, and we still have some stuff to work through, but nothing has ever felt more right to me, and I didn't hesitate to take this leap with him.

I haven't regretted it, and life is about as perfect as it can be.

Except I left the store without the parmesan. Duh. Facepalm.

Grabbing my keys and my coat, I shout up the stairs, hoping Jackson can hear me. He isn't back long from his run, and I'm unsure if he's still in the shower or not. "I'm running to the store for parmesan," I yell. "I'll be back soon."

"Make sure Dawson goes with you," my ever-protective husband shouts back.

"Of course," I yell, before pulling the door closed behind me, because we don't go anywhere without bodyguards these days.

I'm thinking about my apartment and what to do with it as I climb into my Lexus, waving at Dawson as he fires up his blacked-out Land Rover, ready to trail me.

Jackson

Having a bodyguard gives me peace of mind. I thought I'd hate the intrusion, but these guys are the best. They have a way of blending in so you hardly ever see them, and it's easy to forget they're there.

Mom readily agreed to bodyguard protection, and it gives me comfort knowing my brother and sister are safe too. Now that the elite reorganization is almost complete, and commitments will resume in due course, we are all on edge, and everyone is taking precautions. Especially us, because we have taken out a founding father and Jackson was also responsible for Trent Montgomery's death.

I don't refer to him as my brother or Christian as my father because that's not who they were to me. We shared DNA. Period. Christian was a monster, and from the stories Abby and Jackson have shared, I know Trent was too. I'm not sorry they're dead, and I've made sure my husband knows that too in case he's sheltering any stupid feelings like remorse or guilt for killing my blood relatives.

I drive to the store under the dark nighttime sky, parking out front and hurrying inside. Our guests will be with us in an hour, and I want everything perfect for when they arrive. It will be my first time meeting Demi, and I'm keen to make a good first impression. She and Charlie have reunited after the sad passing of her father. She hasn't felt like going out, so I'm delighted she has decided to come to our pre-Christmas Eve bash.

Rushing out of the store with my purchase, I make a beeline for my car when someone grabs me from behind, shoving something heavy and dark over my head. Panic blasts through me, but I remember my self-defense training, reaching my hand down between our bodies, grabbing the guy's balls and squeezing tight while I simultaneously lift my knee and slam my boot into his foot. He curses, releasing me, and I stumble forward, reaching for the bag over my head as the screeching of brakes and slamming of doors confirm this dude isn't alone.

I whip the bag off my head and run, swatting at the hair covering my face. Something or someone hard and heavy crashes into me from behind, knocking me to the asphalt. My lungs compress under the weight pressing me down, and the instant my head thuds against the solid ground, I black out.

Drip, drip, drip.

Muted sounds of arguing greet my ears, mixing with a steady dripping sound, as I slowly come to with a groan. My body aches everywhere, my limbs are throbbing with pain, and my arms feel like they've been wrenched from their sockets. Alarm shoots through my veins when I slowly blink my eyes open, taking in the dank, dark, dirty room I'm in. Although, calling it a room is generous. The space is small, almost claustrophobic, with bloodstained brick walls, a low ceiling with a solitary low-hanging light fitting that casts scant illumination, and a dirty asphalt floor that looks as if it's never been swept or cleaned.

My body jolts involuntarily as the two men in the corner come into sharper view. Fear, thick and cloying, blankets me from head to toe, and I shiver in a way that has nothing to do with the dampness seeping into my bones.

Fuck. This is bad. Real bad.

My butt is numb, my bare feet are like blocks of ice, and it's no wonder I can hardly feel my arms—they are stretched over my head at an awkward angle and my wrists are bound, tied to a steel bolt on the wall. One side of my face hurts, and the metallic taste of blood fills my mouth. My lips are dry and cracked, and the pounding pain in my skull suggests I might have a concussion.

But nothing feels broken, so that's a plus.

"Did you scan her for tracking devices?" William Hamilton asks, staring at me as he talks to Denton Mathers. Both men are dressed in expensive tuxedos, so they've either come from some event or they're in the middle of it.

"She's clean now. We disposed of her bag, her cell, and her shoes back in MA. Those were the only trackers on her." Denton slaps him on the back. "Don't worry. They won't find her in time."

Feeling the weight on my ring finger does little to contain my panic. I have no idea how long I was passed out, what has been done to me during that time, or where the hell I am.

"This would not have been necessary if you hadn't baited Lauder at the ball." Hamilton's jaw clenches as he continues staring at me.

"Come now. It's not like this is unwanted," Mathers coolly replies, his eyes raking over me. They are both talking like I'm not even here, but I don't interrupt, letting them discuss me like I don't lie injured and chained to the wall across from them.

"Right now, it is!" Hamilton barks. "The media and the authorities are still breathing down our necks. If the cunt had talked to the media about your little tête-à-tête in the bathroom, it would bring too much heat on us. We can't afford to fuck this up, and your actions were out of line!"

"You'll give yourself a coronary with all this stress." Mathers squeezes his shoulders. "I've rectified the situation." He pins me with a sick grin, and a shudder works its way through me. "This is a win-win. No PR nightmare to deal with, and we send those meddling kids a warning."

Hamilton kneads his brow, shooting daggers at Mathers. "Remind me again why I got into bed with you, because I'm

failing to see the benefits of partnering with a fucking idiot!"
Hamilton shoves Mathers into the wall, baring his teeth as he
snaps at him. "Those *meddling kids* almost brought our organization to its knees. She just married that prick Lauder, giving
them another vote. Wake up and smell the roses!" He shoves
Mathers again before taking a step back, rubbing his smooth
jaw. "They are a threat. One we must deal with, in the right
way, at the right time." He prods him in the chest. "This is *not*
the right time. You've poked the beast and forced our hand.
That is not what was agreed."

Mathers straightens his bow tie, smoothing his hands down
the front of his jacket. "You forget who you're speaking to,
Hamilton." His eyes narrow. "You would not be where you are
now without me. I can withdraw my support and the support of
others like that." He snaps his fingers in the president's face.
"This will be handled, and we'll handle the fallout in the same
thorough manner."

Hamilton fumes, his hands balling at his sides. I can tell
he'd love to lay Mathers flat on his ass. "Have your fun with her
tonight, because I want her on a transporter first thing in the
morning," he spits out. He runs a hand over his hair, flattening
it back into place. "I'm rejoining the party, and I expect to see
you shortly. Your absence will be noted, and we can't invite
suspicion."

"I'll save the fun for later when I won't be interrupted. I
just want to have a few words with Ms. Montgomery first. I'll
rejoin you in due course."

"Very well." Hamilton shoots me one last look before
exiting the dungeon. The steel door clangs shut, and I startle,
jumping as Mathers stalks toward me, slightly dragging his
right leg behind him.

Crouching in front of me, he lifts his hand, brushing matted
strands of hair back off my face. He tips my head to the side,

probing my sore cheek with his fingers. I flinch at his touch, unable to stop my body's natural reaction. His evil grin sends shards of fear shuttling up my spine. "Thankfully, the damage isn't permanent. Our clients prefer their whores in pristine condition." His hand sweeps down over my body, pausing to cup my breast through my shirt. "We'll pretty you up before we place you into our auction."

I gulp over the panic clogging my throat and the painful knots twisting and turning my insides.

He squeezes my breast hard, tweaking my nipple, and tears spring to my eyes. "I've fucked a lot of women and young girls in my time, but your pussy was one of the sweetest." His hand drops from my breast to my crotch, and he cups me through my jeans. "I can't wait to taste you again. As soon as my guests are gone, and my wife and daughters are in bed, I'll come to claim what is rightfully mine." He rubs his palm back and forth against my groin, pressing the denim against my sensitive flesh.

I pray Jackson gets here soon before they send me away and I'm lost to him forever. But I fear it may not be in time to save me from ruination, because if that monster puts his cock inside me again, I won't survive it a second time.

Chapter Forty-Six
Vanessa

"Aaron knew all along who you were," I surmise, hoping to deflect the wild lust in his eyes. I know what he just said, but I don't trust him not to rape me now. Maybe, if I can keep him talking, and feed his ego, enough time will have passed and he'll be forced to return to his party.

"Of course, he did, but he had no idea who *you* were." His dark chuckle reverberates off the walls. "Christian sent me to keep an eye on you."

My eyes startle at that admission.

"Ah, Christian never told you he found out about you when you were thirteen."

I shake my head. "He told me nothing about how he knew my mom or why he didn't come looking for me."

"Your mom was living rough on the streets when Christian found her at fifteen."

That must have been shortly after Mom's parents died in the plane crash and after she'd been sent to live with her aunt and her husband. Mom doesn't speak about her childhood often, but I know she was happy with her parents, because she speaks fondly of them.

"He took her in, cleaned her up, trained her as an elite whore." Mathers licks his lips, and I'm sickened at the sight of the bulge in his pants. "She almost tasted as sweet as you, but she was weak, crying and screaming, even when doped up. Ruined fucking her for me." He drags his thumb along my lower lip. "She wasn't a good girl like you. You just shut up and took my cock up the ass. What a trooper."

I school my features into a neutral line, not wanting to think about how he tore into a part of my body that had been untainted until then. Or the fact I cried rivers of silent tears as they abused my body for their sick pleasure.

"Christian got sick of her, sold her, but somehow, she managed to escape. That pissed him off for a long time, so imagine his surprise when he discovered her strolling arm in arm with a man along Main Beach in The Hamptons some years later. She was of no use to us then, but you..." He rubs his thumb back and forth along my dry lips. "You were a beauty. All long legs, blonde hair, and these big trusting eyes. Fuck, men will pay a fortune for you."

"What did he do?" I prompt, urging him to continue because I don't want to hear about or think about the twisted perverts who pay for women.

"We watched you for a while. Recognized that Aaron would make a perfect elite member. He came from old money, ran a successful business, and he shared the same desires. Of course, Ruth was an addict by then, but we have ways of dealing with troublesome females."

I know all about how they deal with females, thanks to Abby's mom. The things she's had to endure are truly sickening. Sylvia too. She spent years abused and raped by her husband and others. I cried for a solid twenty-four hours after they shared their stories with me, terrifying Jackson. But it wasn't all horrid. Their stories give me hope I can overcome what's been done to me with time, therapy, and love, and I'm already making progress.

"We had no idea you were Christian's offspring until after I'd befriended Aaron. He let it slip that his whore of a wife had had a kid when he met her. The math added up. We knew an elite had to be your father, so I stole your hairbrush, and we ran a DNA test, which confirmed it."

"If he knew, why didn't he rescue me?" I know why, but keeping the monster talking until my husband gets here is my sole priority.

He looks at me as if I'm some stupid naïve kid. "Trent was Christian's heir. You were female, and he didn't need you. Aaron was doing a decent job training you, so Christian decided he'd let him continue his good work until he had a use for you. We nominated Aaron for elite membership, to keep him on our side, and it meant I had access to keep an eye on you. We were celebrating the day I fucked you. Aaron's nomination had just been approved."

Nausea swims up my throat at his words. There isn't even an accompanying evil glint or lustful look on his face. He's telling me this as if he's telling me what he'd like for supper. He is the classic definition of a psychopath, and the enormity of the danger I'm in hits me full force.

I've got to keep him talking, keep him distracted, until Jackson shows up.

"Did my mom know?" If Ruth knew this too, if she turned a blind eye to this as well, I am done with her. She is dead to me.

"We kept her out of it. She was always unstable, and even though she was a shitty mother, we couldn't risk her going to the cops. That's why I visited when she wasn't there."

Mom was a victim too, and now I understand I am the

result of rape, I can kind of understand her. She chose to ignore what was happening to me because she never faced up to what'd happened to her. I imagine looking at me reminded her every day of what she'd been through.

Maybe she blamed me.

But I was an innocent child.

At some point, she must have loved me, because she didn't go through with the adoption, but I don't understand why she kept me when she never cared for me or protected me the way a mother should.

"I paid your mother a visit after Aaron died," he continues, and shock splays across my face. "I filled her in on everything, including how we staged his death to look like an accident. I fucked her until she bled, until she was so scared, she would've agreed to anything. She fed you those lies about Christian on my instruction. She sent you to him, knowing what he would do." Now his grin is downright evil. "How does it feel to know even your own mother doesn't love you? That she put her other children's welfare above yours?"

"I stopped caring about that a long time ago." I reinforce my mental shields, pulling them up around my heart, to avoid the painful onslaught. I can deal with that another time.

"And Aaron hated you too. Especially after you ruined his chances with the elite. Your arrest and mental breakdown caused too many waves. It wouldn't have mattered if it'd been kept behind the scenes, but everyone at your private school and in the community knew what a wild, reckless, junkie whore you had become. The elite didn't want the bad press."

Shocker.

I'm glad I managed to mess up his carefully laid plans even though I suffered for it.

"Aaron kicked you out after I told him Christian Montgomery was your father and threatened to ruin him if he didn't.

Christian needed you weak and vulnerable so he could manipulate you into doing his bidding."

"Except it didn't quite go according to plan, did it?" I spit out, unable to stop myself from lashing out.

Mathers chuckles. "No, it didn't. Although, it has worked in *my* favor. Christian had lost his edge, and his support was waning. Now, it's all mine, and I'm perfectly positioned to become the next president after we dispose of Hamilton. Guess I should thank you."

"You won't get away with this," I hiss as he stands, straightening out his legs, wincing a little as he rubs his upper right thigh in the place where Abby shot him. She told me what he tried to do to her, and I'm glad she inflicted pain on him and that he still bears the scars of that night. "My husband will gut you to shreds just like he did your friend."

Mathers laughs, like the very idea is preposterous. "You really are quite delusional. But tell yourself what you need to. It's no skin off my back. Now, if you'll excuse me, I really must get back to my guests."

"Eat shit and die, asshole," I shout as he walks off. His limp is more pronounced now as he hobbles away, and his deep voice rumbles with laughter as he exits my prison.

Laugh while you can, dickhead, because you're about to go down.

Chapter Forty-Seven
Jackson

"How much fucking longer do we have to wait?" I hiss, shaking my leg to loosen the cramp that's set in. We've been hiding on the grounds of Mather's Alabama home for the past two hours, and although we have eyes on Nessa, and she's not in any danger right this second, I'm itching to get her the fuck out of that basement dungeon. I don't trust that prick with my wife, and I need to get her to safety ASAP.

Thank fuck for Techxet's new micro-micro-chip technology that enabled me to embed an undetectable tracking device in the band of her engagement and wedding rings. Nessa approved of the idea when I suggested it—there's one embedded in my platinum wedding band too—and it's given me some comfort to know she knows we're aware of her location and that we're coming for her. However, I know she arrived with facial injuries, and I hate the thought of her in there, all alone, in pain, while I'm out here twiddling my thumbs.

Okay, I know it's because there's a right and wrong way of doing this.

The wrong way is to bust into a house full of elite with enough weapons to sink a ship, especially when they loathe our guts.

So, we've had to sit it out while the house clears of partygoers.

"Our man on the inside says the last of the guests are departing now. Remember, Mathers is the only one with a key to the dungeon. We need to wait for him to go to her," Hunt says in my ear.

We are decked out in Techxet's latest prototype, an all-black combat ensemble, consisting of cargo pants and molded long-sleeved body-hugging shirts that are resistant to infrared lasers as well as bulletproof, and we are all carrying guns and knives.

It's just Hunt, Anderson, me, and three guys from the security firm I'm using waiting to ambush that sick fucker as soon as he rears his ugly head. Xavier is in one of the SUVs, stashed in the alleyway at the back of the house, monitoring the camera feeds and keeping in constant communication with our rat on the inside. Charlie can't leave Demi right now, and Drew was needed to watch over the girls, so they both stayed behind in Rydeville.

After Mathers revealed himself at the elite ball, we worked hard to get a man on his security detail. I don't know how Dad found this new security firm, but they have eyes and ears everywhere, and they monitored Mathers until he had a vacancy on the team, and they got a man inside.

Pity their guy hadn't discovered Mathers's plans to come to Rydeville and abduct my wife in time to stop him and to save his colleague's life. I don't understand how Mathers's men got the moves on Dawson, but we found him locked in the trunk of his Land Rover with a bullet embedded in his skull. Dude was a good dude, and I hate that we've lost him. Nessa was fond of him, and she'll be devastated when she finds out.

We all knew Mathers would come after Nessa, but we didn't think he'd strike two days before Christmas in our own backyard.

Lesson learned.

"The deranged sociopath is on the move," Xavier says in my ear, using a deliberately robotic voice. "I repeat, the deranged sociopath is on the move."

I can't tell for definite from this angle, but I'm pretty sure Hunt is rolling his eyes at his lover right now.

"Let's move," Anderson says, and I know he's itching to get his hands on Mathers as much as me. He owes him payback for what the prick did to Abby.

We follow Diesel—the bodyguard's team lead, a guy who was flown here especially to help out, and a veteran of countless covert ops—around the side of the garden, inching toward the outside entrance to the basement level. It's telling this part of the basement can only be accessed from outside and it's cut off from the main basement part of the house. God only knows what kind of sick, morally corrupt shit has gone down in here.

Blood rushes to my head as we wait for Mathers to make an appearance, and I'm getting more antsy by the minute. Every second I'm away from my wife is sheer hell, and I just want this to be over.

Two shadowy forms round the corner, and I stop breathing. Mathers says something to his bodyguard before climbing down the stairs and disappearing. The burly bodyguard stands in front of the steps with his arms crossed, scanning the surrounding grounds.

"What the fuck, man?" I hiss, digging Diesel in the back.

"Stay calm," Diesel advises, and I flip him the bird behind his back.

"You fucking calm down," I hiss. "That's my wife down there, and I don't want her left alone with that prick for a solitary second."

The guard standing watch at the stairs lifts his hand, making a two-fingered salute.

"And we're a go." Diesel scoots forward, crouching down, sticking to the shadows. There are other guards manning the exterior of the property, and it's imperative we're not caught.

"Last room at the end of the hallway," the guard says as we move past him.

"Thanks, Johnson." Diesel slaps him on the back.

I'm guessing he's our spy.

"Walk slowly, avoid any debris in the corridor that might alert him to our presence, and stay back until I confirm it's all clear," Diesel instructs before carefully and quietly opening the door.

We slip inside, and the instant I hear Nessa scream, I take off like a bat out of hell, pushing Diesel out of my way as I blatantly ignore his command, racing down the hallway, past several closed doors on both sides, barreling my way into the room.

"Get the fuck away from my wife," I roar, lunging at Mathers. His pants are bunched around his ankles, his dick bobbing from side to side, which gives me an advantage. I throw myself at him, knocking him to the floor and pounding my fists into his face as the fucker laughs.

What is with these delusional assholes laughing in the face of death?

"Lauder." Diesel hauls me to my feet, and his snippy tone confirms he's pissed.

Oops. Guess he's not used to men disobeying his orders.

Jackson

"Nessa needs you," Anderson says. "We've got this."

I race to my wife's side, kneeling beside her and wrapping my arms around her slim form as Hunt works to untie her hands. "Are you okay? Did he hurt you?" Her shirt is ripped down the front, exposing her bra, one side of her face is bruised, and there's a goose egg on her left temple and a few cuts to her lips. Despite her obvious injuries, her eyes are bright and lucid.

"No. You got here in time." She pecks my lips, wincing a little. "I knew you would."

I rest my forehead against hers as Hunt removes her hands, carefully lowering her arms to her sides. "Christ, this was like déjà vu," I admit. "Hanging around outside while you were hurting. I promised I'd never let that happen again. I'm so sorry, baby."

"Shush, Jackson. You have nothing to apologize for. This isn't your fault, and you got to me in time. They were planning on sending me someplace and selling me as a sex slave."

Behind us, the guys are working to restrain Mathers. We need to get off this property ASAP before any of his men notice us.

"Move out," Diesel commands, a few seconds later, and I watch as the other two bodyguards drag Mathers from the room. His hands are securely cuffed behind his back. A thick silver chain runs from his hands down along his body, linking to the cuffs around his ankles. There's a cloth bag over his head, and considering he's now mute, I'm guessing they gagged him.

"We need to leave," Diesel says to me. "You good?"

"We're good," I say, lifting Nessa into my arms.

Anderson and Hunt flank me on either side as we flee Mather's property.

I only relax when we're back in the car, putting miles between us and the monster's house.

We drive for an hour, pulling into a neglected warehouse

443

on the outskirts of some hick town. Our spy, Johnson, located the place in advance, and it's been prepped for us.

Nessa is asleep in my arms, and I wish I could whisk her back home, clean her up, and tuck her into bed, but we need to deal with Mathers now, because bringing him back to MA is risky as fuck.

"We'll stay with her," Hunt says before I've even asked the question. "You and Anderson need to do this."

Nodding, I kiss Nessa on the forehead before following Anderson out of the SUV and into the derelict building.

Diesel has Mathers securely tied to a chair, and his face is already awash with blood.

"Tell us what we want to know, and we'll make this quick and painless," Diesel is saying.

I snort the same time Anderson does. Yeah, I don't think so. This bastard needs a solid beating and gutting like Montgomery. And we already know he'll tell us jackshit.

We stand behind Diesel watching and listening as he peppers Mathers with question after question about the elite and other stuff that means nothing to us. All the bastard does is smirk and laugh. After five minutes, Diesel gives up, knowing a lost cause when he sees it. "He's all yours, boys. We'll wait for you outside."

"Boys," Mathers says, spitting out blood in the process. "Everyone knows that's all you are."

Anderson cracks his knuckles, ready to inflict damage. "Do I look like I give a fuck, old man?" Kai rams his fist into Mathers's face with such power he sends him flying back, the chair toppling to the ground.

I yank him up by the shirt, repositioning the chair on the ground, before I pummel my fists into his chest, only stopping when I hear the telltale cracking of bones.

Anderson throws another few punches to his face and

lower torso as I strip the bastard naked. Let him see what it's like to be humiliated and beaten to death.

Unsheathing my knife, I trace the tip of my finger along the cool edge of the blade. I press it against Mathers's balls. "I ripped Montgomery's balls to shreds before I sliced off his dick. He bled out like a motherfucker, squealing like a pig, as I gutted him until there was nothing but a mangled, bloody mess on the floor." Leaning down, I put my face right up in Mathers's face. "I was going to do the same to you, but my skills are advancing."

"We're gonna cut you up nice and good," Anderson adds. "But we won't kill you like that."

I lift the can of gasoline, shaking it in front of his face, silently fist pumping the air when his eyes pop wide and his Adam's apple bobs in his throat.

He can't disguise his fear now as realization dawns—he knows he's not getting out of here alive.

"We'll dig a nice big hole in that chest of yours," I say, poking the tip of my knife into his flesh. His anguished roar is music to my ears. "And then, we're gonna set you on fire."

"And watch you burn alive until there is nothing but charred remains," Anderson adds.

"You won't get away with this," he seethes. "I'm a founding father! You can't kill me and expect to go unpunished."

"I killed Montgomery, and I'm still here to tell the tale." I trail the knife down his chest as footsteps thud on the floor behind me.

"Hamilton will never stand for this!" he shrieks.

"Hamilton thinks you're a loose cannon," Nessa says, coming up behind me. "He'll probably thank us for cleaning up the mess—especially when he discovers you were planning to deceive and kill him." Her fingers curl around the knife, and I straighten up, cupping her face.

"You sure you want to do this?"

She nods. "I didn't get the opportunity with Aaron, and I was barely conscious with Montgomery."

I peer into her eyes. "Babe. This isn't something you forget in a hurry." I know what I'm talking about. I still have flashbacks to Trent and Christian. I have no regrets about what I did, but the fact I've murdered two men still plays on my mind. It's not something I'll ever forget, but I figure that's probably a good thing.

"I need to do this for me. The nightmares can't be any worse than what I already deal with."

Nessa looks at Anderson. "Is this okay with you?" I know why she's asking. She knows Anderson wants vengeance for Abby as much as I want this for her.

He folds his arms across his chest, bobbing his head once. "Do it for Abby too."

Nessa nods, and Anderson and I step back to let her work. She circles Mathers, sneering as her eyes roam his naked body.

Blood spurts when she cuts off his nipples, and his tormented screams bounce off the empty walls of the warehouse, going nowhere, because there is no one but us here to listen. She goes to town on his balls, plunging the knife in over and over again until there's nothing left but shredded skin. She doesn't touch his cock as she slices it clear off, and then, she rips through his chest, venting all her pain, anger, and frustration as she tears him to shreds.

She screams and shouts as she brutalizes him, and maybe, I shouldn't support this, but she fucking needs it. She's not just killing Mathers here today—she's killing Montgomery and Breen too.

When the frenzy stops, she stands upright, swiping her arm along her brow. "Check to see if he has a pulse. I refuse to touch him."

Anderson presses his fingers to his bloody neck, nodding.

Nessa grabs the can from the table, wordlessly handing it to my best friend. Then, she joins me, stripping out of her bloody clothes as we watch Anderson douse a moaning Mathers with gasoline. Removing my top, I put it on my wife. It only barely covers her panties, but it'll have to do until we find somewhere to stop and freshen up.

"Burn in hell, motherfucker," Anderson says, setting Mathers's body alight.

We watch from a safe distance until the fire dies out and all that's left are charred remains and dust on the debris-strewn ground.

It's a little after seven a.m. when we eventually crawl into our own bed after showering away the final remnants of last night. We are both exhausted, and Nessa is covered in bruises, but she's not complaining even though she's got to be sore. "Take these, babe. They are homeopathic pain pills I picked up from this woman Sylvia recommends." I bought them a couple weeks ago to have on hand because Nessa refuses to take regular pain pills.

She sits up, fighting a grimace, popping the pills, and washing them down with a glass of water. I grab the lotion from my bedside table. "I also have arnica cream if you want me to put that on."

She slides back into the bed, wincing a little. "There's only one thing I need. Your arms around me."

"I think I can manage that." I'm careful not to hold her too tight as I hug her to me. She rests her head on my chest and her arm on my leg. "You doing okay?" I ask before kissing the top of her head.

"I am," she quietly admits, looking up at me. "I was kinda crazy back there."

"If you're crazy, then, so am I."

"Is it crazy to admit I feel lighter?"

"No. I think it's only natural."

"I should feel remorse or guilt though, right? I mean, I killed someone tonight, and I don't feel bad about it at all."

"Why would you? He hurt you, and he'd planned even worse things for you. He hurt countless people. He was a complete bastard, and the world is a better place without him."

"He was a monster," she whispers, snuggling into my chest. "And I'm not sorry he's dead."

"Two monsters down," I say. "Three counting Hearst."

"And many more to come," she adds in a matter-of-fact voice. "But we'll be ready for them, and no one is taking me from you or you from me." She stares into my eyes with loving adoration and fierce determination as she laces her fingers in mine. "It's me and you against the world, Jackson, and we will always win because we're an unbreakable team."

Epilogue
Vanessa - Three months later

"A re you nervous?" I ask my husband as we get closer to our destination. We've been driving across the state for an hour with the top down on Jackson's BMW, appreciating the sunny day. It's not usually this warm at the end of March, but we're not complaining as it's made for a more enjoyable spring break.

Every morning, we run on the beach before enjoying a brisk swim in the ocean. Our days have been spent relaxing around the house—in between redecorating, because now my name is on the deeds I'm determined to stamp my mark on our home—and savoring long lunches by the pool, and most nights, we get together with our friends for dinner, either at one of our houses or one of Rydeville's top restaurants.

It's the most relaxed we've been in ages, and I never want this week to end.

"I'm not sure I can properly explain how I'm feeling," Jackson says, moving his hand to my knee.

I rub soothing circles on the back of his hand with my

thumb. "Whatever Selena has to tell us, we'll get through it together."

Keven Kennedy didn't find any evidence confirming Dani was held on Senator Allen's island, but he has identified some links between the elite and Allen's crew, which the FBI are looking into on the QT. True to his word, Keven spoke to his sister-in-law, Selena, about her time as a sex slave on the island, and she agreed to meet with us.

So, here we are. En route to rendezvous with Selena and her husband Keanu at the sanctuary they are building for survivors of sexual abuse.

"I'm scared she'll confirm Dani was there," Jackson admits. "Because I watched Selena's interview on *60 Minutes,* and the things that girl endured were heartbreaking. The thoughts of Dani being treated like that..." His Adam's apple bobs in his throat, and pain races across his handsome face.

I squeeze his hand in solidarity, understanding how difficult this day is for him. "We can always turn around. It's okay to change your mind." I remind him of his options, even though I know he won't back down. Not knowing the full story has been killing my husband, and I firmly believe he needs to understand what happened to his sister to properly move on.

"I've considered it," he says, removing his hand from mine and placing it on the wheel as we take a sharp left turn. "But I'd always wonder what she knows. As much as it might kill me to hear it, I want the truth. I need it." His expression is somber when he looks at me, but the usual love and adoration glistens in his eyes. "I couldn't do this without you. Thanks for being here."

"I will always be by your side, Jackson. There is nowhere else I ever want to be." I lean across the console and kiss his cheek. "I love you."

"Love you too, babe." A reverential smile graces his

delectable mouth, helping to relieve some of the mounting anxiety.

I settle back in my seat, watching the pretty landscape flash by. We can't be too far away now. "Abby told me Kai's younger brothers received invitations to the next elite initiation program," I say, thinking it might help to switch the subject.

"I know. He called this morning to tell me. He's spitting blood."

"Can't we do anything? Maybe, another conversation needs to happen with Hamilton."

Thankfully, Abby and I didn't have to attend initiation. Hamilton confirmed the new female rule will only apply to single woman descendants of founding families. If you are married, your husband assumes the responsibility, as is the tradition, and that's what has happened in our cases. But it doesn't bode well for other women even if the initiation program the guys attended was a formal program with no nefarious tasks required. Hamilton is going to huge trouble to legitimize the process and the order, but we all know it's bullshit. We know things will change once the full spotlight is off the elite.

"You heard what he said at the meeting in January," Jackson says, signaling to turn right. "He's playing ball provided we don't interfere in official elite business. We could try and influence him, but I doubt it'll do any good. He can't be seen to make allowances as it sets a precedent, plus it would indicate he's made some deal with us. We're not popular within the elite because of what went down last year in Wyoming. We may be full members now, but we're still on the outside. Hamilton won't do anything to draw attention to the fact he's negotiated an agreement with us."

"We should've made that a condition of our truce at the time," I murmur. "Why didn't we?"

"Protecting your life was our number one goal and getting him to agree to drop his agenda against us was the other. There is no way he would've agreed to anything else. Not when he knows we took out Montgomery and Mathers, and he was in the audience when I shot Trent."

"He has no proof. We told him Montgomery was alive and well when I left Lanzarote and that Mathers took off into hiding once you rescued me, because he knew the cat was out of the bag, that we'd tell Hamilton of his plot to kill him and take the presidency."

"Hamilton didn't buy that, babe. That whole conversation was a farce, but it fulfilled its purpose, and that's all that matters."

"He could still come after me." Bile pools at the base of my throat. "I know he approved of Mathers's plans for me. That he wanted me sold ASAP. How does he know I won't go to the media or the police?"

"He doesn't, which is why he'll uphold the truce, for now. He knows if he comes after us that we have him on that. He knows it would incite another war with us. He doesn't need it when things are still tentative within the order. He needs peace to foster loyalty. He won't risk anything right now."

"But he could come after us in the future."

Jackson takes my hand, squeezing my fingers. "Babe, you're safe. Trust me, you have nothing to worry about. We have that entire meeting recorded thanks to Techxet's fucking genius technology." A shit-eating grin crosses his mouth. "Hamilton thought he was the bomb frisking us, thinking he was safe to talk freely." He chuckles. "The look on his face when Anderson played it back at the end of the meeting was price-less. Trust me, he won't be doing anything to push our buttons. That tape will hang him."

"What if he finds proof we killed those bastards? It wouldn't really matter then."

"There is no evidence to find. Anything that's left of Montgomery lies at the bottom of the ocean. Mathers's charred remains are dust particles floating in the wind, and Johnson smashed his teeth and fed them to an incinerator. There is no way to prove those bastards are even dead let alone that we're responsible."

"I hope you're right."

"He'll come after us, at some point, because he won't appreciate that we have him over a barrel, but we'll be ready for him, and you're well protected, my love. I promised you no one would ever hurt you again and I meant it."

We still have twenty-four-seven bodyguard protection, and I know we will until the elite threat is no longer a risk, but I welcome it. It makes me feel safe, as does my husband and his friends. They are smart, and they would all kill if anyone came near us. However, it doesn't stop doubts from infiltrating my happy bubble from time to time.

"We're here," Jackson says, slowing to a halt in front of large wooden entrance gates. The property is bordered on both sides by tall cream brick walls and leafy woodland. Barbed wire and security cameras reside atop the walls confirming they take the safety of their residents seriously. The overhead sign reads "Moonlight," and underneath it is "Support. Survive. Thrive."

Jackson presses the button on the keypad at the gates, confirming our identity into the speaker, and the gates slowly open. The driveway is long and winding, surrounded by fledgling trees and shrubs on both sides.

"Holy shit," I exclaim when we pull up in front of the compound. The space in front of us is massive, clearly spanning acres and acres of private land, extending beyond what my eyes can see. It's a giant construction site with men in hardhats working on scaffolds while others wander the foot-trampled grass, talking into walkie-talkies. Several buildings are under construction, some at more advanced stages than others.

Jackson pulls the car into the space beside a mud-spattered black Lincoln Navigator, killing the engine. "Wow. Rick said this place was something else, but I still wasn't expecting something on this scale."

"Nor me," I agree, climbing out of the car. "It's really impressive, especially since they are both still at college." Selena and Keanu walked away from successful modeling careers, and there has been much discussion online as to the reasons why. Now that I see this place, it all makes sense. There is no way they could take on a project of this size while at college and still working.

They are such an inspiration, and I'm grateful for today. Not just so Jackson can hear what Selena has to say but for the opportunity to see this place with my own eyes.

Jackson takes my hand, and we walk over the gravel surface of the parking lot, heading toward the site. Nerves prickle the back of my neck, because I'm anxious for my husband, hoping what he hears today will help him and not gset him back. I hold his hand tighter, my heart bursting with love and concern.

A familiar face steps out of a trailer as we approach the building site. Dark hair peeks out from under his hard hat, matching the dark scruff on his chin and cheeks. He's tall and broad with toned muscles and dazzling blue eyes that give him away as a Kennedy. Wearing a warm smile, he heads in our direction. "You must be Jackson and Vanessa. Keven told us to expect you today," he says, extending his arm. "I'm his brother, Kalvin."

Holy hotness. He is drop dead gorgeous, and I don't say that lightly, because my husband is sex on legs. The Kennedys are a big deal in Massachusetts, and the media can't get enough of them. They are pictured most everywhere they go, and I knew he was one of the brothers the instant I saw him, but, honestly, the pictures I've seen haven't done him justice.

"Nessa." Jackson tugs on my hand, his lips pulled into a lopsided grin. He gestures to where Kalvin has his hand in front of me.

My cheeks heat as I shake his hand. "Sorry. I was daydreaming. This place is incredible."

Jackson's smirk grows. He knows I'm lying—that I was caught drooling. Even though he's secure in my love, my husband is still prone to bouts of jealousy, so I'm surprised he's amused. Although that could be the fact Kalvin has a wedding band on his finger and it's widely known he's married to his childhood sweetheart, the bestselling author Lana Kennedy.

Jackson knows there is no reason to feel threatened.

Now or any other time.

My heart belongs to him for eternity.

"It is." Kalvin turns around, and we drink everything in. "What Selena is doing here is phenomenal. The whole family is involved because we all believe in it and her."

Jackson pulls me into his side, circling his arm around me. "We think what you're doing here is amazing."

"The sheer scale of it is mind-blowing," I add, as a couple walk toward us from the other side of the field.

"And here's the woman of the hour," Kalvin says, lifting a shoulder and urging us to walk with him. "I know Sel's keen to talk with you," he adds as we advance toward Keanu and Selena. "But I'm sure she'd love to give you a tour first."

"That sounds perfect," I admit because Jackson is tense, and that might help ease him into this.

"Hey, man." Kalvin pulls his brother into a hug. "I was just calling it a day when I stumbled across your guests."

"We're a little early," Jackson says. "I hope that's okay."

"It's no problem," Keanu says, offering Jackson his hand. "Thanks for dropping by."

There is a striking resemblance between the brothers. Keanu is slightly taller and leaner, and he's sporting impressive ink on one arm, but he's equally as hot as his older brother. The Kennedy gene pool really is something else.

Selena tucks herself into Keanu's side, smiling shyly at me. "This is my wife, Selena," Keanu says, beaming proudly at the gorgeous willowy blonde.

"Nice to meet you," Jackson says. "And this is my wife, Vanessa."

I smile. "It's lovely to meet you both."

"Likewise," Keanu says.

"Thank you for agreeing to talk with us," Jackson says.

"Any friend of Kev's is a friend of ours," Keanu confirms, pinning me with a gorgeous smile.

"I thought we could show you around first and then talk back at the house?" Selena suggests.

"I would love a tour," I confirm, squeezing Jackson's hand.

"I hate to bail," Kalvin says. "But I have a little princess at home waiting for me to take her to the playground."

"Aw, that's so sweet. How old is she?" I inquire.

"Hayley turned one a few weeks ago," Kalvin proudly confirms.

"And she has her daddy wrapped around her pinkie," Keanu adds.

Selena smiles. "She has every Kennedy wrapped around her pinkie. She's a cutie."

Kalvin whips out his cell, pulling up a pic of a gorgeous dark-haired little girl and an older boy who is the spitting image of him with the same twinkle in his eye. "This is my little princess Hayley with her brother Hewson."

"You have a beautiful family," Jackson says.

"I'm a lucky bastard," Kalvin says, leaning in to give Selena a quick hug. "Call me if you need me for anything."

"Enjoy your date with your daughter," Keanu says. "I'm sure we can manage without you for a few hours."

"Nice meeting you," Kalvin says, waving to everyone as he walks off.

I walk beside Selena as she gives us the grand tour with the guys trailing behind us, chatting away as if they are lifelong friends. Selena explains the purpose of each building as we walk around the site, talking about their plans and dreams that the sanctuary will offer a haven for victims of sexual abuse to heal. They have thought of everything, and they are offering a whole host of therapies, alternative therapies, schooling, sports, hobbies, and crafts.

We walk beyond the main construction area, leaving the noise behind the farther we go. I ask Selena questions about her modeling career and college as we trek across open fields. She asks me about RU, and we discuss our shared psychology studies. "This is us," she says, after twenty minutes, her steps slowing when we reach our destination. Nestled in front of thick woodland is a row of houses with pretty gardens out front. "We are building apartments and houses for our families closer to the main building," Selena explains. "These will be the resident cottages."

"They are beautiful. You really have put so much thought into everything."

"I want this to feel like a home away from home," she adds, opening the door to one of the houses. "And for guests to understand they can stay here as long as they need to."

"I wish there had been somewhere like this for my sister," Jackson says, following us into the open-plan living and dining area. "She was so broken when she returned home, and a peaceful place like this might've made all the difference."

"Why don't you sit down and talk, and I'll make coffee," Keanu suggests.

I take my husband's hand as we sit down on the couch across from Selena.

"I'm sorry for what happened to Dani," she says in that soft tone of hers. "She was a wonderful person."

Jackson's entire body turns rigid. "You knew her?" Selena nods. "So, it's true. She was on that island?" he croaks.

"For a few months, yes," Selena confirms.

Jackson's chest heaves, and his Adam's apple bobs in his throat. He stares at Selena, but I'm not sure he's even seeing her. I don't know where his mind has gone.

Selena and I share a look as we wait for Jackson to continue.

"Was she ... Did they ... What happened to her there?" he asks in a low voice.

I scoot in closer to his side, wrapping my arms around him, letting him know I'm here for him.

"I'll tell you everything I know, which isn't much, because she wasn't kept with the rest of us."

"Why not?" Jackson asks.

"I didn't know at the time, but now, I think it's because of who she was. Most all of the girls and boys taken to that island were invisibles. Street kids or kids from poor homes. Kids no one would miss or spend too much time looking for."

"Except for Dani," I say, putting it together. "She was the daughter of a wealthy, successful businessman. A man well known in a lot of circles."

Selena nods. "Dani might've been recognizable to someone on the island, so she was kept in isolation." She pins sympathetic eyes on Jackson. "I don't know what was done to her, Jackson, because I only met her twice, and we didn't talk about that. Most times, none of us did." She clasps her hands in her lap, looking at the floor when she adds, "No one wanted to relive those horrors."

Jackson grabs onto my arm, clinging to me in a way that breaks my heart.

"I met her twice on the beach," Selena says, as Keanu walks across the room, depositing a tray on the coffee table. There is a pot of coffee, some mugs, cookies, and some bottles of water.

I take a bottle of water, handing it to Jackson as Keanu pours coffee into mugs.

"What was she like?" Jackson asks.

"Strong," Selena says. "She was talking to some of the younger kids, trying her best to console them when I first met her. She had this quiet strength about her, and she naturally drew people to her." Keanu slides his arm around Selena. "She talked to me about her life in New York. She talked about you." She smiles. "I could tell she adored you. Her eyes used to light up anytime she mentioned her brother."

A strangled sound rips from Jackson's throat, and he hangs his head, his body shaking. Carefully, I take the bottle from his hands, putting it back on the table. Tears prick my eyes as I hug him close, nodding at a concerned Selena to continue. "She told me she wanted to be a dancer like your mom."

Jackson sobs, and tears stream down my face. Keanu hugs Selena close, and I can tell this is hard for her too. "She told me you were going to be the greatest Formula 1 racer the world has ever known. How it was in your genes."

Jackson totally breaks down, clinging to me as he cries unashamedly, and I'm glad he is getting this out. He spent far too long bottling all his feelings inside, and it was slowly killing him.

Keanu wipes tears from Selena's cheeks, pinning me with a sad look.

"Did she say anything else?" I ask because I don't think my husband can go on.

Selena shakes her head. "We talked about her family and her life. That was it. I didn't contribute a lot to the conversation, but I was content to listen to her speak. She never said it outright, but I knew she believed she'd see her family again. She had hope, and that helped me hang on to the last vestiges of my hope. I thought of her often over the years. Wondered what had happened to her."

Dani's suicide wasn't reported in the press because Travis, with Ethan Hunt's help, kept it contained. The family wanted to mourn in private, not have gossipmongers debating what had caused a beautiful, smart girl with a bright future to take her own life.

Selena closes her eyes, leaning her head on Keanu's shoulder.

"Selena was very upset when Keven confirmed what'd happened," Keanu admits.

"I'm so sorry for your loss, Jackson," Selena continues, in a soft tone. "Dani was an amazing person, and I'm sorry she never got to fulfil her dream. With your permission, I would like to name our dance studio in her honor."

Jackson looks up, swiping at his red eyes. "The honor would be all ours." His pained eyes meet mine, and I hold him closer. "I think my mom would love that."

She would, and I'm sure she'll want to get involved in a more active way. Abby too. This cause is close to all our hearts, and there isn't anyone in our network of friends who hasn't been impacted by the atrocities the elite has committed. I think everyone will want to donate or volunteer when we explain about this place.

"We would like to donate," I blurt, confident in offering this even though Jackson and I haven't discussed it yet. I sold my apartment last month, and I'd already decided I wanted to donate the proceeds to charity. There is no better recipient than Moonlight. "And I'd like to volunteer my time. If there is anything I can do to help, either now or after I'm qualified, I would love to get involved."

"Anything we can both do," Jackson adds, lifting his head. "It's too late to help my sister, but the best thing I can do to honor Dani's memory is to support others who have endured similar traumas. Just let us know what we can do to help and we're there."

"These ones," Jackson says, pointing at the pink, purple, and white bouquet just inside the door of the flower shop. "Dani loved pink and purple." I take the scented bouquet, handing it to the girl behind the register, and pay for it with my card.

"I love pink and purple too," I supply, looping my arm in his as he takes the bouquet from my hand. "Your mom has been pestering me about choosing a color scheme for the wedding, and now, the decision is made." The date has been set for July, and we're getting married at this gorgeous hotel in The Hamptons. Laurena is so excited you'd think she was the bride, but I love her enthusiasm, and all her ideas so far have been fantastic, so I'm happy to let her take the reins.

He presses a kiss to the top of my head before opening the door. "I wish Dani could be there."

"She'll be with us in spirit," I say as we walk to the car.

Twenty minutes later, we are standing in front of Dani's grave at New York City Marble Cemetery. Jackson crouches down, placing the flowers in front of the headstone. He's been quiet since our visit to the Kennedys yesterday, and I know he's processing everything. I didn't pry, knowing he'd talk when he's ready. Instead, I let him bury himself inside me for hours last night, offering him the comfort he needed. I sat for hours watching him sleep, praying for him to find peace. When he woke up this morning and asked me if I'd mind a trip to New York to visit his sister's grave, I saw it as a good sign.

"Yesterday helped," he admits, straightening up and pulling me under his arm. "It's good to know it was her life and her family that kept her going during that time, and that she was able to put aside her own shit to help the younger kids. That's who my sister was."

"She had the best heart." I rest my head on his shoulder. "And the best brother." I kiss his cheek. "Did you mention the dance studio to your parents?" I know he called them last night after we got home.

He nods. "They like the idea, and they are going to donate too." I knew they would. "Mom's going to contact Selena to see if she can teach some dance classes."

"That would be incredible. I mentioned it to Abby, and she's keen to get involved too."

"We have good people in our lives," Jackson says, kissing the top of my head.

I nod as he releases me, holding my ground when he steps forward. "I'm proud of you, sis, for the way you helped others on that island. That you put aside your own pain to be there for the younger kids." He lays his hand on top of the headstone. "I will never stop missing you, Dani. You will always be in my heart."

We walk out of the cemetery, arm in arm, and there's a newfound calmness surrounding my husband. I know he will always miss his sister and that a part of him will still feel like he could have done more, but he's come to terms with her death in a way that doesn't overshadow all the good in his life. I think volunteering and donating to Selena's sanctuary will go a long way toward keeping any lingering demons at bay. I certainly know it will for me.

"Where are we going?" I ask when Jackson veers left instead of taking the exit on our right, the one that will take us back home. "I called Ruth before we left Rydeville, and she's agreed we can take the twins out for dinner."

I have as little involvement with my mother as possible these days. After learning how she threw me under the bus, I never want to see her face again. But I love my sister and brother, and I need them in my life. Jackson is the go-between, and he handles all communications with the woman formerly known as my mother. He established a weekly visitation schedule, and the twins stay with us one weekend a month. We either come up to the city and stay at Hunt's penthouse with them or they stay with us at the house in Rydeville.

My heart swells to bursting point. I stretch across the console and plant a big smacker on his lips. "You are the most considerate husband ever."

His lips curve up at the corners. "Does that mean I don't have to beat on Kalvin Kennedy's ass the next time I see him?" he teases.

I swat his arm. "You know the only man for me is you, but I still have eyes in my head. He's hot. All those Kennedys are, but no one is hotter or sexier than you."

"You better believe it, babe." He waggles his brows. "And in case you need further demonstration, I'll prove it tonight."

Heat pools in my belly, and I squirm on my seat. "Now, I'm imagining all kinds of things."

"Wear your heels. We can role play again."

I swat his arm again. "Stop it! Now, I'm going to be sitting in a puddle of my own making the entire way through dinner."

"My devious plan worked," he quips, pulling up at the curb outside Mom's house.

"Why are we stopping here?" I ask, wondering why he's not driving up the driveway.

"Because I have something I need to say." He takes my hand in his, kissing my knuckles.

Worry furrows my brow. "What's wrong?"

"Absolutely nothing." Unbuckling my seat belt, he hauls me over onto his lap. "For the first time in a long time, I'm happy, truly happy, and that is all thanks to you."

"Ditto, lover." I run my hands through his gorgeous, soft hair. "Thank you for loving me, Jackson. Thank you for giving me this life we live."

He brushes his lips against mine. "It's I who should be thanking you for showing me how to live. For showing me how to love. With you by my side, I feel like I can conquer anything."

I circle my arms around his neck. "Together we're invincible, and it will remain like that until the end of time."

"I love the sound of that." He kisses that sensitive spot just under my ear and I shiver. "And I love you. Now and forever."

Sawyer

My cell vibrates in my pocket, and I groan when I see the name flashing on the screen. I've been dodging Dad's calls all week. *Is it too much to ask to enjoy spring break without some family interference?* I have a feeling I know why he's calling, hence my hesitation to pick up. But I get my stubborn streak from my father, and I know he won't give up until he's said his piece, so I reluctantly accept his call.

"Finally. I was about to send out a search party," Dad deadpans.

"What's up, old man?" I work hard to keep my tone light-hearted.

"I need another favor."

Another groan rips from my mouth. "Dad." My tone carries warning.

"Don't Dad me." I can visualize Ethan Hunt pacing the floor of his office with a scowl on his face. "I don't ask much of you, son, but I need your help with this."

"You said it was one time."

"And that was enough back then when we were courting several partners, but things have changed, and it's become more pressing."

"Why?" I ask, dropping onto the couch with a sigh.

"For reasons I'm not at liberty to disclose just yet, the other parties have pulled out, leaving Shaw Software as the only contender for the merger."

"I still don't get why you want to merge with another tech company. Your new security products are going to blow that market wide-open. Stock prices will shoot through the roof. Why share the profits with another company?"

"We need the investment capital," he says, in a clipped tone. "And this isn't up for debate. Keeping Herman Shaw on our side is mission critical. By all accounts, Sydney Shaw was very taken with you, and Herman approves. You know how concerned he's been over his only daughter. He thinks you're a good influence on her, and it's been suggested you take her out again."

"Fuck, Dad, no. I'll do anything to help, but not that."

I'm lucky Xavier never found out about my date with Sydney the last time. Actually, luck had nothing to do with it. I made sure nothing leaked, because I didn't want to hurt him. I bought every single photo taken of me with the Shaw heiress at The Met that night and wiped every mention of it online.

I probably should've told Xavier, but we weren't even officially seeing one another, and he's a total drama queen at the best of times. I know he would've made a big deal out of it. With all the other shit I had on my plate at the time, I didn't want the additional stress, so I said nothing. Quietly took the girl out and promptly forgot our date. It's not like I wanted to be there or it meant anything to me. Jackson is the only other person who knows, and that's because the asshole eavesdropped on a call with my dad and overheard the whole thing.

But things are different now. While Xavier and I still aren't official, things are more serious between us. I shouldn't have let it get this far, because there is no scenario where it ends well, but I can't turn back the clock.

Truth is, I have strong feelings for the guy. Even though he irritates the fuck out of me half the time, I care about him, and this would hurt him.

"I'm not asking, Sawyer," Dad says, using that assertive tone he deploys when he wants to get his own way. "It's already agreed. You're taking her out Saturday night. Herman is expecting you at eight o'clock sharp."

"I have plans," I hiss between gritted teeth.

"Unmake them," he shouts. "This is more important. Our entire future is hanging on the line, son. This merger needs to happen, or everything I've worked for is lost."

I'm wondering if Dad's been taking lessons in melodrama from my lover. "Let's not overreact."

"Do you think I'd be forcing you into this if I had any other choice?!" he roars down the line. "Stop being a selfish punk, and think of your mother. God, anyone would think Sydney Shaw was an ogre. She's a beautiful, highly educated woman. It's not a hardship."

"One date," I growl.

"It will be as many dates as are necessary," he says in a

more even-keeled voice, having calmed his temper. "Your mother and I will see you for dinner on Sunday, and I expect a full report. Enjoy your date," he adds before hanging up.

"Motherfucker!" Frustration wells inside me, and I throw my cell across the room, before burying my head in my hands. *What the fuck am I going to do now?*

The End

The story continues in **Sawyer**. Available now in ebook, paperback, alternate paperback and audiobook format.

Want to read the details of Nessa and Jackson's Las Vegas elopement? Copy and paste this link into your browser: https://bit.ly/JacksonBonusScene

Want to read more about Selena, Keanu, Keven, Kalvin, and all the Kennedys? Check out **Finding Kyler**, book one in the series, or **Releasing Keanu**, Selena and Keanu's **standalone second chance romance**.

Torn between duty and desire…

Sawyer Hunt has always been confident with his place in the world. He knows what he wants, conceals his painful truths behind a mask of cool indifference and keeps his circle small. The only person who has ever come close to smashing through his inner walls is the one person his parents will never accept.

Xavier Daniels is sick of being Hunt's dirty little secret. When he fled the ugliness of his past, he swore he would never again hide who he is. Or let anyone hurt him or make him feel ashamed. So, discovering the man he's in love with is engaged to some mystery woman devastates him. Forced into making the only decision he can, Xavier locks up his heart, determined to keep Hunt out for good.

Sydney Shaw is the bane of her father's existence. But he's finally found a way to end her rebellious streak—marry a virtual stranger or be cut off forever. Hunt could be a great husband, if he wasn't such a cold, moody jerk and she wasn't still hung up on the guy who broke her heart at fifteen.

Marrying Sydney to save his father's company is a sacrifice Hunt will make because he suspects the elite is involved, and it's up to him and his friends to stop them. With his heart also on the line, Hunt is determined to end the threat quickly or risk losing the one person he now realizes he can't live without. Consequences be damned.

CLAIM YOUR FREE EBOOK – ONLY AVAILABLE TO NEWSLETTER SUBSCRIBERS!

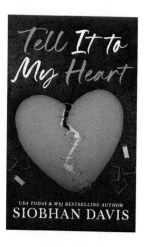

The boy who broke my heart is now the man who wants to mend it.

Jared was my everything until an ocean separated us and he abandoned me when I needed him most.

He forgot the promises he made.

Forgot the love he swore was eternal.

It was over before it began.

Now, he's a hot commodity, universally adored, and I'm the woman no one wants.

Pining for a boy who no longer exists is pathetic. Years pass, men come and go, but I cannot move on.

I didn't believe my fractured heart and broken soul could endure any more pain. Until Jared rocks up to the art gallery where I work, with his fiancée in tow, and I'm drowning again.

Seeing him brings everything to the surface, so I flee. Placing distance between us again, I'm determined to put him behind me once and for all.

Then he reappears at my door, begging me for another chance.

I know I should turn him away.

Try telling that to my heart.

———————————

This angsty, new adult romance is a FREE full-length ebook, exclusively available to newsletter subscribers.

Type this link into your browser to claim your free copy:
https://bit.ly/TITMHFBB

OR

Scan this code to claim your free copy:

About the Author

Siobhan Davis is a *USA Today, Wall Street Journal,* and Amazon Top 5 bestselling romance author. **Siobhan** writes emotionally intense stories with swoon-worthy romance, complex characters, and tons of unexpected plot twists and turns that will have you flipping the pages beyond bedtime! She has sold over 2 million books, and her titles are translated into several languages.

Prior to becoming a full-time writer, Siobhan forged a successful corporate career in human resource management.

She lives in the Garden County of Ireland with her husband and two sons.

You can connect with Siobhan in the following ways:

Website: www.siobhandavis.com
Facebook: AuthorSiobhanDavis
Instagram: @siobhandavisauthor
Tiktok: @siobhandavisauthor
Email: siobhan@siobhandavis.com

Books By Siobhan Davis

NEW ADULT ROMANCE
The One I Want Duet
Kennedy Boys Series
Rydeville Elite Series
All of Me Series
Forever Love Duet

NEW ADULT ROMANCE STAND-ALONES
Inseparable
Incognito
Still Falling for You
Holding on to Forever
Always Meant to Be
Tell It to My Heart

REVERSE HAREM
Sainthood Series
Dirty Crazy Bad Duet
Surviving Amber Springs (stand-alone)
Alinthia Series ^

DARK MAFIA ROMANCE

Mazzone Mafia Series
Vengeance of a Mafia Queen (stand-alone)
*The Accardi Twins**

YA SCI-FI & PARANORMAL ROMANCE

Saven Series
True Calling Series ^

---

*Coming 2024
^Currently unpublished but will be republished in due course.

www.siobhandavis.com

Made in United States
North Haven, CT
17 May 2024

52619079R00293